SHADES OF BLACK

A novel

By Terrance Johnson

7-Fold Publishing

7-Fold Publishing
7732 S. Cottage Grove Ave.
Suite 121
Chicago, IL. 60619
http://www.7foldpublishing.com
email: VIIfoldTerrance@aol.com

Library of Congress Catalog Card Number: 98-94008

ISBN: 0-9667938-1-1

Cover Model: Jon Eric Simmons
Cover Illustration: Justin Jordan Photography and Digital Imaging
Web Page Designer: electronicmediafactory.com

This novel is a work of fiction. Names, characters, places, establishments, events and incidents are the product of the author's imagination or are used fictitiously to give this novel a sense of reality and authenticity. Any resemblance to real persons, living or dead, events, or locales is entirely coincidental.

I wish you could have gotten this dedication on this side, Dad.

Dr. Travis T. Johnson, 1936-1997

ACKNOWLEDGMENTS

First and foremost I would like to thank the Great, Gracious God for my life, experiences, testimonies, opportunities, lessons, motivation and determination, failures and triumphs, good times and bad, and for sticking with me and putting me down with His winning team. I'm not worthy and all glory goes to Him. With a million tongues I can't thank my best friend, confidant and mother, Daisy Johnson, enough. Can't say enough about you. You are a living epistle and true Proverb 31 woman of God. You've stuck by me through it all and supported me even if you didn't support my endeavors. When you had the chance to say, "I told you so" and let my wallow in my mess, you didn't. They say that behind every great man there's a great woman. Well I'm not great, but you are. Love you Ma. I want to thank my biggest and most important supporter--my father, Dr. Travis Johnson. Thanks for all the encouragement, the genes, and intelligent insight, Dad. Special thanks to the Johnson Five: Travis, Bertram, Darnell, Lyonel and my ace when I'm in a hole, my homey when I'm standing alone, and my closest blood and spiritual brother, Trent. When we fight and when we slap fives you're always down and you always got my back. It doesn't go unnoticed and it won't go unrewarded. Stick around T. My sister and editor Spring, a critic who found no fault in what I wrote. Thanks to my oldest brother Kenneth and my oldest sibling Albreta. You are good teachers even from afar. Sister Saint Linda Murphy, the praying warrior who has interceded for me when I was going through. Sister Saint Katherine Bush, who swapped inspiring testimonies with me that illustrated that God is great and that there's at least one other crazy person besides myself walking around. Eva, one of the closest and durable friends in my life even when not present. Despite our differences you have been a blessing and positive inspiration. J. Denise Johnson (as of yet we are not officially related...smile), my spiritual sister who has touched the deepest crevice of my heart. Thanks for proofing my manuscript and encouraging my narrator. Susan Blakes, a good friend and colleague who believed in my dream despite a three-year struggle. Sherry G, my fellow penster who has been the source of a lot of insight and confirmation. We're there Sherry. Let's go for some more. Andrea, my fraternal genre twin...hurry up and birth your work. My first and most pivotal writing instructor, Bernice Williams, who paid me the ultimate compliment even before Shades was conceived. The statement "You're a good writer" was a seed that sprouted into a tree and your instruction was sunshine. Mary Jones, who saw the writer in me before I answered the call. Special thanks to model Jon Eric Simmons and illustrator Justin Jordan for making the cover concept in my head a vivid reality. Also special thanks to Eric Johnson for bringing my web page to life at the last minute. I owe you one brother. Special special thanks to the undershepherds that have touched my life and provided me with a Christian education: Pastor Dwight Craig and Pastor Leon Edwards--who is in the presence of the Lord--and my Southwestern Baptist Church family; Pastor Dr. John E. Hopkins and the New Nazareth Baptist Church family. Last, but always First, I thank my Lord and Savior Jesus Christ. There was a time when I didn't see the beauty in being black even though my tone was brown. That's when You guided me through the humbling wilderness of unemployment and foreclosure. It is in that desert that I saw You. When I looked up, there you were: the Bright and Morning Star; When I fell to my face, there you were: the Lily in *my* valley. Through the intense heat You guided me as my best Friend. In my exodus from the bondage of fear, you feed me with manna steak, provided me with manna money and preserved my clothes. When there was a sea of debt before me and my old nemesis—fear—behind me, you parted that sea and I walked through on dry land. Fear pursued me and You drowned it in the sea and gave me a friend in faith. And then I came to my Promised Land. Before I entered, I beheld myself. My tone was deeper. Through the season of adversity, the gracious Sun of Righteousness shined on me and Your glory tanned me a darker shade of black. That's when I enter the Mansion with an open Door where I now abide. For that I'm in your debt forever. Blessing, and glory, and wisdom, and thanksgiving, and honor, and power, and might, be unto my God for ever and ever. Amen.

Can a black man change the color of his skin?--Jeremiah 13:23. Good News Translation.

I *am* black, but comely, O ye daughters of Jerusalem, as the tents of Kedar, as the curtains of Solomon. Look not upon me, because I am black, because the sun hath looked upon me: my mother's children were angry with me; they made me the keeper of the vineyards; *but* mine own vineyard have I not kept.--The Song of Solomon 1:5-6. King James Version.

PROLOGUE

Mel takes a long look at the glass building that less than an hour ago he called work. The suddenness of the layoff made him feel helpless as he shivers from anxiety and the Chicago hawk. The air causes tears to stream from his eyes. He wouldn't cry under any other circumstances, even though weeping would be an honest manifestation of the sorrow he's feeling at the moment. It's the same sorrow that comes from being dumped by a significant other. After all, he was practically married to Horizon for seven years, albeit a typical, rough marriage that ended in divorce. Rage is something he can't display right now, especially the rage he's experiencing. He imagines launching a missile at the structure—shattering it into a billion pieces of fine glass—and then plowing over the pile. Now would be a good time for him to be the proud owner of a high-powered assault tank. Brad would drop all the way down from his 20th floor office and land baffled on his flat, pampered butt. Only after he looked up at Mel in his tank would he realize that for the last few seconds of his privileged life, that Mel was going to have his way with him. Then he would proceed to demolish him and the rest of the glass buildings in the northern suburbs that he's learned to despise with a hellish passion. To him they represent red-face, white collar, blue suit corporate America—just another institution of United States racism. Everything out in the area is white (anti-black). Even the workers of color are forced to conform to the white mindset. The building looks fragile enough to be fractured by a stone, but since the Chicago area was blanketed with six inches of snow the day before (which translates into about 9 inches for the northern suburbs) there are no stones in sight to test the theory.

His cousin, Earl, had to do some running around town, so Mel agreed to let him keep his car for the day and be dropped off and picked up. The bus pulls up after he waited 45 minutes, which is two hours with the wind chill factor. It's nice, warm and comfortable on there, in stark contrast to what he is experiencing in his heart. The bus pulls off after he makes it to the back and he doesn't look back at Horizon, even though there's nothing to see in front of him. A biblical tract rests on the seat next to him, but he's too bemused to pick it up. The ride home is going to be a long one.

Chapter 1

Mel is so insulted he's nauseous. And the dinner at Bennigan's ain't making things better. It's a good thing Horizon did let him go. He didn't have sense enough to leave on his own or when he had the opportunity. If he had stayed there much longer, he would have either had a stroke or thrown somebody out of a window. He gave nearly eight years of his life to Horizon Electronics, and what do they give him in return? A backhand slap in the face and a swift kick in the rear. His blood pressure is probably about 220 over 130 right now. The clock on the wall indicates that it is his scheduled quitting time. There's solace in knowing that he doesn't have to work like an African-American slave and he won't have to sweat for them anymore, even though he doesn't know how he's going to pay the bills from now on.

As he sits at a window booth, peeling thick crust away from a small piece of imitation fish, his lady—Memory Jones—seems to be enjoying the evening and the meal, despite the latest development in his life. What she likes about this place is a mystery to him. And how can she be so nonchalant when his destiny looks bleak? Maybe she's into breading. And maybe she doesn't give a damn. They're not married, and sometimes they don't even seem like a couple, so he's not her problem. "I don't believe they gave me a plate of crust!" he says dejectedly. "We're going to Docks after this."

"Calm down," she says as she cuts her steak, seemingly oblivious to the real problem.

He perceives she's antagonizing him, but he's not going to bite. Not today. "I am calm. It's just that if I wanted bread, I would've gone to the bakery."

"You're just under a lot of stress," she suggests, falling miles short of sounding sympathetic, and hitting the mark of impatience. "Maybe we should go and catch a movie or something."

"Death row inmates get a decent last meal, so I think I'm entitled to one on the worse day of my life," he declares as he looks out at the busy rush of people and cars on a gloomy Michigan Avenue and reflects on his early days with the company.

He started there fresh out of high school in their sales department as a data entry rep, and within a year he moved from sales into credit and collections. Since he was majoring in accounting at Chicago State University and the original human resources manager—Steve Henderson—catered to all the guys requests, every class he took was approved for tuition reimbursement with no questions asked. At Steve's suggestion, Mel was given credit for an internship for the position that he was in. He even approved a literature class Mel took that had nothing to do with the business world. It was a good experience and he wanted every part of the company and "Corporate America". He sampled every business discipline he could, from marketing and management to business law and finance. Needless to say, he aced every one with nothing less than an occasional B, but more often than not with strong A's. He was on the Dean's List for two straight years, which is where he finished the last four semesters. His intentions were to get his Bachelors in accounting, continue through graduate school, and move way up in the company. He had his sights set for the top. Then they started tripping and soon his instincts (not to mention their insolent stares) were telling him that they didn't want any parts of a "Nigger" in a meaningful position. After all, there were exactly ZERO black mid to upper level managers out of 25 positions in the company and they didn't seem eager to change the status quo. It was funny how they would praise him for his hard work—knowing they couldn't stand his ambition. It didn't matter that he could've been a financial asset to the company.

Steve left town for another position and they promoted Margaret "Military" Daley from trainer. They were adamant for upgrading from within, which is one reason why he was interested in sticking with them. Soon after she took the position, she stopped paying for all of his classes, reasoning, "They're not directly related to your current position." There were only so many classes he could take that were related to credit that would apply towards graduation. What a b-witch. He thought she was pretty cool—although sergeant-like—when he first started. She turned out to be another corporate bureaucrat.

It's kind of funny, since it was through Margaret (indirectly) that he met Memory three years ago. Margaret hired her as a summer intern to assist her in the office with publishing the company newsletter and other public relations tasks. At the time, she was majoring in communications at Northern Illinois with another year remaining.

As he looks at her now, he can't help but consider her metamorphosis. She looks the same, but her spirit has gradually deteriorated. It almost seems like she has lost the softness and tenderness that was always present. Her heart, which was displayed in everything she did, seems to have freeze-dried.

One good look at her is all it took, and he was hooked like a sweet tooth latched on a Milky Way. He'll never forget the day he had to go to human resources to fill out some tuition reimbursement forms and cut through some of the red tape Margaret stretched out in his way. He dreaded her presence because she had a way of trying to patronize black people, and he had to keep himself from giving her the ghetto ignorance that she was hunting for. When he walked in, he was surprised to see a short, young, black lady on the phone behind Margaret's desk. She had a smooth, golden-brown complexion, with seductive orange-brown (not quite hazel) eyes surrounded by long black eyelashes. Her girlish, high-pitched voice didn't overshadow her lady-like demeanor. He walked in frowning, but when he saw her, his mouth dropped open, his expression displayed shock, and his heart grinned. She was fine with a capital o.

As he stepped up to the desk, she smiled at him and stuck her index finger up as if to say, "One minute." He nodded in agreement as his heart raced like the engine of a dragster and he paced over to the bulletin board on the other side of the reception area. He would've waited one year for her. Her smile lit into him like sunshine. She had perfectly straight teeth that were whiter than chalk. Her walnut colored hair was short in the back and on the sides and styled like Anita Baker's. Although she was petite, her figure was notable. It was Friday—a company-wide casual day—and she was wearing firm-butt-revealing, bleach-faded white Levi's shorts with a sky blue tank top that hugged her small chest. He knew he had to hug her.

He didn't read anything on the board because he was pondering the smoothest line of communication without sounding frantic or calculating. As her phone conversation was coming to an end, he walked back over with his hands folded behind his back. As soon as she hung up, he leaned forward and rested his hands on the desk as she asked, "How may I help you?"

He started to be honest and tell her what was really on his lustful mind, but he just nervously replied, "I'm here to pick up my tuition reimbursement forms from Margaret."

"Okay. And what is your name?" she asked, with the same smile intact that she displayed while she was on the phone. He wasn't taking it as a hint of interest, but he wasn't going to leave without finding out something intimate about her.

"I'm Mel. Melvin Adams," he said with a bit of restless hesitation.

"Melvin Adams...Let's see..." she said as she went over to the file cabinet and thumbed through it. "Uh huh. She had it right at the front."

"Yes. She was expecting me," he said without any idea of what to say next that could keep the conversation going. He wasn't thinking fast at all.

"So what are you studying?" she asked, catching him a bit off guard, because he was gaping at her like a love sick teenager.

"Who me? Accounting," he responded, even more skittishly. He didn't know he could still get that uneasy over a fine female.

"Oh really. That's pretty good. Where are you going?"

At that point he was smiling and tapping his fingers on the desk as if he was playing an organ. He couldn't look at her and talk to her at the same time without his tongue getting tied and his knees buckling, so he glanced to the side as he said, "I go to Chicago State."

"Do you like it? I almost ended up going there."

"It's okay, but I'm just in it to get out of it."

"I heard that."

They both paused for a moment as they grinned and nodded. Then he finally got the nerve to do a little probing. "I haven't seen you before. How long have you been here?"

"I started Monday. I'm here on an internship."

"O' yeah."

"Yep. I'm coming out of Northern next December."

"What are you going into?"

"Communications."

"Impressive," he said as he began to get a little more comfortable.

"By the way, I'm Memory Jones."

"Memory—as in good memory, bad memory?"

"Just like it sounds."

"It's pretty...and I'll never forget it."

"Thank you," she said, blushing slightly.

At that point, the butterflies in his belly died and flew to heaven and Memory became a part of Mel's mind by agreeing to go to lunch together that afternoon. They've been going to lunch together ever since. The big bang from the heart-on collision was deafening; the flames spread quickly, and the heat was intense. He believes that a good relationship starts from an instant attraction, which some people use synonymously with love at first sight. He doesn't think it should take months or even weeks to determine if someone is right. Usually the first conversation is telling enough for him. They've had their contrasting ups and downs, but they've weathered the storms under the same umbrella.

He stopped by human resources quite often during that summer to see her (and take care of paper work). Horizon's corporate crap didn't stop him from finishing up and getting his BA in accounting that following July (the semester before Memory came out) and going to the accounting department as the bookkeeper. Six months after graduation, he took the CPA exam and he passed—of course. He was seriously considering leaving just before they offered him a supervisory position in the accounts payable department. Shortly after, they promoted him to manager of the credit department. Minoring in management turned out to be a profitable move. However, he made the mistake of taking the promotion personally—believing that they were fond of him—reasoning, "If they didn't like me, they wouldn't have promoted me". Oh, but the deceptively racist Corporate America quickly killed that okiedokie mindset.

He immediately sold his run-a-day, broke-a-day hoopty Crown Victoria for $50 and bought a new IROC. Later he had the engine and body customized to look like a Ferrari on the sides and fly like a 'Vette. He didn't drag race for money, but there wasn't a GT that could outrun him. Shortly after, he fulfilled a lifelong goal and bought his dream home: a Georgian with a big yard and a two-car garage. He got a good deal on it because it needed some work (he thought it was minor, but it turned out to be more than he bargained for) and came with an FHA insured loan.

At 22, he was living large and comfortable with a house, a sport car, a $30,000 a year job and one of Chicago's finest women. An attitude that he could conquer the world followed. He had all that he could ask for and then some money in the bank, but for some reason, he was *reluctant to relax. It almost didn't seem real—like he was dancing in the wrong music video and everything was an illusion that would pop like a bubble in a cactus patch. Earl joked that he sold out by moving up, but Mel did some serious soul-searching and couldn't find any erroneous compromises. Whenever he could, he would put the word out to someone in need of a job. Horizon had a $500 referral fee for any employee that recommended someone that was hired. Mel never collected on the bounty. Even though he got along well with most of the people in the company (especially the white top managers), he was very uneasy with the arrangements. It didn't take long for Horizon to substantiate his intuition. At first, he thought it was some innate distrust. Later, he understood that his spirit was bracing him for the impact from the fall, much like the brain allows the body to go into shock when it's about to suffer great trauma.*

The company claimed that somebody on the inside was ripping them off, and although they didn't come out and say it, they implied their suspicions of Mel. Pretty soon, he was being watched even when he went to take a leak. The blood loss he suffered from that knife wound to the back would've sent a blood bank into bankruptcy. That was truly personal. It was definitely a black thing. He hasn't stolen since his mother beat him into the following week for stealing a candy bar from the grocery store. If they were really ripped off, he felt their suspicions were rooted in prejudice. After all, black and negativity go hand in hand to some. If there was anyone that fit the physical profile of a thief, it was Mel: the darkest thing in the company. He didn't get the nickname Black Male because of his race and gender. The moniker was descriptive. He happens to be one of the darkest brothers outside of Africa. He's not blue, but he is black. And seeing that he was the only person of color with that type of knowledge and access, he stood out like a black lamb in a flock of white sheep. He was the easiest scapegoat and tallest fall guy. And fall he did.

Although he was expecting them to do something off-the-wall, when they moved—or demoted—him to order entry manager, the well-forecasted sucker-punch floored him anyway (he was promoted in 1992 and demoted just over a year later). The insulting move demoralized him. His experience and degree is in the financial matters of business, not sales. And he hates sales. He hates salesmen and order entry goes hand-in-hand with sales. There are no parallels with order entry and accounting. Order entry emphasizes customer service and kissing too much customer butt; accounting stresses kicking customer butt until payment is received. They insisted that he would better serve their needs in the customer service department. That's when he realized that no matter how much he was making and how hard he worked and how many degrees he got and how many people he recommended for jobs in the company, he wasn't benefiting himself or his community by working for them...not in the long run. While people were able to support themselves with the menial jobs that he hooked them up with, there was no growth opportunity for them and the company was actually getting over like a lazy plantation owner with an abundance of slaves. Apparently, Mel wasn't part of their long-range plans either, which was made obvious after the layoff. Although he came to that realization a long time ago, he was still determined to break through the low, glass ceiling.

Memory is just finishing the last of her meal as he slouches in his chair, daydreaming about the day's events. "Let's go before you fall asleep on me. And are you going to pout if I don't feel like going to Docks?" she asks with a touch of animosity in her voice.

He has the urge to slap the food loose that's caught in between her two front teeth, but he just looks at her without even changing his expression and says, "Whatever."

"You don't have to get an attitude with me," she says, raising her voice slightly.

"I'm not getting an attitude with you," he defends.

"I just asked you a simple question and you act like you don't want to be bothered. Maybe I should catch a cab home since you're acting funky," she says as she tosses the napkin she was wiping her lips with on the plate.

Now he does have an attitude, but he just sits pokerfaced with his mouth open slightly. She amazes him like a miracle. This can't be the same woman he met in human resources. *That* woman was more sensitive and understanding and didn't have a vile disposition like the woman sitting across from him. Here he is at the crossroads in his life—not knowing what he's going to do when his meager savings runs out and the bill collectors come knocking—and she's giving him her thirtieth degree attitude. He knows it's not her style, but she can at least show him the same understanding he shows her when she has problems.

And she has a plethora of issues. Minute in significance, but many in number. Her judgment is beyond bad. She just assumes that whenever he says something is bothering him or that he has an issue, that he's seeking an immediate response or solution. In this case, he can't even get a word in or talk about his concerns because she's tripping and lipping like she's jobless. She doesn't know when he just needs her to zip her lips and listen, providing the free therapy that comes with the relationship. He has his problems and all, but he's no whining basket case. She should know how convenient an open ear is. No matter what her problem is (whether it's something as trivial as a broken nail and the color she should put in her hair, or as serious as her friend getting cancer or her mother throwing her out of the house), his empathetic ear is always open for her to dump her burdens in. When she seeks his insight, he gives her an objective take on the situation. If they speak after today, he's going to start charging her for his counseling services. He's been up 'til wee hours in the morning listening to her spill her guts, moaning about things so insignificant that he questions her mental stability at times. He almost tells her to *'catch the bus'*, but he just takes a deep breath and says, "Let's go home. It's been a long day for both of us."

She springs up with a frown and doesn't say anything as he helps her with her coat. For the sake of being polite, he leaves the tip, since she doesn't (even though the meal seemed to satisfy her), pays for the dinner and heads out behind her. The wind is blowing and there's a blatant chill in the air—in more ways than one. So far he's singing a poor version of the holiday blues (which is closer to black), and is anticipating the end of the Christmas season. Not only is he contemplating taking the gifts he bought back (especially Memory's), but the thought of jumping into the icy Chicago River is very appealing (it's more tempting to throw Memory in instead).

They don't say anything to each other as they walk down State Street to the parking lot four blocks away on Congress Avenue. She just peers in the department store windows while he glances at the people passing them going in the opposite direction, studying their expressions and wondering if any of them have it half as bad as he does right now. Judging from their gleeful casts, they don't. While everybody is drunk off of the holiday spirit, Mel is stewing in Scrooge soup. His mind is so cluttered with Memory's stupidity and the drama from the former job, that it feels like it's going to blow any minute. The needle on his rage gauge goes up a couple of notches as he recalls how Horizon's scheme took form.

He was strongly cogitating graduate school, when they did something notably peculiar and out of character. They hired a supervisor for the credit department from the outside without running an ad. And it was a black woman. Light as a white person, but black nonetheless. They seemed to pamper and cater to her, which prompted Mel to peep them on the sly. However, he knew she was for his eyes anyway. He put graduate school on hold, since he was becoming disenchanted with the corporate world and he figured that his days at Horizon were numbered. They gave her a big whip and she was cracking it like her name was Masa'. He found out her name was Gina Johnson, and she immediately became known as G, as in Gangsta'. In less than three months, three guys—three hardworking, able brothers (all friends of Mel's that he hired)—were whacked like rats by the gat she was packing. The angel of death was a pleasant last sight. With sandy-brown, shoulder-length hair and big, pretty, green eyes, she resembled Vanessa Williams from a distance, which is where Mel kept her. Under normal circumstances, he would've been tempted to talk to her, but she sent him the ominous vibe that she may have his head on a platter one day, a la John the Baptist by the urging of Herodias.

Mel and G talked for the first time a day after she fired one of his boys. Not once did the termination come up in the conversation—as if the day before never happened. It was no question that their conversation had some ulterior motive. Previously, she never even as much as looked his way.

She talked about her past work experiences and how she was glad to be with the company. Her voice was nice and precise like that of a newscaster, which reminded him of Memory. She spoke with proper English like she was raised in suburbia by white English teachers, but it was phony, whiny and condescending and Mel could hear right through it. Yep: she was definitely bought merchandise. During their lunch time chat, he found out that she was his age and getting her BA in Management over the summer. When she told him that her fiancé—who happens to be Jewish—and Benjamin Scheib (the vice president of the company) are good friends, he knew that they brought her in to do (without Vaseline) as many brothers as she could, especially him. She was going to be played against him. He couldn't figure out for the life of him if she was supposed to tell him all of that as a way of gloating or if she was just plain clueless.

When Mel was still fairly new to the company, Ben stopped him in the hallway and questioned his dress attire, noting that it was "borderline casual" in a playful, yet objecting tone that was over-the-line idiotic. Mel was perplexed by the gall of that short, preppy, sandy-brown white boy with the big head and boyish mug that had probably never been punched before. Who the hell was he? Later that day he described him to one of his coworkers and discovered that he was the VP. Well then, what was his problem? Mel was wearing baggy gray slacks, a black button-up short-sleeve shirt with a metal, cowboy string-tie, and black Giorgio Brutini snakeskins with tassels. And at the time, it wasn't like Mel was an executive. He was just a lowly, bottom-of-the-pay-scale data entry rep. Nobody impressionable saw or even talked to him. His outfit complied with the dress code. Yet, they still wanted to give him grief. They revised the dress code within weeks of that run-in. Although the memo was for the whole company, it was quite obvious who it applied to. It stated that baggy slacks can't be worn unless it's a company-wide casual day. They even outlawed stylish haircuts, like high-top fades and parts. Blue suits and preppy haircuts weren't Mel's style, but he conformed because he thought that the job was of equal value to his soul. He didn't realize right away that by taking that without protest that a little bit of his pride was broken off.

That was Ben's first shot at Mel. Mel hadn't seen nor spoken to him before that. Often, Ben didn't even acknowledge him, but when he did speak to Mel, his speech was full of haughty statements in passing, such as "I wish I could trade positions with you" and "I don't see how people can live in the city." That's when Mel became wary of the petty dictator with a racist chip on his shoulder. It was obvious the sight of a black man made him see red. He wasn't man enough to address him the way that he saw him: Nigger. Mel tried to convince himself that it wasn't personal and that Ben just didn't like blacks, but he wasn't so sure.

Mel's suspicions of Ben's personal vendetta against him were confirmed from a female summer intern at the company. High yellow and as cute as a smiley-face button, Beverly worked in the accounting department with him and she was in her third year at Chicago State. It was a big coincidence to Mel, and soon they found themselves talking about all of the professors and the school in general...neutral conversation that could've been taken the wrong way by an invidious executive. Mel was attracted to her in an innocent way, and they became sibling-like. Ben apparently had a slave master-to-female slave thing for her. Mel thought nothing of it when Ben walked passed and cut him a malevolent glance as he was yacking it up with her on his lunch break. He was used to it. Beverly confided in him a week later that Ben told her to "Watch out for Mel...he's no good and you can do better than that." Mel was seething for a month after he heard that. For a long time, the white man in a blue suit intimidated Mel. From that moment on, he was too ireful towards Ben and any other white man to be hectored by the image. The urge to stomp him into ground turkey was almost too strong to resist. Evidently, he thought every young, light-skinned sister was impressionable enough to turn against her darker siblings at the urging of "the man". Beverly didn't come back the next semester (as the company promised she could), but she did go on to complete her studies and get a lucrative position at a bank. Of course, Ben was behind the rejection. He gave more respect to the minorities that knew their menial role in life. As long as they excepted the subordinate lot that was bestowed upon them by the powers that be, they were okay with Ben. Mel was upward bound and considered a problem. Mel was noticing the games the company played and the influence they had on quite a few people, including those of his color who were poisoned by the subtle Willie Lynch doctrine.

A man selling "StreetWise" newspapers is in their path. "StreetWise! StreetWise! Get your StreetWise here! The newspaper for the homeless! Would you like to buy a copy of StreetWise Ma'am? It's only a dollar," he spiels to Memory as she does her deaf and blind woman imitation and turns her nose up at the man. "What about you Sir? It's only a dollar."

Mel starts to politely decline and keep stepping like he usually does—since he hates digging into his pocket when it's cold—but the Christmas Spirit bites him. And he's tired of trying to keep pace with Memory. "Hold up Memory," he yells as he digs into his pocket and pulls out a loose five. She doesn't even respond or hesitate as he hands the bill to the shivering man, who's wearing no gloves, a dirty, black skull cap that's seen better days, some blue moon boots with the thick soles, and a wool jacket that doesn't look warm. The man takes it into his soiled, dusky hand and digs into his pocket for the change. He pulls out a thin wad of bills and tries to count out four dollars with his numb fingers, as he looks anxiously down the block at the fading Memory. "Don't worry about her. She's upset because her man broke up with her today," Mel jokes.

"Hey hey. I see. She looks like she could use some good ol' fashion Christmas cheer."

"She could use something else too. Keep the change," Mel says as he hands the man his leather gloves, trying to get off the subject of the idiot princess walking down the street.

"Thank you brother."

"Don't mention it."

"God bless you."

"God bless you, too."

"Now go keep that young lady warm."

"I will."

"And have a Merry Christmas."

"You too," Mel says as he breaks away from the man's good, frantic cheer. He has to run to catch up with her. It wasn't long ago that he had a bad bout with the flu and bronchitis, and running in the elements is how he got it. He was without a car for a few months since his brother crashed it and wasn't insured. The bronchitis kept him out of commission for the month of October and part of November.

He catches up to Memory at the corner of Congress Parkway and questions, "Why didn't you slow down?"

"Didn't nobody tell you to stop," she hisses.

He doesn't even have a response to that as the urge to dump her in the icy slush intensifies with his temperature.

What may have set him back more than the illness, was the postponement of the trip to Mexico he and Memory had planned. That put even more strain on him and the relationship. Memory reacted as if Mel got sick with the purpose of getting out of it and agitating her. He almost told her to "Go by yourself", but she may have called his bluff. They were planning to grow closer, since their involvement—mostly hers—in their careers dug a valley in between them. It got to the point where her disposition was too robotic for an actual breathing person—asking generic questions just to catch up on the latest with him. There was no spontaneity, just formality. Her planner shouldn't govern their relationship. Before she got into her career in public relations (making more than him, so of course her job was more important and she had more authority in the relationship than he did), they would drive up to the Dells in the summer and fly to Florida for the weekend in the winter without thinking twice. Now they can't even go out to lunch at Burger King without fitting it into her schedule. Her polite discussions lacked genuine interest. She was consumed by her buppy, 90's-black-woman-on-the-move lifestyle. The relationship was more interesting when they didn't have all the money to do all that they could.

Mel was foolishly planning to propose on the trip. They both wanted to be married, although Mel wasn't sure if Memory would accept at that moment. She always wanted husband, one girl, a big house with a fence, a BMW, a Jeep and a cat (although she knew he was allergic to cats). On the rare occasions when they talked intimately about eloping, it was obvious that she still loved him, and he still loved her, but they were drifting apart. Unfortunately, while he was supposed to be vacationing in Acapulco, snorkeling in the Pacific, crooning about ole' senorita, and rekindling the romance, he was at home hacking up an unlimited supply of gold jelly while she berated him for being sick.

During his two months off, Mel did a lot of soul searching and he did a lot of soul finding. He realized he was doing things that others considered right instead of what was comfortable to him. His ol' man pushed him to become an accountant because he was good at math. Memory made for a good arm-piece for any brother. A lot of guys thought she was drop dead fine, but when he looks closely at her now, he doesn't see much to get excited over any more. And her disposition was left as desolate as a ghost town in the desert, so he started questioning his feelings for her. If he didn't have it made up in his mind that he's in love with her, he would've left her many light years ago.

Sure, he was living the American dream (he even had a dog), but who determined what the American dream was? One's dream is another's nightmare, and it was hard to tell the difference for him. The buppy lifestyle wasn't all that great. It was a struggle that wasn't worth the time or money. He wanted a more fulfilling life; a reason to be excited every day he woke up. But after being tailored for a business world that didn't want him, he didn't have a clue, so he sulked for the first week he was out, then he went on a shopping spree with the new VISA gold that came in the mail.

After he pays the attendant and gets his keys, he goes to the hatchback and pulls out one of the prizes from the buying binge: his camcorder. For the longest time, he wanted one. Service Merchandise carries a large selection, all with seemingly the same functions. After spending about thirty minutes going over the different features of five different cameras, he decided on an RCA. Model CC540. It was roughly $800...the most expensive one they carried. It didn't take long for him to start playing with it. Before the week was over, he only had about ten home movies. He fell in love with it. Everywhere he went, so did his camera. He started filming trips to the grocery store and his dog releasing on the lawn. Anything that could be recorded, was. The footage of him taping everything could've been sent in to America's Funniest Home Videos.

He presses the 'on' button and points it at Memory as she waits unsuspectingly by the passenger door. "I want to remember you just like this," he says looking through the lens with a goofy grin at her.

She turns around glaring as if she's about to punch the camera and growls, "Not tonight, all right. I'm very tired and I want to go home."

He lets the camera drop to his side and looks at her for a few seconds—still grinning, while she's still frowning. Neither one of them says a thing as he shakes his head in disbelief and opens the door for her. After he sits the camera in the back, he rests his arms on the top of the raised door to ponder the mood. The crack he made to the newspaper man was actually a joke. Now it's gotten real serious. He needs closure to the day and the relationship. Since things are going so great for him, he might as well start all over in every area of his life. What else can he be rid of today? First his job, now his woman. It doesn't get any better than this.

After jumping in and turning the ignition, nothing happens. He has to get used to driving a stick. He presses down on the clutch pedal of the biggest toy of the infamous shopping spree. *He got an advance to add to the down payment. The car is only four weeks and 737 miles old. It still has the new smell in it. He hasn't even made the first of 48 payments of $496.82. Under the assumption that he would be bringing home at least $550 a week, Mel went all out and got the '94 Dodge Stealth. He was torn between the Stealth and the Camaro with the new body design. The Z24 was about $10,000 less, which meant that it was more affordable. Intuition told him he didn't want any parts of another*

Camaro, because it was too popular and car-jacking was on the rise for that ride. It seems that after Menace II Society came out every wanna-be-thug in Chicago got geeked up. During the previous summer, there were about three car-jackings involving Camaros in his neighborhood, with one a couple of blocks from his parent's house. A brother was sitting in the car with his girlfriend and they shot him in the head—just like in the movie. The difference is the victim was rolling legit and unarmed, and he didn't get a chance to give the car up without a fight. His Camaro wasn't even an IROC. And to think a couple of years ago car-jacking and drive-by's were strictly a Los Angeles thing. If the sounds of NWA and the rest of the West Coast gangster rappers didn't reach the mid-west, Chicago wouldn't have to contend with that element of crime.

Of course, he needed some accessories with a new car. In other words, he had to replenish his wardrobe. Clothes always gave him a sense of importance, so the first stop was Bachrach's in Ford City. He restored his wardrobe with several blazers, suits, shirts and shoes. His closet contained a change of clothes for at least three weeks. And that was just the out on the town wear. Then he headed to the Plaza for some casual and sports wear. He remembered his high school days when he used to go up there on Saturdays just to hang out and girl watch. Now he can't stand to be there for the same reason he loved it almost ten years ago: the youngsters hanging out. He held back on the gym shoes and sweat suits. He was like a poor man that won the lottery, except everything was done on credit, which meant that he'll still be paying for the stuff when it's nothing but rags. His gold card almost melted. Instead of breaking it in, he broke it. There was $600 worth of credit left, give or take a dollar. Through it all, he was content, and for the first time in a long time, he felt happy.

The newfound serenity carried over to his first day back to work. As soon as he walked in the door, he noticed something that he hadn't done in a long time: smile upon entering. It almost seemed like he was at a new job. He had showed no animosity, despite being totally disgusted with the organization. He even spoke to G like she was somebody on his Christmas gift list. Well, of course if she were, he would give her something along the lines of a poisonous snake. Ben's face didn't even ruin his happy high. So what if he imagined filming his fist connecting with Ben's jaw, he was still unmoved by his presence. His work seemed more enjoyable. He was above the world on a cloud for the whole week. Then they announced that G was the manager of Accounts Payable...Mel's old position. That's when his cloud disintegrated and he crashed back to Earth. They didn't even post the opening. They just literally gave it to her like her name was on it. Apparently, that was their plan in the first place when they hired her. Everybody was surprised and they knew that Mel was faded, although he tried not to let his disgust show. He got out before anyone could see him blow up. It wasn't so much him losing the position as it was the principle behind their decision to give it to her. He had given the company seven, long, hard years of his life and he had invested most of his energy into it, and they diss him by replacing him with someone less qualified and educated. He's not a person that uses profanity often, but that day he was cussing like a Pirate.

Today it's crystal clear that they were setting him up to knock him down like a bowling pin. The question—that really doesn't matter at this point—is how long were they planning their little caper? It was a master plan: they figured that Mel would probably sue for wrongful discharge since he (and they) knew that he was innocent of what they insinuated he did; they moved him to the customer service department; they knew they were going to be moving five months later; they were planning to implement E.D.I. (Electronic Data Interchange) as soon as they got to the new location, and they forecasted the phasing out of the department. All of that to get rid of him and a few other people. Let Horizon tell it, he was just a casualty of technology. E.D.I. was going to save money by doing most of the work of the order department. Their major customers could input their orders on their terminals and it would automatically print out at Horizon's distribution center, where it would ship out. As if they just came up with that idea. Since Jan "don't call me Marsha" Brady has been in the customer service department since creation, and it was necessary to have some lines of communications with the customers that wanted to phone an order in with a live operator, Mel was the black man out.

He floors it down the Dan Ryan. The department of streets and sanitation did a good job of clearing the snow off the expressway. It's a good thing too, because all-wheel drive wouldn't have kept him from sliding into the cement embankment while trying to get Memory home and out of his life. Tension is sitting between them during the ride. Not one word is uttered. She frowns for the duration of the ride. It is so uncomfortable, that he forgets that he has a car stereo. He shouldn't have thrown out his little black book. It was the righteous, fair thing to do, but he's regretful now. Oh yes, there was a time when he had a fair share of female admirers. That was one of the fringe benefits of working for Horizon. With black males making up less than five percent of the employees, coupled with the fact that two thirds of them were gay, tripled with his intellect and trendy complexion, he had favor with the many beautiful black women that they employed. He had a couple of flings during one of their many drops of the roller coaster relationship. It was a matter of checks and balances. The competition kept her in or close to the line. He suspected that she was running around more than she let on. Judging by this latest episode, she may be messing around now, for all he knows.

He smiles whenever he recalls the 9 1/2 weeks Rita Wright was a willing fill-in. It was perfect timing for both of them. Her fiancé was in the dog pound ready to be put to sleep and Memory decided she needed some air, so she was in the process of sucking in some oxygen with the help of a couple of airmen. Maybe it was a full moon, because Mel and Rita rarely spoke to each other before they started going out. However, they secretly admired each other from a distance, since they were both devoted. They looked like a perfect couple. Actually, they resembled each other like soap opera siblings. She was a darker shade of black, with skin so soft and smooth that he thought she had a velvet epidermis. Her hair was jet-black and long and usually worn in an enticing ponytail. When she let it down, she looked like an Egyptian queen. Her eyes were big, black and petrified looking. She was about two inches shorter than Mel (which made her about towering five ten) and had a lean, curvaceous model-type figure with absolutely no blemishes. It was perfectly sooty and the exact same color as her face. She was a shadow of excellence; a silhouette of grace. Everything about her was black and beautiful, as if she coined the phrase.

During those two and a half months, they were perpetually intimate. Friendship was their foundation and they satisfied each other's needs. She provided the ear that Memory was lacking. He romanced her like Romeo (flowers, cards, and chivalry) since her so-called man missed Gentleman 101. They always said the right things to each other. He never mentioned dark and beautiful in the same breath, because she was so much like him, that he imagined that she had a hang-

up with such well-meaning, yet insulting, comments—like black coupled with beauty is an exception. The newness and passion never wore off. Perhaps they both subconsciously knew that it wasn't a permanent accommodation. They flirted with the idea of staying together, and almost didn't make it back to their "real" relationships. She offered to change her master plan with her man if he lost his Memory. It was one of the hardest decisions he had to make in his life. He was still in love with Memory and he really loved the intimacy that he and Rita shared, so he told her that he wanted to leave the dream in the frozen frame and wake up to reality. And they did, walking away without looking back, although he's peeking over his shoulder. She got married two months later and moved to LA. He hasn't heard from her since, and that was two years ago. Now he regrets the decision.

As he exits on 83rd Street and makes a left hand turn, wicked thoughts of Darlene come to mind and an impish grin forms on his face. Darlene is to Memory what steak is to hamburger: an envious step up. They are arch rivals. Memory hates Darlene and Darlene loves to make Memory hate her even more. And she lives on the same block as Memory. And she started at Horizon at the same time as Memory. Darlene pushed Memory's buttons by flirting with Mel, representing Memory's worse nightmare. She is a shade lighter than Memory, an inch taller and her eyes are forest green. Her hair is shoulder length and sandy colored. She has a voluptuous body that every man—white and black—lusts, and she knows it. Her chest sticks out and proud and her waist is slender with hips exploding out like living liberation.

Whenever Darlene had the chance, she would walk by him switching and looking seductive as she flattered him in front of Memory. Memory would turn rose red and threaten to "kick that bitch in the ass if she don't keep her eyes and compliments to herself." It was amusing to play along with it once-in-a-while when Memory got into one of her anti-Mel moods. Whenever she saw Darlene talking to him, she would start worshipping him. It didn't matter if they cussed each other out the night before and professed a mutual hate. When Memory would get a glimpse of Darlene messing with him, her mind would go to her worse gutter. She would picture them "boning" and Mel "enjoying it." When she told him that, she gave him the trump card.

After she called herself breaking up with him a year ago because he was "too nice", he plotted to earn a bad reputation for her. Darlene was always begging to take him out, so he accepted her offer and allowed her to seduce him. He knew it would get back to Memory because Darlene was a trophy hunter and rated every kill she made. Needless to say, she rated him a ten in the verbal tabloids in the beauty shop that they both go to and pretty soon, the word echoed off the walls of Horizon like a super ball. There were quite a few females that wanted to ride the "Black Stallion"—as Darlene dubbed him. How original. She was pretty good, too, and if he was gullible, she would've turned him inside-out.

It got back to Memory within 48 hours, and her feathers were ruffled, fizzled and plucked out. She didn't come out and say it, but she was too humble when she called him—especially considering she walked away with an attitude the week before, saying, "You should find somebody else, because I want to go out with other people." He was too hardheaded and soft-hearted to leave well enough and Memory alone. She said that she "did some thinking and that she was sorry and wanted to get back together." Instead of telling her what to do and where to go after she did it, he took her back with open arms.

That was then, this is now, and it will pass in a few seconds. His grin grows wider as he passes Darlene's house. The ignorant thought of video taping an erotic scene with Darlene and mailing it to her—just to refresh her *memory* (no pun intended) of a good thing she took for granted—crosses his mind. As he pulls into the entrance to the Chatham Park Place townhouses and up to her door, he glances at her. She's gazing trance-like out of the window. The frown is gone, replaced by a look of gloom. Neither one of them says a word or looks at each other. Mel just gazes straight ahead while she continues to peer out of the side window. It's almost like they're waiting for the other to pull the trigger. Maybe she's reading his mind. Maybe she senses the end coming, just as a dog senses when he is on his way to the gas chamber. As a cue, he takes a loud, deep breath and lets it out through his nose so that she can hear his anticipation. She doesn't say anything. When he looks over at her, he notices a tear rolling down her face. He almost reaches over to hug her on impulse, telling her everything is all right. But things are all wrong, so he plays like he doesn't see her and stares at the bushes just outside the drivers-side window. After sitting in the same position for about five minutes, she sniffles real loud—obviously trying to bring attention to her tears—but he ignores her, even though he wants to turn his head if for nothing else but to shift positions.

"I guess after tonight you're not going to see me again," she says, breaking the fifteen-minute silence and seeking a reaction from him, but to no avail. He doesn't even look her way.

"I don't blame you if you don't ever speak to me again," she says contritely. "I know I've been a real bitch today. I'm surprised you didn't slap me."

He wants to agree with her, but he still doesn't answer her. He wants her to beg a little more...to wallow in discomfort.

"I was having a real bad case of PMS," she rationalizes—as if that's supposed to make everything okay.

"Do you want me to leave?" she huffs.

He still doesn't respond, however, there are a few things he wants to tell her to do.

"Are you going to answer me?" she asks timidly.

He still doesn't speak and he gets the vibe that she's about to break down and start acting silly.

"Don't be like that," she whines as she embraces him around the neck and tries to kiss him on the cheek.

He turns his face away.

"So you not gonna gimme my sugar?" she whispers in his ear.

Turned off totally, he pushes her away and frees his mind. "Why would I want you to kiss me after the way you've been playing me the whole evening?" he questions. She looks real pitiful and remorseful while growing mute. What can she say? He is right. "When I wanted to be in a good mood, you played me off and right now the only thing you can do is get out of my face. Here I was having the worst day of my life and you make it an even worse night. I needed consoling, and you gave me grief instead."

By now, she can't even look at him as her eyes drop down and well up again. But he's not through with her yet. "It was just like you to blame everything on me. I lose my job: it's my fault; You lose your job: why, Melvin? Why? A bird died: See what you did; It rained today: make it go away Melvin; The world ended today: that damn Mel. How can you blame me for being 'funky' because I was blackballed out of work? And then for you to down play my issues and suggest that I was just under a lot of stress. You're damn right I'm under stress. Right now, I'm too outdone with you and that job. There's no middle ground. I can't win, so I'm not going to play or be played anymore."

The tears start falling again as she penitently murmurs, “Sorry”.

He’s sorry he even saw her today as he buries his chin in his hand and rests his elbow on the armrest. They don’t say anything for the next five minutes. His intentions of talking to her after tonight remain NA. Enough is enough and he’s had enough. And he’s had enough of sitting in this car talking about nothing and wasting gas. He doesn’t have a job anymore, so gas is like gold.

She clears her throat and says, “Would you wait here for me? I have to use the bathroom.”

He can feel her staring at him, but he doesn’t acknowledge it with a glance or a word.

She opens the car door, saying, “Wait right here,” as she closes it real quickly and runs through the door and up the stairs. Just when he was about to cut her loose, she runs off. He made it up in his mind that it’s best that they part, love or no love. The mood is awkward. Maybe because his heart is saying otherwise. He turns on the radio and they’re playing “Yours” by Shai, so he immediately turns it off.

He waits in the running car for about five minutes, when he watches her run down the stairs through the glass windows that stretch all the way up the building, giving a clear view of the hallway. The temptation to be ornery and pull off hit him hard. Sunshine seems to be radiating from her as she jumps in the car with more pep and gazes at him. She flashes that same wily smile from when they first met, however, it’s not effective now. She deep-froze him today and she won’t have the opportunity to thaw him out with her seductive simper. His sedated glare makes it apparent as she folds.

“Merry Christmas” she says as she pulls a long, thin box wrapped in green paper and a red bow from inside her jacket.

He successfully strains to keep his blank expression, taking the box and facetiously holding it up to his ear as if he is checking to see if it was ticking. To his surprise, “It really is ticking,” he says in a reserved tone.

“Of course it is silly,” she says as she rolls her eyes at him.

Determined to give her a cup of the bitter medicine that she doled out to him earlier, he suggests, “So you’re trying to blow me up” as he tosses the box in her lap, realizing that it’s probably a watch.

“You know what it is.”

“No I don’t.”

"Well open it. I'm not going to be able to spend Christmas Eve with you anyway and I want to see your expression. I want you to have it even if you don't ever speak to me again," she says as she extends it to him again.

He looks at her as if her mind ran away and reluctantly takes it from her. Gently, he tears the wrapping paper away from the white jewelry box. He slowly opens the box and inside is the nicest gold watch that he's ever seen. Of course it's gorgeous: it's a Rolex. Only the rich and privileged have Rolex's. She knew that he needed a watch, although he doesn't like wearing jewelry. He's struck with a case of taciturnity. His eyes get misty as he just stares dumfounded at her.

"You like?" she asks through her beautiful smirk.

The ice is melted and he's on fire. "It's nice," he says nervously.

"Put it on," she urges.

He gladly obliges.

"My time is your time, and I don't ever want you to lose time."

She is clever with her spellbinding tactics. At that moment the days events are gone from his memory (pun intended).

"I really want to spend Christmas with you—and since your birthday is next week, I'll have your gift wrapped early in a G-string...that is if you still want me," she says sincerely.

"Yeah, that's cool," he says, somewhat choked up. Now he can't gaze in her eyes, so he focuses on her door straight ahead.

"So does this mean you forgive me?" she questions in a seductive tone as she leans a warm breath away.

What could he say but "I forgive you." She has him whipped like a defiant stepchild.

Suddenly, she grabs his chin, turns his head towards her and dives lip first for his mouth, their lips locking like suction cups as they embrace. Every hair from the top of his head to the tips of his toes seems to be standing at attention. Her lips are savory and arresting. After a short eternity of being welded together, they separate for air. They continue to hug each other tightly for a few moments, and although his arms are getting tired, he doesn't want to let go. They fit together like puzzle pieces.

"Don't ever leave me," she moans. "I don't know what I would do without you."

He just squeezes her real hard and gently lets her go, which was the only response he could give.

"I'll see you around noon on Christmas. I'm going to make your 25th birthday a very happy one."

"You already have."

"It gets better," she declares devilishly.

"I look forward to it."

"So do I," she says as she plants a kiss on his lips and opens the door. "I'll call you tomorrow. See you in my dreams."

"Goodnight," he mumbles under his breath, still overwhelmed by the last half-hour. She slams the door and waves at him as she gets to her doorway—still brandishing that killer smile. He just sits there for another five minutes trying to figure out what just happened. It's like he was conned into love...into the relationship. His heart is racing with anxiety and he has to leak. His body is numb as he gazes at the door she walked in five minutes ago. He looks at his watch—the $2,500-plus Rolex she just gave him. It's a quarter to ten. He smiles and shakes his head as he finally backs out.

While driving down 83rd Street, he yawns loudly, but doesn't realize how tired he is. The effects of being unemployed are masked. The past few lackadaisical months's with Memory are forgotten. Love is a journey. As he pulls up to the stop light at Cottage Grove, another car rolls up next to him. He glances over at the three young female occupants in a new Cavalier. That's when he notices that he's sporting a goofy grin, and he immediately straightens it to a more neutral, less suggestive expression as they start cackling. Wouldn't they love to have the same reason to cheese? He pulls off just as the light turns green.

He hasn't eaten all day and as the Kentucky Fried Chicken sign comes into sight, his appetite convinces himself that he wants some chicken nuggets. There's no one in the drive through, but since his bladder is about to explode, he opts to go in. After releasing himself, he steps up to the counter to order. However, Carlota the cashier is on the phone, apparently on a personal call. Carlota puts her caller on hold, and in a dry tone reeking attitude, she recites the national fast food script: "Welcome to bogga, bogga bogga. May I help you?" He requests nuggets, but they're all out for the night, so he orders an original meal with all white meat, but he has to compromise again, since the only thing left is original dark and three spicy wings. He opts for the spicy wings, although they always give him diarrhea. It doesn't matter, since he can sit on the toilet at home all week, if he has to.

Before he can get to the car, he tears into the box like an animal and pulls the biscuit out. He takes one bit and spits it out. It must have been sitting up there since yesterday, because it's as dry as sandpaper. Oh well. He should've expected it, since it was the last one. He's not going to act ignorant and throw it through the window. A good nights sleep is on the menu, since the chicken tastes like they soaked it in old hair grease. Thirty dollars is what he spent on food today and he hasn't even eaten. Instead of throwing it out of the window, he wraps it up for his dogs, although he wonders if it'll make them puke.

For as long as he can remember, he wanted to breed. The appeal was more in the universal infatuation with puppies than the actual business. The prospect of getting rid of them for a profit before they grew into big, ugly canines, made the idea even more attractive. Of course, his mother knew what kind of responsibility came with a puppy, and that's why she never let him have one. Now that he's on his own, he's going to get a chance to have a couple of litters. He bought two AKC registered female Rottweilers about a month ago. They were part of the spoil of his false sense of purchasing power. He already had a show quality male with 20 champions in his pedigree that he bought just after he closed on his house. Since he was going to be living alone, and he wouldn't have time to train a puppy, he decided to buy the best. His name is Jeremy Von Homey and he doesn't play.

Mel's cousin, Earl, made the mistake of walking too close to the gate once and had his shirt ripped. Homey stalked him like a hired killer. Homey knows Mel's little brother, but he won't allow David in the yard without Mel being present. He got him for a cheap $400, too. He was two years old and 130 pounds, with a head the size of a milk crate. Mel was very reluctant when he bought him. It took about three weeks of feeding and talking to him before he could take him home. It didn't take him long to get used to his new home either. He got comfortable in the big yard, since he had to share limited space with a Miniature Pincher at his old home. Rottweilers are the dog of choice these days and the going rate for a full blooded, AKC registered puppy is $500 and up. He considered doing it for a living. The females are do to go in heat in either December or the first of January. Homey is going to have a good holiday season.

He's surprised that they're not jumping at the fence as he pulls into the driveway and up to the garage. There's nothing like the loyalty of a dog that's always glad to see his master. Maybe they had a long day, too. He tosses the empty bag in the garbage and takes his camera out of the back. After he pushes the button to the automatic garage door, he steps out onto the patio, careful not to step in any dung. Dana (one of his females) comes running up to the gate from the outside. She must have a bit of cat in her, because she has no problem hopping the fence. He lets her in, rubs her head when she gets up to him and tosses her the snack. "Homey! Bridgette!" he calls. He's not surprised to see them come out trotting side by side from the back of the house, but after a double-take, the cadence of their lope makes them look like Siamese twins connected at the tail wick. It then dawns on him that they're in the middle of sex. He looks at them and they both seem to be smiling and enjoying it as they pant away. "Must be the season of love," he says as he lets out a confidential chuckle. "I could've been tied up like that, too."

After observing them for a few moments, he gets the crazy idea of dog porn (something for "Americas Funniest Home Videos"). He pushes the ON button on his camcorder and tapes them for about ten minutes before they break loose, exhausted, yet ready for another round. He wonders would it be too explicit for kids. He smiles and forgets about his hunger pangs as he walks into the house. He immediately heads upstairs to his bedroom and puts his camera on the closet shelf. After walking out of his clothes (he'll pick them up and throw them away tomorrow), he notices the light blinking on his answering machine on the nightstand. The indicator says there are eight messages. Damn. He's popular tonight. Usually he can expect two messages at the most. He slips on his shorts as it plays back. The first three messages are from bill collectors, so he starts singing love songs off key to drown out the voices. The fourth message is from Darlene. She said she is sorry that he got laid off and to call her. The fifth and sixth are from Earl and David. They just said to give them a call, so apparently Earl wants to hook him up with somebody and David wants to borrow his wheels. The last two are from Memory, so he turns the volume all the way up and beams with joy as she says, "It's just me. I'm wondering how long you're going to sit out there in front of my house. Why don't you come on in.

Seriously. Anyway, I just wanted to tell you goodnight and I love you. Talk to you tomorrow."

"I love you, too," he whispers as the machine announces the date and time.

"It's me again. I couldn't wait until tomorrow. I just wanted to apologize again for tonight and for the past few months. I'm very lucky to have a man like you and I'll try to show you more appreciation. Anyway, if you're not too tired when you get in, give me a call to tell me that you made it home safely. If not, sweet dreams and I'll talk to you again tomorrow."

The machine says that she called five minutes ago, so he *69's and she picks up on the first ring. "Mel?"

"Yeah."

"You made it in, huh?"

"Yep. Thanks for calling. It was a pleasant surprise."

"It's my pleasure. I wanted to hear your voice before I go to sleep."

"I wish you were here."

"Really? I could've spent the night. I didn't think you were in the mood, so I didn't ask."

"I'm always in the mood for you," he lies. Almost always, though.

"Awe Mel. I hope you're in the mood Christmas, because you're gonna be stuck with me for the whole day."

"I can't wait and I don't think that'll be enough."

"Anyway. You get some rest, because you're gonna need it. I'm gonna literally wear you like a tailored garment during the holidays," she says seductively.

"A Memory suit...I like the way you sound."

"You'll like the way I feel, too."

"I'll hold you to that."

"You promise."

"I promise."

"Okay. I'll call you tomorrow. Are you going to be home all day?"

"Probably."

"I'll call you from work."

"Okay. Talk to you tomorrow then."

"Goodnight."

"Night," he says as he hangs up the phone, falls back on the bed and shouts, "Yes!"

Chapter 2

What does a man get the special woman in his life that will go beyond the mundane? How are the needs of a woman who has everything appeased? Mel pondered those questions all night and throughout the afternoon as he made his way through several malls, searching for the perfect gift for Memory—whatever perfect is for her. There's no way he can come back weak after she bought him a Rolex—presumably between the price ranges of $2,500 and $5,000. Originally, he intended to give her a modest Herringbone gold bracelet he bought from Service Merchandise, but the watch put it to shame and snickered at it. It might as well have been a rusty tin toy that can be bought from one of those 25 cent gum machines in the grocery store. He wants to give her the sky, but his budget won't get him an acorn from the top of an oak tree and his credit is incriminating and condemns him to a lone choice of dirt from a ditch. Materialistically, she already has the sky, so anything short of Heaven is an unworthy gift. Since Heaven isn't his to give, and murder isn't an option (at the moment), he has to get something economical and creative.

As he walks through the Water Tower, he feels the anxiety from conflicting emotions. The shock of getting a pink slip for Christmas and the blissfulness coming from the reality of freedom simultaneously sets in. He feels light, like a cement jacket was snatched from off of his back. Scrutinizing eyes, intense, two-hour, multi-vehicle trips (an unpredictable CTA bus, a crowded El-train, a smoky subway, and a stringent PACE bus), and early bedtimes and risings weigh a ton. He would normally be stressing it out and praying for the end of the day and the start of the long holiday weekend at this very moment. His stomach and Rolex indicate that it is his assigned lunch break for the past three years.

He hit the malls late in the morning, and the last minute Christmas crowds were right on schedule. The elevator's versions of the Christmas carols are a soothing, subliminal backdrop. The ascent up the Water Tower starts on the second level. He bypasses The Sharper Image because the high tech gadgets they carry are geared towards his electronic appetite. She would end up getting a card if he's not careful. It didn't help matters when he saw Deacon Bradford and trustee Smith's daughter, LaTonya from his former church in there, because he sure isn't in the mood for church folks today. Is the congregation here on a shopping spree? The third level isn't offering anything either. Victoria's Secret has some nice bed gear, but Memory has a whole collection of their underwear in her wardrobe. He even spotted a mannequin sporting the last set of lingerie that Memory modeled for him, in the display window. He plays Lundstrom's off when he gets off of the escalator to the fourth level since jewelry doesn't feel right, unless it's a $5,000 engagement ring that he really can't afford. For his own sanity, he stops in Aventura's (the men's shoe store) and Sam Goody's Music. Both have a limited selection of what he likes, so he proceeds to the fifth level, where Bath & Body Works is calling him. Since Memory loves apples, he picks up a basket of Country Apple soap, body lotion, body splash and shower gel. At least he can pamper her like a queen and clean her up in the process, before he takes a bite out of her. Wentworth Gallery doesn't have anything Afrocentric enough for her tastes. Memory would have a laughing fit if he gave her a portrait from out of there. "Printed toilet paper, is it?" she would ask. The prints in Wentworth would be so foreign and out of place in her living room, that the ambiance would be thrown off'er than the combination of a yellow shirt with green polka dots and a pair of red and white stripe pants. As if her townhouse needs coloring. Her art collection is mystical and captivating, enhancing the home like a turbo charger would quicken a muscle car. Mel could look at it all day and still not get tired of studying it. Behind every piece on her wall is a story that black people can relate to. Often, if she's lip tripping, he'll get lost in one of the pictures until she settles down. Usually one of several portraits of the fine, black women—with their mouth's closed—takes him away from the noise.

Hallmark and the White Sox Clubhouse are the only shops on the sixth level that catch his eyes, although they miss the mark on his interest. The floor might as well be a vacant. The seventh level has everything—for him, that is. He kills about thirty minutes in Shutterbug and checks out all of the video cameras and other electronics. It's too bad they don't share the same interests. Otherwise, he could get her a digital camera that they both could use. Memory loves the Bulls' players, but he isn't about to pay for anything with another man's signature on it. Four hundred fifty dollars for Walter Payton's autographed jersey is stupid. Anything over the cost of the jersey because of a signature is stupid. She wouldn't have a Christmas if Field of Dreams were the only shopping option. Perhaps he should have brought her with him and given her a field trip for Christmas. She would've just loved Michael Jordan's Golf. He contemplates how asinine the concept is as he bypasses it on his way to the WTTW Store of Knowledge, where he plays with some of the toys for nerds. In no time he's bored and walks through the Knot Shop, as if he or she needs a necktie. He doesn't waste his time going up to the eighth floor to Marshall Fields. When he checks his watch, he realizes that it took him two hours to go up seven flights of escalator. Two hours, and nothing to show but bubble bath. He peers over the banister overlooking the second floor and wonders if he would survive a jump. Not that he's considering it, although there was a time many seasons ago when he gave death serious consideration. It almost seems like something he dreamed about. Wallowing in self-pity was his favorite past time. Now if he considered taking a life, it would be somebody else's. If he did jump, he would make sure he landed on someone soft and despicable.

Now he wonders how long it would take him to hit the floor from up there as he stares at the watch again. Perhaps she put a spell on it, because he can't keep his eyes off it and his mind away from Memory. And that's what prompts him to keep searching. Instead of the long, scenic route down, he opts for the elevator. When it reaches him, an unassuming white woman inadvertently cuts in front of him—just like a rude motorist—causing him to stumble over his own feet. For a split second, the temptation to slap the back of her head rises with his temperature. The surge of ire makes his head throb slightly. He realizes the quick temper and the migraine hint indicate an empty stomach. When he got up this morning, he remembered to wash up and put on his clothes, but he forgot to eat breakfast. Not even a slice of bread. Lunchtime is in order, otherwise he may just break his fall on some poor, unsuspecting soul.

He picks up a Sun-Times from the East Indian Magazine merchant in the lower level, orders a grape pop and two, $3.50 slices of sausage pizza from Foodlife Pizzeria, and parks in a corner in the Mezzanine. As soon as he opens his eyes from saying grace, his appetite flies south. BJ Thomas, the biggest religious skeptic and critic he's ever had the displeasure of meeting in person, is slithering towards him. Mel maneuvers his pop between them and ducks his head in the paper with hopes that he won't spot him and come over antagonizing him. Hopefully he'll keep going even if he does see him. Of course he comes and flops down *uninvited*—with his big, phony grin and gargantuan head with the Count Dracula widows peak—right across from Mel, and asks, "What's up, man" in a debate baiting tone. "Long time no see."

"Oh," Mel plays it off, wishing it was a longer time and that he had a cross to repel him with as he asks, through clenched teeth and not truly caring one way or another, "How you doing, BJ?"

"I'm living, Bro. I'm living."

"That's a good start." Now don't get started.

BJ is a little darker than he remembers. Canary yellow is how he used to characterize him, but now he has a gold tint—like he spent a week in a tanning parlor. When Mel was a senior in high school, he worked on the north side at Time Incorporated. Being the youngest person in the department made him restive, so when it appeared that BJ was in his age range, he thought he could relax a little. An aisle is all that separated them, but it was obvious from the way he avoided eye contact with Mel, that he was stuck up like a lost tourist in Florida. He would hold his nose high—as if he was sniffing the clouds—when he walked past Mel. Mel had wrongly concluded that BJ would never say a word to him. When BJ saw him pull his Sunday school book out to read during the idle time that they were accustomed to having, he was too provoked to hold his peace. The first conversation they had was a debate. Actually, since BJ was doing most of the fussing—with his irritating, articulate voice—it was more like a lambasting of Mel. He leaned over and asked, "So you go to church" in a very condescending tone.

Mel just looked up and nodded.

He went back to reading when BJ asked, "Do you think you could answer some questions for me about God and church?"

Mel had a bad feeling about talking to him about religion, but he put his book down and said, "Possibly."

That's when he started setting him up with obvious, rhetorical questions: "Is God perfect? Is God everywhere? Is man made in God's own image? Is God all knowing?..." Mel answered yes to all of his rapid fire questions and then he dropped the bomb: "If God is perfect and all knowing, and he made man in his own image, why did he create man, knowing that man would fall?"

Mel didn't even play like he knew the answer to that question. "I'm not sure," he said as he humped his shoulders up.

"Doesn't the fall of man prove that God is not perfect?"

Mel took the bait. "No, that proves that man is not perfect."

"Doesn't that prove that God is not all knowing?

"I don't believe it does."

"Okay then, the Scriptures state that God is a loving God and that He doesn't want to see any man perish in hell. Well, let's say that he is all knowing. If he's all loving, why did he create man, knowing that man would fall?"

Mel just shook his head nervily at not knowing how to answer this skilled deliberator. He wasn't sure if he was interrogating him for personal amusement or if he was trying to draw him to atheism, but he was sure the source was Lucifer.

"Why did he put the Tree of Knowledge in the Garden of Eden? That's like me putting a wolf in my basement and telling my toddler not to go down there because you'll die—knowing that toddlers are pretty curious anyway, not to mention they don't truly understand the concept of danger. That would be pretty irresponsible of me and I would—and rightly so—be prosecuted for it," he said as he intensified. "Another thing: you mentioned that man was imperfect. Why in the hell would God give his message to a man to give to mankind if man is imperfect? I don't know, but if I was God, I would have just come down to earth and spoke to mankind myself, rather than relying on an unreliable creature such as a man."

Mel got warmer and BJ got hotter: "And why did he separate man when they were building the Tower of Babel...we were getting along just fine, working together, trying to reach God, and what does he do? He confuses us and separates us, which is contradictory to what the scriptures teach. 'God is not the author of confusion.' It sounds like God is a little flaky and confused to me."

He was on such a role that he didn't give Mel the opportunity to respond to anything. Not that Mel was prepared or confident enough to rebuke this mad man. After he got a little audience, he closed out, putting Mel on the spot with "How can you worship a God that you don't understand and that can't even answer a mere mortal like me? That's downright doltish, dimwitted, dumb," as he turned back around in his seat, self gratified. Mel turned around too, picked up his Sunday school book and perpetrated like he was reading. His faith wasn't shaken, but he was a little unsettled. That was actually the last conversation they had at work. For his embarrassment, Mel added the word doltish to his vocabulary. Often BJ would only greet him with a self-satisfied, glancing grin. Mel was horrified when he found out that he was one of the editors of Chicago State's student newspaper when he arrived as a freshman. BJ was still at it, although they missed each other on campus. He earned his notoriety on campus through the paper. Once, he wrote a blistering commentary denouncing gospel music on campus. To Mel's surprise, he had a lot of supporters.

"So what are you doing with yourself? Didn't you study accounting?"

"That's what I studied, but right now I'm on an extended vacation. I'm considering a career change."

"Really? What are you considering—the ministry?" he asks with covert sarcasm.

"I'm considering something along the lines of Broadcasting or video graphics. I would like to do some things with the camera. But right now I'm still weighing my options."

"Cool. That's not half bad. You know that's along my lines of journalism. Have you considered Columbia?"

"Not yet."

"You hinted that you're in between jobs."

"Yeah, you can say that."

"Well check it out," he says reaching into his inside jacket pocket. He hands him a business card, telling him "Give me a call and I'll let you know if there are any openings around town. You might want to come to the Chicago Association of Black Journalists' meeting on the second Wednesday of next month. It's a good source of information and an opportunity to get the inside details of the field."

"Does it cost anything?"

"Membership is something like $25 dollars a year, but if you just want to come to the meeting it's $5. It's well worth it."

"I'll consider it," he says with a bit of disinclination as he peeks into his paper and bites into his pizza. BJ was never at a loss of words, so the pause in the conversation baffles Mel as he glances over at him. He shakes his head because he thinks he's seeing a mirage: BJ had his head bowed in a praying posture. Is he mocking him? Is a religious debate going to start? Mel isn't going for it today. He'll get up and leave if he attempts.

"I'm going to be interviewing Horace Grant in a few hours," he offers as Mel reads over an article on the Bulls in the Sun-Times.

"Really. For the Defender?"

"It's a freelance assignment for a Christian athletic publication called Sports Spectrum."

"Horace Grant is a Christian?"

"A new convert."

"Interesting," Mel says, nodding his head. What's even more interesting is who's giving him this info.

They pause again to nibble on their food.

"So, do you still go to church?"

Here goes the verbal assault. "Not really," he grunts.

"How ironic that you don't go any more and I go all the time now."

"I still believe in God, it's just that I had a rough time at my last church."

"I hear you. The Lord had to humble me. Now I can't get enough of Him. I can remember when I used to denounce people's beliefs in God—even yours—and look at me now. Whatever you do, don't compromise your relationship or beliefs, no matter *who* or what you go up against, because I know that I've rocked some people's faith in my dark days. And I know it's been a few years, but seeing you now brings back some memories that the Spirit won't let me ignore. I apologize for the way I came to you when we worked together at Time and I hope you find it in your heart to forgive me."

Mel feels like he's in the Twilight Zone. Five minutes ago he was waiting to be provoked, calling him everything but the child of God under his breath—which is exactly what he is now—and prepared to leave him hanging here at the slightest offense. Now he has to embrace him as his brother. Life is full of surprises. "Everything is cool," he says with a welcoming grin as he extends his hand. BJ obliges by slapping his into it and clasps' it. "I guess it's good to know that there's a good potential lawyer on God's side."

They both laugh at that and throw out some names of mutual people they knew from work and school, in order to get updated on what everybody is doing. To Mel's surprise, BJ has another talent: the ability to absorb food like a sponge while talking. Before he knows it and finishes his first slice of Pizza, BJ is done. "Well, I hate to eat and run, but I have a hot date, Bro," he says, collecting his tray. "You still got that Christmas shopping to do, huh?"

"Yeah, you know how it is. Shopping for the ol' lady."

"I know. I'm not envious. Well, give me a call and I'll let you know what's happening in the field. And try to make the CABJ meeting."

"All right. I should make it next month."

"Peace out."

"Later," he says as he scans the business card he left. It reads, "Bartholomew "Believing" Thomas Jackson: Freelance Writer. *And Thomas answered and said unto him, My Lord and my God."* He didn't know his name is Bartholomew. For some silly reason, he thought BJ was on his birth certificate. Well, Bartholomew is a long name. He would've probably abbreviated it too. It must be nice getting into the games, and even nicer interviewing the players. If Memory knew that he was going to the game and interviewing her favorite player, she would drop Mel like a sack of empty White Castles and try to swindle BJ. She would sell her soul to go to tomorrow's game. If Mel took her, they would be even in the Christmas present department. He glances at the headline of the coming game and flips to the classified section that he never reads. He finds what he was looking for and it's the perfect Christmas present for her. Excited and pressed for time, he wolfs down the rest of his pizza, gathers his things and jets home.

††

The petite lady with smooth brown skin applies a crimson shade of lipstick to her full lips and studies her face. No blemishes; No misplaced hair; Polished teeth. Then she admires her bare, health-club body in the full-length mirror. Firm breasts', a 70-degree curve to her hips and an ass appropriately named irresistible. She looks and feels good and begins to smell good as she sprays Charlie—Mel's favorite fragrance—in all the vital places. He should be here any minute to surprise her. She was told that they would be going out and that it would be wise to dress down. Why does that not surprise her? Because Mel always likes to dress down in casual wear, which makes sense when a typical night out with him would be spent at the show or on the couch. He's not into the clubs, which is too bad. It would make him and their nights out more exciting. She struts back into her bedroom to the cadence of the Boys to Men sound from over the CD and slips on her panties, loose fitting jeans that hug her waist, size 32B bra, onyx, cashmere, pullover turtleneck and her black riding boots. Now she's ready for a typical date with a normal guy on the biggest night of the year.

She likes Mel. He's a good boy. Eventually, when she's ready to settle down and finishes living a life that is befitting a choice bachelorette; when she's had her fun, she will probably marry him. He would be the type that a good girl would bring home to Momma, if *her* mother was normal. Mel is a prototypical family man. But she's not Ma homemaker, she's not a good girl, and she's not the quintessential family woman. She's a lady of the '90's; A queen in her own right; A goddess to some; *the* Jones' to all. She needs a perfect man to worship her, meaning he needs to be rich, fine, ambitious, eccentric, macho, and a freak and a half. A manly man. All she can say about Mel is, he's nice. Too nice. She can run over him when she wants. She has her way with him, with one exception: He doesn't do oral sex...yet.

He's good for bringing her spirits up. She's never without a date because he's totally devoted to her. He would take his heart out and give it to her if their relationship depended on it. He even does pretty good in bed. But he's too darn traditional. Too dull. With the exception of his car, his house is dull and in need of major rehab, his career is dull (a stiff ass, unemployed accountant/manager), and his hairstyle is dull (just a fade that's faded to the point where it's unseen). His life is dull. All he does is go to work—that is, when he's employed—and buy electronic devices like he's Inspector Gadget. He has gotten on her last nerve with his prized video camera. All he does is make stupid home movies. Why isn't she jumping up and down as Mel knocks at the door?

He comes in and looks nice enough to suck on as he hands her a basket of soap. Is that *the* Christmas present? He better go and come again after she bought him a $5,000 Rolex (on sale and with O.P.M.: other people's money). She gives him a small peck and a phony thank you. The phone rings and she excuses herself to her bedroom to answer it. It's Roger. The man that Mel isn't. He's wealthy (If he wasn't paying her mortgage and car note, Mel wouldn't know what time it is); works as a model; fine (deep dark brown with a long, black pony tail); and a big freak (the things he can do with his tongue). He had her climbing the ceiling last night. She considers sending Mel home and going out with him, but decides against it and promises to call back. She turns around startled as Mel followed her back here. He's wearing a goofy grin that's begging for a returned pleasant expression. She fakes it as he hands her TWO BULLS TICKETS TO TONIGHT'S GAME AGAINST

ORLANDO. Now she's smiling for real and now he's real manly. She's never been to a Bulls' game and has been dying to get to one all of her life. She tries to squeeze the life out of him. Maybe it's time to start taking him serious and tell Roger to hop on his merry way. Eventually she will, but not now.

††

Mel pays the parking attendant and turns smiling to Memory. She beams back and plants a light kiss on his lips. They blend into one of the many veins of people pouring into the giant building. The wind blows slightly, making the air seem colder than it actually is, and prompting them to recede into their coats like turtles. She latches on to his arm, which sends a surge of warmth to his heart that gives him a good feeling of appreciation. They make it to the door where she pulls the tickets out of her purse. The bow is still on them. "Thank you," she says as she takes the bow off and hands it to the usher. "This is one of the best presents I've ever gotten."

He grins with pride as he reiterates, "Just don't make me go down there and embarrass you, Horace, and myself." She kisses his cheek, leaving her mark on him. They walk up some stairs and the scene is breathtaking, as the court seems to glow like gold. The arena aura is a constant buzz, like the engine of a muscle car. The players are on the court warming up and Memory's mouth drags the floor as she walks in a state of awe. The sold out crowd is already charged from the electricity-laced air. They walk all the way down to their seats on the first level. The good seats...about twenty steps up. They can actually see the whites of the player's eyes as they settle down. "You want anything to eat...to drink?"

She turns to him and nods. "I'll have a coke and a hot dog with no relish."

He throws up the okay sign and maneuvers through the crowd. Without sweating the outrageous prices, he orders and carefully carries it back, avoiding any contact. When he gets back, she has an expectant look. Her eyes are wide open as she takes in the whole scene. She's so excited that she nibbled away the hotdog in record time. She usually takes her time eating, chewing each bite thirty times. "Dagge, when was the last time you ate?" he jokes.

She glances at him and elbows him in the arm. "I'm just a little charged up," she says as she scans the crowd.

"A little?"

"Okay Melvin. I'm bursting with anticipation," she says exasperated. "See what you did?"

"No. See what you did," he says as he shows her the watch. "Don't worry...they should be getting started any minute."

"I hope so. I can't take this. You think the players are this nervous?"

"With the exception of Horace, I doubt it."

She rolls her eyes at him.

"Well you know he wants to look good for you."

"I'm not thinking about you, Mel."

"Yes you are."

"I know. These are good seats. You shouldn't have. How did you manage to get them?"

"I had to take out a second mortgage."

"I'm not worthy."

"Yes you are. Besides, if I fall behind, I'll just move in with you."

"That sounds like a win-win situation to me."

"It does, doesn't it?" When Mel got home, he called a couple of ticket brokers and compared prices and seats. He wanted to get as close as possible without spending over $1,000. Jordan isn't even playing. He got close enough for $800. Now he should get even closer to Memory.

The players gather at their benches and Memory asks, "Is it starting?"

Mel winks at her and smiles. The announcer introduces the Magic and the crowd gives Nick Anderson—a Chicago native—a loud cheer, but pepper the ovation of the other players with boos. "That Shaq is a big thing," she comments as he comes out to the mixed applause.

The lights go out, the stadium rises, "Sirius" comes on and Ray Clay introduces the Bulls as the noise goes up a few octaves. Who does he call first? Horace Grant of course. A woman sitting two rows up goes crazy and Mel watches Memory cut the unsuspecting woman a virulent glare. "Don't have me act a fool with her," she threatens over the roar of the crowd. The rest of the players are introduced. When the lights come back on, Memory is facing Mel with a smile. "Thank you."

He just smiles back at her.

Chapter 3

She was just going to say good-bye. Coleman Jackson was a dream: Golden brown like cornbread; devil red eyes; hair straighter than a fresh-ironed crease; lips as sweet as cole slaw. Cole Slaw was a nightmare: He broke her heart. With those same enticing lips that he used to take her to heaven with; that he bewitched her with all kinds of promises, he told her it was best that she moved on because someone else was enjoying the picnic. She left her unfinished business and Louisville immediately.

She found herself in Chicago with her own job as a clerk and her independence—and no man...for a while. There was a Simple Simon of a man that delivered the mail. No flash about him. Just a proper speaking, walnut colored northerner with a nappy grade of hair. Said he was working his way through law school. He was nice enough. After two years of politeness, he insisted on taking her out. She said no. The eighth time she said yes. The ninth time she said yes. The tenth time she said yes. Soon she was saying yes to marriage. He was so old fashioned. Didn't even want to jump in the sack until they tied the knot. His call into the ministry didn't help. Sometimes a double dose of misfortune is on the heels of good fortune.

Poppa went home from Louisville. That was the glorious news. He knew the Lord, planted physical seeds of righteousness, and lived a good, prosperous life with no regrets. Cole Slaw was the bad news. The second she realized that she had to go to Louisville, her mind was on the unfinished business. She didn't have to go see him. She had a divine order not to. But she just wanted to say good-bye on her terms. Before the funeral, she paid him a visit, determined that nothing would happen. She was actually mad when she started on her way from Chicago. When he opened the door, her determination flew further south. He was caught in a time warp. Nothing changed about him, except his allure. It was more potent. An embrace led to a kiss. The kiss led to a close look. Never has she had a vision before, but she saw Satan in his red eyes. She also saw her fiancé's back. She tried to turn back, but he had her hemmed down. She pleaded, but he wasn't hearing it. She cried the blues at the funeral. Everybody thought she was distraught over Poppa's death. The real distress came that next week. She was truthful and expected to see his back. And she did. But he came back and he's still here. She hasn't seen Cole Slaw since. Only a reminder remains, who didn't show up for the Christmas dinner. She's been saying good-bye for 24 years now, going on 25.

++

David is sprawled on the living room sofa talking to one of his female associates when Mel walks in. He cracks an astounded smirk and acknowledges Mel by nodding his head up. With the exception of the TV playing low and David rapping even lower, the house is serene. Mel can only imagine what it was like yesterday around this time. If he's going to be read the "Missing-on-Christmas" riot act, he might as well get it over with. "Where's Momma," he asks as he stands just to the side of him. He points to the back with his thumb. "In the kitchen?" David nods his head without missing a word in his conversation. That means that she probably heard him come in. "What about Dad?" He points down, which means that he's in his basement study (probably reading religious material). He's relieved that the worst comes first as he heads to the back.

The sliding door to the kitchen isn't closed, but just as he gets to the doorway and observes her washing dishes with her back to him, he realizes that there is—as expected—a door of tension right in front of him. Before he knocks or rings the doorbell, she opens that door (not necessarily welcoming him in), as if she is expecting him, with a non-eye contact "Merry Christmas, or should I say belated Merry Christmas. How are you?"

"I'm okay," he says as he comes in and heads toward the table.

"The turkey and macaroni are downstairs and the greens are in the big pot up here with the ham. Wash the stuff you use when you're finished."

Did he ask her all of that? Why can't he be over here to talk? Here goes Monsoon Momma. "I'm not hungry right now Momma."

"That's a surprise, considering you missed the big feast yesterday. Did you get your present from under the tree?" she queries, finally looking at him. For all she knew he could've walked in without a head and she would've just realized it.

"No I didn't." As usual, he is really biting his tongue and he is wondering if he has severed it from the years of holding his peace with her. She needs to be told off in the worst way and he wonders if it's ever been done. She's gorgeous, he's often thought as he peers at her, but her sharp tongue offsets what's pleasing to the eyes with deafening ignorance that can hurt the heart. She's extremely dark, shiny, and smooth. Her face is plump and her five foot figure is meaty (not fat) in the feminine places. She resembles a walking, ripe plum. With the exception of his below average build, they are splitting images. And for that, Mel is thankful. "Did you like your gift?"

She doesn't answer and she doesn't look at him. It has the making of a lecture and, sure enough—"That was very rude and downright ignorant of you. And you still haven't apologized or explained yourself," she starts, with more—much more—to come, and an escalation of voice pitch and word speed, as Mel rolls his eyes up in his head and takes a deep breath. She continues: "You have relatives that traveled across the country that only get to see you once every two years and you shun them like you would shun an enemy. Not even a call. You could've just dropped by to say hi. That's your blood. I bet you wouldn't disrespect that fickle girlfriend of yours like that. That's probably why you forgot your way over here. How do you live with yourself? I raised you better than that *har-har-har-har-har...*" is all he is starting to hear. This is when he mentally evacuates. He developed a tough skin from the years upon years of tongue-lashings from Momma. Some of them were deserved, while most were just to satisfy Momma's desire to gab. How dad has put up with it for 26 years is a mystery to him. Why he hasn't done anything about it in that time is the eighth great wonder.

Mel grew up early, but it wasn't by choice. There's so much expected from a preacher's kid. So much pressure from Draconian rule. Dad wasn't too bad. However, Momma was like an armed tyrant. She wasn't strict; she was downright mean, putting any fairy tale stepmother to shame. Today, if she beat David the way she beat Mel, she would be executed for child abuse. It was that bad. He lost count of the number of times she laid into him with an extension cord. Some of it was well earned. Most of it was over zealousness on Momma's part. It was the way of life that he excepted as something that all Christian children must go through (For whom the Lord loveth he correcteth), just as his parents punished him in the name of love—how ever tough that love may have been.

Yes, without a doubt, Momma loved him and still does. It was almost obsessive, but typical motherly love. When he was hit by a car (Nothing serious—just the wind knocked out of him, a bruised thigh and a scraped elbow.), she freaked out. It really wasn't a hit. He was running across the street to where his mother was on the wide, multi-directional intersection on Stoney Island, when a car came out of nowhere. He saw the horror in Momma's face as she watched helplessly as the accident unfolded. The way she screamed, "LOOK OUT!" was her will stopping the car. It screeched to a halt, and just as it stopped, it tapped Mel. He's been punched harder. It was one of the only times he witnessed her crying. He cherishes that memory, because in that brief moment, he saw her heart beneath the crusty exterior. There have been many more instances of her evident soft side, but that one stands out the most.

Introversion and independence are the results in stages of that tough love. The fear of rejection or messing up and being punished mentally or physically, afflicted him all the way through high school. The only policy at the time was reservation. Being unseen meant being undisturbed in his mind, but in reality, that wasn't always the case. It didn't take long for him to discover fantasies. In his dreams, he was in control and he was happy. He didn't have to answer to no one and he was bigger than life. Fantasizing fueled the desire to be alone and to be able to provide for himself. His Declaration of Independence came after he graduated from high school. He got a job doing data entry and moved into a studio apartment on 73rd and Wabash—close to public transportation (since he didn't have a car yet) and a lot of fast food restaurants and greasy spoons (since at the time, he despised his mother's cooking, although he loves it now). It is a thin line between the Introverted Mel that is submissive to the Spirit of God and the Independent Mel that is a raw, tormented soul that can kill with thought. Somehow, they coexist within him. He happens to be in control of them, because his actions lean toward meekness.

"...And furthermore, you come over here like you're the Emperor of the world—as if somebody is supposed to be glad to see you and kiss your behind. You need to get rid of that attitude of yours. I'm very disgusted with you...Get out of my presence before you make me madder," she huffs.

Gladly. Mel heads downstairs to stiller waters. To Mel, Momma was like the law: he could never satisfy it or her. She was a teacher by trade, but she showed little patience for Mel, even though he was a good, reserved student. It's hard to believe that such a little woman can hold so much hot air. Dad, on the other hand, was like the new covenant or salvation by faith and the gift of grace. He was gentle, understanding and always present to uplift and encourage Mel when he messed up. Dad was his favorite out of the two—hands down.

He can see the light on in his father's reading room at the back when he gets to the bottom. The door is open and he walks light-footed back there. He stops in the doorway and his father has his reading glasses on, perusing over a couple of biblical reference books and a Bible that lays on top of his big, walnut, executive desk that's facing the door. Mahalia Jackson is playing softly over the CD player that David convinced him to accept as a gift last Christmas.

Mel has always been impressed by his little office/library. Dad has matching walnut, seven-shelf bookcases forming a 'C' and engulfing the desk. All types of books line the walls: Religious references make up the bulk behind him (about twenty different Bibles); World Book Encyclopedia's for every six years since 1970 line the wall to the left; Legal books from his aspired career as a lawyer rest in some of the cases to the right; A variety of business, sports how to's and athletic biographies (he loves sports), black history and literature, and even some Biology books pepper the cases throughout. Dad is an avid reader and is knowledgeable about many of things. He spends much of his time down here. Often, he would be down here reading from dusk to dawn. Mel recalls that he averaged about four hours of sleep a night. Some nights he wouldn't sleep.

There's a 50-gallon fish tank with—what else—angelfish floating in it, along with a few other colorful marine creatures just inside the door to the left side. Mel spent a lot of time down here just watching the fish when he was a kid. He wished that he could shrink down in size, grow gills, and retire there for the rest of his life. It's so tranquil—like an oasis in the middle of a war zone. Momma never made noise down here. Often he would come down to stay out of her eyesight. Sometimes he would read some of the books; most of the time he would come down and relax on the sofa just inside the door and opposite the fish tank. It was his paradise. Dad never objected to him coming in here, even when he was studying. As long as the serenity was respected, anyone was welcome. Reverence is something Mel has for this room. To him, it represents a holy place. He didn't learn to appreciate the library until he got into college and needed to do extensive research, but this is where he had his first vivid encounter with God.

"Hey hey: there he is," Dad finally acknowledges with a typically warm smile as he sets his book down, removes his glasses and rises from his seat.

Mel comes towards him smiling as Dad comes from around the desk. "How you doing," he inquires as they exchange firm handshakes and embrace.

"I'm blessed. What about you? I heard your mother jumping on you up there. We missed you yesterday. How was your Christmas?"

"It was real enjoyable," he says as he peaks over the literature his dad was studying. "Preparing a sermon?"

"No, just down here relaxing. It's been busy the last couple of days with all of the family in, and I haven't been able to get down here, so I'm catching up," he says as he ejects the CD, signifying the coming of a long talk.

"I can imagine," he agrees, grabbing a peppermint from the candy dish on his desk. "How do you like the briefcase?"

"I love it. Now I can carry more than one reference book at a time," he testifies of the expandable briefcase Mel bought him for Christmas that's sitting next to his desk. "Did you open yours from us yet? You know your mother got you something else at the last minute?"

"Naw. Not yet." He doesn't even respond to the last question as he steps from around the desk and falls into the sofa.

"How's that girl of yours?"

"She's fine. That's why I wasn't here yesterday," he recalls, smiling and hinting at his very merry Christmas and honeymoon rehearsal.

"Y'all still fighting?"

"Naw. We were actually making amends and rediscovering the feelings that were lost over the last year. It was nice for a change. Who knows, maybe you'll be going to a wedding in the near future."

"I see. As long as I don't have to perform it, that's fine with me," he jokes, heading to the bathroom just on the side of the coat rack. "Don't leave yet...turn on the TV, while I rinse out these glasses."

Mel obliges as he gets up and turns on the big, antique-like, floor-model television with a wood frame, and two channel knobs that Mel has never figured out how to coordinate. The channel five news is on and Warner Saunders is anchoring. It's not cable compatible, but 20 years ago there was something out of this world on it that is priceless, although he would've paid anything to view it. That moment was the beginning of a special line of communication from the Almighty to Melvin Adams Jr.

Momma and Dad left him home alone for the first time (he doesn't remember why, but he does remember that they came back with McDonalds). They told him to stay in the study in the basement, which, at the time, he was afraid of, because the furnace on the other side of the paneling made so much noise when it came on in the winter, that he imagined that there was a monster that lived in it. They told him to stay in there and watch Sesame Street and not to answer the phone or the door—not that he would if they didn't tell him. The second he heard the front door close shut, a black man appeared on the screen. A flick in the screen and Big Bird was gone. It was uncanny. A plain faced black man was in front of him—literally inside the television, not on it (he knew the difference, even at that young age)—in back of a counter or a table with a plain, neutral colored background. Then the uncanny went into the bizarre. The man started talking to Mel, and Mel was talking back. They were actually having a conversation. He remembers the man asking him his name and then repeating it back when Mel told him.

He doesn't remember all of the dialogue that took place or how long they talked, but he knows that they talked extensively. In retrospect, before he understood what happened, he realized that it wasn't a video trick his parents played on him—as some supernatural skeptics may suggest—because they didn't have a VCR at the time. Too much improvisation took place. There were too many questions on both sides that were answered with a lot of insight. And he wasn't dreaming or hallucinating.

When he recalls the experience, four things confirm the authenticity of the discussion. First, he told Mel to open the Bible on his fathers desk to Luke 18 and 16 (at the time he couldn't even read his name, let alone understand the King James version, but he started reading the scripture as plain and clear as the sun is bright and hot); The scripture addressed his issue with low self esteem and humility; He foretold the coming of his younger brother, David, two years before his birth; He told Mel that he wouldn't see him again for a long time, but he would hear from him from that day forth. Those four recollections have manifest themselves in an ability to read with an understanding from that point on; a proud to be humble disposition; a brother that gets on his last nerve sometimes (but he loves), and a unique line of communication from the Lord. By the way, his fear of the basement was gone at that moment.

Although the communication isn't as frequent as it was when he was very active in church and spiritually motivated, it hasn't disappeared. Sometimes he doesn't pay attention. Other moments he's unaware of the message. No matter what type of problem he goes through, he finds comfort, guidance, encouragement, wisdom, and the right answer from the Lord. Again, he realizes that unbelievers will easily dismiss it as pure coincidence, but he recognizes the truth.

About two weeks after the great television encounter, he was do to be baptized. Of course, he was a believer in Jesus Christ after that. His parents came in on him reading the scripture and were astonished. He confessed his belief in Jesus to them and they didn't ask for an explanation, assuming that it was the Holy Spirit—because it was.

He was riding his bicycle on the block with a neighbor. Bob was a few years older, about 30 pounds heavier, and had a big-time five speed. At the time, it might as well have been an 18-wheeler. They were racing up and down the street, and—of course—Mel lost every time on his converted two-wheeler that only weeks before was a quadcycle. To make things competitive, Bob gave him a head start. It still wasn't even close. Bob gave Mel a five-second lead and almost had it erased half way down the block. Mel's mistake was looking back as Bob gained on him. It seemed like the sidewalk was too narrow for both of their bikes as Bob bore down on him. Mel panicked and veered off into the street. When he looked up, there was a car coming at him. It seemed like the driver was in a hurry, too. Mel froze and forgot that he had breaks as he braced for impact and sure death. How the car managed to come to a swerving stop could only be attributed to the hand of God. Mel knew nothing about physics, but he knew that car was too close and going too fast to miss him. The driver seemed just as amazed and scared as Mel. The only thing Mel could do after that was walk—barely—his bike home and lay down. He didn't even realize that he peed on himself.

He was too traumatized about the prospect of going to the Devil. The only reason God kept him from getting hit was because he wasn't baptized yet and He didn't want him to go to Hell. The prospect of an accident kept him in the house, in his father's study where it was safe, *for two, hot summer days. He couldn't risk it again. Then he was watching the television again. While he was going through the channels, trying to get to the cartoons, he happened upon some station that had a preacher talking about confessing with your mouth and baptism. He said as bold and clear as ever that 'if a sinner confesses with his mouth and is killed before he's baptized, he's still saved!' Then he made reference to Romans the 10th chapter and the 9th and 10th verses:* ***If you confess with your mouth the Lord Jesus and believe in your heart that God has raised Him from the dead, you will be saved. For with the heart one believes to righteousness, and with the mouth confession is made to salvation.***

That was enough, but Dad's big bible was turned to Luke, the 23rd chapter, and verses 42 and 43 were highlighted and read: ***And he said unto Jesus, Lord, remember me when thou comest into thy kingdom. And Jesus said unto him, Verily I say unto thee, Today shalt thou be with me in paradise.*** *That was all the reassurance he needed and he has held that scripture in his heart ever since. Mel was overcome with joy and went outside smiling uncontrollably. From that point, whenever he needed a concern or problem addressed, the Lord would use the TV, newspapers, magazines, radio stations, tape recordings, records, and CD's to talk to him, confirming it with the Bible. The answer would always be too clear to compromise and second-guess. As amazing an experience as it was, to this day, he has told no one. He's not ashamed of it or afraid that someone may recommend a head shrink. If and when the time comes for him to share the testimony, he will.*

Dad emerges from the bathroom drying his glass with a towel, so Mel turns the television off. He asks Mel, "So how has life been treating you," as he pours some water from the pitcher, sits down and leans back in the reclining chair.

Mel sinks comfortably into the sofa and tells him what he already knew: "Outside of the layoff—which I consider a blessing and a much needed vacation—I'm doing well. I could complain, but it wouldn't help, would it?"

His father doesn't answer that, but just nods to confirm that he's listening. "Where are you going to go from there—are you going to sit on unemployment for a year?"

Mel smiles because he can't help it. For some reason, Dad always elicits a grin from Mel, even when the subject is serious. It's a nervous smirk (not out of intimidation or fear), from being out of his normal discomfort zone. "Well, that's what I'm planning."

His father pauses for a moment, like he always does when he talks to somebody. It's almost as if the words take a long time to register. Mel knows that that's not the case, seeing that his father is the smartest man he knows. He has the utmost respect for him—not just as a parent and elder, but as a person. "Is that going to cover all of your bills for the duration?"

"Well, on paper I'll be about two hundred dollars short of all of my expenses. Since I'm the worse manager of money with an accounting degree, multiply that by two, which means that I may have to get a part-time job in a couple of months. In the meantime, the puppy profits should hold me over until the summer. Would you like to prepay for your dog now?"

He pauses, but doesn't answer, asking another question instead: "Have you figured in the possibility of bad business, lack of employment opportunities, and unexpected expenses?"

Mel knows where the conversation is going, but he doesn't really mind. "I'll just cross that bridge if and when I get to it. And if necessary, I'll make a withdrawal from my account with Dad National Bank."

Dad just stares at him and decides to go along with his wit. "What if I die and will everything to your mother and brother...where are you going to go from there?"

"I'll go to the Lord in prayer."

Dad just looks at him.

Mel gets defensive as he struggles with himself, but pleads his case with his father. "I'm really not ready to come back to church," he says matter-of-factly.

"What about when God is ready for you to come back?"

Mel sighs, knowing that he can't win this one. "When God prepares me to deal with the hypocrites, I'll be there. They would've drove Moses to the grave. Right now I don't think He's given me the patience to handle the congregation."

"I'm sorry to hear that," he says solemnly.

"Yeah...I'm sorry to say it," he says as he pauses to ponder the drama that drove him out the door and almost to the nut house.

Never mind his mother's lack of respect for him, the church was worse than a beauty shop or a nightclub. The problems were everywhere: Drunk deacons that didn't want to pay their tithes, yet can stand up at the front begging for money and criticizing the congregation for "robbing God"; Bickering choir members trying to out-sing and out-control each other; and the back-stabbing trustees, who care about nothing but money, not spiritual growth. It's hard to break bread with a bunch of religious Pharisees'. One of the last straws was when some money came up missing and the trustees suggested that based on the time Mel stole something from the store when he was a child, that maybe he did it again. What really disturbed Mel about that incident, was that those lying devils exploited him and his testimony. It was only a month prior when Mel testified that if his mother didn't beat him for stealing, he would've eventually graduated to robbing people. Not only did they spread it in a malicious way, but slandered the whole family—even suggesting that his father knew about it. Mel left shortly after, because he was going to hurt somebody in the Holy of Holies on the Sabbath. He was totally disenchanted with the church. "I'm going to be back eventually. I just don't know when."

"Well, you know it's not my style to ride somebody to come to church, but I will tell you that things are not going to get any easier for you out there. Trust me on that. If I can borrow a worldly cliché—there's no better time than the present, while things are a little mellow. But I understand people come when things get a little rough. Although I did the same thing, I don't condone it."

Mel just nods at that as he gets up to examine some new books in the bookcase. He pulls out a Bible, confirming, "You've added a couple of new swords to your collection," as he flips through it.

"You know me. I can't get enough of them. You can take that one if you want it. It's a good study Bible."

Mel usually turns things down by instinct, but as he goes through the pages, he notices it has good illustrations and a good commentary on the scriptures. "You know, I think I will."

"By all means do," he says as he watches his son scan the pages. "Still considering grad school?"

"Yeah, for the wrong reasons."

"What are the wrong reasons?"

"For a status symbol and a higher income. To tell you the truth, I don't know if I want to go back to Corporate America."

"What are you considering for a career? You know the ministry can support you."

Mel looks over at him and smiles because he used to always tell Mel that he had a calling on his life. Not necessarily as a preacher, but not excluding that, either. "To be honest, I'm not exactly sure, but I'm considering computer graphics or video production or photography. I don't know yet."

"Have you considered starting a business? You definitely have the knowledge."

"I considered opening a training facility for ministers," he jokes as they both laugh. "I'll figure it out within the next few months. Who knows, maybe I'll end up at Bible school to prepare me for my ministry."

His father nods his approval, adding, "Well, let me know if and when you're ready to do it" for support. "Did you see the Bulls' game on Christmas?"

"Did I see it? I was there. Close enough to hear the players talk trash."

"Is that right?"

"I took Memory as a Christmas present. This was her first game," Mel says as he recalls the time his father took him to his first game. It was way back in '82. Dr. J, Moses Malone and Maurice Cheeks came to town with the Sixers. It was actually closer than everyone expected. Philly won by six. Mel was so happy to finally see the Doc dunk in person, not to mention getting a glimpse of their championship run. "Pippen went crazy and Memory went crazier."

"She likes Pippen, huh?"

"She actually likes Horace Grant, but since Pippen went off, he was her man that night...no pun intended."

"It was close. I would've loved to have been there. That was a nice shot by Kukoc. Of course it wouldn't have been necessary or close if Jordan was playing, but it was a good one anyway."

"I guess that's why Nick Anderson had a good game, too. He almost sent it into overtime. And O'Neal is a monster. He looks like King Kong."

"Yeah. He's the biggest boy on the playground. I would hate to have to guard him in the post."

They both pause as Mel surveys the room and all the books. "You oughta open this room up to the congregation...make it the church library."

"It's funny that you should mention that. We are going to add on a part to the building and use it as a library for the church and the Christian Education Department. It's long over due."

Mel nods and checks his new watch.

"Nice watch. I thought you didn't wear jewelry."

"I didn't, until Memory hooked me up for Christmas. It's a Rolex."

"Really? She spent that kind of money on you? You're right to amend your constitution and wear it."

"Now we're relating," he chuckles. "Well...I'm going to be going now."

"Okay," he says, rising. "Take care and consider coming to the Watch Service next Saturday night."

"I'll consider it," he says as he shakes hands and embrace like they always do. Then he's gone, knowing that it's very unlikely that he'll show up.

††

Talk about a powerful anointing. Mel's father saw it when he was born. He was always full of joy. He wasn't a crying baby. Often, he would hear him playing with the angels, just having a good time in the Lord. It was confirmed when he came home and saw how the Holy Spirit blessed him with the ability to read the Bible at the age of five. It was confounding even to him, and he's seen many miracles in his days on the battlefield for Christ. He even heard him speak in tongues in his sleep. All the Christ-like character traits were there: meekness, humility, long-suffering, and patience. There were times when he submitted to his peers, when he could have easily fought—and won because he wasn't a coward—or made a big fuss about what was fair. Once, he observed Mel in a minor dispute with his cousin about a portion of Mel's birthday cake. Instead of claiming what was rightfully his, he let his cousin have the larger portion without even bickering about it. He just smiled at him and thanked the Lord for his son. And Dad has never seen a more loving and forgiving heart than his son has. The fact that Mel still respects his mother is a testimony in itself, because she was hard on him. She still is. He and his ministerial staff should take lessons from him.

Dad gave him a test in high school to see how obedient he was and if he was still interested in the scriptures. High school could bring more than enough temptations. Dad wanted to see if he was still grounded in the Word. He bought a set of individual, pocketsize books of the bible with study aids and commentaries included in them. Over a three and a half-year period, he gave him one book of the bible to read at a time, starting with Genesis and ending with Revelations. At the end of each book, he taped a $20 bill. The funny thing is Mel never told him when he finished the books. He would ask him if he finished and Mel would casually say, "Yes". Then he would give him the next book.

He checked the books just before he gave him the book of Proverbs, and noticed that the money was still taped at the end of each edition, but he didn't say anything. He decided that he would give him a chance to redeem himself. He got all the way to the book of Revelations and the money was behind each and every volume, so he showed him a desk sized African Heritage Bible with a check for $3300 taped to the back of the inside cover, and asked him why did he lie about reading the books. But Mel insisted that he read them all. He showed him the money at the end of each book and Mel said he saw it. He was skeptical, so he quizzed him orally on the contents and specifics of each book, and Mel answered almost every question correctly. He was pleasantly surprised. When he asked him why he didn't take the money, Mel responded, "You didn't tell me the money was mine, and Momma beat the hell out of me for stealing, so I wasn't about to remove it." Before he could tell him what the $3300 represented, Mel figured it out: $50 dollars for each book in the Bible, plus the $20 for each volume, equals $70. Seven is the heavenly number that represents completion. The Heritage Bible was a graduation present—which was a milestone in his life—and the total reward for his obedient reading effort was $4620, which his father told him he could use the way he pleased. He was pleased when Mel put it in the bank. He had accountant written all over him.

Often he wonders does Mel still pray and talk to God. He also wonders does his son realize the potential he has in the service for the Lord. There's only so much he can reveal to him, even though he wants to tell him everything the Lord has showed him. Unfortunately, the Holy Spirit has told him not to disclose every thing he knows just yet, and out of a page from his son's obedience book, he hasn't gone against the Spirit. He can't wait until Mel answers his calling though, because some amazing things are going to happen and a lot of souls are going to be won for Christ.

Chapter 4

When Mel got home from his parent's house, Memory was waiting for him in her BMW. She was as frisky as a Tomcat, which made for a nice, long night. She has been on good behavior for the holiday season, and he's hoping that it carries over into 1994. He got an early start Monday and was pleasantly surprised. He had nightmares about going to the unemployment office. A dull, dim-lit, crowded room with welfare mothers accompanied by three or four bad kids that didn't mind, slow receptionists with bad attitudes, and three different long lines to stand in was all he envisioned. An all day stay was anticipated, so he brought four current magazines and the daily Sun-Times to keep him occupied. After filling out a few short forms, standing in a line with a pleasant clerk and seeing the counselor after a brief wait, he had to pinch himself to make sure he was awake. Total time spent in there: just under an hour and a half. He didn't even finish reading the sports section of the newspaper. She said that he should be getting his first check and certification in about two or three weeks. He hoped for the maximum $250 a week, but she said to expect $240.

When he gets back home, he drops the magazines, walks out of his snow-soiled shoes and starts unfastening his clothes on the way upstairs. Just as he hits the bed, the doorbell rings. On the way down the stairs, he wishes that he had put the lock on the gate and let the dog outside. He's in the mood for a deep sleep, not for socializing with mankind—especially the kind of man at his door: Earl. His first mind is to play like he didn't hear him out there singing, but that wouldn't be right, so he opens the door, hoping that he won't regret it.

"What up, Cuz," he shouts, walking past Mel in his Sherlocke Holmes hat, as if he's sleuthing for clues in the kitchen. "What you got to eat here?"

"How come you're not at work?" he questions as he follows him.

"Awe man. A brother comes over to talk to his blood and he gets treated like a panhandler," he says as he raids the refrigerator. "Why you still in your night stuff?"

Mel doesn't even respond or attempt to play it off as he leans against the door.

"I took the day off. I was wondering if I could borrow your car next week?"

"You got a credit card?"

"Yo Cuz," he says, helping himself to Mel's doughnuts. "I need to make a good impression with this female I met at the club last week. I told her that my car was in the shop and she won't set it out unless I drive some wheels that kill. You gotta help me score, Dog. I'll hook you up later."

Mel just looks at him.

"Naw man, seriously, next week is registration and I need to get there early from work. It's for a good cause."

"You still haven't paid for the parking ticket you got the last time you had to register."

"I'll hook you up next week. I couldn't help you this week because you know things were tight with the holidays and all."

"Whatever," he says. "If I say yes will you leave...now?"

"I'll be a sweet memory."

"Yes, now go."

"Let me finish my doughnut man. Do you treat all of your guests like this?"

"Yes, when they come unannounced and uninvited," Mel cuts.

"Okay, I see how you playing me. You must have your girl up there—speaking of sweet memory," he suggests.

Mel cuts his eyes at him and tells him "My life doesn't revolve around 'my girl', and if she was up there, you best believe I wouldn't have answered the door."

"You sure she's not up there?"

"I think I would know if someone was in my house. Besides, she's at work today, unlike some people who just take off at will."

"Good, I need to tell you something," he says, putting his boisterous side in check and growing a little serious. "I saw her with a dark skinned brother on Christmas."

"Of course you did fool, that was me."

"Well then you cut your ponytail and you're stashing a Lexus in your garage, huh?"

Mel gives him a critical look for a hint of humor, but doesn't find any. "You're serious?"

"No joke man. They were on the Dan Ryan at about one in the morning and—I don't know—they were having what looked like a very endearing talk."

Mel realizes that Earl doesn't like her and his account could be biased, but he doesn't think it is. He believes him, but he doesn't want to jump to conclusions about what she was doing with him, even though she apparently lied about her whereabouts on Christmas Eve. His stomach fills with adrenaline as his heart starts to ache from the familiar anxiety attack he's having right now. Fortunately for his pride, Earl can't see the chemical reactions going on on his insides. "You sure it was her?" he questions, a little embarrassed by her unfaithfulness and his constant insistence that she's a good woman.

He looks Mel in the eyes and doesn't utter an answer to that question. "I know that I have reservations about her, but I ain't trying to jack y'all up, and you know that. I just want you to watch your back, because you're my boy and my blood," he claims with convincing sincerity.

Mel examines his face while imagining the worse she could've been doing that night. She had just given him a $2,500-plus watch and claimed her undying love to him. She reaffirmed it after he took her to her first Bulls' game. Things seemed to be on the path to matrimony. Even if she wasn't cheating on him, why did she lie? Now he's mad and considers pawning the watch. "All right man, thanks for the tip," he says, heading into the living room.

"Don't mention it. Just check your front and I'll watch your back," he says as he exits.

Mel stands motionless for a few minutes after he slams the door shut. The calendar with the daily verses falls to the floor. He reads today's verse from Hebrews four and sixteen, which says, *Let us therefore come boldly unto the throne of grace, that we may obtain mercy, and find grace to help in time of need.* He doesn't feel like praying and he doesn't want to be merciful. He doesn't even feel like sleeping, and although there's a lot to do, he just doesn't have the focus to do it. He wants to call her up and ask her what's going on, but he figures that would cause a lot of friction and break the implied peace treaty that they have. What if it's an innocent situation? He would have to convince himself of that. It is very suspicious, if not incriminating. It wouldn't be the first time she's strayed from him, but it will probably be the last time he puts up with it if that is the case. He decides that he isn't going to dwell on it or her and won't talk to her until his birthday, when she will probably be taking him out—that is, if she isn't too busy with other people. With that thought, a surge of anger overcomes him and he decides to call and curse her out. He picks up the phone, but there's no dial tone, so he switches lines and it's also dead. "Damn," he says as he realizes his phone has been turned off for non-payment. He slams it down and the lights flicker in the kitchen. At first, he thought that maybe it is a short somewhere, but he hears a noise out in the back as the VCR clock goes blank. "Shit! What else," he yells as he watches the guy from Common Wealth Edison exit his yard, leaving his gate open. If only Homey was outside.

His blood pressure rises and his heart races as he realizes he doesn't have any money to get them turned back on. It makes him madder because he spent $800 for those tickets. Catching up with Earl is out of the question, since he's always borrowing from Mel. He'd rather be without a television and a phone than ask his mother. And Memory. It's best that he doesn't even think about her, let alone see her, because he's libel to end up with a murder rap before the year is over with. The only person he can really turn to is his father, although Mel figures he'll give him some hints to come back to church. He's not in the mood for it, but he decides to swallow his pride and go deeper into the $3000 hole with Dad as he starts walking back into the clothes he walked out of thirty minutes ago.

As he opens the car door, he realizes his Christmas presents from his parents are still in the back seat, unopened. He was caught off guard by Memory, so he forgot all about them. He opens the gift from his father first, and isn't surprised that he got him a gold and black checkered sport coat from Bachrach's. It's nice and would go well with his black slacks. The first box from his mother doesn't surprise him either. It's a Bible dictionary. "Thanks a lot, Mom," he says sarcastically as he lays it on the seat. The other package—which is about the size as a shoebox—is very light. As he takes the lid off, there's a lot of confetti to pull out to get to the bottom, where a business envelope is waiting. It figures she would go through all of this trouble to write him a note telling him about himself. He loses his breath as he pulls the paper out of the envelope. He can't believe it. It's a money order for $500. Never has a money order looked better. He lays it down on the seat, closes his eyes and says, "Thank you Lord" as he grins irrepressibly. He wonders why she gave it to him, and feels a little guilty for assuming that she was lecturing him in writing. No matter, he'll have phone and electrical service today...after he pays his *mother* a visit.

††

"Now watch him play like nothing is going on with her," Earl says to himself. Occasionally, he comments out loud to himself. He's having a panel discussion right now. "Think she's the slickest thing in the world. All she needs is a couple of weeks with a brother like me, so she could get what she's dishing out and what she has coming to her. Problem is Mel is too damn nice. What he needs is a double dose of my attitude so he can stop being played by that silly ass woman."

He downplayed what he saw. How could he tell Mel that she was swallowing ol' boys tongue at the stoplight in Greek town, just before they got on the Dan Ryan at Madison? Maybe he was sparing himself the sorry sight and dreadful knowledge of him going back to her after that revelation. Then again, it would've sounded too critical. He made it quite clear what he thought of Memory when he first met her—although he put it in a nice way. To be blunt, she is a "flirtatious, teasing, scoping, unfaithful tramp" in denial. She has Mel thinking that she's this sweet, bashful little tender-roni. "Yeah right. The way she's throwing her stuff around at the clubs, indicates that she ain't hardly shy and she ain't hardly the girl next door Mel wants her to be." She called herself giving him the eye. He let her know in no uncertain terms that gaming on his blood in front of his face could be fatal and she better check herself into Whores Anonymous. Needless to say, she wasn't too fond of him after that. He's considering having one of his slims knock her head off as soon as she gets through dogging Mel out. He knows it's only a matter of time before that happens. Until then, he can't even give her a hard look out of respect for Mel.

††

Mel sits in his kitchen all decked out in a burgundy sport coat, black, loose-fitting slacks and black Giorgio's as he waits quietly for Memory to take him out for his birthday. He's been contemplating the games she's been playing and can care less if she comes or not. In fact, he hopes that she doesn't show up, even though she called him an hour ago and said,

"Be ready." He's not in the mood for her and her charades, and silently wishes that terrorists will abduct her. Why doesn't she just go away and do her own thing? How come she can't take the initiative and go a whoring until her body leaves a smoke trail from here to the West Coast? He's been laboring over the issue for too long. His head starts to ache and his desire to spend his birthday alone intensifies. Although he's out of work, he longs to get away from everything. If he could, he would sell his house and start over. Unfortunately, he's way over his head in debt and the sell of his house would hit him for a loss at its present condition.

The worse kind of blaxploitation is that perpetrated by someone of African descent—such as the three separate contractors that he paid to remodel his home. They're the reason why his kitchen doesn't even have cabinets in it now. Before he moved in, he called two painters to go over the whole house. That marked the beginning of the destruction of his home. The paint on the walls looks like the unfulfilled requirements of a preschool class's mural project with a $1.99 paint set from Walgreen's. He started to have them arrested for vandalism. Not only did they lack skill, but they also lacked common sense. Why a person would paint window seals is way beyond Mel. He's still trying to figure it out and he's still trying to get some of the windows open that were painted shut. It's the same story in his finished basement that's unfinished. The paneling is a joke. The guys who were doing it must have missed the lesson on measurements in school. Maybe they were blowed when they started working. A blind man could've taken better measurements. Mel put up some of the paneling in one of the rooms and it looks 100% better than the contractor's work.

People have killed for a dollar. Imagine what they would do for $15,000? That's 15,000 murders. As he sips on some Lipton Tea and studies the ugly space where there should be cabinetry, Mel imagines how he would execute the contractor that ripped his kitchen up and ripped him off for $10,000. He would cement his feet to the basement floor, marinate him with barbecue sauce and let Homey have his way with him. Better yet, he would blow the pilot light out on the furnace, turn all the gas on, ignite the place, collect the insurance money and start over with another home. Why risk giving his dog food poisoning? Mr. Richards was a low down bastard if there ever was one to be born. He hee'd and hawed about what he was going to do and how nice it was going to look. The dude—who could barely speak English—didn't know *simple math, let alone carpentry, but he sure knew how to cash a check the same day he got it. Apparently, he didn't know the specific uses for the tools, because he did more demolishing than constructing. He tore the old cabinets out and started putting up the countertop when Mel noticed that it was uneven. When he brought it to the contractor's attention, the man requested the rest of the money to finish. Needless to say, he didn't get it, the case is pending in court and the kitchen has been incomplete ever since. If he wanted to sell the house now, he wouldn't be able to ask for top dollar, because the kitchen looks like a junkyard.*

What's worse than the job they all did, is the money he actually paid—in advance, of course. They should've paid him for messing up. "Black people need to give each other a chance" is what they all said in effect. Despite the experiences, he tries to be true to the black businesses. However, unless he gets a referral, he'll go to Sears once he gets some money.

The phone rings and he hopes it's Memory calling to cancel the date, otherwise, he'll call it off himself. "Hello," he answers, making sure his tone tells the story of his mood.

"Happy birthday, Boo," the female on the other end says.

His mood does a 360 as the voice makes him forget everything. "Darlene...it's good to hear from you. I'm surprised you remembered. Thank you. I'm really flattered," he says as thoughts of revenge and a good time flow.

"How's my Boo? What are you doing in the house—you should be celebrating. If Miss Thang ain't doing her job, I'll give you a private party to tell her about."

"She's actually on her way over to take me out, but I'm tempted to stand her up for you."

"Now we're talking."

"You just got it like that."

"Hey now. I miss you up here. That was really a raw deal that they gave you. I've started looking for another job because of it. Who's to say that I'm not next. It's not like they like us out there, anyway."

"Everything is cool on this end. Of course it would be nice if I could see you everyday, but when I lost my job, I lost my benefits. The price you pay for a vacation. You don't have to bail yet. Stay on the inside. We need you in there."

"I don't know about that. Word is they're struggling anyway and I want to jump ship before they sink."

"I hear you."

"So are you looking for another job or are you going to sit on unemployment for a few months?"

"Do you hear me? I'm on vacation. My job is to sit at home all day and watch the talk shows."

"I heard that. I wish they would lay me off. Then we could lay up in the bed all day and all night. You hear what I'm saying?"

"I hear you," he says as the thought got him a little excited. "Where are you?"

"I'm at the hell hole. They got me working late—doing overtime, as if I'm going to see it on my check."

"Yeah. Being salaried can be a real trip. How were your holidays?"

"Oh, they were real good. I went to Vegas. I'm talking 80 degrees. Didn't lose too much money either. Got some nice gifts and all of that. Then I went to the Frankie Beverly & Maze and Toni Braxton concert at the Pavilion. The only thing missing was you," she flirts.

Mel blushes a little, as he gets a little tongue-tied and hot.

"So how were your holidays, Boo? Did girlfriend do you right?"

"It was kinda good. She got me a Rolex."

"Hey now. I can give you the time, but I don't have that much time."

They both laugh at that.

"It's nice. I'll give it to her. She went all out this time, because I was on the verge of chopping her head off."

"That means that I'm going to have to come up with something big. I can't let her outdo me. So where are y'all going tonight?"

"She's supposed to be taking me out to eat and maybe to a movie," he says as he hears her blowing. "Speaking of which, she just arrived."

"Okay, tell her I said hi," she says with a laugh. "Listen, keep in touch. Give me a call sometime."

"I will. And thanks for calling and remembering."

"Anytime Boo. Bye bye."

"So how does it feel to be 25?" Memory asks between bites of lobster.

Mel wants to ask her *how did it feel to be with Mr. Ponytail on Christmas Eve instead of him*, but he just replies, "It feels like 24" without any emotions. She chews like a damn rabbit and he has the urge to shoot out the two front teeth that she lied through. Her presence is a vexation at the moment. Red Lobster is crowded and there is a long line for those that didn't have reservations. They're sitting at a center table for two. Memory did have it together, because they walked right passed all of the patient patrons. The wait is two to four hours and definitely not worth it. The food isn't even warm. It tastes like it came out of a microwave. It's unfortunate that they've resorted to this type of service. They're no different than McDonalds. The waitresses just came over and sung the birthday song, much to Mel's displeasure and embarrassment. He has the urge to throw the cake—candles and all—in her face as she chomps away. As he glares at her, he imagines "LIAR" is stamped across her face.

She continues to try to make small talk. "Gwen told me that she's getting married in June," she says of her sorority sister, as if he really cares.

Mel is not too crazy about her or any of her fellow AKA's. He hasn't met one that isn't stuck up. And that includes the slut sitting across from him. Truth be told, he really can't stand any of the Greek fraternities and sororities. They may have served a meaningful purpose when they originated, but now he looks at them as cliques for childish snobs who overdose on peer pressure. Memory is proof positive of that. She didn't drink and go to clubs until she went over. According to her, she hated liquor and wasn't comfortable at the clubs. Now she can't stay away from either. He wants to ask her if Gwen has been fooling around too, and if so, is she going to continue when she ties the knot (after all, whores of a sorority...), but instead, he claims, "That's nice" with the fervor of a roach husk.

"She asked me to be in the wedding."

"Well are you?"

"Yeah, but I hope it doesn't mess up my marriage plans."

Mel has to tune her out to keep from laughing while she empties her bowels. He wants to congratulate her and Mr. Ponytail, but he stuffs his mouth with french fries and keeps it shut as he chews, because he can't bring himself to fake an agreement. Not only does he want a Christmas wedding—as opposed to a Fourth of July wedding—but he also wants a faithful bride.

"He lives in Atlanta and she's going to move down there with him. The job market is pretty good and that's the place to be."

"Are you going with her," he slips

"Excuse me?"

"I mean, are you going to help her get set up down there?"

"I haven't thought about it, but now that you mention it, I'll ask her if she wants me to go down there with her. That seems like it would be fun."

He wishfully imagines her staying down there as he takes a sip of his Shipwreck, and almost chokes.

"What's wrong?"

"This has alcohol in it," he says disdainfully as he frowns his disapproval.

"Lighten up, Mel. It's not going to kill you."

"Maybe not, but I still don't like it," he says, gesturing for the waitress. "Can you give me the virgin Wreck?"

"I'm sorry," she says as she takes it away.

Mel wants to strangle her. Memory knew better. She ordered for him when he went to the bathroom. Just as his rage builds, something goes down the wrong way and she starts coughing uncontrollably. She buckles over and her eyes flood with water as she tries to dislodge whatever it is that's caught in her throat. He's concerned, but a part of him wants her to die on the spot as he gets up and pats her on the back. It took all of the restraint that he could muster up to keep from acting on the desire to knock a dent in her spine. "You okay?" he questions.

She nods her head as she wipes her face with the napkin.

They finish their meal and he continues to be curt in the conversation on the way home, but she was too tipsy to notice. When they get to his house, she's expecting to come in for the annual back breaking, mind-blowing, inside-out turning, head-spinning a la the exorcist, dehydrating, crippling, throw caution to the wind love marathon, but before she picked him up, he made it up in his mind that it isn't happening. He reaches over, pecks her on the cheek and says, "Thanks for taking me out" and starts out the door.

"Wait a minute," she pleads, grabbing his arm. "Don't you want me to come in?"

"Not really. I'm tired and I just want to chill out."

"You can chill and let me do the work," she says as she slides her hand down and rubs his crotch.

Of course, his body gets aroused, but his mind is still stronger as he rebukes, "Honor my birthday wish and let me go in alone."

"Come on Mellie Mel," she purrs to his disdain as she skillfully unbuckles his belt, pops open the button and unzips his pants, in seemingly one motion. "I want to try something on you."

He would've just left, but she was gripping his firm, weak spot. "Not today Memory," he insists. Before he can utter another sound, he feels her hot, succulent mouth wrapped around him. That silences him. He isn't for giving or receiving oral sex. The first time, the thought alone may have ruined the feeling for him. He had reservations about it when she telegraphed what she was going to do. He always considered it nasty. That's the impression most of his peers gave of a woman that went that far. The first time it didn't do anything for him and he stopped her after a few seconds. Now it feels good and he hates her for it. He doesn't want her to do anything pleasurable to him. She sucks in and pulls out and he shivers like a desert hermit at the North Pole. She looks up at him like a hungry cat and takes it in again, gently bobbing her head up and down. Mel tenses up with the unexpected urge to detonate, as solar power seems to be surging through his body.

She abruptly pulls him out. "Oh no you don't," she says in a tone that a mother would use with her child that was trying to sneak some cookies out of the jar. "Can I come in and finish?"

Mel just nods his head like a zombie. They go in and she finishes him off. He never imagined that his body could feel the delectation it did, especially since it's not what he wanted to do. She must've been practicing on somebody, but it didn't matter at that moment. One thing that struck him as peculiar, is that this time she didn't ask him to do the same. With his suspicions, he wouldn't have anyway. That's an area of concern and disagreement between them. She said she hasn't had it, but wants it. He's never done it and insists he never will. Since their last discussion about it, she got it from somebody and she's addicted to the pipe. It was delightful, but it's something he's determined to live without. He's ecstatic and agitated as they cuddle together. She got her way with him again and it felt terribly good.

Chapter 5

Mel was reluctant to touch Memory ever since he found out about her Christmas Eve tryst with Ponytail. A week has passed since his acidic-soothing birthday present, and he is still seething with pleasure. After he resisted her verbal advances, his determination succumbed to the attrition of her groping, teasing and arousing touches. She got her way again. He was intent on sadistically dishing out some rough love. There's no feeling like bodily pleasure and a broken spirit. It gave him the desire to burn or break something animate, such as her back. He likens it to someone tickling him while someone else is setting his hair on fire. To add vinegar to the bitterness, she enjoyed his assault. After ejaculation, she purred, "I luuuuuv you."

While he lies next to her, he feels...empty. If she really "luuuuuved" him, she wouldn't have ridden the pony. He craves a total body scrub-down with kitchen cleanser and a wire brush as he lays in a fetal position on the edge of the bed with his back to her. For the whole night, he stared straight forward in that spot. At the break of dawn, the "Yes Lord" picture on her wall is highlighted. The ankh has a hypnotic, humbling effect. An aching bladder forces him from the bed as he leaves a sweat delineation on the sheets. He stares down at her when he returns, struggling with the right words to announce his departure. He considers just walking out for good while he quietly slips on his clothes. As he stands over her, studying her innocent looking face, he contemplates overturning the bed. He's a sucker for an angelic face. "I'm going Memory," he murmurs reluctantly.

She grumbles something inaudible as she shifts her body.

He stands there for a moment before he scribbles a message and sticks it on her nightstand: ***I had to leave. I'll call you later. Mel.*** Later could be as late as the millennium.

When he got home, he immediately hit the hot shower and lathered up, even though he had to take the dogs to the vet. That promises to be a messy, hairy job that requires another bath. However, the filthy feeling weighed heavily on him, like a mud epidermis; like he was wearing a layer of dung. He realizes that the true cleansing is to take place in his heart, but he felt that washing her scent and bodily fluids off his body was a start.

He calls U-Haul to verify the van reservation and then catches the 79th Street bus to get it. He loads Homey, who needs a hip X-ray to determine if he's free of hip displasia (some type of bone or joint disorder that plagues big dogs). Bridgette has her certification. If Homey gets his, he could use it as another selling point and get anywhere from $600-800...possibly more. Dana jumped the fence two days ago and hasn't been seen since, so he's going to have to get top dollar. Three hundred fifty dollars is either running around or dead.

After Dr. Floyd sedated Homey for the trip to the facility, Mel went home. It will be about five hours, so he decides to collect dust in front of the television. He finds himself watching Comedy View on BET. There is a comedian performing that professes to be a minister of the Lord who *grew up in the church*. Mel can't determine if it is part of his act or if he is serious. His skit is about how the devil took over his mouth in the pursuit of a woman he wanted to lay with.

"You have a body to die for...I'm willing to take care of you...buy you nice things...what's mine is yours...just give me a chance," he coos dramatically. "She was saved, sanctified and full of the Holy Ghost, but that didn't mean a thing to me. She was a sexy virgin and that was all that mattered to me. She used scriptures like a *'sharp sword'*—as she referred to them from Ephesians 6 and 17. There's nothing like a woman using the Word of God to tell you your game is weak. She said that *'1st Corinthians 13 and 3 says And though I bestow all my goods to feed the poor, and though I give my body to be burned, and have not charity, it profiteth me nothing.'*

"She had a point, but I still had a few tricks up my sleeve. I felt that I could pull a Playboy bunny out of my hat. Charity is synonymous with love—for those who can't decipher that scripture. So, I professed 'I do love you.' What did I say that for. She dissected that line like a mad scientist: *'John 15 and 13 and 14 says Greater love hath no* ***man***—of course she put emphasis on man—*than this, that a man lay down his life for his friends. Ye are my friends, if ye do whatsoever I command you. Jesus commanded not to look upon a woman in lust, let alone commit adultery. I don't know about you, but Jesus is my friend and I choose to obey him.'*

"I thought I was slick, so I said 'If you weren't here in my sight with that nice skirt that highlights that beautiful body of yours, I wouldn't be lusting after you.' Of course, you know she sliced and diced me up into dog food. I spit in the wind and had a bucket of vomit come back in my face. She went on about how Jesus said if my right eye was causing me to sin, that I should pluck it out as opposed to going to hell. That scared me to death and I was ready to gouge my eyes out with a butcher knife because she was fine and I felt that mere man couldn't help but fantasizing about her, and I wasn't trying to go to hell for *nobody's body*. But then she stopped me, informing me that the lust originates from my heart and not from my eyes or anything on the outside. Jesus was using a play of words: If castration could keep you out of hell, then why not do it? But it doesn't. A change of heart is what was necessary.

"That was too deep for me, so I tucked my tail and retreated. A change of strategy was necessary. I had to read up on my scriptures, so I—the devil—could use them effectively. I went home, went to 1st Corinthians 13, and read up on love. And I memorized the fourth verse, because I had been in pursuit of her for about a year. The next week, I came back and told her how patient I was about waiting on her, so that proved my love. I argued that my sex drive was just an extension of my feelings. I was expecting an ethereal comeback, but she got humble and opened up to me like a mere, mortal *wo*man, which really struck me stupid. She told me that she had some of the same urges and feelings...she even commented how I had loved her with the love of Christ by doing things for her and sacrificing my own comforts and pleasures...but then she went to the scriptures again to back her up: *'Since you already love me like a husband is supposed to love a wife—as stated in Ephesians 5 and 29...and 1st Corinthians 7 and 9 says it is better to marry than to burn with passion...'* Good Lord. Ladies, if you want to put a man's love to the litmus test, don't ask him if he'll give up all of his belongings or die for you; ask him if he'll marry you. You can eliminate a lot of drama like that. I didn't know what she hit me with, but I know it was harder than a Mike Tyson uppercut. I couldn't win with sin, so I just gave up...and married her." Mel buckles over in laughter along with the television audience as he closes out: "May the grace of the Lord Jesus Christ, and the love of God, and the communion of the Holy Ghost, be with you all. Amen. I'm Minister Simeon Hall. God bless you."

Mel determines that Simeon *is* one of God's messengers and the message was for him. He couldn't stop laughing and reflecting on his testimony. It was powerful and had a profound effect on him. He cut the TV off and mulled over his relationship with Memory. Is he willing to die for her? Better yet, is he willing to marry her now? At the moment, he can't answer yes to either question. But a more pressing question is does she love him enough to marry him. Does she love him at all?

Mel almost forgot about the monthly CABJ meeting. When he got back from the vet, he happened to look at his daily devotional calendar that read, *"Then saith he to Thomas, Reach hither thy finger, and behold my hands; and reach hither thy hand, and thrust it into my side: and be not faithless, but believing."*—John 20:27. He remembered BJ Thomas invited him, insisting that it would be well worth his time. Mel threw on a light, button-up dress shirt, a floral-design, silk tie and a pair of slacks before taking off. It started at six and it was already a quarter after seven.

He backs into a spot under Wacker Drive and steps out to start the four or so block trek to the NBC Tower, when he notices a mound of gray clothes behind his vehicle. He walks up to make sure it's not dead. The gentle, soiled face of a middle aged black man (presumably homeless) is exposed as he slumbers away. His heart sinks as he stares at the content man that has nothing and is asking for nothing. Countless people have walked over or around him today. People that have homes to go to and beds to sleep in. A flat tire or rush hour traffic would ruin their day. When they don't have enough to get the personal computer or the chic leather outfit or the new furniture, it's obvious God is against them. It would be a crisis for them if they didn't get the promotion or raise. Mel sticks his bare hands in his pockets and ruminates. For the past week, he's been making a dire issue over Memory. As if she's going to make his life better. Perspective. He studies the face of the man and muses if he has more peace. He pulls out a ten—two thirds of his last money until next weeks unemployment check—and slides it just under his bearded chin. God is love, and the affirmation made him feel a lot better.

The lobby leading to the elevator has a wall full of NBC broadcast personalities. The stoic guard directs him to the third floor. Empty Giordano's Pizza boxes are scattered on a counter. Apparently, he missed the refreshments. There are four friendly, professionally dressed individuals sitting at a long folding table with several handouts of the organization. He collects a copy of each and bypasses the membership fee, choosing to scout the meeting out and paying the $5 admission charge. He walks through a door of what appears to be the backstage of a theater. The backside of the paneling seems to make a revolution as he walks up some wooden stairs to a lightened area where he could hear some type of forum. To his surprise, he is in the stands of the Jenny Jones Show and settles in a seat a couple of rows from the back. A discussion about minorities breaking in the media business is going on as he studies the room, looking for BJ. Several camera-ready people loom in the audience. Some of them are probably fresh off of work. They are made up like wax figures. He realizes that the makeup works wonders on a face in front of a sensitive camera lens. Off camera, some of the newscasters look either darker, lighter, heavier or smaller. He recognizes a couple of students from Chicago State. Art Norman is on the stage with the panelists. Mel half-listens to the topic as he peruses the materials he picked up.

Just before they close out, which was 20 minutes after Mel arrived, they update the job listing, mention a national conference, and announce the scholarship banquet as some of the people start self-adjourning. To his dismay, the jobs are all either out of state or require extensive experience. As most of the audience disperses, Mel grabs his things and follows suit. Just as he bypasses all of the networkers in the lobby, a hand grabs him on the shoulder from behind and a voice announces, "I see you made it."

He turns around to greet BJ. "What's going on?" he asks, extending his hand. "I didn't think you made it out today."

He shakes Mel's hand. "I usually make them all," he declares. "So what did you think?"

"I was late, so I wasn't able to get a strong feel of what it's like, but from what I could see, it may just be worth my while and 25 bucks."

"Good. I'm glad you came out and liked it."

"So what are you working on now?"

"Awe man...don't ask."

"Freelancing that bad to you?"

"It's not bad at all. Me...that's a different story."

"Writer's block?"

"Something like that," he says elusively. "Are you headed to the underground?"

"Yeah. Under Wacker," Mel confirms, nodding as the members flow past. He throws a stick of Double Mint in his mouth and offers one to BJ.

"That's where I'm headed," he says as he takes a stick and gestures with his head to start walking.

A hard, icy snow has started pouring from the sky and the brisk wind makes the flakes feel like micro blades as they hunch over. BJ strains out an elaboration through the resistant wind chill. "I'm still being delivered from a lot of worldly things—namely sex. When I first got saved, I didn't think anything of it, since I didn't have anything serious going, just partners. I cut them all off and was into my work and the Lord. But then a couple of weeks ago, I was doing this story on this author—Aura Smith—who wrote this book about relationships."

"I heard about her, but I haven't read any of her work."

"Recycled, non-objective, feminist rhetoric from a bitter woman, if you ask me, but people are gobbling it up—especially black women. One of my colleagues wrote a mordacious commentary about it in Bourgeois Magazine. I mean he ripped the book to pieces, and for the most part, brothers agreed with it. Anyway, she suggested an interview at her high rise apartment on Lake Shore Drive, which I was cool with."

"Her home?" he questions as his eyebrows rise.

"That's not unusual. I interview a lot of celebrities at their homes."

"I'm just surprised that with some of the obvious ill feelings she has towards men, that she would allow one in her place of residence."

"The press doesn't have a gender or race—on paper. In the real world, of course people are partial when they see me. A lot of times I can detect condescension—and that's from other African-Americans. White people occasionally try to mask their prejudice when they see me, resorting to covert put-downs in the form of big words and rhapsodies that they assume I don't understand, and when they figure that nothing is going over my head, the surprised expression is uniform: *This Nigger is well trained* is written all over their faces. It tickles me how they expect me to come out using a lot of colloquialisms and jive talk with a deep street dialect straight from *'da hood.*"

"I know what you mean," Mel agrees. "I've been there. It's like they see you perform tasks such as math and reading, and they figure you're gifted—like it's phenomenal for a black person to read. I remember when a new manager in another department started at my last job. She came up to my department—at the time I was the manager—and needed an explanation of some account activity. When I told her I was the manager, she gave me a 'Yeah right' look. I kept my cool and proceeded to explain the simple postings that a first grader could have understood. Her mouth just hung open—as if I was a talking dog."

"I know how Corporate America can be. My sister told me a story almost identical to what you just said," he testifies. "Anyway, this was all business with me and Aura...or so I thought," he emphasizes. "Have you seen a picture of her?"

Mel shakes his head.

"I hadn't either," he says. "Let me tell you Mel, she was as fine as a strand of fiberglass."

"Is that right?"

"I'm talking 'bow down to the queen' fine," he stresses. "She came to the door in her housecoat and a glass of wine in her hand. Luther Vandross was playing over her CD and she was already a little tipsy. It was like a romantic scene out of a movie and I was the leading man entering the action. But I wasn't even tripping over that. I was determined to get the interview and get out. I sat on her sofa—at her request—and she sat an uncomfortable breath away, but I didn't protest. I just turned my recorder on and proceeded to talk in depth with her. She was actually doing all of the talking, or confessing—for lack of a better term. Five hours of guts—on tape. I felt like a therapist."

"I'm sure that made for an interesting story."

"Actually, I haven't even transcribed it yet," he states matter-of-factly. "My conscious won't let me reveal some of the things she confided in me—me, the journalist. I could get my biggest royalties from the tabloids on the story."

"That deep, huh?"

"She gave me some dirt on a lot of well known people. And trust me, she showed me things that proved that she wasn't lying either. She confirmed a lot of suspicions about them that I already had."

Mel smiles as the man that slept near his car walks towards them, towing his thick, soiled quilt and clasping the financial blessing. He smirks at them and God blesses them as he passes. They both return the wish as Mel's heart warms his whole body.

"This is me," Mel states as they arrive to the space Mel parked in. Mel sets his attaché case on the hood as BJ proceeds to chronicle his story.

"She shifted throughout the interview and with each movement she ended up closer to me, until she was literally in my lap. Mel..." he chuckles as he shakes his head. "In my promiscuous, pre-Jesus days, I've never slept with a woman I've known less than a week, and I ended up in bed with her after a five hour *professional* interview."

"Awe man..." Mel says in a disbelieving chortle for lack of anything else to say.

"Awe man, is right. I let her bewitch me with her wine and body heat. To read her book, you would think that she took an oath to never touch a man again, but as it turns out, she's a meek and lonely creature belied by a bold book."

"Sure she wasn't acting?"

BJ shakes his head. "I've seen shows before—participated in them, and I doubt if she was performing. If she was, why, and who was her audience?"

Mel humps his shoulders.

"I've had a thick block in front of me since. This other female reporter did a story on her for the Defender—minus all of the juice. Every time I try to listen to the interview, my mind drifts to the gutter."

"So what are you gonna do?"

"Well, last week I decided to forget about the whole story and this week I'm on a fast."

"Oh yeah?"

"Every time I get out of fellowship, I have to fast and pray to get my spiritual discernment and creativity back. Writing is a gift from the Lord, and when my communication with God is bad—like now—my communication with man is bad. I can't write a decent sentence. When I walk in obedience, the line of communication with God is open and clear and I'm putting out Pulitzer Prize winning work."

"I hear you," Mel confirms as he chews intently.

"It's like, when I blatantly go against the Spirit, I can feel him grieving...I can't concentrate on anything. I didn't have to sleep with her, but I'll be honest and say that I wanted it bad. In fact, I fasted for the following two days and apologized and begged God's forgiveness, and you know what I did? I went back over there a week later and slept with her again, so I took a step back when I didn't have to and I'm making my way back to my feet."

Mel just nods his head in admiration as his body starts shivering. He's in awe of the change that has taken place, and wonders, "What's your story?"

"Story on what?"

"How you became a Christian. Your conversion rivals that of the Apostle Paul."

He chuckles and staggers. "Well, that's a long testimony and it's too chilly to get into it, but I will tell you that it *was* a Damascus Road conversion: I heard the voice of the Lord in the darkness and I've been a follower ever since," he testifies, promising to "tell you the whole story later."

"Pen me in for next week," Mel urges facetiously. "And don't worry, I won't try to seduce you."

"I got you covered, Bro," he says with an extended hand.

Mel slaps hands with him and promises to "keep you in my prayers" as he jumps in his car and heads home. "Sex Me" by R. Kelly plays lightly, with an overdose of bass. As he cruises and eats up Lake Shore Drive, scenes from his past flash before his eyes, specifically, the episode when he lost his innocence like a man that wanted to be guilty.

Her name was Traci Dukes. The date was November 3, 1988. He was a year into his church hiatus, which meant that if there was an opportunity for him to slip into sin, it was at that moment when he wasn't answering the voice of God. For two years in high school they crossed paths, but never spoke. She was two years ahead of him, and from what he remembered, he didn't have any bad impressions of her...nor any necessarily good one's. She was just a familiar face in the hallway. He was shopping in the Plaza with his little brother, charging some gym shoes for him, and she was there with one of her girlfriends, when they bumped into each other. They immediately recognized each other, chatted briefly and exchanged numbers. At best, Traci was cute; at worse, she was average, yet presentable. She smoked, had a daughter and seemed to enjoy hearing herself talk. From the start, she wasn't a potential mate, yet Mel delighted in listening to her, too. As it turned out, she went to Chicago State also, and likewise, was an accounting major. The irony was that she struggled in school and often sought Mel for private tutorials. It was during one of their late night sessions at her apartment, that he made a mud murky formula (she went through a pack of cigarettes in four hours trying to get it) as clear as a Windexed glass to her, and she insisted on showing her gratitude.

It was about two in the morning and she brought a blanket for him to sleep under on the couch. He wasn't even settled in when she came out and straddled him. Although he wasn't experienced, he wasn't nervous or clumsy. He knew what was going on, but didn't resist. She got him up and jumped him. He was numb and went into auto-sex. It was like he was preprogrammed to go through all of the right motions. From what he heard, it was supposed to be the supreme joy; something to live and die for; the ultimate pleasure. He stroked with the expectation of getting caught up in the seventh heaven. He didn't even reach the clouds. After an hour of union, sweat and the smell of ground in cigarette smoke, he faked an ejaculation. The thunder echoed and lightning flashed, but the rain never came. Not a drop. He could've waited until his honeymoon. It was nothing wrong with her performance, even though initially there was mild sensation when he entered her. He chalked it up as his inexperience.

A few days later, they did it again. Again, not a drop. She seemed to get a lot out of it though. He started wondering if it was his lack of feelings for her that prevented him from getting any joy out of it. He didn't believe a heart was a necessity of ecstasy. After all, his peers spewed tales of one-night stands with girls that they couldn't even remember the names. After a few months of screaming passionately without substance, he lost count of the times they bedded. It became a boring routine. He could relate to Al Bundy.

One day, after she passed a test that he prepared her for, she treated him to a play and dinner. When they got to her apartment, she sat him on the couch and came out in a cop's uniform, complete with handcuffs and a nightstick. Mel was totally surprised and didn't understand the method to the madness. She pranced seductively around him and told him to take the position. He opened his mouth to protest, only to be cut off with a swift slap on the cheek. Then she cuffed him, escorted him to the bedroom and put him under bed arrest—chaining his arms to the headboard. It suddenly clicked that she was giving him a crash course in dramatic foreplay. She read him his Miranda rights, strip searched him and proceeded to grind on top of him. Whenever he moaned, she used it against him, biting him in sensitive places that educed more noise. After she left teeth marks up and down his body, she stripped down to a bikini lingerie set. She danced, teased, and fondled him for what seemed like a couple of days, but he enjoyed every second of it.

He was ready to detonate while she was gnawing on him, but when she grinded on top of him, he felt like a hot air balloon filled to capacity with nitrogen. Then she flirted with that balloon with a white-hot needle: she sucked his toes. He thought he would have a heart attack. It was torturous. It was gratifying. Every atom; every molecule; every cell in his body was fizzling. It was painfully delightful. Then she engulfed him and he immediately exploded, anointing her with his soul juice. The feeling was rapidly rapturous. For a split moment, everything was deceptively perfect. She took him to the mountaintop, but he tumbled down once he got there. Then she collapsed on top of him and he almost forgot who she was. He couldn't hold her because his hands were still cuffed—and he was glad. Instead of beaming with satisfaction, he was burning with regret. That much joy should be reserved for someone special. He vowed to share his next relationship with his lover, which turned out to be Memory. She wishes that she could come close to the empyrean, but she was too trifling. Rita was thrilling and came close because of his admiration for her. Darlene is just an outlet and an instrument for vengeance and isn't even in the valley. Although every encounter after brought him physical satisfaction, no one has ever taken him to his erogenous peak like the Duchess. She had the advantage of deceiving his soul.

As he parks in front of his house, he makes a silent pledge to get closer to God. He is somewhat envious of BJ's relationship with Christ. That envy doesn't manifest itself negatively, but it motivates him to make the necessary sacrifices to clear up his line of communication. When he gets into the house, he lets the dogs out. Before he can get his coat off, the phone rings. "Hello," he answers.

"Put the dog up and let me in," Memory says.

Mel peeks out the window, observing Memory's car behind his. "Give me a second," he says as he lets the dogs in on the side. He opens the door for her and comments, "You must've been following me."

She struts in and around him, grinning in her full-length mink coat and leather riding boots. "I wasn't following you," she remarks as she opens her coat to reveal her bare breasts and all of her anatomy. "I was stalking you."

"Oh my," he says as his mouth drops like a comet and his flesh hops like a rabbit, but then his mouth snaps shut like a mouse trap and his flesh collapses even quicker. Part of him questions where the creative sex drive is coming from, and his mind imagines and suspects the worst, but that isn't the issue.

"Oh my is right," she comments as she strikes a pose with her hands on her hips. "I'm having you for dinner tonight," she announces as she drops her coat and lunges at him.

"Wait a minute," he says as he catches her forearms. "Not today, Memory."

"I'm getting mine," she declares as she manages to get her hands free and grabbles in his pants.

Mel just stands still in frustration as her fondling tickles more than arouses. "I said not today, Memory," he pleads. "I can't do this."

"Why not," she questions as she persists.

He didn't script it, but he hears, "Because it's not pleasing in God's sight" come boldly out of his mouth.

She immediately stops and pulls her hands out of his pants. "Oh really?" she asks as she takes a step back and folds her arms.

"Really."

"So all of a sudden, you're getting religious on me," she assumes.

"Call it religion if you must, but I can't do it anymore."

"What about the other times when you wanted it and got it? What about my needs?"

"I'm sorry for the past. I really am. But I can't go on like this."

"So in other words you're breaking up with me, is that it?"

"No. I'm not breaking up with you," he confirms as he steps toward her and embraces her. Then he explains, "I'm making up with the Lord."

She stands still and doesn't respond to the hug. For a few moments, she just looks at him like his head took off running without the rest of his body. "You might as well be breaking up with me," she reasons in a huff. "What am I supposed to do while you're making up with the Lord?"

"Last night, you said that you luuuuuved me...did you mean it?"

"What kind of question is that?" she begs as she curls her lip up. "Of course I meant it."

"Well in the name of luuuuuv, I would like for you to wait for me."

"Wait for you?"

"Yes. Wait until we get married."

"Married? And how long is that supposed to take? We're not even officially engaged."

"I won't keep you waiting long. I promise you."

She soughs aloud and rolls her eyes as she collects her coat and wraps it around herself. "I wish I had known last night...I would've gotten a years worth."

Mel chuckles, but she doesn't crack a smile. "So does that mean that you're going to wait on me for marriage?"

"Whatever," she blurts.

"Don't be mad," he appeals.

"I need time to think this over."

"I understand."

"Well," she says as she leans to one side. "I guess I'll talk to you later."

"That's fine."

She turns around and marches out of the door without uttering another word. He watches her all the way to her car, and when she peels off, he feels a little relief. Although he doesn't feel that he earned any brownie points with God, he does feel that the line just got clear of all the static. He takes a seat on the sofa and reflects on the stand he just took, realizing that she may not go the distance with him. He hopes she does. If she's willing to abstain for a few months until they elope (he wouldn't keep her—or himself—waiting over a year), he could easily forget that she was messing around. If she can't, then it would be a good thing to find out before they become legal. In that case, he can move on and search for that mountain to climb.

Chapter 6

"Shut up and don't call here no more," Mel mumbles as he turns the volume down low enough on his answering machine to just barely hear Mary Jo ramble on about how late his furniture account is. She's usually the first bill collector to call every working day. She's right on schedule. He knows in about two minutes the phone will ring again—just like clockwork. He lies on his side, staring at the digital display on his clock, waiting for it to hit 8:05 and listening for the phone to ring. The phone rings just before and he rolls over on his other side and blurts out, "How many times have I told you not to call here when they call for me, Momma?"

But it isn't Momma on the line as the message starts to record. It's a man's voice, that doesn't sound demanding or threatening, although Mel can barely hear what he's saying. His eyes pop wide open—as if he's trying to hear with them—and he quickly turns over, knocking the covers on the floor as he cranks the volume all the way up to catch the man say, "...talk to you about a sales position. You can call me at 555-4525. Thank you."

"Sales, Bells, go to Hell...I can call you a fool," Mel mumbles at the thought of working in a sales position. He sent out résumés only to satisfy the requirements of unemployment. He sits up and presses the rewind button to erase the last two messages. He's not sleepy anymore and he decides to start his long, boring day. It didn't take Mel long to get into a tedious, unproductive routine of sleeping until noon, fixing a grilled ham and cheese sandwich for brunch, channel surfing through those pathetic day-time talk shows (he thinks the buffoons on Rikki Lake are especially sad), reading the delivered Sun-Times on the toilet, taking an hour-long bath, taking an evening nap, eating take-out in front of the prime-time cable movies, and going to bed at about two in the morning. An occasional visit or phone call from Memory (which has been almost non-existence since he decided on abstinence) or trips to the store, Memory's apartment (he hasn't been over there in three weeks) or Blockbuster were the only warranted breaks in inaction. Some days he doesn't leave the house. After all, his new job was to wait for his unemployment checks to come in the mail. He got his third check today.

A whopping, untaxed $480 every two weeks. Of course, he had to take a cut in pay. The vacation in the middle of the winter is worth it though, since he has always hated going to work and school during the cold months. But bills are pressing and his lifestyle is suffering. Not that he was living lavishly before the layoff, but he bought clothes, food, and toys when he wanted to. Now he has to really use his accounting knowledge and *budget* his money. That meant actively looking for sales at the grocery stores and not being too meticulous when it comes to food; buying less clothes, which doesn't matter now, since he doesn't go a lot of places, and putting off any of the latest technological gadgets until he has some excess cash. He definitely has to cut down on his fast food. At one time, he was carrying home over $500 a week. And with his minute savings dwindling fast, a harsh reality started to set in: He is going to have to find another job soon. His plan of staying on unemployment for six months while possibly working a part time gig isn't going to work.

Today he's on schedule. He chuckles at the unfaithful transvestites on the Jenny Jones Show. His mind drifts in and out of the pseudo-soap opera as he ponders his life. Soon he finds himself floating to the picture window. A light snow is falling on the six inches of six day-old fluff. Dismal. Restlessness sets in. He paces through the kitchen, into the den and back to the living room. A thought of retrieving something from upstairs comes, but he forgets what he came up there for when he makes it to his bedroom—doing a revolution of the room, without getting a hint. After he gets back down to his living room and settles on the couch, he spots an old People magazine on the floor and remembers that he went up there to fetch the latest issue of Ebony. It's the February, "Black Love Black History" issue with Spike Lee, Bobby Brown and Will Smith on the cover.

He sits on the bed as he peruses it. "The 10 hottest couples" strikes the most interest, Lee and Smith in particular. How did he get to this point in his life? A point of looking in from the outside and a feeling of envy. Disappointment sets in as it usually does when he dwells on dreams unrealized. *He wanted to be a big movie star when he was growing up. The fantasies were unlimited: he was in front of the camera doing his own stunts; his movies were all box office smashes; he raked in 10 million a film; every week he was on the cover of some magazine (Ebony, People, Entertainment Weekly, Time, and even Playboy); the polls in several of those magazines listed him as one of the sexiest men alive; the late night talk shows were after him; and every director wanted to cast him as their leading man.*

However, reality checked in often and early. The first appearance came in the third grade Christmas play. He had the leading role he hoped for: Jesus Christ. Of course he knew the story and the lines and the attitudes and feelings of the whole story. He knew it inside and out in his sleep. It's too bad he wasn't asleep when playtime came. The lights mesmerized him and all of the faces scared him. His lips were moving, but no sounds were coming from his mouth. After a few seconds of excruciating humiliation, he forgot all of his lines and froze up on stage. There were similar flops in the church plays and the day camp events. He never got over it and was traumatized by the spotlight. At the same time, he loved the idea of entertaining. Unfortunately, he didn't have the boldness to match his desire. He wanted to join the drama club in high school, but the thought of having a buffoon's reputation scared him off. High schoolers can make a person want to die. Instead, he opted for the low profile business club and aspired to be an accountant. And that leaves him in his current dilemma: two degrees in a field that he hates.

After he goes through a couple of articles, he drives to the bank to cash his check. He decides to rent "Public Eye" from Blockbuster. When he gets back, he strips down to his shorts and crashes in front of the television. He kicks his heels up and closes his eyes in meditation as the previews flash across the screen. The sounds of the television are easily tuned out as he thinks about what tomorrow has in store. He almost drifts into a blissful blackness, when he hears a piercing cry. His eyes pop open to verify his presence in reality. He hears it again, and it's coming from the basement. He springs up and runs downstairs. Homey meets him at the bottom. He bypasses him to the back, where—to his amazement—there's a rat-like creature squirming around and crying by Bridgette. The puppies are arriving!

He rushes upstairs for his camcorder and grabs his phone on the way back down. When he gets back down there, Homey is sniffing it in a questioning way, as if confirming that it's a baby canine and not a Gremlin. Mel starts rolling as he shoos Homey into another room and places the damp pup in the designated space as Bridgette follows him. He calls Memory's cellular, but there's no answer. Then he phones her home, and her answering machine picks up. He announces excitedly that the puppies are coming and that she should come see them. Bridgette lays down in silent distress and pushes another one out. Quickly, she's back on her feet and she eats the membrane sack from around it as the pup starts squealing with its sibling. There's blood everywhere as she repeats the process nine more times, for a litter of eleven. Mel continues to tape Bridgette while she nurses her offspring. When the tape comes to the end, he continues to watch her, in awe of the creative power that God has given. He is to be revered.

Mel was so excited about the puppies' arrival, that he forgot about the movie that he rented and that he hadn't heard from Memory in about a week. He finally watched "Public Eye" this morning and was well entertained and enlightened. He gave it two thumbs up. The two hours it took him to view it gave him a chance to reflect on the direction he was going with his career. He wrestled with the idea of still photography and video production. Both areas seemed exciting, although he figured photography would be the easier path that would provide more freelance opportunities. Video production would put him close to the drama that he's always relished. The indecisiveness excited him as opposed to stressing him out. There will be a lot to think about at night since his love life was on a leave of absence.

Memory came in with fangs and claws just after the movie went off. It's been a full moon for her ever since his announcement. He was surprised that she didn't brutally rape him. She is in her critical mood as she views the puppies. "It stinks down here," she remarks, turning her lip up.

Mel lets the comment pass as he hands one to her, smiling.

She declines, observing, "It looks like a rodent" as she folds her arms.

"How can you not adore a face like this?" Mel questions as he holds it up to her.

"Get that thing out of my face," she says, leaning back.

"Awe. Boo Memory," he jokes. "You've gotta be the only person alive that shows contempt for a cute, little puppy." She turns away indifferently. Apparently Homey doesn't like the smell of arrogance (which is the fragrance Memory is wearing), because he starts making a big fuss behind the door. Mel considers knocking her upside the head, throwing her in a meat grinder, and putting her in his dish, but that would be inhuman to the dog. "See," he says. "Even Homey is mad at you."

She just huffs. When they get back upstairs, she paces around like a peacock. "When are you going to get this kitchen fixed?" she queries impatiently, as if she's ready to do the work herself.

"I'll gladly get it done...as soon as you provide the financing."

Memory looks around at the mess the contractors made and turns her nose up as she takes a look around the living room—like it was her first time in there. After she determines that Mel has an interest in the basketball game that's on the television, she changes the channel.

Mel cuts her a dirty glance and passes on her bait as he takes a seat on the sofa. Memory purposely sits on the love seat across the room. "I'm not contaminated," Mel announces.

She ignores the comment and focuses on the TV. Mel takes a seat next to her and she immediately shifts to the point where her back is to him. Instead of acting on the impulse to whack the back of her head, he rubs her back—to her dismay. "Would you stop!" she hisses as she turns around frowning at him.

Mel throws his head back and draws his hands up. "Are we okay?"

"I'm fine," she snaps. "Just not in the mood for BS."

"Am I a Boy Scout?"

She burns a hole in him for a long second and announces, "I'm gone," as she springs up.

Mel doesn't even get up to see her to her car, as he bides, "Goodnight" to her. She slams the door as a reply and he turns back to the game.

Chapter 7

Mel has just enough money to get him and Memory in the theater and maybe buy a small, overpriced cup of pop. It's the type of wet, gray Saturday that saps all desire to live from the soul. Unemployment and the stench of dog dung compounded the effect. The thought of seeing "Ace Ventura: Pet Detective" doesn't excite him. They're going just for the date of it, and of course, she suggested the movie. He was planning to wait for it to come on cable—if he was going to see it at all. If he's going to pay to go to the movies, his first choice is "On Deadly Ground". But of course, she's not really interested in high-flying, butt-kicking, blood-pouring action, just sappy dramas or comedies. Why are they together?

He didn't even bother getting fancy. He threw on a pair of faded 501's, a Bulls' sweatshirt, and his black Reeboks. No fancy outfit, no rose (actually, he stopped giving her roses *just because* over a year ago and reserves flowers for special days, such as Valentines day, her birthday and Sweetest day—or when she's acting right), and no excitement. When he gets to the door, he's expecting her to come out dolled up. He isn't even going to try to beat around the bush about his reasons for dressing like a bum. If she doesn't like it, she could go by herself and he could go home and mope. She opens the door and her outfit is telling the same story. She's wearing a maroon, Nike jogging suit, and matching Nike cross-trainers. Her hair is tucked in a Bulls' baseball cap, her make-up consists of a modest red shade of lipstick, and her face looks exhausted. "You ready?"

"Yeah, I guess," she soughs as she gives him a hug and gestures for him to come in. Comic View is on and he can't tell if she was actually watching it or just filling the house with sound as she darts in her kitchen. "Let me finish putting these dishes up."

"Suit yourself," he says as he sinks into the soft, leather sofa. She must have been frying something, because the smell of cooking grease and butter is thick.

"You want some perch?"

"So that's what you were cooking. That's okay. I ate before I came." He tries to get in the mood to go, but Comic View isn't amusing him. The jokes are probably hilarious, but his funny bone is in a cast right now.

She emerges from the kitchen and grabs her navy blue leather jacket. "Let's go," she says as she opens the door.

"Come help me up," he says, extending his arms.

She goes along with it without a word, leaning back as she clasps his hands. Her grip is strong and he's tempted to get a piggyback ride to the car. "How much time do we have?"

Checking his watch, he announces, "We got about 30 minutes, but I'll get you there in 15." He winks at her as he let's her in.

"I know you will," she says blearily.

He pulls off and just before he reaches the Dan Ryan expressway, she whines, "I want you to promise not to get mad if I ask you something" as she rests her head on his shoulder.

He just looks straight ahead, waiting for the light to change.

"Promise me."

"All right!"

"Say I promise not to get mad."

"I don't know if I should, but for the sake of moving the conversation on, I promise not to get mad."

"I really don't want to go to the show. Can we just rent a movie and go watch it at my house?"

He pauses and she looks up at him. "I had my fingers crossed, so the promise is null and void," he says as he holds his hand up to her face.

She clicks her tongue and sighs, "Mel," as she slaps his arm.

"But I don't feel like going to the show either, so Blockbuster sounds a lot better," he says, peeling off when the light changes and illegally cutting into the straight lane towards video rental place three blocks down.

"Thank you," she says as she plants a soft kiss on his check that unlocks the chain of endurance and releases the resentment from doing something he isn't in the mood for. "How about if you pick the movie and I go get the doughnuts?" she suggests as he comes to a stop.

"Now you know our tastes are different and more than likely you're not going to want to see what I pick."

"I know, but tonight I'll go with what you choose since you compromised with me."

Mel can't say anything to that.

He strolls the new releases row and the action, horror, and drama aisles, looking for something that he hasn't seen that will hold his attention and keep Memory in a decent mood and in the living room with him. Although she gave him her blessings on the choice, he realizes that he can't get too outrageous. Extreme violence, blood and gore are out of the question, which eliminates most of the movies he entertains. He figures the only way to be fair is to get three movies: one of his preference, one of her liking, and something in between—like a sports video. He chose Lethal Weapon III for himself and a sports bloopers tape for the both of them. He's strolling the romance section when she comes up behind him and touches him on the shoulder. "I picked out two so far, so if you want to get something..."

She holds her hand up and assures, "What you got is fine," as she peeks at the titles. "I think Lethal Weapon should be pretty good and the bloopers tape should cure the ho hums. I'll go with that."

Mel is surprised...pleasantly surprised.

When they get back to her townhouse, she pops the microwave popcorn they picked up at Blockbuster and warms up the fish that Mel now has a taste for. Mel kicks off his shoes and jeans, slips into a pair of shorts that he leaves at her house and stretches out on the couch, getting comfortable as he channel surfs. She comes in, places a bowl of popcorn on the coffee table, and asks, "What do you want to drink?"

"I'll take red wine."

She rolls her eyes and smirks. "Silly."

"Is there any Kool-Aid made?"

"Nope, but I'll make some. What kind do you want?"

"You don't have to. I'll drink pop."

"I'll make grape for you," she says as she dashes back into the kitchen.

Days like this should come more often. Not that everything has to be picture perfect, but this disposition should be the standard, and not the exception. He's holding out, and she's trying. Eventually, they'll get the consistency down. Today marks another step. Normally she doesn't allow people to suck on a mint—let alone eat—in her living room, but she threw the rulebook out of the window when she compromised her video preference.

As he savors the tranquillity, he glances around her living room at her art. Each piece is like a still documentary. He gets lost in her "Attitude" portrait. Sometimes he wonders if the artist had Memory in sight when he painted it. Surely, he knows her. The resemblance is eerie. The honey brown complexion, short, feathered hair, and orange, exotic eyes bring the picture to life and captures the essence of his woman. The title defines her—most of the time. Memory tilts her head to the side like the figure in the painting, except she does it out of humility. If he wasn't sane, he would be enticed to kiss it.

Memory comes in, sets the fish and hot sauce on coasters on the table and pops Mel on the thigh. "I told you about looking at that woman...and if you say she looks like me, we're going to be fighting this evening," she threatens as she darts back into the kitchen before he can justify himself. She returns with the pitcher of Kool-Aid and two glasses and plants a kiss on his lips. "Now say the grace."

He does and she pops the bloopers tape in first. They nibbled on the fish and popcorn and laughed in between bites at the video, commenting and sticking their own humor in. "Lethal Weapon" follows as they snuggle up and mellow out. "There's Homey," she exclaims of the Rottweiler in the film.

"I didn't tell you he was in the movie?"

"You think he'll give me his autograph?"

"For a small fee."

"What's that fee?"

"A kiss on my cheek and smile to melt my heart."

"In that case," she says as she smooches both checks and gives him an inebriated smile. "Now I should get two autographs."

Not once did she jump at a violent scene. She didn't even turn her head at the sight of blood. If she was only acting like she was amused, she was ready for Hollywood. After the movie went off, they both headed for one of the bathrooms and met back at the sofa. She turned on the lamp and collected the dishes. When she gets back, she flops on the other end of the couch and rests her legs on his lap. Saturday Night Live is on and they glance at it occasionally, but can't follow the skits as they talk. "I liked it better when they had Eddie Murphy," she comments.

"I know what you mean. My favorite act was his portrayal of Gumby. It used to have me rolling. 'Get out of here before I rip your throat out. You stink,'" he mimics in a high pitch tone.

"I liked Mr. Robinson's neighborhood. Chris Rock is good, but the show isn't what it used to be," she observes as she clicks the TV off and turns her stereo on to V103. "Everything I Miss at Home" by Cherrelle is playing. "I can't say that I miss anything at home."

"Amen to that. I think I'd rather live at the YMCA than go back home."

"Tell me about it. All I could think about when I was growing up, was getting out of my mother's house. Sometimes I wonder does spite come with age and children; does childbearing and rearing bring out the worst in people. She was a real bitch when I was living with her."

"I know what you mean. I know one thing: I may tear them up at home if they get out of line, but I'm not going to slap my kids in school."

She agrees. "Some of the stuff my mother did to me was totally unnecessary, and I'm still not over it yet. I talked to her today and she made me feel real small, as usual. I can't do anything to make her happy. I used to get good grades, but all she would do was say 'that's nice.' I stayed home and kept my room clean, but she acted like it didn't matter. But let one sock be out of line and she would hit me and the roof," she whines as she starts getting pitiful and upset. "Maybe my death would bring her a little joy," she wonders as a tear drops.

Mel slides down to her end of the couch and puts his arm around her. "It's okay. Cry if you must. I know how you feel," he whispers in her ear. *He remembers the days of not wanting to wake up. That was his prayer every night. He would sleep peacefully, which was the only time and place that he had serenity, and then wake up to hell all over again. He didn't dream: he fantasized. As he got older, his mental illusions got more realistic and modest. His imagination is still an occasional escape, but he prefers to deal with reality, now that he's the decision-maker of his life. The need to dream is unnecessary, since his biggest dream is being fulfilled everyday: adulthood. Once in every eclipse, he'll think about a career in showbiz. Most of his escapes have to do with real life drama, such as rescuing a woman from attackers (even though he doesn't know anything about self-defense) or reviving a child (although he wouldn't know were to start CPR). Now he dreams about attainable things, such as a nice wife and kids, a satisfying career, and somehow influencing a lot of people in a positive way. He's come a long way from the "Hollywood" vision.*

"What did I do to deserve that, Mel?" she moans.

"Nothing sweetheart. You didn't deserve it."

She sobs as she plants her head in his chest. "Why, Mel? Why is she so mean to me? Why does she act like she hates me? I tried to please her. I wasn't fast; I never disrespected her house by bringing any boys over and coming home pregnant. I stayed pure so she wouldn't be disgraced. I didn't even have a boyfriend until I got out of high school. What does she want?"

"I don't know. We're still trying to figure our mothers out."

She regains her composure and confides, "I felt all alone growing up" as she sits up and scans the room. "I could never understand why she would hit me. Sometimes she would give a trivial reason, other times she would come in and knock fire from me and tell me to figure out why. I still haven't figured out why."

"I know what you mean, but don't let it bother you." She isn't lying.

Ms. Jones is deranged. He doesn't know for sure, but that's probably why she was dismissed from her job as a Chicago patrol officer. Memory told him that she shot not one, but two people. The first was apparently a self-defense situation. Some guy that was disruptive on the El charged her with a switchblade. But there were questions surrounding that incident. Word was the man was too drunk to stand, let alone attack someone. There were reports in the Sun-Times in which witnesses said the second dude said something she didn't like and turned his back on her. Others say that there was a struggle when she tried to handcuff him. One thing is fact: she shot him in the butt. Shortly after, she was fired.

Memory claims that she was a werewolf before that point, but afterwards she morphed into a devil who had her gas turned off in the winter. It was around that time when they first went out and she brought him home a couple of times. At first, her mother seemed like good people, until one time she snapped on Memory about having too many credit cards. Memory reasoned that she was paying them and that they were in her name. They were two rooms over, but Mel heard her mother tell her to "Stop getting smart at the mouth," as the sound of skin connecting with skin echoed through the house. Memory emerged grimacing seconds later with a red hand print on her cheek and tears coming down her face as she breathlessly whispered, "Let's go."

Before Mel could rise or even say anything, her mother charged in and interrogated her about what she had just said to him. Memory was a wreck on unstable legs as her mother came up in her face, yelling and threatening to knock her down again. Mel was totally dumfounded as Memory cringed in anticipation of more punishment. Apparently, Memory didn't answer quick enough for her mother, because she threw a straight right to her mouth—knocking her over a love seat. Her mother jumped on top of her and had a handful of hair in one hand and her throat in the other. "What did you say," she growled.

Mel jumped up with the intentions of interceding and insisted, "She just said let's go, Ms. Jones," as he gently grabbed her shoulder.

"Get your fucking hands off of me and mind your own business, or I'll blow your damn head off," she said as she pulled her revolver from the holster on her hip and pointed it at his face as he backed up. "Now get the fuck out of my house."

Mel must have peed his brains out, because he heard himself say, "I'll leave, but not without Memory," as he just knew he was about to lose his head.

She paused and sneered as she got up and walked up an arms' with-a-gun-in-it length away, still pointing at him. "You stupid ass fool...you realize that I can send you out of here in a body bag—without her—just for putting your hands on me in my house. I carried her for nine months, and I've lived with her for 19 years, and I can tell you she ain't worth the price of a funeral. Now are you gonna walk, or should I call the morgue," she asked as she cocked the hammer. Since she put it that way, Mel walked passed her and Memory—who was curled up in a fetal position—without saying another word. Mel could've been a hero and ate a bullet, but why? She didn't have any intentions of killing Memory—just slapping her around for whatever sadistic reason she did. It would've been romantic to tell her to "Shoot me...I'm willing to live and die for that woman." It would've also been stupid. Why die when he had a choice to live?

"She'll be out after I finish talking to her," she assured caustically. She didn't seem to mind him waiting on the porch. From what he could hear, she did just talk to her, ordering her to get her things and get out. Memory huffed out five minutes later dragging an over-size, stuffed

suitcase with clothes hanging out. He carried the suitcase to the trunk. She sobbed on the car door all the way to his apartment before she whimpered, "Can I stay with you for a couple of days?" As if he had any reservations. She stayed with him two days and one night before she found a studio in the Hyde Park. She never stayed under her mother's roof again. She graduated a few months later and she's been flying since.

"Outside of you, I don't have anybody, not even my two-faced sorority sisters."

Mel rubs her back and doesn't say anything. He grins slightly as he thinks about his parallel sentiments that he kept to himself for so long.

"I never thanked you for sticking up for me when my mother hit me. I was truly honored and grateful," she says as she recalls the event with a simper. "It was also a little foolish."

"I guess I'm a fool for you."

She rewards that statement with a kiss.

They simultaneously peer at the "Soul Mates" print hanging on the wall over the television and get stuck in the image. "I used to wonder who I would end up with...if I had a soul mate. I used to think that no one would want me, or that whoever I found would be someone I settled for," she recalls.

"I always felt that there was a perfect match out there for me, but I never knew if I would meet her...that is until I met you."

"I'm glad I met you when I did, especially with graduation coming up and the situation at home. I couldn't have made it without you," she says as her voice gets lower. "When you first came up there to Margaret's office, I thought I was having a heart attack. I was so nervous. I didn't know if you would be interested in me. You caught me totally off guard. I was so glad when you went along with my corny conversation, and I was even happier when you turned out to be who you are."

"Is that right?"

"Umhmm," she confirms as she drifts off to sleep. He has never seen anyone cross over into slumber as quickly as she does. She could be talking one moment, and in the next second, snoring lightly. It's little imperfections like that that make her so perfect for him. For the instant, everything is right with them. He wants to freeze the moment like a picture frame and inscribe "Happily Ever After" beneath it.

"I don't know the first thing about this," Mel testifies. "So you're going to have to guide me through it." Feelings don't get more amalgamated than Mel's. He should feel excited and happy—and he thinks he is, but he also feels insecure and hesitant, which is a natural reaction when a big step in life is going to be taken. If a decision is big enough to affect the rest of a person's life, anxiety is part of the package. And a marriage proposal will turn the manliest men into cowering cowards.

"Sure. You said that you wanted to spend between $1500 and $2500, right?" the friendly sales woman verifies. Of course she's friendly; she's getting a commission from the sale.

"I heard someone say that it was appropriate to spend a months salary on it."

Mel price-shopped and went to the ATM to withdraw the remaining amounts from his VISA and Savings. His account is emaciated now. Earl paid him back $400 that he owed him and his Unemployment check came Wednesday, so he's pocketing $2,200 cash.

"You can do it that way," she offers.

"Well in that case, I would be spending a little less than nothing. I'm going by my salary from when I was actually working."

"I don't know if we have anything in that range," she goes along with the wit.

"So what can I get in the fifteen to twenty-five range?"

"Well over here in this section, we have the engagement sets. Is she the flamboyant type or would you say that she's modest?"

"Flamboyant by all means. She loves jewelry."

"Well, this one right here," she says, pulling out a ring that he was eyeing from under the counter. "...has a 1 karat diamond in it. I think she would love it. And it's priced on sale at $1995," she says as she hands it to him.

He rotates and examines it as if he was looking for a symbol of approval. Although he's not a ring expert or critic, it does look nice...like something she would wear. In fact, it looks like something he would give her after she stole his heart. It's not the biggest thing by far, but it's not microscopic either. A potential suitor would definitely be able to see it from a distance. If he was a stranger and spotted it on her finger, he would assume that she is in love with someone and someone is in love with her. He smiles and pulls out his wallet.

"So you like that one?"

He nods.

"Do you want to look at any others?"

He shakes his head. "This one is perfect," he says, arrested by the dual reality of the decision to seal last night's moment with a commitment. It is both expensive and sentimental. He's made bigger decisions with less time and knowledge of a subject. He didn't study real estate before he bought his house. He couldn't decipher the whole contract and barely skimmed over the whole document. Gut feeling, with a touch of naiveté and a dose of foolishness, is what he went on—which is the norm for him. Occasionally, a little egging on from his confidants influences the decision. His gut is hurting and he hasn't even told Earl yet. It *is* a big risk. If they don't work, his feelings will be hurt and his bank account will be broken. Isn't it a risk to walk out of the door everyday? A person trotting down the street could easily get killed in a drive-by or a robbery; an airplane can crash on a person's house, killing the occupants, so life is a risk. He pulls out twenty-one straight $100 bills as the cashier rings up the sale. It mysteriously sticks to his hand as he tries to give it to her. When she pulls it from his grasp, he gets a sinking feeling, like his heart is being flushed down the toilet.

Mel slept until 1:30. He watched the late night movies until they watched him. There is no food in the refrigerator and no cash in his pockets. With $2100 invested in an engagement ring, there is no guarantee the marriage would ever take place. On any given day, the odds could shift either way, and at the present, they're not in Mel's favor. Last night Memory took her evil alter ego to a whole new level. She was just the opposite of the Memory he sat and talked with at her house on that gloomy Saturday eight days ago. Amnesia reared her ugly head. She came over bitching about everything under the sun. From the smell of the puppies and the unfinished kitchen (which was a rerun of what she fusses about whenever the moon is full or when she breaks a nail or whatever sets her off), to the few seconds it took to answer the door and the shorts he was wearing, there was nothing visible or imagined that she didn't complain about.

Last week he ran the first ad for the puppies for $50, and so far, it has yielded two calls and no sales. The other twenty ads probably have something to do with it. Now he's broke with 13 dogs to feed. He *started second and third guessing his decision to breed. With no job to go to, he has no reason to get up or go out, but he is still somewhat optimistic. Luke 12 and 29 through 30 is in his daily reading, because he was worried about where his next meal was going to come from. It is Thursday—Payday, if things are going his way. When things aren't going his way with Unemployment, it could be another week if they found one "i" undotted or a "t" uncrossed. The only thing he looks forward to today is the mailman.*

When he gets up, his eyes are still foggy, his feet are heavy and he can barely focus as he makes his way down the stairs, carefully holding on to the banister. He is definitely bed drunk. He reaches into the mailbox and pulls in a big clump of mail rolled up in a rubber band. The April edition of Ebony, with Mariah Carey on the cover; an invoice from MasterCard; a bill from his furniture company; a gas bill that's as heavy as a sewer cap; a credit card solicitation; a missing child flyer (did it come or what?); a phone bill; another phone bill; a sales flyer and an envelope—hopefully a check—from the Department of Employment Security. He drops the rest of the stack and opens it.

His heart sinks. There's nothing like the disappointing feeling of expecting some much needed money, only to get a note in it's place. He was denied because something was missing and he has to come into the office and talk with one of the counselors. Now he knows how people go postal. He throws the letter down and grimaces as he holds in a few curse words. "DAMN! JUST GIVE ME THE MONEY AND STOP BITCHING OVER EVERYTHING!" he snaps as he stomps up the stairs and into his bedroom. He slams his back on the bed and fumes as he looks up at the ceiling that's turning bloody red from his indignation. The room's temperature is even and comfortable, but he starts emitting heat and raises it about fifty degrees. Furious energy races through his body, making him very alert as he lays sprawled out and motionless. His heart rapidly pounds on his chest as his lungs rush air out and sucks it in with authority. He has no reason to get up or move for the rest of the day...except the sudden ringing of the telephone, which elicits a reflex to pick it up. "Hello," he snaps.

"Melvin?" the professional, nasally voice asks.

It doesn't register quickly, but when he realizes that it's one of the bill collectors from the furniture financiers posing as someone close and personal, it evokes the reaction to slam the phone down, almost breaking it. "Dumb ass. My friends call me Mel," he huffs.

The phone immediately rings again and a surge of nervous fuel is added to the rage. The answering machine picks up and Jon Baxter starts his attitude-tainted spiel: "That wasn't nice or smart Mister Adams. I'll tell you what: If I don't get a call back in five days, I'm going to turn this account over to a collection agency and..."

Mel snatches up the phone and yells, *"YOU AND THAT FURNITURE CAN GO TO HELL! NOW STOP CALLING HERE! STOP CALLING HERE OR I'LL COME DOWN THERE AND WHOOP YOUR SEVEN DOLLAR AN HOUR PUNK ASS!"* and slams it back down as he jumps up out of the bed. Mel realizes that wasn't really wise, but he doesn't care...and it isn't a threat: it's a promise, at the moment. It's bad enough being broke, but hunger compounds the anguish. He feels trapped like an animal; like a wolf with his leg caught in a steel trap with teeth—snapping at any and every body that gets close, even if they mean well. In the case of Jon, he's the poacher—antagonizing him before he puts the bullet through the heart, so he can mount his head on his wall and add to his trophy display. For that, Mel is ready and willing to gnaw his leg off just to get a chance to rip out Jon's jugular. All he needs is a chance to inflict some pain before he goes down. Burning the furniture, the house and the car is one of the options. By no means did he want to just give it up—knowing that after all the money he put into it, all the heart and emotions he bled, someone is going to get it at a non-sentimental bargain.

His temples are pulsing when the phone rings again. He turns the volume down on the answering machine and storms out into the hallway and into his office, where all the bills are piled up on his desk. Before he knows what he's doing, he savagely brushes the mound of letters off his desk, takes a seat and lays his head down—totally exasperated from the struggle. "Why don't you just let me die right now," he murmurs. "Why do you let me linger in this hellified life? I'm tired...just tired of the up and down situation—mostly down. How can I be strong on an empty stomach? I tried to be faithful..." he stops himself from insulting Him and lays hushed, trying to calm down. The air he's breathing is hot, burning the hairs in his nostrils and the insulation in his chest. He throws himself back into the chair and stretches out into a bad sitting posture as he fixes his eyes on the pile of paper on the floor, wishing his line of vision was a laser beam, like Superman's. The stare is so hard it almost seems like the paper is animated; like it's full of life. That's when he notices that the Good News Bible his brother got him for his birthday last year (as if he didn't have enough Bibles, being a PK and all) is peering through the paper at him. Out of respect for the Word (even the physical Bible should be revered), he picks it up by the page that it is open to (page 310: James 1). Of course—as is the case when he reads an already open Bible—there's a scripture that draws his eyes. Unless the verses are going to miraculously turn into money, he can't imagine what God has to say to him that will be more moving than a check.

The subject heading reads, ***"Poverty and Riches"*** in bold italics. It's definitely for him. He glances upward and then reads the whole chapter. He places it on the desk—still opened to the scripture—and ponders the speed of darkness...that is, how fast darkness leaves the room when a light is turned on. He reflects on how a storm cloud can pour out an ocean in one area—as furious as a hungry man on unemployment, with tree snapping winds—yet ten yards away it can be as calm as paradise, with squirrels playing, the sun beaming, and a rainbow glowing with the promise of a pot of gold. It's like stepping out of one room into another; coming in from the outside. No doubt, he's still in a financial grave, so he's semi-funkatose. However, it's amazing how he can go from rage to serenity in two minutes. He studies the ninth verse—as if it's a new, scientific concept—and he addresses God: "I promise I'll be glad when You lift me up."

A bold indifference overcomes him, so he grabs an envelope sent by his mortgage company from the pile. He let's out a sharp, uncontrollable giggle and nearly goes into shock when he pulls the contents out. Suddenly, he has energy to burn, the sun is shinning bright, the city is warm and he hears angels singing. Then his heart starts singing, "Thank You Lord, For All You've Done For Me" with them. Is it a dream? He places the envelope and the documents that were in it on the desk, casually steps over the pile of paper and heads downstairs to collect the mail that came today. For the first time in a long time, he opens the vertical blinds, so the outside can get a good look at the glorious inside. After a long stretch, he shakes his head and goes back into his office. With great care, he takes a seat—as if there was some type of hazard to avoid. He verifies the check: *$278.14.* Then he verifies the scripture: ***The Christian who is poor must be glad when God lifts him up.***

"Thank You! Thank You!" he yells over and over as he reads over the accompanying statement. Apparently he had too much in escrow (he never imagined) and they sent the refund check about eight weeks ago. It is due to expire in another three weeks. Talk about manna from heaven. It isn't enough to cover his delinquent mortgage, pay the past due car note, or cover the balance of the furniture. The creditors are still around. The debt is still thick. He doesn't even have a job yet, and unemployment is barely paying for his food, electricity and phone. Despite it all, he knows that everything is going to be okay. How many people get revelations like this? Still, how many people actually recognize them as the voice of God? He recognizes. The check and the timing represent God's perfect will. It means that God is providing him with his every need. For the month, he is going to have food in the refrigerator. He feels like he could walk across Lake Michigan if Jesus was on the other side.

Now Mel doesn't have any qualms about opening the mail that came—even the gas bill that's probably close to two thousand. Only $1585.39. Things are still going good. He piles all of the envelopes on the edge of the desk and opens the business-size hand-addressed envelope from 6963 South Euclid (good lake front property not too far from the country club). The letter was typed and apparently reproduced for mass mailing. It's dated March 10, 1994, and it reads:

> **It is with a heavy heart and a troubled spirit that I prayerfully write this open letter to the Holy Family of Love of God. A series of appalling and troublesome events have taken place within our Tabernacle of Worship, which can no longer go unrecognized, unaddressed, nor unresolved. This is not a letter of solicitation for support for Pastor Adams or Deacon Bradford.**

He shakes his head and blurts, "Figures," as he recalls some of the many engagements with Deacon Donald Bradford and family. *The clan has been on their power trip since Lucifer's mutiny in heaven. Instead of focusing on building relationships and promoting spiritual growth within the church, the whole family has focused on acquiring titles and holding positions at Love of God as if they're buying shares in a business. They mimic a royal family. Their pursuit of an earthly throne (specifically at Love of God) is axiomatic. For the Adams—which are few in number at LOG—Bradford is synonymous with adversary.*

What can Mel say about Donald? He has a bag of descriptive adjectives to chose from, but his experience sums up his feelings. On a church trip, Donald pushed him into the deep end of the hotel swimming pool—even though he knew Mel couldn't swim. He laughed as Mel fought the pull of the water and sunk like a rock. Mel hadn't finished coughing up the chlorine doctored water from his lungs after another patron pulled him out, before Donald got busy relaying his account of the prank to their peers. Donald and his sister—Rachel—are two of the most arrogant beings in creation. It's almost as if they feel like they are self-existent for the purpose of being admired. Mel was caught in between their ages (He's two years older and she's two years younger), so at different points, he was at odds with both of them.

They really have a strong pull of the genes. Donald was the main irritation. Just like a mosquito bite, he just kept on aggravating him. Outside of the pool incident, he didn't do anything treacherous, although if all the trips, flicks of the ear, slaps on the head, annoying pranks and jesting were added up, they would amount to a capital offense. Immaturity aside, Donald has a good religious base. He was put on the Deacon Board (at the prodding of Trustee Bradford) at the same time Mel was voted in as a Trustee. His position didn't change his attitude, though. Mel couldn't fathom how such an imbecile could be as gifted as Donald. Not only was he a good singer, but he could send up some powerful, eloquent, scripture-laced, dead-raising prayers. Perhaps it wasn't from the heart. If that was the case, he had everybody fooled.

He continues.

> **However, it is a letter prayerfully written to inform the Church Body, as a Holy Family, of the many serious concerns, issues, and problems that have arisen in this, our church, which threatens the spiritual growth of every member of Love of God, as which must be aired, addressed and resolved in an open, fair, and unbiased emergency church forum.**
>
> **This is a call to every blood bought born again Christian and member of Love of God Missionary Baptist Church to call our Pastor and Church Officials to meet with the Church Body in efforts to avert a split and to stop the**

spread of character assassination, confusion, disrespect, evil, and hatred that has taken hold of our church. As believers, Christians, and Heirs to our Father's throne we are fighting a very unpleasant, difficult, and painful fight, yet fight we must, in spite of those who would prefer that the wrongs perpetrated against our brothers and sisters, within this Church, not be brought to light. A hateful wrong has been perpetrated against Deacon Bradford, and there is sufficient cause to warrant a Church-wide review of Deacon Bradford's dismissal from the deacon board.

On Wednesday, February 9, 1994, Pastor Melvin Adams had a heated exchange with Trustee Bradford in regards to the building of the church library. The following Sunday, he met with Deacon Bradford privately in his study, and then dismissed him from the deacon board.

Several members of the church body have unanimously, openly, and fervently protested and opposed this action because of the work in and around the church that Deacon Bradford has performed. His worth to the body of Love of God is invaluable. To dismiss him from the deacon board is tantamount to removing a leg from the body, which will restrict the spiritual mobility and growth of Love of God since that leaves just three ordained deacons. The reasons for Deacon Bradford's dismissal were suspect, vague, invalid, unsubstantiated, and seemingly rooted in bias and vindication, not act.

Deacon Bradford's dismissal follows a series of strategic, rather than spiritual, decisions by Pastor Adams that have reeked of a one-sided vendetta, including the denial of a permanent seat in the pulpit for and the silencing of Minister Adrian Irving, the passing over Reverend Bradford as assistant pastor in favor of Reverend Jones, among many other instances. Brothers and sisters in Christ, this cannot go on. I beseech Pastor Adams and the official board, to address these crippling decisions to the whole church in the name of unity.

There needs to be an open church meeting and hearing addressing present as well as past injustices that

have taken place at the hands of the Pastor and the official board. In lieu of the meeting, the church constitution needs to be reviewed and amended to prevent future injustices and abuse of authority. In love.

It's signed by Sister Margaret Bradford: Reverend Bradford's wife and the mother of Deacon Bradford. "Not soliciting support" it read. Mel considers calling his father, but decides that the miracle and the letter warrant a personal visit.

As expected, everyone is gone except dad, so Mel lets himself in. His father is in his study talking to Minister John Robinson (the non-ordained preacher) and apparently they both got a letter, because based on what he read, they're discussing it. Mel surprises them when he enters. "Hey son," his father greets.

"How you doing. What's going on, Jay?" he says as he extends his hand—only to have John shift it in all types of clasps, clenches and locks with the craftiness of a freestyle wrestler, in mock hipology. John likes to be called by his nickname and prefers informally open discussions about everything (especially sports), rather than rigidly religious talk, justifying that it's nothing wrong with it, but one's life style sends a louder message than scripture quoting. He can be a joker sometimes, but when it comes to bringing the word, he's strictly spiritual.

"Melvin, my good friend, when are you going to give me a chance to school you on the fundamentals of ball?"

Mel shakes his head and promises, "Soon, my buddy...just don't take it too personal when I teach *you* a few lessons." John is a funny guy. He's about 10 years older than Mel, four inches shorter and 25 pounds lighter (which makes him an old 35 or so, a towering 5'8" and a loose 130), and he's always bragging about his basketball skills. He has a nice set shot and head moves, but his game stops there. Mel is no superstar by any means, but he jumps higher, runs faster, and shoots better than his anointed friend.

"Teach me? Please. Imagine: after I beat you, that means that I would have conquered two-thirds of the family...Mrs. Adams doesn't count. Ain't that right, Pastor?"

"Say it ain't so, dad. Tell me you didn't let *Jay* beat you. Bust out with the sackcloth, the whole family has been disgraced. Let me go put a paper bag over my head. Now I'm going to have to find another father."

"It was by the grace of God that he hit that last free-throw after I went back down to 13 twice—*twice*. I'm a 90 percent free throw shooter. Explain how I could miss twice in the clutch," his father interjects.

They all laugh. Mel loves this side of the pastor, his father. The side that relaxes. The buddy side. Everybody has their own perception of what he's like. Demigod—with scriptures in his blood and scriptures out of his mouth—is a popular myth. That's how he's viewed, until people get to know him. He has a soul. He makes mistakes. Other things intrigue him. He likes to watch the games on Sunday, like most brothers. The difference is, he has mastered perspective. God first; everything else second, including self.

"Well Melvin, hopefully I'll see you in church soon, and then on the court," Jay hints. "And hopefully I'll see you back in church after I see you on the court."

"We'll see."

"I'm out. Later Pastor."

He nods as Jay exits through the basement door. Mel takes a seat and gets lost in the fish tank, dodging the subject. "What's the good word?"

"I got two for you: Miracle and letter."

"You know I like miracles. Talk to me."

Mel explains what happened and then places the letter on his desk. "Then this came. I guess *you* can talk about this," he states.

True to form, he looks at the letter and takes a deep breath. "Well, without going into details, I'll give you an account of myself, and best believe that God will affirm. And I have the two witnesses as an illustration."

Mel shifts in his seat. When his father addresses a serious matter, he's brief and he always references the scriptures. His accounts are not direct, but with an honest, mental effort, the message can be deciphered. He makes you think.

"You're familiar with the account of how Moses disobeyed God by striking the rock twice without speaking to it, and how he wasn't able to enter the Promised Land because he took the credit for bringing the water out of it. Well, there was a time when I took credit for the growth of the church; that I assumed all the glory for which God was due. He taught me a lesson though—like he does for all of His children—but it wasn't as harsh as it should have been. Instead of sitting me down, he let me work like a slave dog—you know, since I wanted to take credit for everything. He allowed me to work and work just to keep things up, but it always seemed like when one problem or situation was worked out, two different, more complex one's would come up. You should have seen me. This was before we moved to the new building. It was by God's grace and mercy that I made it. He could have let some other pastor bring the congregation into the Promised Land. I was like the bear making all of the tracks and getting nowhere. Better yet, I was like the Israelites marching in the desert for forty years when it should have taken forty days. I had my hand in the situation, so God withdrew His. I wanted to do all of the preaching, even when I knew the Lord gave a message to the other ministers. I wanted to do all of the counseling and supervise the Sunday school.

"There's a scripture in 1st Kings in which Elijah wished to die when he got discouraged after Jezebel threatened his life. Moses also had a death wish when the children of Israel kept complaining. That was me. I got so tired in working with a hardheaded congregation, that I prayed for death. I said *'Lord, it's too much. Take my life away. I might as well be dead.'* But there was still a work to be done. It was when I cried out—just like you did today before you got the manna money—that God stepped in and took over. I bet I wasn't burned out any more. Don't get me wrong, there are trying times and it is work, but the burden isn't on my shoulders," he pauses to close up as he leans back in his chair. "I say all of that to say this: In the past, I've been guilty of self-reliance and pride in over-drive. Since then, I've repented, yet I've been falsely accused of many of the same things since. If there's one thing that I'm not guilty of, it's trying to monopolize. I'm no power ranger."

Mel nods, looking intently at him without commenting. The big grandfather clock tick-tocks away as his father returns the stare.

"I will tell you that those who are putting their mouths on me are guilty of what they're accusing me of. You're aware that some people are interested in authority. Well, again, I'll go to the scriptures and leave it alone. When Miriam spoke out against Moses, she turned colors and the 400 false prophets of Baal were put to death when it was proven that they were frauds. I'm not cursing anyone. As a matter of fact, I pray that they will get it together and get on accord with the Lord—but when you go speaking against God's anointed and speaking on your own accord, stuff happens," he says with a slight smirk. "When you're wrong, you will be corrected; secrets will be revealed; what's done in the darkness shall be brought to light. The Lord sees in the dark just as easy as we see in the shade. What was done was very bold and defiant to the Lord in the name of fooling mankind. The letter was even bolder. If they're able to sell their argument to the whole congregation, it still doesn't make them right. Remember, Satan convinced a third of the angels to rebel, so it wouldn't surprise me to see some of the carnal, weak Christians take the wrong side. However, the victory is already won."

Mel matches his smirk with a grin. "Well, I just wanted to share that testimony and hear your side of the letter," he says as he casually brings up another point. "By the way, I'm going to propose to Memory."

"Really? So you're going to give me a daughter-in-law. I guess pretty soon you're going to make me a grandfather," he says with jubilation that turns into reservation. "She's not pregnant now, is she?"

"No. I'm trying to do things the right way, that's why I decided to abstain and get closer to Christ."

"Well, I really can't express how happy that makes me. The mess at the church pales in comparison. Whatever you do, don't let it keep you away."

"If anything, it'll draw me nearer, seeing that my ol' man is involved in a family feud. What would tribal warfare be without the oldest son."

His father smiles. "Your mother is going to be thrilled about the news."

"About me getting married or coming back to church?"

"Both, but especially about you getting married. She always wanted a daughter."

"Is that why she treats me like a step child?"

He doesn't even respond or look at him.

"Why is it that David doesn't catch the wrath of not being a girl like I do? Is he a transvestite or something?"

His father looks up and flashes him the "You know better" expression.

"I just don't understand her."

"You need to talk to her."

"I've been trying all of my life."

"Have you tried since you've been an adult?"

"I try all the time. Every time I attempt it, I get verbally crucified for any and everything...and I usually forget what I wanted to talk about. I don't even know if I'm going to tell her. She'll probably find some fault in me taking that step."

"Now give her a break."

"Give her a break? What I'll do is let you tell her. You're better prepared to handle the onslaught of criticism than I am."

"If that's what you wish, I'll tell her, but I think she would rather hear it from you."

"Yeah, she would rather ball me out. I guess I'll let Memory tell her."

He doesn't say anything. When he holds his peace like that he has an answer, but it's too emotional and passionate, although it may be true. He tries to speak in love, not passion. A lot of times, the Spirit will speak to that person for him, and this instance is no exception.

"I'll be back over later. Then I'll give her the news," he resolves. "Later."

His father just nods and smiles at him.

When Mel gets to the front door, David is creeping in, stained with guilt. "Aren't you a little early?"

David shakes his head in disgust.

"What happened this time?"

"A fight, man," he says. "Got three days off."

"David, David, David," Mel says, shaking his head. "Are you actually going to graduate on time?"

"I should," he guesses.

"You should?" Mel questions in disbelief. "There shouldn't even be a question about that. I don't know what we're going to do with you, but I'll let Dad handle it. He's in the basement."

David heads to his room with his head down as his denims sag like a soggy diaper.

Sometimes Mel wonders where David came from. He's not quite a man after God's own heart. In fact, he's very defiant and unrepentant, like the poster boy for the Hip-Hopping Generation X. He has put God to the test like no other. Mel caught him in dad's study getting a blow job when his parents left town on vacation a couple of years ago. This happened a day after a big party he threw. After his parents called Mel and told him to check on the house to see why the phone wasn't being answered, he was shocked at how many people were crammed inside. Mel had to dig through several bodies before he found David in the study having an orgy. Mel put everyone out and preached the gospel of respect for God and sacred things. David seemed sorrowful when Mel left. The very next day he showed how sorry he was by fornicating with just one person as opposed to three.

Rebellious and proud. It can't be justified by the company he keeps, because he's charismatic and sets the trend for nonconformity. He would be considered a pretty boy: Light skin (the source is a genetic mystery), soft hair, and exotic eyes, like an Asian. Last year, he staged a walkout in his Chemistry class, because the teacher was from Jamaica and spoke with a heavy accent that was hard to understand. Surprisingly, the whole class followed him. Most of them wouldn't do anything like that on their own, and more than likely a lot of them got the beating of their lives when their parents found out why they were suspended. David got off unscathed. He may not even tell his parents that he's suspended. For the most part, he does what he wants, which baffles Mel. Curfew is a big joke for him. Mel is grown, yet he's usually in before David. Once, Mel was out at Walgreen's at two in the morning to get some NyQuil for a cold that wouldn't quit. When he got to the line, there was David, waiting for some idiot to pay for some beer for him. He couldn't believe it. Still can't. And the way he talks back to his mother is amazing. It's not so much that he is vulgar—just disrespectful. It seems like he always gets the last word in. When Mel was coming up, he didn't have a word when it came to being lectured. He resents his parent's lax attitude towards David, especially since he couldn't—rightly so—get away with the things that David does. David actually shows more reverence to Mel than he does to his parents.

Mel calls his mother instead of going back over, and when David answers, he suggests, "You ought to give me one of those puppies."

Mel is surprised that David still has the privilege to answer the phone and how relaxed he sounds in doing it, but he doesn't even mention the suspension, since his parents already know. He talked to his father when he got home and they were in the middle of a discussion about what happened. "I thought about keeping one from the litter in the family. Of course you would have to take that up with your folks."

"So you would give me one if they say yes?"

"I would think about it."

"Good, 'cause my boy got this big Pit that I want to see get whooped."

"So you want to train it to fight?"

"It's a lot of money in it."

"In that case, I wouldn't even sell you a dog."

"Man...why you gonna be like that?"

"Put Momma on the phone," Mel orders.

"Hello," she says.

"How are you?"

"I'm doing fine."

"How do you feel about having a daughter in-law?"

"I feel that there are some women that are not ready to be daughters-in-law," she claims. "Why?"

"Well, someone near and dear to you is going to propose pretty soon."

"Does this near and dear someone realize that they're not ready for marriage?"

Mel bites his tongue and pauses as the heat seeps out through his pores. He wants to hang up. Why is she so damn difficult? "Did I get any mail over there?" he shifts.

"Of course you didn't. You've been gone for six years. Everybody knows not to send anything to you at this address."

"Okay then. I'll talk to you later."

"Bye," she says and hangs up.

Chapter 8

"Lord, I thank you for this moment that you've blessed me with. I thank you for blessing me not according to what I've done and what I deserve, but according to Your unconditional love and everlasting grace and mercy. Right now, I ask that you order my steps in your word. Touch my heart so that I won't act, think or speak against Your will. If there's a situation that I'm ignorant of, I ask that you open my eyes. I ask that your will—not my will—be done. Strengthen my relationship with You and remove anything that's a hindrance, because all I want to do is please you. In the name of Jesus, I bind up all unrighteousness in my life and I claim Your Holy Spirit as my Guide and Comforter. Heavenly Father, I ask that You bless my proposal and anoint the marriage, unite us spiritually my Lord, in the name of Jesus. Your Word says that it is not good for man to be alone. From the beginning, You ordained marriage as a divine institution that's a model of Your relationship with me. It is written that whoso findeth a wife findeth a good thing, and obtaineth favor of the Lord. Lord, I want to obtain favor of You. If it be your will my Lord...Your will, not my will. In the name of Jesus, I pray. Amen."

Mel opens his eyes and continues to kneel for a few moments to get his equilibrium. Last night, he tossed and turned as he rehearsed the proposal in his head. Even though he barely closed his eyes last night and seems to be lacking the energy to go on with the day, once he rises from his kneeling position, steps out of his shorts and jumps in the shower, he gets galvanized with the anticipation of a life-changing, busy day.

Yesterday evening, he sold the first puppy, and he's still riding the high. About five roughnecks from Harvey came to look at them. Mel was a bit apprehensive about letting the Hip Hoppish group in his home—even though he had his big dog watching his back. It was all business though, and to his surprise—after they tried to bargain down to $250 from $350 (to no avail)—they didn't take the biggest one from the litter. He was a little sad to see him (it was a male) go from his siblings and parents, but the grief was oh so brief. He filled out the certificate and tallied his record with the registration number and the new owner's information. When the money changed hands, he was ready to get rid of them all.

His day promises to be quick, since waiting for Memory to get home is the main task on the agenda. All he has to do is pick up the cake and tranquilize Earl—so he won't do or say anything crazy to Memory—since he's filling in for Mel's broken tripod. He got two calls before he left the house. The first guy (who sounded white) said that he'd think about it after Mel went through the sales pitch. The second man promised to stop by after he got off work around three.

The day passes without incident. He picked up the cake from The Abundance Bakery on 47th Street around noon. While he waited, he ordered a couple of cupcakes—which is all that he's running on. He jetted downtown, picked up a catalogue and admission application from Columbia, and swung over to Chicago State for their information. On his way home, he mailed some resumés at the post office on 75th Street. When he got home, the phone was ringing and he was happy to hear the gentleman announce that he was on his way. When he arrives, Mel eagerly shows him all of the papers, the ribbons and the parents, and allows him to play with the puppies briefly. Mel isn't surprised when he chooses the biggest one—which Mel sells for $50 more than the first. "I figured you would probably want this big Goliath," Mel says as he fills in the papers.

"You know what, I may just name him that," the guy announces.

"It sure is fitting. He's almost twice the size of the rest of them."

"The bigger the better. I need something intimidating for my house."

"Well, he has potential to outgrow the father, who weighs 130," he predicts as he escorts him to the door. "Listen, tell me how things are going with this big guy."

"Okay, I'll stay in touch, buddy," he says as he totes the dog to his car. Mel is in good spirits, but is a little low on energy, so he decides to take a nap. He snoozes peacefully and dreams about the puppies and the proposal scenario. When he wakes up, it's time to get Earl and he has an abundance of happiness and energy. They are taking Earl's '87 Mustang 5.0 that he bought last week, so that Memory won't recognize Mel's car. Earl starts the minute they get in. "Why do you want to video tape this?" Earl questions.

"Because I want to be able to look at this cherished memory—no pun intended."

"What's to cherish, Cuz? You're losing your freedom. What...are you going to pop corn, call friends and family over and watch it? What if she says no?"

"Then I'll mail it in to America's Funniest Home Videos."

Earl shakes his head as he cruises down 79th Street to the sounds of an old EPMD album. "Is there any way I can talk you out of it?"

"Nope."

"Just checking."

"You really need to consider getting a CD installed in here. The sound quality is much better."

"Oh shut up."

Mel advises him not to steal or break anything when they pull in front of her house. The curtains are drawn and no light from the outside comes through, making it pitch black. Mel dims the Halogen lamp and places the cake in the kitchen. Earl flops down on the couch—as if it's his home—and turns on the television. "Keep your ears peeled," Mel yells from the kitchen.

"What time is she due in?"

"Around now, give or take thirty minutes," Mel confirms.

"Do you think she would miss any of these pictures on the wall?"

"She would notice if there was a finger print on them." Earl cuts the TV off and gives himself a tour of her townhouse as Mel fiddles around twiddling his thumbs.

An hour passes and finally he hears her pull into the driveway. "This is it," Mel announces with excitement. "Get behind the door and roll the camera," he says as he cuts the lamp off and grabs the cake from the kitchen.

Mel is grinning from ear to ear as he hears her fumbling with her keys. The door clicks and she staggers in with the grace of a drunkard just after happy hour. "Surprise," he shouts as he clicks on the light. She turns to him with a look of an animal stupefied by the headlight glare of an oncoming truck on the highway. Surprise indeed. There are two sets of eyes caught on tape: Memory's alarmed eyes, and the unsuspecting eyes of the infamous, dark-skin man with the ponytail, whose lips are fused to hers. "What the..." Earl starts as he continues to roll the camera.

There is a long moment of screaming muteness as Memory and Ponytail slowly part. Mel is still grinning, but lateral stress marks form on his brow and his concentrative eyes distort his countenance. Ponytail raises his eyebrows and creases his lips into a little smirk as he turns his head to the side and steps a few feet away from her—as if he was disassociating himself with her. She breaks her stillness, putting her purse down on the couch, greeting, "How are you Melvin," as she looks away, like she's searching for her keys or something.

The chorus line from "Jane" is ringing in Mel's head as his tongue is struck with paralysis. *"Like Anita Baker; Like Anita Baker"* chimes in his mind's ear as he flashes back to that day in Margaret's office when they first met; up a month when Memory said that he was her soul mate. When he gets that question, it's appropriate to answer "Fine" even when things are bad. Right now, he knows what it's like to be shot in the heart and have his blood spray out everywhere. This is so bad, that "fine" would be an inappropriate crutch word. He just stands petrified with a fading smirk as he can feel his heart thumping against his chest and the air in his lungs seeping out. Earl answers for him: "What kind of question is that?"

"Mel, this is Roger; Roger...this is Mel," she says, visibly flustered and oblivious to Earl's instigation as she throws her hands up to her sides. Roger speaks to Mel, but doesn't get recognized. His arms are as thick as tree trunks and his chest sticks out like a soldier's. He reminds Mel of a pretty Wesley Snipes on steroids, representing everything that Memory wanted Melvin to be: Buffed, flashy (Roger has a gold hoop in his nose and a diamond stud in his ear, a Rolex on his wrist, and a thick herringbone around his neck), and eccentric (look at that ponytail). Mel is a modest 160 while toting groceries and pocketing bricks; he hates jewelry (Memory insisted on him getting his ear pierced; he told her to take him or leave him without any extra holes in his body); and she wanted Mel to have a crazy hairstyle (dreads are the last thing she suggested). Well, she went out and found her prototypic Melvin. Would Mel be able to match blows with him? Probably not, but it would be in Ponytail's best interest to keep his words to himself, otherwise he and his nice, gray, silk suit may get messed up.

"Ain't this a bitch..." Earl starts as Mel holds up his hand to slow him down.

Mel sets the cake on her coffee table and wishes her "Happy birthday," as he plucks the ring out of the center. "This is Rogers and Hollands," he proclaims, holding the box out.

Memory's mouth gapes open. "Can you excuse us, Roger?" she asks.

He gives her a smug expression and nods as she leads Mel into the kitchen, closing the door behind him.

Mel makes up in his mind that although he wants to break down and cry, asking for an explanation that is beside the point—even begging her to apologize and get right—he isn't going to let her blow her nose on his pride. This will *never* happen again. He isn't going to show any signs of pain. None whatsoever. He wants his disposition to be the slap in her face that he wants to physically deliver, just like a pimp. Memory takes a seat at the table and folds her hands. Mel sticks his hands in his pockets and slowly paces without looking at her. "I don't know what to say," she concedes.

He shakes his head as he faces the floor. "You don't have to say anything. A video tape is worth a thousand words," he murmurs through clenched teeth. The grin is long gone.

She clicks her tongue and whines, "I got weak. My body needed to be satisfied—especially today. It was hard for me to live with your decision of abstinence. It's hard for me to adjust to celibacy."

He cuts through her with his glare. "It was hard for you to adjust to celibacy? Don't you mean it's hard for you to adjust to monogamy? What's your excuse for Christmas Eve?" he interrogates, straining to keep a confidential tone. She doesn't even try to defend herself as she rests her chin in her palms. "That's right, I found out that you were with Mister Ponytail on Christmas Eve, after you gassed me up with that *'don't ever leave me'* crap. You're wrong: You didn't get weak, you *are* weak."

"We weren't working out, Mel," she justifies with a huff.

"Wah-weren't working?" he questions with a deceptive guffaw as he stops at the other end of the table and rests his hands on the chair. She looks up at him with regretful, sagging eyes. Is it Emmy time? He quickly shifts back to the somber ambiance as he lectures her with staggered breath, poking his finger at her intensely: "Last month, you said that you were happy with who I was...talking about soul mates and I'm the only one you could depend on. I must be suffering from a

Memory loss. Or maybe just a bad Memory. I know I do have a case of Amnesia: No Memory whatsoever. I hope you're happy," he says as he strolls past her and through the door.

Earl is eyeing a seemingly unknowing, magazine flipping Ponytail through the camera lens in an annoying way. "Let's go," Mel commands as he sticks his finger in the cake, licks the frosting off and tells Ponytail—or Roger—to "Enjoy."

The air seems colder than it is and sends a chill up his body. He can feel the change of atmosphere sapping his strength. Everything about his being seems to be going crazy—like his organs have minds of their own. His knees feel like rubber; his lungs are quivering; his stomach is doing cartwheels; his whole body is quaking. It feels like his entrails were yanked out of his ass. He's faint, so he rushes to the car so he can be supported. He notices a dazzling black Lexus in front of them with "RAHJ" on the vanity plate. He blinks and turns his head away as the tears form in his eyes.

"Don't sweat her, man," Earl says as he pats him on the shoulder and unlocks the door.

Mel just nods, collapsing in the seat as his throat tightens up. He examines the ring and it starts to look real small and cheap to him. As Earl starts the ignition, "Who's Booty" comes blasting through the speakers. Damn. Appropriate backdrop. Earl turns it off, because he doesn't feel that Mel wants to hear that. The silence is loud and focused on the moment, so Mel turns it back on. Women-bashing rap music sounds good to him right now and serves as a good transition from the moment. It makes him wrathful instead of sorrowful. He likes it that way. Don't get sad; get mad. He tries to relax his taut face, taking a deep breath and blowing it out of his nostrils.

"If you want to get even, I'll gladly help you hook her up," Earl says, because that's what he figures Mel wants to hear.

"I'm all right. A little embarrassed—shoot, it hurts like hell—but this will pass. It's probably best that we part. I would've rather it been a mutual split, but what the heck," he says and pauses for a few seconds as he peers out of the window. "I'm tempted to go back there and kill them both, but she's not worth the jail time."

"I hear you, Cuz."

"Did you see that long ponytail? Looked like the back of a horse's ass. I started to grab it and sling him out of the window when he spoke to me. Oh well. I don't have a beef with him, whoever he is. She probably deserves him."

"I agree. It's scary how we think alike sometimes...like mental twins. I was waiting for you to make a move—haul off and slap her. I had your back. That pretty, buffed, ponytail wearing punk would've gotten a haircut and concussion for the weekend, if he would've jumped. You would've probably lost your camera in addition to your unfaithful ulcer. I hate pretty boys. He called his-self nodding at me. I just looked at him like he was crazy, wishing he would say something. And between you and me, I think that was a weave."

They cover the short distance from Memory's to Mel's house at a snails pace. Mel looks out of the passenger-side window, but only has hindsight. He wouldn't even notice a towering inferno if it were in front of him. Already, Mel has replayed the whole dramatic scene no less than a hundred times. It gets worse with each rerun. It's like a slow, torturous death; like someone is tearing him apart small piece-by-piece. He starts regretting his reactions. There should have been a fight. There should have been bloodshed. He was too cool and composed about it.

"What a waste. I should've put my money to use and plastered the cake on her face. If I wasn't afraid she would've swallowed the ring, she would've been wearing it. I swear she would," he huffs with a half smirk, still gazing out of the window. He chuckles a little and shakes his head. "You were right again. I need to start listening to your words of wisdom."

"I wasn't right—she was wrong."

It's the little things that people take for granted, yet matter the most, like the use of their limbs, peripheral vision, and breath. Mel is having trouble with them all. Although he was as stiff as a corpse, he managed to make it through his front door without assistance. Now he can let go and grieve in privacy. He sets the camera on his sofa and lets out an implausible giggle. He is drained, but jittery. The ordeal knocked the spiritual wind out of him, but he can't keep still. Without thinking, he proceeds to the basement and feeds the parents, filling Homey's bowl first. Apparently, a day without eating made Dana impatient, because she sticks her head in the bowl, even though Homey already has his in it. Homey growls raucously. In his language, he must have told her "You made a big mistake," because without giving her a chance to step back, he chomps into Dana's face. She yelps and snaps back as they both jostle like grizzly bears before she submits, tucks her tail stub and prances off. "Serves her right. I would have bit the bitch too, Homey," Mel hears himself utter. He fills her bowl and notices a gash on the top of her head. "It should've been..." He stops himself from wishing that on Memory, and he tends to the puppies. They're in a playfully social mood as usual, but he gets in and out and leaves them to their food.

He fixes a ham sandwich when he gets back upstairs, takes one bite and tosses the rest in the garbage. He hasn't had anything all day—except the cupcakes—so he's hungry, but he feels like he had eaten the whole pig and wants to vomit. He knows what it's like to jump into deep waters without a life jacket. The grip of consternation overcomes him as he sinks into the couch. The lights are off and the blinds are pulled shut. It's been four years since he's been single. At the time, he didn't particularly mind too much. He was young and dumb and not even close to settling down. There were many dates to go on; many women to get to know. He was figuring out what made them tick. Still is. Is he ready for the deep, turbulent waters of dating? Does he want to go through the drama? The suddenness of the breakup makes him feel so detached; so alone.

He sucks in the dry, room air, trying to relieve the pressure on his chest. Yokozuna might as well be standing on it. A car periodically zooms by his house, breaking the monotonous silence. Part of him wants it to be Memory driving up in her Beamer. His disposition alternates between a vengeful rage to a helpless self-pity. Perhaps a character change is long over due. The moment he saw her kissing Roger, his heart turned into ice. Cold and hard. He loved her with all of his heart—pouring his soul into her—yet she excreted his affections like potent urine...as if his emotions were worthless. He doesn't have anything to give to anyone, not even himself. He's too hurt to cry. After Earl dropped him off, he thought about going for a long walk, but he was too tired and his legs were still numb from the shock. All of this pain on account of a guy name "Rah Rah Roger", he yells, kicking the coffee table over and slinging a stack of magazines across the floor. What a name. Roger, as in "What's Happening", Roger Rabbit, Mr. Roger's neighborhood, Rogers and Hollands. The name will forever remain in his Memory as a designation for pain and insult.

For the most part, his meek temperament has taken him through the bowels of the love game. If he didn't care, he wouldn't be here. But he can't resolve to go on a whoring tour of destruction. The idea seems perfect, but it doesn't fit him. It's a size too big. Perhaps a little masturbation would increase his sexual appetite and he could grow into the role of canine, but it seems like too much work for him. And work is something he doesn't want to do. He just wants to die right now.

He springs up and paces the living room. What if she marries Ponytail and lives happily ever after? More than likely, he'll run into her later, having the time of her life with her family that was supposed to be *their* family. He doesn't want happiness for her; He wants her to get dogged over; He wants her to come back to him—begging for another chance; He wants to still be angry, so he can tell her what to do and where to go after she does it. What if she is his soul mate...the woman God has chosen for him? That means that he's going to have to swallow his pride and forgive her. What if he does run into her eight years and four kids later, and he is still lonely? She would be like a seven-course meal to a famished child to him. He would rather die of starvation, but he knows it would be good for him. He resolves that he would just disobey God than get back with her.

Will he have to settle for a woman—possibly much worse than Memory—if he wants to get married? As it stands now, he would rather stay alone than to go back to her. "Now is a good time to die," he yawns as he crashes back into the sofa and turns on the TV. "When Harry Met Sally" is on HBO; "Loverboy" is on The Movie Channel and something uninteresting that he didn't recognize is on Showtime. Nothing was on the tube, but love—lost love—is on his mind. He doesn't know what love is any more. He flicks through all 50 channels several times and turns it off. For about ten minutes, he sits in the darkness, dwelling on what happened about an hour ago—steady rewinding that kissing scene. The words she said stick in his head like a thought bubble in a comic strip: "We weren't working;" "I got weak;" "Mel, this is Roger." It's making his chest hurt even more as he doses off and reverses the dialogue "regoR si siht ,leM;" "kaew tog I;" "gnikrow t'nerew eW." He can't tell if he's dreaming the whole sequence or thinking too deeply on it, but he snaps out of his daze—hyperventilating.

He leaps from the sofa and dashes upstairs. Out of habit, he goes to the bathroom. He stands over the toilet and only a trickle comes out.

Eventually he'll relax enough for a good ol' fashion leak, so he closes his eyes and lets it hang for a moment. The floodwaters do come and he decides to make use of the brief moment of repose. He comes out of his clothes and leaves them in a pile at the foot of the bed. Without a prayer, he crawls under the covers. Whether he slept or not is a mystery. Usually peace is the main element in the land of slumber. Even when he has nightmares, he's oblivious of what's going on around him. This night, however—from bed-resting to bed-rising—he was tormented by his awareness of what happened.

Mel is in a zombie state when he crawls out of bed at nine. He doesn't bother with breakfast, and tea is absolutely out of the question—with the way his heart has been racing for the past 13 hours. Although he still feels like the discarded gum on the ground that eventually ends up on somebody's shoe—ripped, stretched and smeared all over the pavement—he doesn't want to die. He isn't going to waste any time getting over it. That's why he planned to be at Rogers and Hollands before noon. A bath is in order after he sat on the toilet for a half-hour reading Jet. After the water ran, he stuck his foot in and almost hit the ceiling. It's ice cold. The pilot light must be out, so he runs downstairs in the nude, with a book of matches and the funk of well-worked bowels leaving a trail. "Oh shit!" he exclaims as he discovers that there is no flame in the furnace. No gas. It's a good thing that Memory did break up with him. The bill is probably the same as the cost of the ring.

He throws on a pair of sweat pants, a tee shirt and his Bulls' Starter jacket. Today he decides to enjoy the fresh spring air by busing it downtown, since his legs felt good enough for the walk to the bus stop. Besides, he didn't feel like dealing with the city traffic and the outrageous parking prices.

He notices that he has bounce in his step when he gets outside and he's stronger and rejuvenated. The circulation got going in his legs as he makes it up to 79th Street in no time and in time for the bus. He settles all the way in the back and stretches his legs out as he faces the front. A couple of dudes glare intently at him from the side seats on the right. Based on the right tilt of their caps and the identical, deep-blue Cubs' Starter jackets, they're GD's: Gangster Disciples. Their faces are frozen with frowns. The oldest looking one has long, permed hair and a toothpick in his poked out mouth. The younger one has shopping bags under his eyes and what appears to be a joint in his ear. Mel glances at them both and chortles as they whisper to each other. A brawl would be right on time and he almost hopes that they start something. He can picture the screaming headlines: "Two Thugs Thrashed on Bus". All of his wrath would be unleashed on them if they get froggish. Originally, he planned to go all the way to the Dan Ryan, but decides to get off on Jeffrey and spare them a potentially bad day. He just shakes his head when he exits as they follow him with their eyes.

The Big Ben bus is just arriving. He buys a paper, boards and takes a window seat closer to the front. The ride through South Shore and Hyde Park is pleasant and uneventful, not that he would have noticed, since his head is buried in the daily. He looks up just in time to see 53rd Street. The Hyde Park Theater is two blocks down (the site of his first date with Memory).

She was so reluctant to go, that he had to almost kidnap her. He grabbed her by the arm after work and towed her all the way to the ticket booth. Of course, his car was in the shop that day—like it was most days—so they caught this same bus there, just going in the opposite direction. He had to struggle to come up with small talk. She was so humble then. She wouldn't be caught dead on a bus now. They saw "Mo' Better Blues." She laughed reluctantly at some of the scenes, trying to hold it in and not sound like a horse. The romantic moments had her engrossed and spellbound. Needless to say that although he was really into her and wanted to put his arm around her, he refrained. It seemed like if he barely touched her, she would have jumped out of her seat. Ironically, he was just as tense.

After the movie, she relaxed a little and opened up—even going as far as dubbing Mel "Shadow," and adding the compliment that turned him out: "Wesley Snipes is nice looking, but you're much sexier than him." He was ready to cut his heart out of his chest and give it to her on a silver platter. He treated her to Giordano's Pizza instead. She was so easy to please and impress (she had never had Giordano's). The small talk came abundantly as they sat at the window seat, watching (and even joking about) the patrons that were coming and going. Full from the laughter, they couldn't finish half of the stuffed pizza, so they boxed it up and left.

Then came his real test of the comfort level: he invited her to stop by his apartment. To his surprise, she showed trust in him and obliged.

He was glad that he straightened it up the day before. He showed her around the one room and brought out old pictures and mementos. She seemed impressed and got cozy as they watched television and opened up their hearts like mystery novels. Sometime during Arsenio, they dozed off—he with his arms wrapped around her, and she with her head planted in his chest. The connection was made. When they woke up at about two in the morning with the television blaring at them, he called her a cab. He walked her out to the car and for an endless moment, they were frozen in an innocent, perfect stare. No words were exchanged. He embraced her and she gave him a peck on the cheek. He wishes that he could erase the good memories of her...especially that one.

"NO REFUNDS AFTER 30 DAYS!?" Mel didn't hear that. He isn't trying to hear that. The cold, hard message the clerk is telling him is shrouded in sympathy. *"You're out of luck, because it has been 34 days since the purchase of the ring"* is what she said, although she dressed it up. Mel likens it to terms used synonymously with somebody dying: he passed away; he went home; he's sleeping; he expired; he departed; he's with God. The way people play with words. HE'S DEAD, when it's all said and done. And Mel is out of $2000 dollars. Never mind the fact that the ring hasn't been removed from the box. 34 days is the reason he's out of $2000. A $500 a day late fee. Doesn't she realize that lives are at stake? The 30-day policy can be the difference between someone living and dying, namely Memory. He has to get his gas turned back on, because he smells like a skunk after a good workout. An exchange is hardly the consolation they expect it to be. As if he has another prospect for a wife hanging in the rafters in case of a situation like this. *"Just go find another fiancée and we'll gladly exchange the ring for one more appropriate for your new love."* As if the love of his life comes with the seasons. As if the affairs of his heart are some type of annual ceremony. His heart is ravaged like a vacant lot in the ghetto. There may not ever be another engagement for him. And as it stands now, his financial status is as desolate as a ghost town. He hears the sales woman murmuring on, but it's not registering. Her lips seem to be spieling in slow motion. She sounds sincere offering her apologies, but it has no weight. "It's okay," he hears himself say as he walks out. It's far from okay though. There's only one remedy that will even come close to giving him solace: Making Memory a memory.

Mel strolls in the house and heads straight for the refrigerator. Now is one of those times to get sloppy drunk. It's a good thing he doesn't have a tolerance for alcohol, otherwise anything could happen. He pours a glass of apple juice instead and finishes it in four, loud gulps. He slams the glass down and parks in one of his kitchen chairs. Life is not fair. Why is it that the conniving women end up with nice brothers that won't carry out the dastardly acts of stalking and throat slashing? How come Memory didn't end up with an obsessive, macho-man type that would've broken her neck if she thought about leaving him, let alone cheating? Mel was infuriated when he left Rogers and Hollands. For that moment, he didn't care. Unfortunately, the moment couldn't last a good 20 minutes. The anger poured out like the sands of a busted hourglass. By the time he made it to Memory's job, his rage had depleted to a rational level, so he was only going to give her a piece of his mind and try to lay a guilt trip on her...that is, if she was there. She called in sick today. That figures. He was going to pop in and make her sicker if he could, but the long El ride liquidated all hostility. It was an emotional avalanche that had him so frustrated, that he almost broke down in tears when he got to 79th Street. He went from stoic to seething to sorrow in such a short amount of time.

Now he's somewhat settled, although he can go in any direction at the slightest reminder of her. Out of habit, he checks his watch...the watch Memory gave him as she professed her undying love and devotion, knowing that the next day she was going to sack with Ponytail. *Damn!* She could have given him something. Mel rips the watch from his wrist—taking some skin with it—and stomps out to his car, leaving a trail of charred footprints. He can barely get the key in the ignition as he grits his teeth. He revs the engine and peels off before the indicator lights go off. As long as he's moving, he's hot. About a quarter-block away from the intersection, the light turns red and he comes to a screeching halt. He's only three blocks from his house, and already the rage is easing up. *"DAMN!"* he yells, punching the horn. With that outburst, his anger gushed out and he finds himself in front of his house two minutes later, with his head resting against the steering wheel. He can hear his heart racing, even though he's panting like a hot dog. A thread from his jacket gives the sensation that something is crawling on his hand, so he jumps and checks for bugs. When he realizes it's just a string and his flustered imagination, he starts giggling fractiously. Internally, he is weeping. "Hour 19 of the Amnesia Age and I'm going crazy," he says as he composes himself and goes in his house for the day.

He checks the mail, lets the dog out, and plays his messages back. To his pleasant surprise, he has a call from a prospective employer. With the roll that he has been on for the last few months—the last 24 hours in particular—he thought it would be forever before there was any glimmer of light. A slight smirk forms as he freezes up. The professionally pleasant Olivia Clark from Spark Incorporated informs him via voice message that they would be interested in talking to him about the supervisory position. If he's not mistaken, he mailed that resumé about two months ago. Replaying it, he jots down the information and checks the old classifieds in his office. The ad was from February 20th—the eve of Memory's infamous "When are you going to get your kitchen remodeled—it stinks in here" tirade.

Spark is just west of downtown. They manufacture and sell educational material, from books to software. The position is for a department supervisor and they don't have the salary listed. It doesn't matter. He's almost regretting not returning the call from the insurance company in Waukegan. Benevolence left a message on his machine two weeks ago in regards to a management position. The pay and benefits were competitive, but the distance left much to be desired. It would be over a two-hour commute on public transportation (He could drive to Kalamazoo Michigan in that time), which entailed catching two trains, and a rigid PACE bus (which left no time for morning mistakes). If he needed to sit on the toilet an extra five minutes in the morning or if the El was thirty seconds slow, he would miss the bus, and would therefore end up an hour late. Devoting 12 hours a day to somebody's company isn't in his plan. He calls and sets up an appointment with Spark for Monday.

Mel was surprised when he snapped out of a dreamless, peaceful sleep and the clock read 11:59, indicating that he missed the X-men. He got up because it felt like he slept through the whole night and he couldn't sleep any more. Of course he tossed and turned for a while before he faded into the mysterious world of slumber. Memory was on his mind when he dozed off and she greeted him when he woke up, but he decides he isn't going to sit in the house all day. Although he can't afford it, he is going to treat himself to the show. Thank God "Sugar Hill" is playing at Ford City, because he didn't feel up to being in a sentimental spot like Hyde Park. The next showing is in thirty minutes, so he decides to go at 2:30. He washed up (using a big pot of heated water—thank God he has an electric stove—pouring some over his body, scrubbing down with a rag, and then rinsing with the remaining water, which is like a quick shower), threw some laundry in the machine, and went out for brunch. While he was out, he dropped his suit in the cleaners, picked up an early edition of the Sunday Tribune, and had his car washed. By the time he gets back, it is time to head out to the movie theater.

When he arrives, the crowd is modest for a Saturday, but it's still more people for his liking. He buys the ticket and bypasses the concession stands to the dim, half-empty theater. He takes a few steps down the aisle and decides on a seat all the way in the corner of an empty row, so he can use both armrests' and fart in peace. As the patrons pace the aisles (mostly couples), Mel ponders his next move. Darlene is out of the question, since sex is not part of the answer. How long can he go without it though? It could take forever for his bride to come in his life. And when she does, she may want a long, complicated courtship. Celibacy is not easy, and he worries about making a hasty decision based on his hunger.

He doesn't want to eat at a greasy spoon full of truckers and bugs because it's the first eatery on the road. After all, a four-star, award winning restaurant with fine waitresses, candles, soft music and lobsters in a fish tank that he could choose to dine on, could be just over the hill. Of course, it would cost much more, not to mention the image he would have to keep up. That's a concept he's having a hard time accepting. Fast food and gourmet cooking serve the same purpose: satisfying hunger. McDonalds and Red Lobster both turn into feces. With Maxwell Street polish's, he knows what he's getting—whether the cook digs in his butt just before serving the food—and that he'll have money left over to come back the next day. He'll get his food quick and hot—most of the time. Occasionally, indigestion and heartburn will follow, but nothing to hard for Pepto Bismol. Mel's problem is that he has been eating at the Signature Room on the top of the John Hancock Center. He didn't know what went in the food, if the waitress hated him and spit in the dish, and if his credit would be good the next time he came. The wait can spoil his appetite, and if that doesn't do it, the teasing appetizers will quench the hunger. He has his answer now. It's unfortunate that it took years of Salmonella poisoning.

As the previews come on, he realizes that the food metaphors have given him an appetite, so he gives in to the $4 a slice frozen pizza (a whole pizza from a good pizzeria costs about $4 more) and an oversized pail of pop. When he gets back, a couple is sitting in his seat. Envy surges through his veins, followed by the heartache that comes from the void left by the abrupt departure of love. The petty urge to ask for his seat is strong, but the threat of getting embarrassed is stronger, so he goes a few rows down and settles in an aisle seat as the movie starts.

He has a problem following the storyline, the pizza is too stale and expensive to enjoy, and after a few gulps of pop, he is freezing with the need to go leak. By the time the movie is over, he regrets wasting his time and money. For his troubles, he has a headache, which is magnified by the sun when he steps out.

He picks up his suit from the dry cleaners on his way home and calls it a day. It's only 5:30, but seems like it should be next month. Time has been really constipated since Thursday. The only thing he could occupy himself with is lounging around the house and channel surfing. Unfortunately, Memory is in every room and on every channel. At six o'clock, he finds himself sitting in his office, flipping through the classifieds out of habit and for safe measures—since he doesn't have a job yet. Before he realizes it, he skimmed through the whole section and is looking at the personal ads on the back. *This is ridiculous.* He vowed to never go this route. Those dating services are for desperate people...like him. His curiosity gets the best of him as he reads over an ad titled **"Seeking Blackberry": Attractive SBCF, 25, voluptuous and outgoing, enjoys movies, church and spending quiet times at home. Seeking dark, chivalrous gentleman over 24 for friendship, possible ltr.** A slight smirk forms on his face as he tries to picture this person. He studies the features in the profile and puts a check mark by it. After perusing the whole "Women Seeking Men" side, he marks off nine similar ads with a few variations in weight, height, age, and hobbies, but for the most part they are identical on paper: **SBF; 20's; under 5'8" and shapely (125-160).** He listens to the voice greetings and eliminates the prospects that contain statements like: I *like dancing and partying; spending time with my KIDS; occasional drinker; I smoke, so smoking is okay; MUST BE FINANCIALLY SECURE; I'm seeking a white professional* *male (which wasn't indicated in the ad); I'm extremely attractive and I'm looking for the same; must be over 6'3" and have an excellent body.*

Some of them sound identical, like computerized voices reading from a script. Those that put all the emphasis on superficial qualities are ignored. Mommas are out of the question. A lady name Janice has a sexy bedroom voice...and two kids as a result, that were crying in the background (which she failed to mention in the ad). He thought Shanaynay was a myth, but he's listening to a woman with that name and sounds every bit Shanaynay; Lolita wants a Denzel look-a-like with a bank account to match; Loretta puts emphasis on partying at the clubs; Kim sounds like she just broke up with her man and would settle for anything male. Seeking Blackberry, along with Sensitive and Sexy sound nice, so he left a description that included his height and weight, along with his hobbies, and dreams. He's optimistic and hopeful when he hangs up. What if one of them turns out to be everything that he wants in a woman? He's also aware of the risk. The chance of mutual disapproval of looks is strong. He knows all to well from experience.

When Mel got his driver's license just before his junior year of high school ended, Earl insisted on him meeting this girl from his school. They spoke a few times on the phone and they seemed to hit it off well. Crystal described herself as high yellow with short hair...pretty generic, although he formed a mental image based on light being right. At the time, he equated light complexions with pretty, so he anticipated meeting a super nova. They picked a neutral place to meet. The McDonalds on Downtown State Street was convenient for her, since she worked in the area. She—along with Earl and two of her girlfriends—was waiting for him when he arrived—as if Mel wasn't self-conscious already. Before he had a chance to evaluate her profile, she looked at him as if he had just climbed out of the sewer. She actually had a startled/repulsed expression and an attitude to match. She was curt and nasty as her friends whispered unflatteries and giggled to acknowledge the nightmarish moment. They spoke for all of two minutes before Mel said his good-bye to her and her ignorant friends. His feelings were too hurt to notice that she had the height of Big Bird and a humongous head like Tweety, reminding him of a winner in the San Diego Chicken lookalike contest. Apparently, she equated her complexion to beauty also. That day, he drove his father's Cadillac and Earl was anticipating a ride home. His expectations weren't met that day either.

Instead of learning from the experience, Mel allowed Earl to hook him up again. It was close to prom and Mel didn't have a date, so he figured there wasn't much to lose, and much to gain. Again, it was a girl from his school and again, they talked and hit it off on the phone (although she wasn't that talkative, she was pleasant) before they met. Her name was Felicia, and when they did meet, Earl was the mediator. He was actually trying to be nosy, seeing if his cupid skills had improved and if Mel would finally lose his virginity. Outside of the initial introduction of "Nice to meet you", the dialogue was strained. Felicia's appearance was okay, and from what he could discern, she wasn't displeased with the way he looked. Mel chalked it up as crowd shyness, because Earl made it crowded.

She agreed to go on prom with him. Two things he discovered on that night: the prom was an over-hyped fashion show and Felicia was shy to the tenth power. They were late for prom (which didn't matter, since the only thing people were doing were styling and profiling) and stood around the whole time. Since neither one of them was a dancer, holding down their chairs was the only option. When they were alone in the car, he tried to get her to open up, but she was wrapped tight. She didn't want to eat or go to the Lake or to the show or anything. It was excruciating. Melvin was bashful too, but he knew how to hold a conversation and get distracted during an uncomfortable first date. He couldn't stand it. It was worse than standing naked in the display window at Carson Pirie Scott on State Street during rush hour. After driving around for a couple of hours, he dropped her off. He ended up in bed before one. They talked a couple of times after the prom, but then they just faded. He vowed never to let Earl "hook him up" or go on a blind date again.

Mel slept until two in the afternoon and was still drowsy. He missed the Bulls/Knicks game, but was able to catch Denver and Houston. A nice couple came by and bought one of the females around six, and he is giving his farewells to them when the phone rings. He is expecting it to be another potential buyer, but it isn't. "Hello," he answers.

"May I speak to Melvin?" the female voice asks.

"This is he speaking," he says as he strains his brain to place the voice.

"Hi Melvin, this is Vernita," she announces. Mel pauses. He doesn't know any Vernita's. Then it clicks just as she says, "from the Date Line in the Tribune."

"Oh I'm sorry," he says, recalling that just yesterday he responded to her ad. He's surprised that she got back to him this fast. "How you doing, Vernita?"

"I'm doing good," she says. "How about yourself?"

"I can't complain...not that it would help anyway."

"You got that right," she affirms. "So Melvin...what did you do today?"

"Let's see...what did I do? It was so long ago, that I'm having a hard time recalling."

"One of those days, huh?"

"You know it."

As the pattern would go, he warms up to her quickly. They chatted until nine—about nothing in particular, just loose, smooth dialogue. He found out that she works downtown and they agreed to have dinner after work the next day, since he is going to be in the area for his interview. It was going too well, so he is expecting some kind of flaw in the chemistry once they meet.

Mel was calm and precise throughout the interview. He seemed to answer all of the questions correctly. Based on the body language and verbal feedback from Olivia (as she likes to be called), it is promising. They talked like old friends, as opposed to potential fellow workers. She brought in a couple of the current supervisors to talk to him and then she showed him around the different departments, even pointing out where he would sit. After she finished briefing him, she assured him that they will be calling him within a week to set up a second and final interview with the department manager, who was away on a business trip. From what he observed, he could work comfortably there. The building is magnificently structured—something that's worthy of an architecture award. There was even a cutie giving him the eye when he was touring. He didn't want to get his hopes up, but he couldn't help but be optimistic. Perhaps the positive interview will carry over to the date he has with Vernita in about an hour.

They agreed to meet at Food Mart in the Merchandise Mart. She told him that she will be wearing a sky-blue skirt suit with a royal blue blouse. After he buys a friendly card from Carlton Cards, he browses the stores for the hour he has to kill, and winds up perusing a couple of books from B Daltons, which is right across from the Food Mart. As he makes his way out, he notices a woman dressed in a light-blue skirt suit cross his path on her way into the dinning area. If that's her, from what he can see, he will be well pleased with her looks. She is the color of a Hershey bar, with a short, feathered haircut and thick (in the right places) build. Now Mel is starting to get nervous. Technically, they have 15 minutes before their date. He walks just inside and watches her as she steps up to the sbarro line. From behind, she looks excellent. She casually glances to the side, revealing a picture perfect right profile. Now all he has to do is be himself. He decides to wait for her to sit down before he approaches her. He darts over to Mart News and buys a pack of DOUBLEMINT and a copy of Jet. He gets back in time to see her leave the front of the counter and head over to a seat in the back overlooking the first floor. He takes a deep, anticipatory breath as he goes over what he's going to say to her. As he shifts and starts towards her, someone touches his shoulder as a soft voice says, "Melvin?"

He turns around to face his blue clad date and verifies, "Vernita," as a smile spreads across his face.

"How are you?" she says, embracing him.

"I'm okay," he declares as he's engulfed by her. He figures Vernita's circumference has to be at least 226 inches as he tries unsuccessfully to return the hug. "How about you," he questions after she releases him.

"I'm doing good," she says as she grins approvingly at him.

He returns the grin as he nods his head and takes all of her in, noting that she has at least three inches on him without heals. She is a lot bigger than him. Actually, she is a lot bigger than three of him, but the surprise doesn't register on his face or in his speech as he asks, "So how was work today?"

"Work was good," she announces. "What about you...How was your interview?"

She's cute, with a sweet disposition, but her massive body sends all types of thoughts through his head: Big surprise, big package. He can't imagine himself carrying her through the door on his wedding day.

That would be next to impossible. He can't imagine talking back to her in a disagreement. If size carries authority, she would rule him and the world with an iron fist. Woe unto thee that makes her mad. "The interview was real good," he attests. "There's a strong possibility that I'll be working down here with you."

"Good, I'm glad to hear that."

"You want to go order?"

"Sure. Why not."

She orders a modest salad and a baked potato—admitting that she is on a diet—and he has the sirloin steak dinner from The Great Steak & Potato Company. They settle at a window seat overlooking the cafés on Kinzi and have a freelance discussion. Her confidence is admirable as she speaks with passion about her job as an inside sales representative and her goal to be a fashion designer. Although she is sure of herself, she isn't imposing or pushy. She is currently attending Columbia, with another two years to go. Mel mentions how he's stuck in career purgatory as he narrows down his broadcasting path. Of course, they get on the subject of church.

"I lead 'His Eye is on the Sparrow' in the choir," she comments, adding, "and I'm working on another one called 'He's all over Me.'"

"I've heard them both...very pretty songs. Your voice seems somewhat low for those songs. Can you get it up?"

"That's what people keep saying."

"Does your choir sing a lot of the contemporary stuff?"

"It's like 50/50. We're trying not to ostracize the old school, you know what I mean?"

"I hear you," he says, cleaning up his garbage. "I'm on my way back to church, but I'm not sure what office I'm going to serve in. Singing is out of the question, though."

"What's wrong with singing?"

"Nothing. I just don't like to do it."

They gather their things and start out. Who would Mel see as they walk along the North corridor? None other than Earl—walking in the same direction in the adjacent hall. They catch each other's eyes at the same time, just as Mel is getting to the beginning of the post and Earl is just reaching the opening. At the next gap, they are walking parallel to each other and Earl is grinning like a mad man. At the next outlet, Earl heads them off and crosses over. He can't seem to have a blind date without his presence.

"What's up Cuz," he greets when he gets up to them, showing no partiality to Vernita's girth—although Mel knows it's in his heart. When they're alone, he's going to let Mel have it.

Mel cuts him a "Don't embarrass me" look as he introduces them. Earl is polite and pleasant in his brief exchange before leaving and wishing them a good evening. Mel will have a message waiting when he gets home. On the way to the parking lot, Mel struggles with his fondness of her while they discuss the problems of the black family. When she speaks, her statements carry authority—not necessarily dictatorship—since she always asks, "What do you think" when she would make a point. She reminds him of a big sister—no pun intended. He always imagined that he would get along with the woman he wound up with, like a sibling. He's even starting to get a little past her size. After all, she isn't a sloppy, blubber-hanging-from-everywhere, large; she is just large.

"Gin and Juice" by Snoop Doggy Dogg comes over the radio when he starts the car and she comments, "If their lyrics were centered around Christian morals, I think it would have an influence on those with a weaker resistance to the temptation to survive by any means necessary. What do you think?"

"Well, I never gave it much thought, but off the top of my head, I think that with positive lyrics to the gangster sound, it could reach some," he states. "But I'm not sure if it could reach those that are hard core criminals."

"Maybe, maybe not," she compromises. "I think that it could have a subliminal effect on the hard core listener if enough of the artists that made it would change their message."

"What are the chances of that?"

"Good point."

He switches the station to V103 and "Jesus Is Love" by Lionelle Richie and the Commodores is playing. She comments that that is one of her all time favorites as they both enjoy the tune. As he makes it to her Lake Shore Drive apartment just before Sheridan (Mel hates the North side), he ponders the potential kiss. Usually the first kiss or non-kiss dictates where the relationship goes. He doesn't even know if it is appropriate. All he knows is that in the past, if a kiss was given on the first date (usually a peck on the cheek, which is perfect for him), there was excitement ahead. If not, usually it was strictly platonic. Truthfully, it wouldn't devastate him either way.

He pulls to the side and puts on his hazard lights as he announces, "Well, this is it."

"Yep," she confirms. "Thank you, Melvin. I had a nice time."

"My pleasure."

"Well, hopefully I can get you to my church within the next few Sundays."

"That shouldn't be a problem."

"Okay then," she says, pausing briefly. "I'll call you later this week," she promises.

"Okay. I look forward to it."

"Well, goodnight," she says, reaching over and hugging him.

She exits, saunters through the lobby door and out of sight. Mel chuckles and blurts, "Platonic all the way" as he pulls off.

When Mel gets home, he opened his brief case to remove some of the literature he collected from Spark, when the Chick tract that he picked up on the bus last December falls out. Up to that point, he hadn't read it. It's titled, "A Love Story." There was a message for him in it five months ago that he chose to ignore. Now he's compelled to read it. It takes less than five minutes to get through it. The message is redundant to what he was hearing since the New Year. At that moment, he answers, "Affirmative," and makes a commitment to his first love.

Chapter 9

After a night of tossing and turning and about an hour of anxiety filled sleep, Mel wakes up as if it was a good year's rest. He doesn't feel sleepy at all. His heart isn't racing and his chest isn't aching. He sits up, verifying that he's not dreaming or dead, and scans the room as if he's in a strange place. It's the same place, but then again, it's not. Sure it's 2506 East 80th Street, his bedroom, with the same old furniture and the same year. But the feeling is totally different. For the first time in a long time, he notices a lot of things...a lot of simple things. It's like he doesn't have any peripheral vision—he doesn't notice the things that are going on around him. Straight up the mountaintop is what he is focused on. The bills that are piling up all over the house, might as well have been paid off. He'll pay them when he pays them. The shame of being unemployed is his badge of honor. He doesn't have to deal with the headaches of a 9 to 5. His savings are dead, his net worth is in the negative red, he has no job, no hot water, no woman (God, no woman at a time like this) and no desire to go back to a white collar, office situation. But he has a life, and for that, he's grateful, despite wanting to crawl under a rock for the last week.

The whole week was gloomy and/or wet, but today—Sunday—is so bright and calm, it looks like a promotional picture for a day in paradise. Funny enough, the sun always seems to shine on a Sunday. It could've been a Tornado watch forecast; hurricanes could've ravaged the city the night before; the whole Midwest could've been blanketed with snow and deep freeze conditions; thunderstorms could've rumbled and lightening could've illuminated the sky at dawn, but the sun always comes through on it's designated day. Today Mel really takes notice of it.

He looks over at the clock and smiles. It's only eight, which means he can still make it to Sunday school. He rolls out of bed and proceeds to the bathroom. After taking a long, loud stretch, he beams at the reflection in the mirror. It's been a long time since he's felt this mentally, physically and spiritually good at once. A makeshift shower will only enhance the feeling. He warms the water in the pot and drops his shorts to the floor before he darts carefree and nude to his bedroom. He punches the ON button of the radio and tunes in to college radio station WKKC. They play the best Gospel music on Sundays and

Thursdays. As soon as he hits it, he cranks the volume all the way up and bounces back to the bathroom singing Kirk Franklin's "The Reason Why We Sing" along with the radio.

The water is just right after he cools it from the faucet. He steps in, lathers up with Irish Spring and sings off key as loud as he thought he could without being heard by the neighbors. He pours some water over his head and shampoos his hair. As some of the Head and Shoulders streams its way down his face, he closes his eyes and envisions Memory, but it doesn't hurt to see her. At the same time, it doesn't bring him pleasure. He quickly opens his eyes and the shampoo stings them shut, so he reaches for a face rag and wipes them clear. After rinsing off from head to toe, he jumps out and goes through the hygiene routine of trimming the excess whiskers from his chin, brushing his teeth, deodorizing his under arms and oiling his scalp. He avoids cologne, because it messes with his sinuses, especially in the spring.

The phone rings when he gets back in his bedroom—presumably someone inquiring about the puppies. "Hello," he greets cheerfully.

"Uhhhh...I'm calling about the puppies," the nasally woman's voice says on the other end with apprehensiveness in excess.

And sure enough, as he gets into his spiel, "Yes, I still have a male and two females; both parents are registered and..." she hangs up. At least he didn't have to sing the whole song. *Usually they'll listen to the whole script—as if they were interested—maybe ask a few more questions, and then hang up. His answers were correct: Papers on the parents; both parents on the premises; descent sizes; dysplasia certification; competitive price. The answers came from the wrong person, though. On a few occasions, they would promise to "be right over" to buy one. Only thing, they were so eager to get off the phone with him, that they usually didn't even get the address. One idiot left a message on his machine that said, "I was calling about the puppies, but you sound like a queer ape that should be for sale, too." Mel was coming in the door when he got that message, so he *69ed, but because the number was out of the area—in suburbia, no doubt—he was unable to get through.* This is the first cloud of the day, but he just blows it away, humping his shoulders as he hangs up.

With conveyor belt precision, he slips into his beige, button-up shirt, pulls up his sand colored slacks, slides into his socks and loafers and steps to the bathroom mirror to evaluate the neck ties. After deciding on the blue and brown silk with the vacation resort print that blends well with the outfit, he starts reflecting while he ties it around his neck. If there's one thing that he's learned from working in Corporate America and entrepreneuring himself, it's that Caucasians will rarely do business with a black proprietor when they can go to another white person. That point was nailed home ever since he's been advertising. The concept is logical, if not wrong: If a lot of black people think that the white man's ice is colder, of course the white man is going to feel even stronger about that misconception.

One stand that his father takes that others may not agree with or have a negative opinion about, is his STRONG support of his race. It almost sounds pro-Nation of Islam, since the community thinks that they coined the philosophy of brotherly support. Reverend Adams is as far from serving Allah as he is to calling Satan the Son of God. But he does believe in supporting black people, because of the lack of support they get outside of the race. Mel will never forget the time he told the congregation that "if there was a black man and a white man in separate rooms of a burning high-rise, but there was only one ladder he could send up, that white man better jump or prepare to go to his funeral." Mel realizes that evil comes in all colors, but when it comes down to going with a black business and a white business with equal credentials, he'll always take his chances with the brother with a higher price.

He grabs his blazer and Bible, jets downstairs and starts out the door, when Memory's picture on the end table catches his eye. Cloud number two needs to be blown off, so he casually and impassively walks over and puts the picture inside the drawer of the table. As he pushes the drawer in, the sun simultaneously shines directly in his face through the window and vertical blinds. "Ain't No Need to Worry" by the Winans featuring Anita Baker comes on the radio upstairs (he always leaves it on while he's out, to ward off potential intruders, for his pets to hear and to leave on a positive note). He pauses, then beams as he shakes his head and strolls out the door with the feeling that he's walking on a cloud, as opposed to a storm cloud hovering over his head.

Mel stopped at Jackie's Place on 71st and Vernon for a pancake, bacon, and hash brown breakfast. He said his grace before and after. Sometimes, grace becomes a brief routine—like it has for him in the past few years. Not that he wasn't thankful or took food for granted, but this morning he was bowed in prayer a little longer than an ordinary *"God is great, God is good, let me thank Him, for our food, Amen"* grace. He gave some praise to God that was long over due. The night before, he didn't pray before bed. A good night's sleep and a touch of divine peace can make a world of difference.

Gospel music rang in his ears all the way to church. It's 9:06 when he steps out of the car. They should be just finishing up the opening prayer and songs and dispersing the members to their respective classes. It's been over two years since Mel has been to a church. Over six years since he's been a faithful member of his father's church. The thought makes him feel funny—almost like a visitor. He doesn't count the times that he had to drop something off or pick David up on some Saturdays after usher board meetings. Things still look the same. The smell of food cooking in the kitchen is the same (fried and smothered chicken, collard greens, cabbage, string beans, roast beef, macaroni and cheese, homemade rolls, cornbread, sweet potato pie and all kinds of cakes). Church kitchen food makes a long sermon worth the while. And Deacon Joseph Lewis is still the oldest person in the church. He's older than George Burns, yet sharper than a switchblade. That has been Mel's Sunday school teacher his whole life. He notices that he still is as he enters the sanctuary. Amazing.

His short, white hair looks like it was sprinkled on his head with a salt shaker and it contrasts against his dark, leathery-brown skin. Tall and venerable like a statue, he stands a lean 6'1"—and he doesn't lean. The class is all the way in the front. Mel will be sure to sit as close as possible during service, because the walk down the aisle can be an uncomfortably long one, with all the members turning around watching, as if it's a wedding march. There are about 10 fellows in the class ranging in age from 19 to about 45, and they're reading the lesson verses coming from Luke 15. The subject is redemption. Mel knows it well. He read over it the night before he lost his Memory, not realizing that it is today's lesson.

He stealthily sits in the pew three rows from the front, just as Deacon Lewis looks up from his reading. He bows his head and peers over the top of his glasses to confirm his vision is still accurate. They both smile at each other as Deacon Lewis shakes his head and passes a handwritten copy of the lesson outline back to him. Apparently, he's going on a topic different from what's in the book. Occasionally, Deacon

Lewis will improvise and teach outside of what was assigned. He only does that "When the Spirit leads me that way". Mel always gets confirmation from another source. The Lord always uses another vessel to hammer a message home, so Mel knows it's not something that originated in his mind.

The lesson goes by fast and when the classes gather at the front for the review of their lesson, everyone that knows Mel gives him a ghostly once over before beaming. It makes him a little uneasy, although he expected it and smiled at every acknowledging eye. Of course, Deacon Lewis wants him to do the summary for the class. Normally, Mel prefers advanced notice when he is going to summarize—not that he was going to refuse—so he could prepare an organized, written presentation to refer to, but under the circumstances, he has it written in his heart, since he has lived the lesson to a degree. When he gets up to address the Sunday school, his temperature rises, his body stiffens up, and his peripheral vision ceases as the words come quick, clear and smooth. Before he knows it, he's saying, "and that's our lesson for today" and taking his seat as the church applauds. He really doesn't hear the "Amens" and clapping as his metabolism returns back to normal.

After the clerk reads the minutes of the school and Deacon Lewis prays them out, everybody—starting with Deacon Lewis—comes to greet Mel. "Good to see," he says, extending a firm hand and pulling him into an embrace.

"It's good to be here."

"How have you been? You're looking good."

"I'm living, so you won't get any complaints from me."

"Amen, brother. It's good to be in the land of the living. That's a blessing in itself," he says, still gripping Mel's hand. "That was a good review you gave. Thanks for doing it."

"Thank you. I was glad to. I needed to anyway—that was just a testimony."

"That's good. Say, you still got the house?"

"Yeah, I'm still there."

"Now that's good. I'm so proud of you. It's good to see a young man making it like that. We need more young men like you, because my generation ain't gonna be here forever."

"Well, I'm just glad to have good role models like you to show me the way I should go," he compliments as he gets blitzed by older ladies, a couple of the elders, and some of the younger members that were toddlers when he left. He answers the same questions repeatedly as fast as he could, kisses the cheeks of respectable, lovable women that could be his great-grandmother, and jokes with the teenagers. He loves them all, but prefers to keep a low profile. If he didn't have to use the bathroom, he would have stayed in the sanctuary and avoided more attention by going into the basement, where everyone gathers during the break between Sunday school and morning service.

He manages to slip through the people and make it downstairs unscathed and unnoticed. There is a guy with his back to Mel in the stall, fixing a child's pants as he releases in the urinal. The man sends the child out after he washes his hands and they both look into the mirror at the sink at the same time. Their eyes meet and Mel realizes that it's his childhood friend, Lamont Hudson—the Reverend Lamont Hudson—who he hasn't seen in five years. "What's up man," he says gleefully as he punctuates it with a hug.

"What's going on, Mel? Long time no see, partner," Lamont says, equally pleasantly surprised.

"Man. It has been too long. The last time I was here, you were a deacon in training and I was a trustee, and now you're a member of the clergy. Time flies," he says as he looks him over. Lamont looks shorter than the two inches Mel gained on him after high school. He grew a light mustache and beard, but still looks like a fresh teenager. His body is more solid and stable from a little marriage weight and conditioning from keeping up with his children.

"You better believe it. I got the calling and I answered it, so here I am. So what have you been doing with yourself, now that you're all grown up with a house and all?"

"You heard, huh?"

"You know I did. Your father was probably more excited about it than you."

"Really?"

"Man, he told everybody he could. He was just short of putting the announcement in the bulletin."

Mel is surprised the news is around the whole church, although it didn't bother him. "Yeah, I had to move out on my own. I needed the space. It's nothing like having all that space to yourself."

"I know what you mean. Are you ready to tie the knot; Ready to settle down?"

"Don't ask," he says as he rolls his eyes up in his head, shaking his head.

"Awe man, it couldn't be that bad. You know black is in vogue now."

"That's what they say, but so is stupidity," he remarks as he jumps focus. "So was that one of your sons that left out of here?" he asks.

"Yeah, that was Lamont Junior," he says as he rubs his chin and beams with pride. "I got two more around here somewhere."

"Three? You ain't wasting no time being fruitful, are you?"

"No time to waste. I have a daughter—Pearl—that's four and a two-year-old son, Nathan. Lamont just made six last month. I think that's all I'm going to put out though. I know it'll be a while before I put some more out if I decide to have more."

"I hear you. I still have to work on my first, but of course I have to find a wife first."

Lamont nods at him as he washes his hands. "So I heard you got your degrees and took Corporate America by storm."

"Man," Mel says, shaking his head. "I'm out of Corporate America currently and I don't know if I want to go back. It's a long story, but I can tell you it's not the nicest place for a black man to be."

"People keep telling me that. I hear that it doesn't matter how many degrees you get, you still have to prove yourself on a daily basis. That's too bad. What are you thinking about getting into now?"

"I'm really not sure what my next move is, but I'm considering taking some visual communications classes."

"That's a big change from business."

"I know, but right now, it's a thought."

"I know what you mean. Have you considered teaching?"

"Everybody asks me that."

"Maybe we see that as your calling. You know we were like twins: close birthdays, same likes and dislikes, good students and strong beliefs in God. Maybe *He's* calling you out."

"I don't know about that. I think God would have to catch me, 'cause I would definitely flee from teaching."

They both laugh as they continue to catch up and reminisce.

From the fifth grade to their last year of high school, they were close. They were best and only friends. Both shared the burden of being talked about, although they felt like the Lone Ranger at times. Whenever Mel could get out of the overly protective grasp of his parents, they would go to the show downtown and see the scary movies. Both had strained relationships with their mothers and would often complain about them to each other, although Mel thought Lamont's mom was like a Fairy godparent compared to his Broom Hilda. They would often make imaginary swap and trades. They were always at the head of the class and planned to be business partners when they finished school. Since they were both good at management, they considered a consulting firm. Lamont studied finance and marketing in college. The most important area that Lamont mirrored Mel was in his relationship to God. Lamont was baptized the same Sunday and got a phone call from the Lord before he accepted Him. It was a literal phone call that he hasn't shared with anyone, not even his twin in the gospel who's standing before him.

Not only was he the only one that heard it, but at the time, he wasn't even allowed to answer the phone. When it rang, he answered it, because it was for him. The deep, gentle voice on the other end called him by name, saying, ***"You are loved and I am always with you. Call me. I am Love."***

"Okay," he responded and hung up. He didn't know how to use a telephone, but he knew how to pray at that point, and pray he did—in tongues. He didn't know what was happening or what he was saying, but he didn't stop. Whenever he opened his mouth to speak, something foreign came out. He stopped and went to the old Bible that belonged to his great grand mother and opened it as if he knew what he was doing, where he was going and how to read. Finally, he heard the voice again, and it began to read the passage to him as he looked at the words: ***"As the Father hath loved me, so have I loved you: continue ye in my love. If you keep my commandments, you shall abide in my love; even as I have kept my Father's commandments, and abide in his love. These things have I spoken unto you, that my joy might remain in you, and that your joy might be full. This is my commandment, That you love one another, as I have loved you. Greater love hath no man than this, that a man lay down his life for his friends. You are my friend, if you do whatsoever I command you. Henceforth I call you not servant; for the servant knoweth not what his lord doeth: but I have called you friend; for all things that I have heard of my Father I have made known unto you. You have not chosen me, but I have chosen you, and ordained you, that you should go and bring forth fruit, and that your fruit should remain:***

that whatsoever you shall ask of the Father in my name, he may give it you. These things I command you, that you love one another."

He turned the page over that day. The Lord still reads to him from that Bible. Of course, he learned how to read for himself, but it's nothing like the Lord reciting the Word. That day he asked for his mothers' love and salvation in the name of Jesus, and had the faith that He wouldn't deny him, although that faith was tried and tested for almost 15 years.

Prior to the call, he didn't feel any love. Liquor was his mother's child that she cherished and adored. There were many men, but he didn't know which one was his father. "You ain't got no daddy, bastard" is what she slurred to him when he asked. It was a cold existence. The men were on a mission and would not be distracted by him. They were in and out quickly, sometimes Lamont wouldn't even get a look at them. He may have seen his father, but he'll never know for sure. No one claimed him. When he was old enough to realize what was going on, he had to bear that cross. He couldn't vouch for her honor when people would label her a whore. Sometimes he wished that he was big and imposing, so he could've stumped anyone that talked about her. It wasn't until later that the last part of the scripture really enlightened him. Despite the neglect, icy disposition and downright disdain Ms. Hudson displayed to him, Lamont would have walked through a fiery furnace for her. His patient, unconditional love manifested itself in her deathbed salvation five years ago. Right after his call from God, he went and told his mother "I love you, Momma."

She gave him a bizarre look, as if that's the first time anyone confessed love to and for her. Then she dismissed him and asked, "What do you know about love?" He was always obedient and never disrespectful to her. It was the little things, such as remembering her on her birthday with gifts and the little "just because I love you" letters that wore her down. After 20 years of alcoholic saturation, her liver was devastated and she was on her way out. She got sober enough to tell Lamont that she noticed all of the things he did and that God was going to truly bless him. "I'm going to get what I deserve and go to hell, now that I've raised it for so many years," she said regretfully.

Lamont wasn't trying to hear it and told her that everyone deserves to die and go to hell. "Jesus loves you as much as he loves me. It's up to you to accept Him as your Savior before you leave."

"I don't know how," she cried, turning her head to the side.

Lamont laid his hands on her and prayed the sinner's prayer of faith. The next week she was up and out of the hospital, in the church and being baptized. She was with him for seven more weeks and in that time, she introduced ten souls to Christ—some of them her drinking, partying and fornicating men friends. The Lord used him to bring her to salvation. That was His perfect will. Lamont wanted to curse her and leave a long time ago, but he was obedient. She could've been saved through God's permissive will even if he left, but he wasn't trying to put God to the test. Patience is a hard virtue to get down, and the Lord often permitted him to do things that weren't in his perfect will because he didn't want to wait. And that's what he's going to speak about today: waiting on the Lord's perfect will. Last night he dreamed of the message and that Mel was there to receive it. He doesn't know what Mel is going through, but he knows that it's in God's perfect will for him to be here. "I'm really glad you're here, man," he says with overwhelming joy.

"I'm glad to be here. It's good to see you're doing good. Now when am I going to here ya preach?"

"Today."

"Are you serious?"

Lamont nods with a slight grin on his face.

"You mean to tell me my ol' man is giving the pulpit up for you?"

"Whenever the Lord gives us a message, he lets us bring it without any dispute. That's one reason why I admire him: he doesn't try to hog prime time. Not that I'm knocking the old school pastors, but I like the idea of him allowing God's word to come from any one of us."

"Well, I was planning to anyway, but I'm going to definitely get on the front row now."

They both laugh at that and head out, Mel to the sanctuary and Lamont to the Pastor's office. Mel enters, gives his brother on the door a pound and takes his seat comfortably near the front. Mel is glad to see David back in church. Earlier in the week, he stopped by the house and David was in a heated discussion with Momma. He had gotten word that day in school that he wasn't going to be graduating with the class and that summer school was necessary. Mel never imagined David screaming at Momma, but there he was that day, defiantly blaring out at the top of his lungs. Mel wondered what his father would have done if he had been present. As wrong as Mel thought his mother was on certain disciplinary occasions with himself, he sided with her and pulled David outside for a verbal chastening. It worked, because David calmed down and went in and apologized.

As the deacons begin the devotional hymn a cappella at the front, he ponders his past at LOG. *He was always popular, although he tried to keep a low profile. Everyone considered him the choirboy that he was—everything a PK was supposed to be. He resented the tag and the pressure that went along with it. As if he was ssssooooo perfect. As low key and active as he was, if he didn't have to go to church, he probably wouldn't have. The idea of going because it was expected of him because of the office his father held, never sat well with him. He didn't enjoy the days of cotton bell bottoms, fat clip-on ties, hot polyester robes, choir rehearsals on Fridays (of all days), long, steamy services throughout the day and the whole ritual of being a PK. It was as if he was a wild animal on a leash. He was almost hurting to sin. High school graduation marked the start of his backslide. He actually doesn't really consider it backsliding. He justifies the leave with a need to find God for himself and not because it was the rule for living under his parent's roof.*

As the procession music for the choir plays, the changes that have taken place start to really hit home. *A guitarist and a flutist were added for a more contemporary sound in the music department. Of course they replaced the old organ too, and added a set of keyboards, an equalizer, more speakers and a whole lot of sophisticated digital/electronic equipment. It's hard to believe how far the department has come in six years. The choir starts marching in and the concept of six years starts to sink in. The choir robe colors went from blood red and dull white to bright navy blue on soft baby blue. Kids got bigger. Actually, some of them grew up. A child goes from 12 to 18 in six years. Toddlers grew into grammar schoolers. Some of them look the same, except they have adult size bodies. It tickles him to see someone who was in the junior choir when he left, now singing in the Angelic Choir.*

The bulletins are different. Instead of a letter-size one pager, it's now ten 5 X 8 pages. His father has an updated picture on the front, which was due when his first mug shot was taken. He used the same shot for 15 years. It was a bad picture that didn't look like him. It was reproduced to the point where he looked like a person in blackface. Often, members would draw all types of exaggerated features on his visage, such as pointed beards, thick, hairy mustaches, ridiculous bifocals, black eyes, fangs, horns, afros and rolling eyes by cutting out the real ones. They traded in the old van that was falling apart years before he left. The paint was peeling off and the church name was bastardized when the letters "V", "E", "O", "F", and "D" fell off. "Lo Go" it read. Their broadcast time even changed from four to five. Love of God has surely prospered.

The irony is that it started after Mel left—after years of his suggestions. They wouldn't listen to him though. It's like they heard what he was saying after he left, or they decided to do it all after he was gone. He realizes that it wasn't planned as a personal vendetta against him, but it still pissed him off, since he didn't get to reap the luxuries (yet he had worked like an Egyptian slave around here). He makes it up in his mind that he's not going to be bothered by the past, as the service proceeds through the songs, offering, alter call and announcements. For the first time in his life, it truly feels good and relaxing to be in church. It's spiritually satisfying, as opposed to religiously tiring. As a child, he didn't pay much attention to the sermons, because he would hear it from his father at home anyway. He would usually sleep through it with apple wine candy or strawberry Now/Laters in his mouth. Now he's eager to hear the message, especially since his friend is bringing it.

Two new ministers are on the roster, for a total of five. Lamont is one of them and the husband of the letter writer is the other. Now the church seems to have a minister that has a specialty in every area of the Word. Reverend Jones is the old school, whooping preacher. He's over 80. Sometimes it gets hard to understand what he's saying, let alone preaching, but he knows the Word. He's very chauvinistic and his position of women preachers is NO. He feels they should be having babies. Out of all of them, he's the Pastor's strongest supporter. Often his messages come from the Old Testament. Many times, he focuses on the Mosaic books. He's skilled at it. Perhaps he could have been an attorney, with his ability to discern, decipher and dissect the books of the law and the prophetic books, cross referencing them to the New Testament, comparing and paralleling the law and the Spirit.

Minister Robinson is an encouraging, motivational minister. He understands how people can make mistakes and give in to temptation, so he's always encouraging the congregation and people to be strong and repent, and that God is a loving God, Who's willing to forgive. His messages focus on the personalities of the biblical characters and he compares them with people today, bringing out their imperfect nature and illustrating how God still showed love to and use for them. He usually opens up with "Hello Peter", if he's going to talk about the Apostle who cut off someone's ear and denied Jesus three times; "Let me introduce you to Jonah", if he's going to discuss the disobedient Prophet who was swallowed by a fish; or "You are the Pharisees", when he addresses the hypocrites.

Reverend Bradford, the former deacon and backstabbing, power-hungry spouse of the letter writer, tends to focus on the book of Revelation. Mel has heard his father say in private that Minister Robinson needs to introduce him to Judas Iscariot: "Hello Reverend Back-stabber...You are Judas the traitor." The congregation refers to him as the apocalyptic minister, because he's always talking about the last days and how hot hell is. His messages are always composed of criticism of Christians. He always calls them to put in the work, instead of deceiving themselves into thinking that saving faith means sitting down and not exercising that faith in works. He always makes mention of how close we are to the judgment—like one of the Old Testament prophets.

Reverend Williams is everyone's favorite, because of his short, wise sermons. He uses parables and proverbs to bring the message in compact, practical terms that even a child can understand. Straight to the point. Some ministers have a tendency to talk around the world and back before they get to the point. A lot of them enjoy hearing themselves preach and can go seven years past the human attention span. Not Reverend Williams. He's usually through in ten minutes. His record is five. The message is tasty and digestible and the membership is never asleep when he finishes. He could get rich by teaching a class on "Getting to the point with time enough to see the game."

Pastor Adams—Dad—is a teaching preacher. His messages are diverse and spiritually charged. Never predictable, as he obliges to the Spirit's guidance. Sometimes, he tells a story to bring the Word. Other times, he talks about something that's going on in the church that went on in the first century church, and either encourages or chastises from that topic. If there's a subject in the news that's of interest, he'll address that and apply biblical principals to it. He could finish in 15 minutes or an hour and a half; He could be screaming like a raging river or murmuring as low key—yet bold—as a humming bird. Because of his gift of harmonization, he occasionally ministers in a song. He can tickle the congregation or shame them. He is an interesting instrument of God. Mel has seen many ministers bring the Word of God, but he has never seen a minister quote scriptures from the top of his head like his father. It's truly an amazing gift. So far, his father has a 100 percent accuracy rate. When he says that a scripture is in a particular book, chapter and verse, it's there. The Word is in his heart.

The only preacher's style Mel is not familiar with, is that of his friend: Rev. Hudson. His father finishes his announcements and introduces him to the warm applause of the congregation. He wears a smile as he gets to the podium. Instead of the shy, homely teenager that Mel remembers him as, he's a glowing, bold, confident, and comfortable man of God, standing before the church. It seems like the change should have taken a lifetime, instead of just six years.

As the applause dies, he opens with a brief prayer and greeting. As soon as he announces the passage the subject is taken from, he asks the congregation to follow along in their Bibles. It's taken from Lamentations 3, 19 through 39. He puts emphases on the 37th verse: "*'Who is he that saith, and it cometh to pass, when the Lord commandeth it not?'* I'm going to talk to you about the Lord's perfect will, and his permissive will." He proceeds to break down the passage like a true teacher, which reveals his style. He goes into the setting, the mood, the author and the meaning. It almost sounds like he's giving a seminar. Speaking very enthusiastically and clear, asking, "Do you follow me" periodically as the other ministers and deacons encourage him to "Preach on".

He goes on: "Now you know I'm a Jesus freak, so what would a message from me be, without Jesus? I looooovvvvve the Gospels of Jesus Christ. You ladies that like to read romance novels, I recommend the books of Matthew, Mark, Luke, and John. They're highly recommended. The greatest love story ever, with four different points of view. Hallelujah. Follow me to Mark 8, 31 through 33. You know Minister Robinson talked about Peter not so very long ago. We're going to talk about him—and everybody else who wants their own will, instead of the Lord's perfect will—for a while." He stays in the gospels for most of the message, proceeding to cite Peter's insistence on saving Jesus in John 18, 10 and 11, cross referencing it to Matthew 26, 53 and 54 about fulfilling the scriptures and how the Father would have "permitted" Christ to call twelve armies of angels. The "Perfect Will" theme continues with the prayer in Gethsemane in Matthew 26 and 39, in the insults he received on the cross from one of the criminals, and the Salvation promise from

Jesus to the penitent thief (one of Mel's most inspiring scriptures) in Luke 23, 39 through 43.

"Now I'm gonna go back to the old school, as in the Old Testament. Follow me to Jonah," he says as Mel casually flips back to the story that he's very familiar with, knowing where his friend is going with it. His Bible opens up to the Song of Solomon instead, and as his friend explains how God's perfect will occurred, despite Him permitting Jonah to go in the opposite direction, Mel gets flashbacks to his relationship with Rita as he reads over the verses: ***"I am black, but comely, O ye daughters of Jerusalem, as the tents of Kedar, as the curtains of Solomon. Look not upon me because I am black, because the sun hath looked upon me: my mother's children were angry with me; they made me the keeper of the vineyards; but mine own vineyard have I not kept."*** *Rita gave him that scripture when they were flinging around. That was the first scripture he highlighted in the Bible that he carries with him, because it was so poetic and it spoke directly to Mel...and Rita.*

For the longest time, Mel felt that the darker the berry, the greater the curse. There was never any visible advantage to being dark complected. He often prayed for storm clouds as opposed to the sun, because he felt the sun would tan him an even darker shade of black, which would translate into more woes. She awakened his subconscious mind with that scripture. As Lamont continues to preach/teach, Mel starts to wonder if Rita was His perfect will, and if He "permitted" Amnesia—Memory—to be in his life because Mel insisted on it. He did have a chance to marry her, and even before this sermon, he always second-guessed the decision. She always made him happy and they got along like a fairy tale couple. And he was attracted to her. Why did this verse pop up now if there isn't a message in it? He gets excited and resolves to write her when he gets home, when Lamont declares, **"We have to take our hands off of a situation before God will move in it"** as if he is addressing Mel. It's kind of ironic that it seems like Lamont and his father are peering at him at that moment.

"Now in closing, I want the congregation to address God with me right now. I don't know what you have your hand in or on; I don't know what He has permitted to happen against His perfect will, but we all have something that we're interfering with," he proclaims, seemingly to Mel again. Mel can only chuckle, "Amen", and shake his head as he repeats after Lamont: "Lord—I thank You for having mercy on me—when I had my hand in Your perfect will. Lord—I ask that you forgive me—for doing anything against your perfect will. Lord—I promise to take my hand off of a situation—that I know I shouldn't have my hand on—and let You have Your perfect will." Mel notices that like himself, there are a few reluctant people that want to be in control of things. But he smiles, looks up to the sky and vows with his minds mouth to "remain celibate until You deliver me my wife—whoever she is," with the hunch that it's Rita, even though she is already in a marriage. He also resolves not to write her and wait on the Lord to move.

"Now I'm going to extend the invitation to those who may not have a church home, or who may not have salvation," he says as the musicians start playing and the choir sings "Nobody Like Jesus." Up until that point, Mel was relaxed and didn't think it would be a tense situation when the invitation was extended. He already made up his mind to join. But here he is, as stiff as a board as his temperature rises about twenty degrees. He is four rows from the front, but it still seems like a country mile's walk. He can't move. It feels like all eyes are on him as the choir switches to "Come To Jesus" and Lamont proceeds to plead for someone (Mel) to walk the aisle. All the ministers and deacons are scanning the audience. Mel closes his eyes and when he opens them again, he is in the aisle, walking towards the front as his mother and other members start shouting and clapping. Dad is the first to greet him with a big hug and tears in his eyes, followed by Lamont and the rest of the ministers and deacons. He doesn't have the love of a woman, but with the love from Christ and the church, he didn't need it. In the Memory era, when he was on the outside, he never felt this much affection before.

Although everyone knows him, they still go through the formality of taking his name, former church, and status, announcing it to the congregation and then officially taking him in. His father lead him to his office—alone—while the associate ministers closed out the service with the last offering and other announcements.

"When you were here, I felt that your place was the Deacon Board, as a Junior Deacon."

Mel nods and is surprised to hear it. That's where he wanted to go anyway.

"But they voted you on the Trustee board. Well, I'm not going to give them that chance again. Even though you're not married—yet—I'm going to make you a Deacon in training and I'll keep you there until the Lord promotes you, but you will perform all of the duties of a regular deacon," he affirms to Mel's delight. "And I'm going to put you to work today at our visitation to Saving Grace Baptist Church. It starts at four o'clock, and since you got that fast car, I'm sure you'll beat us all there. I also want you to assist Deacon Lewis with the Sunday school class and fill in when he's out or tired. Eventually you will take over full-time."

Mel's eyebrows rise with excitement.

"Welcome back, son," he says with a smile as he puts his hand on his shoulder and anoints his forehead with oil.

It's amazing how far a little faith will take a person. Monday, Mel got a call from HUD. He was informed that the account was turned over because of the delinquency. From what he understood, they were going to start the foreclosure process. For a moment, he got anxious. To say that he didn't, would be a lie. But then he said, "Your will, not mine" and started listening to some inspirational music. He was calm and collected and even started Praising the Lord in song. Not even an hour had passed before he got a call back from HUD, informing him that they wanted him to come downtown that Thursday to give an explanation to the delinquency and to possibly sign some type of forbearance agreement. He didn't totally understand what it entailed, but apparently he would be able to work out a payment plan and keep his home. He immediately called the devil a liar, blasted the music and started dancing, despite his lack of rhythm.

Before he even broke a sweat, Paul Webber, the department manager at Spark, called to set up a second interview for Thursday—just before his appointment with HUD. As it turned out, the Power that is had it all worked out: The interview was just a formality in the hiring process (when he walked into Spark, the same young lady that was checking him out was coming in at the same time and congratulated him—before he had the interview—insisting that "You got it locked up." He was scheduled for the drug test the same day) and HUD gave him a pass on the $2,500 delinquency and a grace period of two month's to start making payments (since he informed them that he was starting a new job in about three weeks). And to think that he was on the verge of taking a job at Mickey D's like a guy name Calvin. The goodness of God *made him forget about all of his troubles over the last four months. He praised God that whole week.*

Saturday, his joy and faith inspired him to attend the prison ministry at Cook County Jail. He vowed to never, ever go to jail, whether by his choice or not. *Whoever lands there deserves it. Why waste time on them, when they did something that they shouldn't have?* That was his reasoning, but God's grace changed his heart as he finds himself walking along side the barb wired fences on Sacramento to the entrance to men's division 5: one of the medium security divisions. He doesn't know what to expect. What if there is a prison riot during the service? What if some of them try to escape? What if they take him and the rest of the congregation hostage? He chuckles to himself at the ridiculous thoughts and prays for an open mind. The prison guards in the booth at the gate direct him in, after he mentions the church he is with. He is almost expecting a strip search. When he gets in, the guards are friendly about informing him that some of the members just arrived. After telling them what he has in his pockets, they let him walk through the metal detector and lightly pat him down. One guard directs him through a long, white corridor, with several doors on each side that remind him of a hospital.

"Is this your first time here?" the guard inquires.

"Sure is."

"It should be a good experience for you," he suggests as they reach the doorway to a gymnasium full of inmates that are facing the podium with the membership of LOG. "Take care," he says.

"You too."

Pastor Adams greets him with a smile, and the other members (about 15 total) shake hands with him as his friend, Lamont, is enthusiastically addressing the audience. Mel takes his seat and studies the faces: predominately colored faces, since the system is marketed towards them; hardened faces, from a trying life; young faces, that weren't schooled enough in the art of being slick; innocent faces, that had a story to tell, but no ears that mattered that would listen. Some of them chose that particular path to walk. Others were born into a situation. Many were probably caught up in negative affairs. A handful were probably persecuted for no reason at all. A constant with all of the faces, are the eyes that reveal receptive and penitent souls. From the mightiest to the meekest, they all have lowly, sorrowful eyes looking towards the sparrow and seeking Jesus. If only those who are privileged would be just as open to the Gospel of Jesus Christ. Humility. Mel thought he knew all about it, but he realizes that it was just hammered home when his eyes meet the eyes of the multitude looking to the podium. Eyes just like his. Mel could have been here. He has broken laws that could've landed him in jail. God was gracious. God is gracious. After Lamont finishes greeting them, he announces that Brother Melvin Adams will open up with a prayer. Gladly. They all need it, especially the congregation. It marks the second time in the week that he's opened a service with prayer. Sunday afternoon at Saving Grace, he was one of only three deacons from Love of God present. Although he would've lead the song if asked, singing isn't his forté. They asked him to pray. He did. And he laid it all out. It is an honor to talk to God on behalf of himself and so many others.

Chapter 10

Training starts at 8:30. Mel arrived at eight. The night was pacific and the morning is welcoming. After thirty minutes of devotional time, he had a filling breakfast and a hot, expedient, makeshift shower. He was never readier to start work than today. The receptionist—who is already on a friendly, first name basis with him—directed him to the training room, where there will be an orientation. Later they are to tour the whole building—each and every department—and meet key persons in the company. Training is scheduled for two weeks, which Mel considers good and necessary. At Horizon, they just threw new supervisors from off of the street into the war-zone without any product training. Often, they would appear to be power-tripping buffoons out on the floor. Some of them couldn't answer simple policy and product questions, which really wasn't their fault since they were learning on the job. It was like teaching a weakling how to fight by putting him in a highly visible prizefight with a seasoned champion. And predictably, they got knocked out.

There are three other people in there when he arrives: a studious looking white girl that appears to be fresh out of high school; an obese black lady wearing a nice gray business suit; and a short, chubby, black woman with a weave that even Mel could identify. The room is divided in two, with six rows of long, folding, conference tables on each side. There is room in each row for three people. A computer terminal, manual, pad, writing utensils, self-promotional key chain with matching coffee mug, and benefits package is placed in each space. The two black ladies sit in the second row next to each other, chatting. The white girl sits on the other side in the front, perusing the manual. Mel settles in the back, studying the room and meditating. A taut, blond woman comes in and identifies herself as the human resources representative, Jackie Burke. She informs them that training will start shortly.

"Are you going to help us fill out these benefit forms?" hair weave asks.

Ms. Burke confirms she will. Gradually, others pour in, settling in rows to themselves until they all fill up, with the exception of about four or five seats. Everyone keeps quiet and to themselves, except for the two women in the front who continue to chatter. At 8:25 Ms. Burke comes back in and passes out nametags.

"We'll wait a few more minutes for anyone else coming before we get started," she announces. "In the meantime, if you want to go to the cafeteria for some coffee, you may do so."

Mel takes the opportunity to go to the rest room. When he gets back, there is a buppyish man sitting next to his space. "What's up," he says as Mel takes a seat.

"Nothing much. How you feel?"

"Truthfully? I'd rather be at home right now," he confides.

"I hear you," Mel confirms.

The last person staggers in a couple of minutes late and Ms. Burke proceeds. "Okay, the first thing I want you to do is write your name on the name tag and stick it on your person, where it will be visible," she says gleefully. "Now what I want is for the class to introduce yourselves and tell us something about yourself. We'll go around the room, starting with myself, and I'll introduce the trainers. For those who weren't here, my name is Jackie Burke, and I'm the human resources assistant. I've been here for about five years. I'm a newlywed, and me and my husband are expecting our first child in seven months. I'm a graduate student at Northwestern University and I'll be getting my Masters in Business Administration in January. I enjoy softball and swimming, and I plan to indulge myself a lot this summer. I would like to introduce the other trainers: Gregory Jackson, Melony McDonald and Donald Hofmann. Gregory will start," she says as the guy sitting next to Mel gets up and walks to the front.

"Hello. My name is Gregory Jackson," he announces. "You can call me Big Gee or Jay Bird or Beggin' Greg or Black Jack—whichever is easiest. Just don't call me Bob," he jokes as the class collectively chuckles. "I'm in the Billing and Collections department. I've been in the department for eight months. When I started here, I worked in manufacturing as a supervisor, and I stayed there for two years. I've been with the company for three years. When we have systems training or new employees—like today—I moonlight as a trainer. I will be training you on the procedures of billing and how to navigate on the system. Sometime in the near future, I will be attending law school, and so that the company will have a reason to pay for it, I will study labor law. For all of the ladies, I'm available...I mean I'm single and I enjoy nightclubs and hooping, so if you're interested in a good night out on the town or if you want to get smoked on court, see me during the break. Seriously, I look forward to working with all of you. Melony McDonald is up next," he says as he starts toward his seat.

Hair weave raises her hand and announces, "I have a question, Greg."

"I have an answer," he responds.

"Are you free this evening?"

"Nope. This evening I'm $1.99 plus tax," he claims as he takes his seat to laughter. He leans over and whispers to Mel, "I hope she doesn't come up to me with $2.14 after class."

Mel looks at him and giggles as Melony goes through her straight forward, no-nonsense routine, followed by a brief introduction from Donald. The training group commences to introduce themselves, starting with hair weave, formally known as "Sandra Gibson", whose "background is in customer service," she says as she presents her resume, dramatizes her autobiography and goes into an oratorical about why she likes the company. It is supposed to be brief. She goes for a long five minutes. "...and that's why I want to work here full-time."

"With a mouth like that, she won't get past probation," Greg comments as she sits down and allows the rest of the class to introduce themselves. A handful of them are part-timers in the order department, like the ambitious and cheerfully suave Marcus Wells, who is "fresh off of prom weekend and soon to be a graduate of Hales Franciscan Catholic High School (Friday is the commencement exercises) and on [his] way to DePaul University to study Finance and Economics." Some are in the billing and collections department, including the baby-faced white girl at the front (Karen Jordan), who's working on her Masters in business management at Roosevelt University and who happens to be another supervisor in training. A few are in manufacturing, such as the bull-built, blatantly butch Brenda Cassidy, who coincidentally has three male Rottweilers. When Mel's turn comes up, he briefs everybody on his schooling and experience and takes the opportunity to mention his work in the church. "I'm involved in an outreach ministry at my church and the Sunday school," he claims, adding, "and although I'm not as good as I used to be, I play ball, so Greg may have a challenger."

"Bet on Black Jack," Greg interjects as Mel takes his seat. "Do you sell those peanuts on the El?" he asks confidentially.

Mel laughs at his misconception of outreach ministries. "No, but I know what you're talking about. The Victory Outreach Ministries reaches out to the addicts, gang members and felons and sends them out with a message on the El's...and they sell the peanuts to fund the Ministry. What our church does is offer the plan of salvation and a plan for survival to inmates who are on the verge of being released at the Penitentiary—which is along the same lines, but we don't sell peanuts on the El—not that I'm knocking or downing it. Our methods are different, but our God and goals are the same."

"Really? That's a good thing you're doing. I have a cousin that's in and out of jail and he always tells me about how the churches come in to try and encourage them. He says that the visits are the only bright spot to being in there: knowing that somebody cares."

"That's what it's all about," he says approvingly.

After toiling through the tedious process of filling out the benefit and tax forms, the class breaks. Different bonds develop and several cliques form as they gingerly converse in the cafeteria. Mel goes his own separate way and sits alone, reading the paper on one of the comfortable, lounge chairs in the lobby. From all physical appearances, Greg is a lot like Mel: Dark, slim, young and educated. Based on Greg's absence, they are from the same private, independent mold. When they return, they tour the building. Mel keeps up the caboose with Greg, lagging a few feet behind the rest of the group. Greg gives commentary on every department and some of the people in each of them.

"Nothing but a bunch of silly white guys that goof off all day," he remarks of the marketing department. "The brothers in here work like horses, but they're cool and they would hold your back if you got into it with the powers that be," he says of the black and Hispanic dudes in the warehouse, where some of the items are manufactured. "The view will be enough to get you in here everyday, but the gossip will make you want to quit," he remarks of the black beauty beset customer service department, adding, "You'll like being single down here, brother." Indeed he will. No sooner than he says it, the young woman that greeted him with seductive glances on his interviews, smiles at him as he looks her way. He almost runs into the back of the rest of the group. When they get to the cafeteria, Greg notes, "The guys in here look like they just got out of prison."

"I noticed."

"Just who you would want on your side in a fight. They're all down with me though, since they be throwing down in the kitchen."

Mel confirms with a nod.

Jackie announces lunchtime—an hour-and-a-half during training—and dismisses them on the spot. The group breaks up, including Mel and Greg. Mel decides to go take a spin around the area and bring his lunch back. He settles for a roast beef sandwich on wheat bread from Mr. Beef on Orleans and wastes no time returning. When he exits his car, the cutie that keeps holding his eyes captive is coming his way. His stomach drops like he was taking a dip on the American Eagle.

"Went and got you some take out, huh," she comments through her grin.

"Yeah...since we get an hour and a half for lunch, might as well make use of the time," he responds.

"So you're one of the new supervisors?"

"Yep. That's what they say."

"What's your name?"

"Melvin. Melvin Adams."

"Nice to meet you Melvin," she says with an extended hand. "I'm Deidra."

"Nice to meet you too, Deidra," he says, gripping her firm hand.

"Well, I'm not going to keep you," she proclaims walking away. "I'll talk to you later. Enjoy your lunch."

"You do the same," he says as he lets her hold his eyes with her confident smile and magnetic gaze all the way to her car. He finally looks away due to optic fatigue.

When they come back from lunch, the afternoon drags on at a dull, snail's pace as Jackie covers the company history and products. Their meals have settled to the bottom of their stomachs and feels like cement. The still air, coupled with the white, windowless walls, makes it the perfect setting for a coma. After about a two-hour yawnathon, Jackie informs everyone that that is it for the day and that Greg will start his presentation tomorrow. It is like getting snapped out of hypnosis. "First, I want everybody to gather their things that they'll be taking home and follow me to the conference room for ID pictures."

It's a little after three when Mel pulls out of the parking lot. If only everyday is as short.

Everything was happening so fast. Mel went from sleeping until his eyes wouldn't stay shut, with nothing to do during the day—except watch the clouds pass—to rising at dawn for his 9 to 5 and tending to church matters. It's only day two, and already he is spending more time away from home than in it. He isn't complaining, though. Today was a full shift. No early dismissal, although there were breaks every hour. From what he could see, Greg is a pretty good trainer. He didn't throw too many technicalities and rhetoric their way at once. However, Hair-weave's mouth was out of control. Thanks to her and all of her petty questions, the class is probably a half-day behind schedule. Greg couldn't even get through the presentation without her asking a question every five minutes. With every point he tried to make, she had a "dumb" question. Some say that there is no such thing as a stupid inquiry. They haven't sat in a training class with Sandra. Either she is trying too hard to make an impression (if there is an impression to be made), or she is as dense as a McDonald's chocolate shake. Greg was gracious enough to answer all of the queries she shot at him while the class was on the verge of napping during Sandra's training session.

Mel killed two hours after work before he heads to go to the board meeting at church. He really isn't looking forward to it. For the brief period that he was a Trustee, he never attended a meeting that was civilized. There was a lot of mud slinging. A couple of times, a few of the members were on the borderline of verbal assault and an all out brawl. This meeting promises to be a real pay-per-view, no-holds-barred prizefight, with the issues in the letter to be addressed. Although Mel is particular about turning the other cheek and prides himself on not losing it, he is ready to take a stand with and for his father, even if it means throwing down with the hypocritical viper clan.

When he walks through the door, the patriarch of the Bradford's is walking down the stairs. Trustee Joseph Bradford is a massive man with all of his wits, even in his old age. He must be about 95. His fortune was made in real estate and other businesses, and he's still as shrewd as a mob boss. He always wore a coat of dignity, which contrasted well with his nine-inch fangs. There is no mistaking: this man is somebody. Although his high-yellow complexion has faded like a 20-year-old coat of paint on a frame house in the Midwest, he is still bright like the morning star. He has snow-white, stringy hair that's as smooth as a perm. His handsome profile got him far with the ladies in his days. Word is he has illegitimate children by at least six different women. At one time, one of them used to attend the church, but that was way before Mel took notice. His eyelids sag over his intense, calculating, black pupils, giving the impression that his aim is still good. Mel is prepared to jump out of the way, in case he spits some venom his way.

"How are you Brother Adams?" he greets in a smooth baritone as he extends his massive hand.

"I'm good," he replies as he clasps his warm hand. Mel notes how unusual it is for a reptile to be warm and sweaty. "How about yourself?"

"Pretty good, thanks. It's good to have you back."

Why? Because he needs some fresh meat to bite into? "It's good to be back," he says with a smile as phony as the old man he's addressing. Jewelry from a street vendor in the ghetto is more authentic than this man and his family. As they descend the flight of stairs to the meeting room in the basement, Mel imagines himself putting his foot on his back and giving a hefty push, only to beg his pardon as he steps on him at the bottom. When Mel was appointed as a Trustee (at Joseph Bradford's urging) it marked the beginning of a series of daggers getting planted in his back. Somehow, Trustee Bradford's fingerprints were always on them.

Mel gave his testimony in Sunday school of how his mother beat him to the path of righteousness after he stole a Twix from the store. The lesson was focused on disciplining a child. A few people in the class didn't advocate corporal punishment, but Mel insisted that if his punishment wasn't physical, he would still be stealing, possibly killing. The story spread and people praised him for his stance. About a month later, Mel had the responsibility of tallying the Sunday collections. During the totaling process, a check was cashed in the office. As a result, he got a little confused and his figures were short $30, due to an inadvertent omission. Behind his back (of course), Trustee Bradford suggested that Mel still had sticky fingers. He reasoned that an accounting major shouldn't make mistakes like that. Although Mel was hurt by the suggestion, he refused to believe that Mr. Bradford said it. After all, he was Mel's biggest fan.

No sooner than the talk died down, another monetary incident occurred about a month later. It started when one of Mel's friends from his school came to church. Corey Anderson was a bona fide Black Gangster Disciple. They were in the same division, and seemed to end up in a lot of the same classes. While most of Corey's associates used to slap Mel across the head and terrorize him, Corey defended him. If Corey was around, Mel wasn't bothered. Of course, Mel let him copy his Economics (among other subjects) homework in the process. One day after church, Mel ran into him at Walgreen's on 75th and State. Corey asked him "You a church boy, ain't you?" Since he was already decked out in church attire, Mel confirmed his suspicions with the name and address of LOG. Then without an invitation, without verbally witnessing, Corey announced, "I'm coming to your church next Sunday." Mel didn't know whether to beg him not to or rejoice. Since he had just graduated, he didn't think that he would ever see Corey or any of the losers from high school again.

Sure enough, that Sunday he was in Sunday school before Mel arrived. Mel was surprised, because he seemed so out of place in a sanctuary. To say that he was thuggish was as understated as labeling Halle Berry fine. He wore a diamond stud earring in the right lobe and it seemed like he made a Samsonian covenant with God to never cut his buttered hair. His face was street hard and his outfit that day (actually everyday) was black: black baggy slacks, black suede bucks, black sport jacket, and a black button up shirt without a necktie. Obviously, he didn't have the luxury of a big, colorful wardrobe. Not all, but a few members (the Pharisees of the church—most of whom are in with the Bradford's) weren't exactly hiding their contempt for him. It was almost enough to drive Mel away. There's nothing like "church folks" that are so self-righteous, that they condemn anyone that doesn't "appear" to be prototypical Christians. That day, Mel stood up for him, although Corey seemed oblivious to the unspoken criticism when he walked the aisle and joined church as a candidate for baptism. Then-deacon Bradford hesitated, as if he didn't want to accept him as a candidate—like he wasn't clean enough to get in the water. Isn't the water for the unclean?

After service, he introduced him to everyone as his "friend" and invited him home for dinner. Corey was respectful and polite, even though he talked candidly in his broken English and street lingo about his dysfunctional family and gang life. He confessed that he was shot—which prompted him to seek an escape—and had seen others shot, but not so lucky. He admitted that he had never been to church and that he loved to drink and smoke weed. He also expressed his plans to leave that lifestyle behind in the near future. The family embraced him like their own. Mel was surprised how friendly his mother was to him, since she can be hard on young men (on him anyway). Before he left, she prayed a deliverance prayer with him and Pastor Adams anointed his head with oil.

The Sunday following his baptism, another Trustee (Brother Davis) was taking the offering for that Sunday to the bank, and he was robbed at gunpoint as he got out of his car. Corey was the prime suspect, although he was in service at the time. Mel was considered an accessory, because he had inside information. Never mind Melvin didn't even tell Corey that he was a Trustee. The Pharisees had them convicted and condemned to rot in hell. This time, Trustee Bradford didn't go behind his back. "It's very ironic that two monetary disasters happened within the two months that you were appointed," he insinuated. At the time, Mel was very reserved and respectful—even when the same respect wasn't shown toward him—but he was so livid that he almost lost his religion and Trustee Bradford almost lost a row of teeth. While he was expressing his suspicions, Mel was tuning him out as best he could. When he finished, Mel left the building and started spewing a few obscenities. From that point on, he hasn't forgiven Trustee Bradford.

No one was ever taken into custody, and Mel started wondering if one of the serpents in the church had something to do with it. He was surprised and relieved that Corey didn't know that people were accusing him of orchestrating the robbery. He actually never found out about it. A month later, Corey graduated from summer school and moved to Atlanta, because his life was in danger since he was leaving the gang. He has written a few times, and the last Melvin heard, he kicked his weed smoking and drinking habit (which he credited to the Lord), joined the choir of a Baptist Church a block from his home, got married and had two kids.

When he enters the room behind Trustee Bradford, he can see that the battle lines are drawn. His dad sits with the gavel in hand at the head of the three, long folding tables that are lined up, and Trustee Bradford takes a seat at the foot of the table (so he's facing Reverend Adams), where his clique is sitting. Reverend Adams smiles as if he has an ace up his sleeve when he sees Mel enter, and Mel returns the knowing grin. There are nine trustees present (seven that are bought off by the Bradford's and a mere two that have some integrity) and five deacons, including the three that are in training. The meeting opens with a short devotion, in which Mel leads in prayer. Reverend Adams brings the meeting underway with a pound of the gavel. The church clerk, Ms. Young, reads the minutes from the last meeting. After a few minor corrections, the financial secretary passes out the financial reports for the month. Mel notices that his father's salary is still the same $45,000 as when he left six years ago. Dad could make that in a quarter of the year working in the legal field. The musician that's on the power trip is making $25,000 a year. Many people would play for free and wouldn't fight to gain control over the universe. After a few minutes of nit-picking over the expenditures, they move on to old business. Deacon Lewis, who's sitting right across from Mel, lights into the Trustee board for dragging their feet on the addition of the church library.

"We brought this up four years ago, and we're still shucking and jiving about getting it done. What's the problem? Wasn't this approved a year and a half ago?"

Trustee Bradford attempts to answer: "We're still talking to the contractor about conforming to certain building codes. We can't just be throwing up additions to the building."

"That's a bunch of garbage," Deacon Lewis interjects. He's not that crazy about Trustee Bradford anyway. "Any contractor in the city could get the permits within days and have the library built within month's. Their job is to build, not talk about something for two years that can be resolved in a day."

"I want the library too, but things have to be done in order."

"It sure doesn't seem like you want the library. It seems like all you want to do is sit on the money that isn't even yours."

"It seems like you should be worried about getting your deacons out of training. How long have they been in training—four years? Don't tell me they're waiting for the library."

"I tell you that's not the issue."

"It needs to be."

"I would like to see the library before I go home to glory."

"I would like to see more ugly deacons before I go to glory."

"Why do you want to see more men?"

And they go on for about fifteen minutes, throwing the parliamentary procedures out of the window. They're supposed to raise their hands to be recognized to speak, but those two seem to be exempt when they get into it. Although they aren't raising their voices, the contents of their speech is the equivalent of profanity. After they jab themselves out, the board unanimously votes against the two loan requests from the members and moves to the juicy issue: what to do about the choir President, Brenda Sims, and the Minister of Music, Gene Fredricks, who wants to be the exalted over God. Bradford flunky Eric Smith motions that Brenda be dismissed and that the Presidency and Minister of Music be one consolidated position. Deacon Lewis suggests that Eric gets excommunicated for threatening Brenda, adding, "Since you're so interested in saving money, you can save a whooping $25,000 on that sophisticated director and get rid of a headache in the process."

"Since you're so adamant about women staying in their place, you all should practice what you preach," Bradford interjects, igniting a flurry of cutting remarks.

Pastor Adams even gets riled up and suggests that "You study the scriptures and consult the Lord before you talk about someone practicing what they preach." Needless to say, the vote is split in half and nothing is resolved. The President is still in office, and the Musician is still there to keep the drama going. For his wasted time and breath, Mel ends up with a migraine with Bradford written all over it.

"Does the system allow us to correct a balance?" Hair weave inquires.

"Yes, Sandra," Greg exclaims, after being interrupted for the twentieth time in the hour. "It does allow you to go behind someone and correct a balance. You would have to post a comment on the account, and a record will remain."

"Well it doesn't say it," she reasons as she can sense the class getting tired of her questioning every thing every minute.

"I didn't get specific," Greg justifies. "But then again, I didn't realize I was going to have you in the class."

The class chuckles at that remark, but Marcus guffaws, insulting Sandra. She cuts him a dirty glare and blurts, "Go back to high school, little boy."

It rolls off him as he continues to laugh for the next thirty seconds. When he gets the laughter out of his system, Greg announces that it's lunchtime.

Mel stops at the rest room and on the way out, he meets up with Greg, who's heading to the cafeteria. Today Mel was running late, so he didn't get a chance to bag a lunch. Since he's starving, today is a good day to try the company's food out. "Could I borrow five dollars from you?" Greg humbly requests as they walk down the stairs.

"Sure," Mel says as he digs his wallet out of his back pocket and hands a crisp bill to him.

"Thanks, man. I'll hook you up on payday," he promises. "I've been cutting it close with my finances ever since I had this accident."

"Don't worry about it," he urges. "I've been there, done that. I'll probably borrow it back from you sometime in the future."

"I hear you. Once I get paid from the lawsuit, I'm gonna be in the money like Lotto."

"Then you're going to buy the company," Mel suggests facetiously.

"Yeah, so I can fire a couple of people. I know I could just strangle Sandra," Greg says.

"Or put some duck tape over her mouth," Mel suggests. "At this rate, we'll get through training next year."

"I don't know why she feels the need to question every thing: '*Why do we have to go through that screen? Why does approval have to go through a different department? Why is the earth round? Why is air clear? Why am I here?*'" he mocks. "As if she's going to remember all of the answers to her tedious questions. A lot of it she'll learn from experience."

"I hear you," he seconds.

"Do you notice how she asks anyone in authority who will listen whether she'll become full-time? Like she needs confirmation from everyone."

"Yeah, I noticed. It tickles me."

"Another one that trips me out is Karen. I can pick up on her supercilious attitude towards me: A mere black man. She sits there in silence with a tight face throughout...dissecting everything I say...waiting for me to make a mistake—which I won't. And then when the manager of production comes in, she perks up and becomes real inquisitive—as if she can finally relate to someone. Like any white organization, you're going to run into those white subordinates and managers that will not respect you as an authoritative figure."

"You don't have to tell me," he says as they turn the corner leading to the cafeteria, coming face to face with Deidra. Mel locks eyes with her and asks, "How are you?"

"I'm fine. Thank you," she responds cheerfully, with all of her teeth showing. "Hi Greg," she greets, with a heap of rancor in her voice as her expression grows sour.

"Hi Deidra," Greg shoots back with mutual contempt.

"I'll talk to you later Melvin," she promises as she saunters off.

Mel turns to Greg with raised eyebrows, seeking the 411 without actually asking. Greg doesn't even look his way as he smirks, waiting for the question. "So," he says. "What's up with Deidra?"

"What can I say about Deidra," Greg chuckles. "Well, my grandmother says if I don't have anything nice to say about somebody, then zip those lips. My lips are zipped," he says as he renders his lips zipped and locked as he throws away the imaginary key.

"Oh," is all Mel can say.

"I'm sure you're asking why they weren't zipped when it came to other people. Let me put it this way, you'll find out about her: just don't find out the *hard* way—if you know what I mean."

Mel just nods as they enter the cafeteria. Today's menu includes fried fish with cole slaw and french fries or mashed potatoes; Lasagna with mixed vegetables; and a taco bar. They both settle on fish with fries. Mel follows him to a table where Marcus is sitting with three other guys that Mel hasn't met formally, but he has seen around the building. Greg greets them all by name, interrupting their discussion about the NBA playoffs. Reggie, a big burly dude with uneven, half-inch hair, spectacles, and a razor bumped face, works in MIS. Felix is a white Puerto Rican from the customer service department that looks like he was dressed by a first grader: wrinkled, navy-blue button up shirt without a tie, unironed Khaki paints and a pair of brown loafers. A little, soft-spoken man with a thick mustache—Mike—sits content. He's from the mailroom.

"My brother's name is Melvin," Marcus offers.

"He has a good name, then," Mel jokes as the fellows resume their debate, dragging Mel into.

"Who do you think is going to take it all this year, Melvin?" Mike queries in proper English.

Mel is a little hesitant in saying it because of the reaction he knows he's going to get, but he claims, "I like the Bulls, but the Knicks look good this year."

Mike, Marcus and Felix groan loudly as Reggie exclaims, "Yes. Another good evaluator of talent." Mel just laughs as the three Bulls' supporters go at Mel and Reggie.

"I got a joke," Felix announces.

"You might want to close your ears, Mel," Greg suggests. "Watch your mouth Felix...this is a man of God."

"It's a tame joke."

"None of your jokes are tame," Reggie insists.

"What does spaghetti and women have in common?"

They all hump their shoulders. "What do they have in common?" Mike asks.

"They both wiggle when you eat them."

Mel chuckles and shakes his head bashfully, although he isn't offended.

"And just how do you know this, Felix?" Greg interrogates.

"What can I say—I love Italian and I love pasta."

"I ain't been there...don't plan on going either," Marcus declares.

"I thought I smelled garlic," Greg jokes, adding, "Go brush 'em," as he fans with his hand in front of his face.

They all laugh as a short, conservative looking white guy joins them. "What's the joke, guys?" he inquires.

"You," Greg blurts under his breath as Felix repeats the joke to him.

As Mel finishes up the last of his fish, he hears Reggie claim, "That's your new supervisor."

Mel looks up to see the white dude (known as Brent Walsh) cutting him a disapproving once over. He can almost hear demons hissing. Mel says, "What's up" to acknowledge him. Brent reluctantly nods his head and changes the subject with the rest of the guys. Mel is glad to shoot his racist ego in the spot where there's supposed to be a heart. Mel silently chuckles at knowing *who* the enemy has decided to use.

When Mel walks in, the church is just finishing the offering, so he fills out his tithe envelope and walks it down to the finance office. He stopped at his parent's house to take a good, old fashion bath. Just before he enters the office, he doesn't see Donald with his hand on LaTonya's behind as they turn to go up the stairs. Donald is very married with two kids going on three at that very moment, and LaTonya is very under-aged at 15 for a man 28. Although he has 20/20 vision, that is a long, dim hallway. That may not have been Donald, since he hasn't seen him since he's been back.

He figures there's a testimony behind every tithe, and his $75 offering is no exception. Trustee Smith comments, "The Lord has been good to you this week" as he notices the amount. Indeed He has.

Yesterday he sold Bridgette and the last puppy for a total of $750. He's going to put down a deposit to get his gas turned back on, so he can take a decent bath at home again. It should be another week before he'll have the rest of the $1700 needed to do it.

Lorraine Kidd is in the office getting an explanation to the loan denial as Mel fills in the money order. She reasons that she tithes faithfully and that all she needs is $650 to catch up on her rent. Trustee Bradford counters that she has been here less than a year, and after a series of loans that haven't been paid back, they generally don't give out any more unless it's a dire emergency. As if a final notice to pay two month's worth of rent isn't dire. Lorraine brushes past Mel in calm disgust. She has two kids and a teenager to feed and no relatives in the city. It seems like some of those board members are missing a heart and the point of the Poor Saints Fund. It's not like she's a crack addict that squanders all of her finances to a bad habit. He recalls Trustee Smith's remark that her little brother, Harold (who she takes care of), got in trouble for fighting in school and that he's a reflection of the whole family. As if that determines a person's need. Mel realizes that Brother Smith is not too fond of Harold, because he's not in the same social class as he. His daughter's romantic association with him doesn't alleviate the animosity. Mel shakes his head as he tosses his offering in the basket and heads up to the front pew, spiritually charged and open to a good sermon that his father has been preparing for two weeks about being good stewards for Christ. The whole church should be convicted today.

When he gets to the top of the steps, he takes notice of one Rachel Bradford: a.k.a. the whore of LOG. At one point, Mel was almost intoxicated by her passion, but he didn't like the taste. My how things change. When he was acquainted with her, she was a pretty, petite thing. After high school, she became very fertile. It's amazing what four kids (by three different men) in a five-year period will do to the female body. She looks like an oil tanker, as she has a child hoisted on each arm with the oldest two hanging on each side of her skirt. When he acknowledges her and speaks, she responds with a dry "Hey"—as if he is the source of world hunger—and enters the sanctuary. He shakes his head and goes in the opposite direction as he enters also.

The two-week training flew by. Melvin set up his desk with all of the necessities, including a daily devotional calendar, a serenity prayer plaque, and a picture of Homey. His phone is functioning and to his delight, he has E-mail and an Instant Message feature on the computer. The spot is cozy. Monday, he met with his new team and had a brief introduction in which he fielded some of their concerns and experiences. He was happy to find out in the meeting that Greg was switched to his team. At least he had someone he could trust to guide him through some of the processes. Things felt good Monday. However, Tuesday was a different world. He found that outside of his little cubicle is Hades. He was on the front line for only four days, and he already longed for a vacation. Three observations of the department made being broke and living on the street seem like paradise: the power tripping supervisors, the complaining employees and the clashing of the two entities.

There are four supervisors (two females, a male, and a shemale). Excluding himself, all of them seem to be vying for the best position to kiss the manager's butt. The funny thing is that Paul—as he likes to be called—shows contempt for the brown nosers, who all happen to be white. They're a good illustration of outdated management styles. An intern could observe how not to manage a department by watching them.

The worst of the trio is Jack O'Connor: a case study in Theory X Management (People do not like work and try to get over, so managers have to keep them in check, which is what people like). Greg, who left his team because they couldn't get along (before Mel started, he was suspended for a week after they had a verbal run-in, in which he threatened to slap Jack), claims that "The Queen of the Pack wants to be an African Slave Driver." And he's right. Never, on any level, in any organization, has Mel seen as bad a case of the "Simon Says" Syndrome as Jack has. "Jackie" is oh so meticulous. With him, the script that's used has to be followed all the way down to the punctuation marks and voice inflection. It seems like he watches the phone monitor all day, making sure no one—out of all the abominable things to do—makes a personal call out. He's rigid about the rules. A young lady on the floor was calling to make sure her daughter was home, so he switched on over to her desk and ordered her to get off the personal call. It's amazing that he's managed to keep from getting his block knocked off for this long, but it is surely in his forecast. He acts like he's God. Mel wants to tell him "You're a first line manager Jackie...just a supervisor." He's typical of someone who hasn't been to school to study modern techniques on how to deal with human beings.

Jackie called himself sending Mel suggestive, silent signals with his eyes when he got out of training. Then he got up the nerve to ask open-ended questions that required a conversation to answer, but Mel slammed the door in his face with each query: What do you think of Spark so far? It's aiight; Do you know how to operate the phone system? Yeah (even though he didn't at the time); Do you want me to show you how to upgrade the system? Naw (he didn't bother telling him that he would rather get somebody else to do it). Mel was very abrupt with him, making it quite clear that there's a big risk that comes with saying the wrong thing to him. Now Jack seems indifferent towards him, which suits Mel just fine.

Teresa Knox, on the other hand, is just the opposite: A driver of the Human Relations Movement. She assumes that when management shows concern for the employees, they will respond with improved performances. While Mel feels strongly about that too, he noted that her performance is analogous to a B-Movie bimbo's theatrics to a sentimental moment. And she's probably too dense from sitting in the sun to realize it. From the way she says, "HI! HOW ARE YOU DOING" in perk overdrive, to her "What do you guys think about this (knowing that the decision is already made)" queries with pseudo-concern, her approach is too okiedoke and phony—even for a satire. She goes through all of the lip service, like she's reading the style from a script, but her dramatics indicate that she doesn't know what she's doing. Everyone feels that she doesn't give a rat's butt about what happens to the employees. As long as they play along with it, then she thinks that she's doing her job. Talk about reverse psychology. Ironically, she's the lesser of the three evils.

Karen is so sophisticated with her high level of education, that she is able to hide behind a little Maslowism and a veil of Theory Y, but Mel could see through the fog. She is a Frederick Taylor disciple with a racist genetic makeup. She believes that money is the biggest motivator, and before she actually knew what was up on the floor, she came in talking about incentive programs, as if people are willing to sell their soul. The way she sees it, she could get the Nation of Islam to make ape sounds and jump through hoops for the right price. What an arrogant, patronizing B-witch with a superiority complex. Mel could count on one hand the number of words they exchanged outside of the department: Hello and See Ya. He would have it no other way with her.

"Is there any chance I can get a new keyboard," the young woman known as Denise Hubbard queries. "The one that I have now is full of dirt, grime and old food. Some of the keys stick, too."

"Give me the serial number off of it and I'll tell the computer room to send another one up."

"Thank you much."

"You're welcome."

She has a point. It looks like somebody mistook his keyboard for a plate. He could actually stick a fork in it and come out with a meal. That was one of the only calm complaints he's gotten since he's been on the floor. Every chick up in here is somebody's mother, which to them is a license to gripe. They all have ugly babies and nasty attitudes. They sit up all day like hens, squawking, "BWAWK BWAWK" and bleating, "BA-A-A-A-A-A" about everything under the sun.

He prints the department reports out and collects them from the alternate printer. Yesterday, the usual printer started malfunctioning, so he asked Devita Harper—who's on his team—if there was an alternate printer. Her reply: "You're a supervisor, so you should know." He couldn't believe she was serious, even after she walked away.

As he passes them out to his team, he notices that a group of women are gathered together, reading over a menu and discussing lunch. All of them are extremely obese. The scene reminds him of the pigpen in a state fair. Their lunch is serious business. They spend at least eight dollars a day on fast food. It seems like that's all they work—or come to work—for: EAT EAT EAT. Life is a smorgasbord to them. Everyday they place a large order for grease and calories. And spend thirty minutes getting it together. But Mel isn't the fool to try to come in between them and their lunch. Woe unto him if he did.

They serve as a reminder of his early lunch break for today, so he gathers his sandwich and newspaper and heads for the cafeteria. He decides to sit off in the corner to himself to enjoy his meal and read. Unfortunately, he's far from peace and quiet. Within earshot is one of the many female cliques of the company. This one is the know-it-all group and they're discussing the gospel of astrology and how it figures into finding their soul mates. It tickles Mel for a moment, but then it starts getting absurd. They're negatively stereotyping people based on their "sign": The Taurus man is stubborn and a terrible lover; Libra men are freaks; Sagitarians are just plain stupid and don't have a clue. When Mel hears that he is a weird MF—among other things—he gets up and finishes reading in his car, where he is tempted to drive off.

Chapter 11

When Mel starts the car, the music from 106 JAMS comes blasting out of the speakers, prompting him to almost self-eject through the roof. David had the volume all the way up. One day Mel is going to remember to turn it down before he starts the ignition. He takes a deep sniff and smells the remnants of reefer. He definitely has to remember to strangle David. It's hot and Mel is running late. Today is picture day and he manages to make up the time on Lake Shore Drive. He reaches his expressway exit on Washington at 8:57. His scheduled time is in three minutes. Despite the congested traffic, he's in good spirits. The "Commissioned" CD has a soothing affect like no other CD he owns. Combined with the boost from the hot Bigelow Raspberry Royale tea, he feels totally edified and ready for the day. He runs the red light and pulls into the parking lot with one minute to spare. A touch of perspiration forms under his arms and in the crease of his back during the ride. He gathers his briefcase and newspaper and jogs to the building across the street, adding to the sweat. The cool air slaps at him when he gets in as he dashes up the stairs to the third floor. There is no time to wait for the slowest elevator in the world. When he makes it to the department, the group that he is going with is waiting for the elevator. He dumps his stuff, stops in the men's room to refresh and release the tea, and runs back downstairs to the conference room, where the photographer is. He breathes a sigh of relief as he walks in just behind the last person: Deidra.

"Cutting it close," she claims jokingly.

"You noticed," is all he can manage as he goes after his breath.

"Well, you're looking good," she says as she straightens his silk tie with the violet flamingo on it.

"Thanks. Thanks a lot. You look nice too," he compliments. She's wearing a black and white checkered skirt and matching collarless jacket, with a white silk blouse. She actually looks better from behind, because the skirt is clinging to her like a nursing baby possesses a full breast.

The whole scene reminds him of picture day from grammar school. Everybody has on their professional best and is groomed to perfection. Not a crooked tie; not one hair out of place. He's wearing a pair of gray slacks, a black blazer (that's probably why he was burning up), and a white shirt. Deidra's outfit actually compliments his, making them look like a stylish couple. It's about twenty specialists, trainers, and supervisors that handled the eastern region. The stodgy white photographer with the big beard lines them up. Of course, he directs Mel and the other men in the back, and as the devil would have it, Deidra is directly in front of him. The photographer commands, "Say cheese", but Mel isn't planning to smile for the picture. With amorous intent, Deidra gently presses her butt in his crotch just before he snaps the shot. He's going to be a big, sunny grin on the photo. As she walks off, she turns around and gives him a sensual glance, like he's going to be her next meal, and purrs, "Cheese" as she licks her lips. Mel is left standing there with a shameful erection and a taste for hot, toasted buns. He shakes his head and chuckles, pleading, "Lord have mercy" as he goes to the bathroom—before somebody spots the growth in his pants. He heads for the same stall he prayed in when he interviewed and supplicates to shrink the hard-on and quench the desire.

He thinks that it's a good thing that she is out of sight, because it means that she isn't on his dirty mind. That thought comes too soon when he sits in his cubicle and switches on his computer. The E-mail prompt sounds when he signs on, and of course it's a message from Seduction herself. She wants to know if he can give her a ride home, since her car is in the shop and he is getting off late, too. If only life is as simple as yes and no; right or wrong.

On one hand, he wants to go behind closed doors and act on every carnal desire he's ever had and turn into an animal one good time with her...and then repent and walk the celibate walk. He knows it can happen if he goes with her flow and gives her a ride. On the other hand, he wants to do the righteous thing, please God and not even flirt with temptation. Giving her a ride will be like walking through a den of hungry lions wearing a sirloin steak suit. At the same time, it wouldn't be the "Christian thing" to let her catch the bus home at night, just because he has an appetite for fornication.

He wrestled with the issues all morning and into lunch, then he bumped into Deidra. He submitted when she body slammed him a couple of times with her charm and pinned him with her sex appeal. "Yeah, I can give you a ride," is what he heard himself saying when she got up close to him and peered into his eyes. He'll play Gospel music all the way home and maybe witness to and bombard her with Jesus. That is the plan, and he prays that he can remain focused.

The rest of the day, he works on pins and needles. His body is simmering, but the Spirit is uneasy. When the twelve-hour day finally ends, the nervous energy makes him forget about how long he was up and how hard his body worked the last two days. She sends him an Instant Message just before he cuts off his computer, informing him that she will be waiting downstairs. He shuts the phone system down, turns the answering system on, and strolls through the department to shut off any computers that are left on. After he packs his things at a reluctant pace, he goes to his stall and prays, ending it with "Give me the strength."

When he turns the corner on the first floor, she is looking out of the window, with her rear facing him and her behind whispering enticing ideas to him, assuring, "One hit won't hurt". She's holding her jacket across her arm and the black pantyhose that went well with the black pumps she was wearing earlier have been shed. He makes it to her undetected and touches her shoulder. She jumps a little as she greets him with a "Hey there," as they proceed to the car.

"Was today long, or what," he questions nervously.

"Yeah. These twelve-hour days feel like whole weeks at a time. I've been in these high heels all day, and when I get home, I'm going to soak these worn out feet. I'm still not used to them."

"I hear you."

"So how do you like it so far, Melvin?"

"Well, so far it's okay. I can't complain at all. I mean, it is paying the bills, you know."

"Yeah, I know what you mean. That's what I work for: to pay bills."

He senses the plot unfolding like a soap opera. The jitters are overwhelming him as he looks around for hidden cameras and camped out, nosy girlfriends. When he lets her in, the flesh perks up, and he forgets all about his Gospel music. Instead, he turns to WGCI, who are playing the dating game. A lady with four kids is on there, grilling some seemingly expectant brother, going down a checklist of superficial high expectations: weight: 160; complexion: dark; height: six feet; occupation: bus driver and education student. He answers wrong on every question except the height. She's looking for a buffed, light skinned, businessman. He retorts she "needs to look for a baby-sitter." They both get a good laugh as Mel relaxes a little.

"Damn, she had a lot of nerves. As if she can be picky with all them kids. She'll be lucky if she can get a short, Jamaican garbage-man. Dumb hoe."

Mel giggles uncomfortably at the profanity, but he feels she has a point.

"Did you ever have to go through complexion discrimination," she fishes.

"Oh yeah. There was a time when dark skin wasn't in—and it wasn't that long ago. There are still some color shy women out here, but it's not as bad—depending on how you perceive yourself. To me, it's just as bad for a person to get caught up in dark skin. It almost seems like a fad. What about what's under the dark skin? What about what's in here," he ponders, patting his chest just over the heart.

"I heard that. I like all complexions of black men."

Mel nods as he plays with the incriminating, suggestive statement in his head.

She pries all the way to her house. It is well scripted: *Do you have a girlfriend? What do you do for fun? Do you get out a lot? Are you going to get married?* It seems like she's going through the song and dance just as a formality. He doesn't have the impression that she really cares about him as a person or even wants to get to know him. She seems to be on a mission to get him in the sack. She is as scheming as a club brother that hasn't had none since last weekend's one night stand. He pulls up to her house and puts the gears in neutral. She continues to romance and interrogate him with the super slickness (so she thinks), as she leans over and gently slides her hand over his. "Never In My Life" by Cherrelle comes on.

"It sure is a nice night. It reminds me of the moonlight on the beach of Jamaica. Have you ever been to the Caribbean?" she asks as her legs inch open.

"I've never been off the continent. Me and my ex-fiancée were supposed to be going on a cruise for our honeymoon, but of course the breakup killed all of that," he says gingerly.

She reclines the seat back and turns on her side so she's facing him. "Do you like kids," she queries boldly.

"Kids? Yeah I like 'em. Why do you ask," he questions, a little puzzled by her curiosity.

"I was just wondering. Do you want to have any?"

He swallows and looks over at her. Her eyes are glazed with liquid lust, but the small talk is confusing him, so he gets a little goofy to try to quench her fire and strategy a little. "Well, since I'm a man, and men can't give birth, I haven't given it much thought."

"You know what I mean," she says as she leans close enough for him to feel her soothing, warm breath.

He tenses up and folds under the subtle wheedling. "Yeah. I want to have kids...five of 'em: three boys and two girls. What about you?" he asks in a hushed tone as he faces her.

"Um hm," she says, nodding as she traps him with her seemingly crossed eyes. She places her hand on the inside of his thigh and gently runs it up, then down and all the way up to his petrified extension. He's spellbound, while she's cocked and aimed at his mouth. In quick slow-motion, she clutches him down low, leans forward until their lips barely touch, and launches her tongue into his mouth—exploring his dental work and voice box. With the surety that it's safe, she pulls out and crawls on top of him like an octopus (no pun intended) on a crab. He goes over her waist and under her skirt with his hands. She's already wet and—to his surprise—pantyless, as she gyrates and grinds her hips over his, provoking him to palm her bare buns. That brings him pleasure, but then she goes to work on his mouth again. Unfortunately for her, tongue kissing isn't the way to his heart or his appetite. Her tongue jolts the Spirit awake and douses the fire in his flesh.

"Wait a minute," he says desperately as he turns his head away from her jaws.

She persists.

He presses her out and into the passenger's seat. "I can't do this," he says, catching his breath.

She frowns up at him in frustration and asks, "What do you mean you can't do this?"

"I just can't. It's not right and I can't go through with it," he says, looking down and shaking his head, as he feels divine eyes watching him.

For a long moment, she stares at him without saying a word with her mouth, but cursing him with her eyes.

He's ashamed, but feels justified in pulling back, as he explains, "I made a promise to the Lord that I would walk in righteousness and that I would stop fornicating. I asked him to bring me a wife and I promised Him obedience. I want to do this—I really do—but I can't go against my Father. I'm sorry Deidra."

Deidra sits speechless, staring at him with her mouth resting in her lap.

"Please don't take it personally. It has nothing to do with you. This is between me and God."

She turns her head and rests her chin on her shoulder as she glares at nothing outside of the passenger's side window. After a sarcastic chuckle, she collects her things and exits without a word. "Affair" goes off, to complete a double dose of Cherrelle, his favorite female vocalist. He watches her all the way to her door. She doesn't look back once. When she gets in he looks up, says, "Thank You" and pulls off.

Mel got about 20 minutes of sleep last night. Vernita called him and they stayed on the phone for a good two hours. She briefly distracted him from the anxiety of the near hit. Her choir is going to be in concert in two weeks and she let him know in advance. After wrestling with the unbeatable solicitude, he dozed off at about six-thirty. Never would he have imagined that he would get that close with a woman with sensuality flowing through her veins and resist. He didn't think it was possible. He's almost ashamed to tell it. The experience proved one point: the conviction of the Holy Spirit is stronger than a rock hard penis and an opportunity to sin. He couldn't even masturbate last night. When he gets to his desk, he's going to send Deidra an Email, apologizing and inviting her to lunch. He hopes that maybe they could get to know each other better, and who knows.

Despite an empty caffeine tank, he walks in alert and preoccupied. Tracy, the security guard, greets him with a smile wider than the horizons. "Good morning, Melvin."

"Good morning. How you doing?"

"Just fine."

"Great," he says, proceeding to the elevator.

He silently prays that he doesn't run into Deidra before he has his Raspberry tea. He arrived early to beat her here, but he saw her car in the lot, which indicates that she may have the same idea. When he gets off the elevator, he thanks God that she isn't around. After unloading his things, he heads to the bathroom and sends up another prayer, then he sets out to the cafeteria. When the elevator arrives, a feminine sounding man from the order department that he doesn't know greets him by name, and he could only give a generic response. He thinks it is somewhat odd. When the doors open to the second floor, Deidra is standing there prating with three of her giggling, attentive girlfriends. It catches him off guard when he exits and they all look curiously at him. Deidra plays like she doesn't see him, and doesn't respond to his greeting. He keeps stepping and he could hear her speaking in a "listen up" tone as the doors close behind him. He fills a cup with hot water for his tea, and buys a bag of chips to go with it.

Karen Green speaks to him in a cheery voice on his way back up. "Good morning, Melvin."

She never really went out of her way to speak to him. He glances at the several young ladies from different departments that occupy the table with her, as he returns the greeting. "Good morning. How are you today?"

"Fine, and you?"

"I'm doing good."

"That's nice to hear," she says through a cat-like grin.

They pause for an uncomfortable, speechless moment, before he says, "Okay, I'll see you upstairs," as he gets back in stride to his desk.

He starts pondering whether he should send the letter or not. Maybe he should give her a chance to cool off and evaluate the situation. He replays the whole incident, weighing if his actions were offensive—realizing that her feelings and pride may have been hurt. That wasn't his purpose. He felt he handled it as best he could, but maybe it wasn't good enough. Perhaps he should've let her catch the bus, making up a place to go in the opposite direction. Sinning to resist sinning wasn't the answer though, so his conscience is justified.

When he makes it to his desk, he switches on his computer, prepares his tea, and unloads his Bible from his briefcase, onto his desk. He decides to put a scripture in the note. After getting things settled, he starts on the letter, since his official starting time is still 30 minutes away. "Dear Deidra" is as far as he can get at the moment, so he opens his Bible to the King Solomon wisdom books (since his practical instructions can stimulate even the worldly minds). As he skims through

Ecclesiastes, he feels someone standing in his cubicle. When he turns around, Geraldin—one of his team members—is standing right on him, with a big, guilty grin on her face. "Let me guess: you need to take a day off?"

"You got it. You must be psychic," she says, handing him the request form.

He scans over and signs it. She has a doctor's appointment, not that it mattered, since she has most of her vacation and personal days, and no one else is off that day. Her eyes dart from the computer screen when he turns around to hand it to her. "Here you go," he says, a little hesitant.

"Thanks," she says, rushing her peculiar air out.

Before he can turn around, one of the older, outspoken women in the department comes in and takes a seat.

"How are you, Janet?"

"I'm fine," she says abruptly as she gapes directly in his face, with her brow wrinkled.

He pauses, waiting for her to state her case, but she just continues to stare through her thick glasses. He hopes she doesn't start tripping. It's not even his starting time. "How can I help you, Janet?"

"Melvin," she says and hesitates. "Are you gay?"

His eyebrows touch his hairline. "What?"

"I was thinking about introducing you to my niece, but I want to know if you're gay, so that nobody will be embarrassed."

He is already embarrassed. And insulted. And shocked. And tickled. And ready to throw her out of his cube for an ignorant, personal question like that. "Hell no. Where did that question come from," he asks, with forced meekness.

"I told you I want to intro..."

"I know what you told me, but I want to know where it came from," he cuts in as his voice rises slightly.

"Somebody suggested it," she offers, a little startled by his forceful demeanor.

"Somebody suggested...give me a name," he demands, although he already has an idea.

"Deidra," she drops. "She said she ain't never seen a man turn her away, and that you kiss like a corpse, but you didn't hear it from me," she says as she dismisses herself.

The statements echo in his head. "Gay" and "kisses like a corpse" bounce around in his skull. His sexuality could be defended easily with a definitive HELL NO, but his kissing flaw is incriminating. Never has he considered sodomy. Oral sex is something that he considered briefly. Three women at a time was a one-time wet dream. He is definitely conservative when it comes to sex, although he feels that he could satisfy most women. It's a matter of preference and opinion. If there's one thing that he's guilty of, it's being a poor kisser. He couldn't argue that fact, based on the poll of two. If it was a capital offense, he would have been executed seven years ago. Sometimes he thinks that death would've been better than having his first love tactlessly tell him that.

Rachel Bradford was two years younger, but she was a generation faster. Word was she was going out with 25-year-old men when she was only 15. Just after he graduated from high school, they started going together—or so he thought. He found out later that she wasn't claiming him and that she was "going with" a couple of other guys—that he knew of. He took her out one evening that summer. Neither her parents nor brother weren't home that night, and he was thrilled to be alone with her. He small talked her to death as the radio played real low. After he ran out of conversation, he got the nerve to ask her for a kiss. She said, "It's about time" and they embraced and locked mouths. From what he heard, he was supposed to stick his tongue down her throat, so he did. He didn't find it particularly arousing—and neither did she. While he was swapping spit, he was wondering what his mother was doing, what was on TV, what classes he would take in the fall, and what he was going to do with his graduation money—among other things. It went on for about ten minutes, until she finally pushed him away and told him "You can't kiss." Time stood still. He was speechless, but he managed to ask, "Can you teach me?" She got raw and told him to go to kissing school and come back to her next year after he graduated. He had never been hit in the face with a brick before, but at that time he knew what it felt like to have a ton of them dropped on him at once. At the moment, he feels like every wheel of a 100-car freight train just ran over him.

He's had kissing inhibitions ever since that episode. For a long time, he thought that it would keep him out of the dating game. Then he met Memory (after his fling with Traci). She was so open when they first met, confiding that she didn't know how to kiss (and she couldn't).

That's when he knew—or thought—he found his soul mate. And that's why it's so hard to get over her.

He closes his Bible and clicks out of the letter with her name on it. A nauseous feeling consumes him, so he puts the tea to the side. Everybody's full-moon behavior makes sense to him now, as he scans the department on the sly to see if he's being watched. How could she go so low? He's hurt, but he's hotter, and decides to address her to see what's behind the madness. When he turns the corner to her department, she's talking to a different set of giggling females. He plays it off as he gets closer, because a scene is not what he's looking for or what he wants to give them. They spot him and do a B-movie routine by pretending that the discussion is about something else, as they get quiet and one of them interjects, "Yeah girl, I can't wait for the weekend, either." When he passes by without eye contact and gets a few feet away, he hears them explode with laughter. Now the question is how soon before the whole company knows.

He retreats to the bathroom to meditate, but it doesn't do anything for him. He needs to have a serious talk—oral, audible talk—with Jesus: the kind that people label as crazy. Since he doesn't want to share his business with everybody, and he doesn't want to add insane to the list of tags, he decides to go to his desk and wait for lunch. Paranoia and anxiety are a terrible mix—probably the drug equivalent of Cocaine and Heroin taken together. It takes a whole month for his lunch break to come, and he manages to get nothing done in that time. He fiddles with papers to perpetrate activity. He hasn't been up at all since sitting, not even to go to the bathroom for a much needed bladder break. Eleven o'clock arrives and he treks to the cafeteria for his morning break, and who would be in there, with a group of guys? Deidra, of course. Is she Omnipresent or is she just following him around like a schrilling shadow, to torment him? They're yucking it up and overtly look in his direction. Even Brent, the short, haughty white boy is feeding on his dirt. Now he's having trouble simultaneously standing and breathing as he gets to the pop machine.

Fortunately, he makes it out unassisted without falling or suffocating, and making a bigger fool of himself. The pain peaks as he presses the up button. Although his department is only a floor up, his legs feel rubbery. Tears well up in his eyes and his composure drains out. When the doors to the elevator open, he silently thanks God that no one is on there. He can only imagine how demolished his face looks. If he looks half as bad as he feels, his countenance is a titanic shipwreck. When the doors open to his floor, he stays on and presses the first floor. Now is a good time for lunch. It's scheduled two hours from now, but he wouldn't be able to get anything done. He brushes past some white, marketing guys without looking up and wanders out the door.

It's gloomy outside, mirroring his insides. The clouds haven't released the rain, and it's a miracle the tears haven't fallen from his eyelids. His body lets him know tired he is when he makes it to the car, and he can't wait to lay back. He notices his hands trembling as he sticks the key in. With dire relief, he falls into the bucket seat, turns on the ignition and cracks the window.

He wants to die—or drive off and never come back, but he remembers he has too many important things at his desk. He also remembers that he left his phone on Ready, but he doesn't care. Maybe the big bosses will find that he's on an early lunch with his phone unattended and fire him. At least he would be able to go home and sleep. And if God is in a gracious, giving mood, he won't wake up.

He reclines until he's as lateral as he can get, and closes his eyes so the lids can absorb the moisture. Then he asks, "Why" as he sniffles. "I tried to be obedient—I *was* obedient. Why do I have to get hurt like this?" He doesn't expect an audible answer, because he's not finished venting, and he knows God knows. He continues: "I don't regret taking a stand for you, Lord...You took a stand for me. Right now I just want to hurt her—I want her to suffer in the worse way, but I know this feeling isn't of You." He pauses as he gets choked up. "Lord, I know that I'm not going to feel this way for long; I know I won't be bitter forever. I've been this way before, but it's still hard to handle. I need you to give me the strength, because I don't think I can go back in there. Lord, they're laughing at me. I don't even know if I want to live anymore. I know Your will is perfect, but life doesn't feel good to me. Forgive me for taking it for granted right now, because I know there are others who are in much worse shape and are still praising You, but I feel bad and I want to come home...if You can put it in Your will."

He pauses as he tries to gather as many thoughts as possible, grouping them into emotional categories. He concentrates on his anger and the urge to get even: "She's a cold blooded tramp in need of a good butt kicking," he says with a bitter pause, hating that he has to bite his tongue. He wants to use stronger, dirtier adjectives. He wants to swear; he wants to cuss like a man that's justified by pain and rage. But he's not that crazy, realizing that God is to be revered, even at a time like this. If he uses language like that, it wouldn't be in his talk with Jesus. "I just want you to let me see her suffer, even if it's not at my hands. I want her to come crawling back to me. I want the same thing to happen to her, but worse. If I can't get her back myself, please allow me to see her downfall, my Lord. Just let me be in a position to say 'now you know how it feels'. Put her at my mercy, Lord."

He dwells on his ill feelings for a while longer and switches to self-pity: "Was I created to be alone? I don't want to be alone. All I want is one good woman. Just one. She doesn't have to be perfect, just perfect for me and pleasing to my eyes. Lord, I don't want to be single out here. I don't want to be out here dating. It's not good for me. Too much temptation. Too many nice looking women. Do I have to wait until I'm elderly?"

He ponders that last question that seemed to demand an answer of "No", realizing that he's not in a position to demand anything. Then he switches to doubt, with a touch of resolve to give up: "I don't know about these women. They're just so difficult. They make things so hard on me and the other decent men. I don't even know if it would be good for me to get married. It's probably just a big headache. Is that what you're trying to tell me?" He contemplates that query and adds, "I hope not, because I like sex too much, however, not more than I like you. Maybe what I want is not what I need or what's in Your will. Should I cross over? These black women have too much attitude. Their favorite retort is *'black men just can't handle a strong woman.'* Why do they equate strength to a big blabbermouth and a nasty attitude? Always ready to fight and unwilling to ever submit. Everything is a power struggle with them. Lord, I don't want a slave that can't think for herself, but I don't want someone that's going to fight for control all of the time. Do I have to act like a chauvinist fool to get that? Women seem to respond better when men treat them like crap. But You know that's not me, God. And You know I'm over-generalizing based on my mood. If it's meant for me to be single, let my life and ministry go by quick."

He's never felt this frustrated and helpless. Actually, the break up with Amnesia comes awfully close. The tears are gone and the tension eases a bit as he lets out a deep breath. He checks the clock, realizing that he's been out here for 30 minutes. It's hard for him to imagine that some people can babble all day, because his mouth is tired of going on and on. Now he's ready to listen, but a voice doesn't echo from the sky. The line isn't like that, so he switches the radio on. But he realizes that it's not going to come from the airwaves, so he clicks it off in the same motion. His Bible, books and calendars are either at home or on his desk, and he's not ready to go back up yet. There's absolutely nothing to read in the car, except a Rules of the Road, a couple of maintenance bills, and the city sticker on the windshield. His thoughts are tired of flowing around in his head and flying out of his mouth. He needs outside stimulation; a fresh sound. Without even thinking, he pushes in the taped broadcast of Thursday Night Inspirations of WKKC from last week. He hasn't heard the whole thing and listened to the first side this morning. Maybe it was his mood, but it sounded mediocre. "Speak to My Heart" by Donnie McClurkin starts in the middle and his stress level immediately drops a notch. He doesn't say a word while the song is playing, as the words saturate his soul. The anger is still lingering, but it's not as intense.

"Hold On Old Soldier" by The Mississippi Mass Choir comes on, giving him another dose of comfort from the Spirit. His heart is still sore, but the lyrics are soothing to his psyche—moving his feet to tap to the beat. The sick feeling in his stomach fades like a gas vapor and the tightness in his throat loosens like a tooth on the receiving end of an upper cut.

He's getting his answers. Although he still has an appetite for revenge, the Spirit is using the melody and the message to spoil it. Now he starts to feel compassion for her, not just because God is not going to let her get away with it (there's nothing like a whooping from the Heavenly Father), but because she's lost. She's miserable. She's the type of person that has to hurt people to feel better. Just a slave to her image—unable to handle peer pressure. It's a shame that her pride won't let her admit that she's wrong...that she's vulnerable. "I'm sorry Lord. I'll let it go, and I repent of the things I said about her. I need you to help me though, because it's hard not to focus on the gaping wound that she left, but I don't want to see her through bitter eyes," he says in response to His encouragement, as "It's Okay" by the Winans starts playing. His eyes well up again, this time with tears of joy. Of course they don't fall. By the time the tape gets to the last song, "Trouble Don't Last" by Reverend Timothy Wright and the Chicago Interdenominational

Mass Choir, he's smiling and singing along with it and shouting Hallelujah. It's 12:30 when the tape stops.

On cue from the hunger pangs, he starts the car and heads for the greasy spoon in Greek Town that makes the best grilled ham and cheese sandwich in the area. Fifteen minutes is all it takes him to get there and back, and to inhale the sandwich, fries and pop. Before he gets out, he addresses the Lord: "My promise to try to stay focused on You is still on, despite this circumstance and what I said and felt earlier. I'm committed to you for better or for worse in my life. Thank You for listening to me and loving me enough to answer me when you didn't have to. Thank you Jesus for being my friend." With that, he saunters proudly back to work, with the last song still ringing in his heart.

A touch of nervous energy is in the pit of his belly, but the Spirit gives him the courage to press on. The wound is still fresh, but the Comforter has him sedated like a lunatic in an insane asylum. He walks into the department with his head up, chest out, smile spread, and eyes sparkling, as if he was complimented instead of slandered. The phone is signed off at his desk and a post-it note with "SEE ME ASAP!!" from Claretha is strategically placed on his computer screen, so he would be sure to see it. She's typing away on her system when he walks into her cubicle. Without looking up, she announces, "I need you to sign this benefit form over here."

He was expecting a warning of some sort. "I forgot to sign it," he says as he steps in. "Now that ain't right. I've got to have my benefits, don't I?"

"You better believe it," she says as she hands it to him, still keeping her eyes focused on the screen.

"Thanks," he says as he endorses it and starts out.

"Wait a minute," she calls out. "Have a seat."

He figures this is where the warning comes in at.

"I turned your phone off about thirty minutes ago," she says in a confidential tone. "You know you have to be careful not to leave it unmanned."

"I know. That was my mistake. I had to step out," he reasons.

"Don't worry about it. I understand. It's just that the big man doesn't always understand."

Mel just nods.

"And listen, don't let these silly girls get to you. They don't know anything about a real man. And the ring leader—your good friend, Deidra—thinks her pussy is made of gold, so to turn her down is an insult to her."

Mel's eyes get bigger. He's surprised that the talk got this far and that she's siding with him.

"I saw you out there praying. That was the right thing to do, because she's just trying to put you on the spot in front of all of her immature girlfriends. Don't let her provoke you. Just ignore her and let the Lord deal with her, because you know He will."

Mel smiles and nods.

"That's all I wanted to say to you, because I know that it was upsetting. Just stay strong and keep your head up."

"Thanks a lot, Claretha. I really appreciate it," he says with total gratitude and humility.

"Hey, you're always welcome," she says with a wink and a smile.

It's good to know that everyone in the company isn't an advocate of Deidra's—the devil's—tactics. At least he knows that somebody stands behind him and doesn't glorify that type of ignorance. Now he knows he can make it through the day. This calls for another prayer of thanksgiving.

When he gets in the bathroom, Greg is brushing his hair in the mirror. "What up, Mel?"

"Nothing much," he says as he heads to the stall.

"Yo...whatever you do, don't compromise your religious convictions for Deidra."

He comes out. "You heard about it, huh?"

"Yeah, I heard, but I know she's tripping. That girl makes me sick. She thinks that she can get have her way with every man she meets, like she's all of that. She's just mad because you're stronger than that and you have a righteous foundation that can't be easily corrupted. Talking about *'he must be gay, because I ain't never seen no man turn it down before.'* I asked her 'are you sure the stench of the decaying corpses in the closet between your legs didn't scare him away?'"

"You asked her that?" he questions with a laugh.

"You better believe I did. I don't bite my tongue. I got called a stupid-ass, dickless bastard, but I turned the little backbiting games she plays around on her, because she tried it on me."

"Did she? What happened?" Mel questions with astonishment.

"We went out a couple of times a few years ago and I saw that she wasn't about nothing, so I told her to hit the road—after we did a few things. She couldn't handle that, and started calling me all kinds of faggots, but I didn't sweat her, because I knew I wasn't the only one."

"Is that right?"

"Man, she's probably spreading STD's faster than rumors. If you would've hit that, your health would've been in worse shape than your rep is now. I mean everybody except her little clique, knows that she's just talking shit...excuse my French. Don't worry about her man. Just play her off and that'll get on her nerves more than anything."

Mel just shakes his head at the revelations. "Thanks man."

"Don't mention it. By the way," he starts as he reaches into his pocket. "Thanks a lot," he says, handing him the ten dollar bill that he owes him.

"Must be my lucky day," Mel suggests as they leave out.

Mel forgets to pray. When he gets to his desk, his eyes are drawn to the calendar. The scripture is taken from James one, the second through the fourth verses: ***"My brethren, count it all joy when ye fall into divers temptations; Knowing this, that the trying of your faith worketh patience. But let patience have her perfect work, that ye may be perfect and entire, wanting nothing."*** Mel just looks to the sky and smiles even wider.

Chapter 12

The notation of the three panel interviews grabs Mel by the shirt collar and causes his belly to churn when he arrives at his desk. He's ten minutes late and two meals behind, since he crashed on an empty stomach last night, only to oversleep and rush out without as much as a Corn Flake. He dumps his things and grabs his pad and questionnaire as he rushes to the conference room. "Yo. You gotta put in a good word for the babe in there now," Greg says, stopping him. "She is *fine.*"

"Does she have any skills, though?" Mel questions.

"It doesn't matter. She could be my wife to be. Hook me up."

Mel shakes his head and promises, "I'll see what I can do," as he walks off.

When he opens the door, Jack and Teresa are casually chatting with the applicant. Greg wasn't lying. The young lady—Carmen Wilkins—is almost a splitting image of Chanté Moore. And Mel is in love with Chanté Moore. He recalls seeing her on Box-Talk giving honor to God. A fine woman who loves the Lord is a gem. It is his wet dream to meet her. Carmen will have to do.

"Well, I guess we can begin now," Teresa announces.

"Sorry I'm late. I'm Melvin Adams," he says, extending his hand.

She stands up and grips his hand. "Carmen Wilkins," she proclaims.

"Has anyone ever told you that you look just like Chanté Moore," Mel questions.

"All the time," she claims with a laugh.

"Can you sing like her?" Mel asks facetiously.

"Why did I know that was going to be your next question," she queries. "As a matter of fact, I sing alto in my church choir."

"Really. Of course Chanté got her start in the church choir," he points out as Jack and Teresa sit clueless. "Chanté Moore is an R & B singer with the nicest voice," he explains to them.

"Oh, that's nice," Teresa adds. "What church do you attend?"

"New Life Baptist."

"Is that right? Isn't that Reverend Maxwell," Mel asks.

"Yep. That's him."

"He and my father are good friends. They grew up together...Reverend Adams, the pastor of..."

"Love Of God," she interjects. "We fellowship with them every year. Reverend Adams is your father?"

"Sure is."

"He's a powerful speaker. I love the way he brings the message. What a small world," she claims.

"Indeed it is," Mel says.

She just unwittingly earned his recommendation for the position. Coupled with her attractive demeanor and appearance, she has his vote even before the interview begins. Teresa asks most of the questions and seems to connect with her. The few questions Mel poses are just formalities. Jack seems to be more critical of her and her answers. He must be operating on an empty stomach, too. Her resume is very impressive: She recently got her degree in Marketing from UIC; She worked three customer service/sales jobs through college and she stayed an average of two years on each; Her communication skills are honed.

Mel escorts her to the elevator when it ends and passes her his card, informing her that she should get a call from them within a week. If not, to give him a call. As he heads back into the conference room for the next interview, Greg gets his attention and just grins from coast to coast as Mel nods his head at him. Three things remain: Jack, Teresa, and the other interviewees. Since the majority vote will determine the outcome, as long as two of them recommends a candidate, she is assured of a position, pending a drug test.

The next candidate is equally, if not more, attractive than Carmen. Kim Johnson is slim and sultry, with a bob haircut. She seems to be dressed for the runway in her long, gray dress that explodes at the bottom and black blazer. Mel doesn't have a problem with the outfit, although it may not be considered traditional "business" attire.

She turns out to be an under-qualified, confident liar. She actually did do some modeling, but she is lacking on meaningful skills and job stability. She has at least seven jobs listed in a three-year period, with a maximum of one year on a job. She explains that they were temporary positions, which all three of them know otherwise. A two-year gap stands out on her resume that she accounts to her schooling—which was for her G.E.D.—even though the resume states she graduated from Chicago Vocational High School. Mel doesn't hold it too personally against her, even though he can't recommend her. His comrades sit tight-lipped as they make comments on their sheets.

Mel escorts her to the elevator, hands her a business card and informs her of the same thing, although he felt that the other two would make it three thumbs down. He looks over at Greg, who is standing with an advocating grin as he throws his hands up to his sides and lips, "Is she in?"

Mel half smirks on the left side of his face and shakes his head. Greg rolls his eyes up in his head as he collapses into his seat.

When Mel gets back in, the last candidate makes him do a double take and almost somersault over the table in the process. It has nice foundation; its eye lining is neat; it wears some type of conditioner to give it a look of soft, wavy hair. It is either an ugly girl, with a slight mustache; a transvestite; or a flame-thrower who is consumed, but isn't burning up. When it speaks, Mel realizes that it's a male. The heat it is emitting boosts the temperature about 90 degrees and the glory of it chars them all. He can't keep a straight face while quizzing him. Teresa is straight to the point and a bit indifferent. Jack, on the other hand, seems to come to life. He is enthusiastic about the eccentric character named Shawn Norris. It truly is a small world. Lo and behold: a gay interviewee and a gay interviewer. They become friendly fast. When it is over, Jack insists on escorting him to the elevator. Now it's evaluation time. Dilemma: three candidates; three votes; one position. It's obvious that two are highly favored.

"Well, I think that Carmen and Shawn are the top two," Teresa declares.

"This is going to be hard," Jack adds.

Mel already knows who he doesn't like. "First, let's narrow it down to the two. I liked Carmen, and Kim wasn't all that bad."

"Kim," Jack questions in disbelief. "Please. She hasn't even worked on a job more than a year."

"And I don't think that she has enough experience for the position," Teresa seconds.

"Okay. We can eliminate Kim. What about Carmen?" Mel asks.

"I think Carmen would be excellent," Teresa reasons.

"I don't know about that. I think that her attire was borderline inappropriate," Jack whines. "It was tight and revealing."

Mel can't believe that he let that come out of his mouth. He was about to let him and his favored candidate have it, when—to Mel's surprise—Teresa defends the outfit, saying, "I think she was very professional, and the outfit was businesslike. I wanted to ask her where she bought it. She looked like an executive."

"It was sluttish to me. It made her look like a whore," Jack states.

Mel snaps: "Compared to LaShawn—I mean Shawn—Carmen was quite conservative and—as Teresa stated—businesslike. It—I mean Shawn—had jewelry in his nose. It sounds like you're showing favoritism to someone that was advertising an alternative lifestyle."

"What?!" he questions in disbelief as his face reddens. "How dare you sit up and accuse me of discriminating!"

"I didn't accuse you of anything. You're the one nitpicking about a well-endowed woman that knows how to wear a business suit. I didn't hear you criticizing how Boyfriend was popping his fingers like he was in a disco and how he manipulated the conversation to the point where we didn't even ask him all of the questions. We didn't even touch on his education, yet he's one of the top candidates."

"Well, it seems like you're showing favoritism towards the attractive, Christian woman, Mister Bachelor."

"Guys, lets not argue about the candidates. It's not like our jobs are hanging on the perfect selection."

"You never know if we get the wrong one in here," Jack reasons.

"In that case, let's go to the resumes," Mel suggests. "That way we can judge them by paper, since the appearances are in question."

"Fine," Jack huffs. "I think Carmen is overqualified."

"Oh c'mon, Jack," Teresa pleads with a chuckle. "Now you're being ridiculous."

"She has a degree in marketing. What does that have to do with our department? She'll probably be gone the minute a better offer in her field comes along. Then what? We wasted the company's money training her."

"That's weak. It's sounds like you got something personal against her," Mel hints. "I mean, there's no difference between the degree'd unemployed and the degreeless unemployed. They both need a job. I've been both."

"Yeah. I mean who's to say that all of us wouldn't jump at a better opportunity. The potential for her to leave is not reason enough not to hire her. Everyone working here has the potential to leave," Teresa adds.

"And who's to say that she wouldn't do a good job before the *'better opportunity in her field came along?'* We have a marketing department that she expressed an interest in going to eventually, so stop trying to blackball her."

Jack just clicks his lips and huffs. "Okay. Fine. We'll go with her," he resolves.

"Majority ruled without you anyway," Mel says under his breath, where Jack apparently is, because he cuts him a nasty glare. Mel chuckles out. Even if Carmen is a slut, like Jack suggested, he can't stand proud homosexuals. Rain or shine, for better or for worse, if he has to choose between a tramp and a fag, the company would be the biggest whorehouse in business. Mel restrains himself as Jack brushes past him on the way out. He starts to yank him back in the room by the hair, close the door and then throw him through the wall, but he's able to catch himself. At this point, Mel and his stomach are growling and craving raw meat.

"The fruit of the righteous is a tree of life; and he that winneth souls is wise."—Proverbs 11:30. Mel reads his calendar on the way to lunch, since he was running late that morning and he didn't even get a chance to sit down. His emotions immediately simmer and the spirit convicts him of wrongful speech and thoughts in the management meeting he just left and the earlier interviews, so he apologizes in silence. He'll make professional peace with Jack when he sees him again.

He made the mistake of leaving the house without his wallet, so he borrowed ten bucks from Greg, since he was also low on gas. He grabs his bagged lunch, newspaper, Bible and Sunday school book and starts towards the door leading downstairs to the cafeteria. The caffeine and his tolerance were depleted two hours ago. He feels as vicious as a hungry Doberman. With the potential to bite into somebody's neck growing strong, he avoids contact with everybody all together. There was already one tense incident today; he just missed missing incident number two.

Before he could get his foot out of his cube, Gayle Appleton—one of the mainstay, outspoken women in the department—apparently isn't satisfied with the job Marcus is doing today. She comes up like a forty-year-old preschooler and actually tricks on him: "Tell him to sign on and take some calls." Apparently, she thinks she's making an impression. Paul is in Mel's cubicle using the computer, since the technician is working on his. However, Paul isn't moved and tactfully tells her it isn't her place to tell somebody what to do or to tattle-tell. Nothing like raw eggs in the face for lunch. Mel doesn't even have to open his mouth.

Mel noticed that she seems to have a problem with a lot of the young men in the department. Perhaps it's because she has a weak pride and children older than Mel. Maybe the nine-year tenure is getting to her. Anyhow, she's one of the biggest gossipers in the world, and somehow finds herself in the middle of everybody's business. She always has something negative to say about somebody. Most of the time, she spews shot-in-the-dark assumptions. When the "Know It All" clique was discussing the Zodiac, she made the blanket statement about the Capricorn male, "because her father is one".

Marcus is seething as he meets Mel at the stairs, and insists that Mel "Move me away from that bitch." Mel promises to place him in a spot out of Gayle's sight.

There are a handful of people in the cafeteria clustered in their coteries. He lays his stuff down at a secluded table far from the grapevine and traffic, and takes his frozen macaroni and chicken breast sandwich to the microwave. He settles down and breezes through his grace (he's not fasting today, so his flesh makes his mouth real hasty). After his first fork-full of macaroni, the tension in his shoulders and head rises. He opens the paper, flipping past all of the O.J. stuff to the comics, which is the same difference. It's been a long time since he's been this wound up. Dad called him at four in the morning, because someone broke into the church. Since he and Momma are eight hundred miles away in Texas for a funeral, he was the appointed family member and church representative that had to be on the spot. If that wasn't enough, he was up until 12:30, counseling one of the new members that was struggling with depression and the issue of whether God would forgive her. The previous Sunday, Lamont announced that he was leaving the church for a season, which left only a handful of capable counselors out of the ministers and deacons. He said that he was going to put some focus on the outreach ministry that God called him to. Coupled with the ride Mel gave David to school at the last minute (since he had to stop at kinko's this morning), he has been going like the

Energizer Bunny all the way up to his late lunch. David had to have his paper in at eight on the head, or he stood a chance of coming out of high school next year, as opposed to the end of the summer. Since he couldn't use the car (he got picked up for curfew and for trying to purchase alcohol the previous weekend), he was really at Mel's mercy. If his graduation weren't riding on it, he would've had to bus it to kinko's.

Mel wolfs down his lunch in less than ten minutes, turns from the cartoons to the back, and then back to the front. After scanning the news, he opens his Sunday School book. Sunday the class has to review the lesson before the whole school (and since he's the back-up teacher and Deacon Lewis was going to be out of town, the review will fall on him), and it marks the beginning of a new unit. The title of the lesson is "Bread from Heaven" and it is focusing on God's provision for His people. After he reads through it, he starts outlining his presentation, simultaneously searching the scriptures for background. He doesn't look up when a group of women pass, stopping a few feet away from him to chatter. As they fade to a table further back, the Spirit leads him to the scripture in 1st Kings, where the ravens brought food to the Prophet Elijah. Then he starts pondering his own testimony of how God kept him well fed and housed when he didn't have a job. Joy overtakes him as he leans back in the chair, closes his eyes and smiles.

"How you doing?" the voice asks. His eyes pop open, as he is startled out of his meditation. Thinking he was the only person in the area, he feels a little foolish to be grinning to himself.

He sits up straight and tells her "I'm fine," as he takes in the young woman that's standing directly across from him. *Onguard.* Although he didn't see her when she passed by a few moments ago, he recognizes her voice as one of the females.

Karen is someone that he speaks to in passing. They haven't sat down for a long discussion. Just a pleasant "Hi" and "Bye". Based on past conversations he's overheard her engaged in, she's naive and impressionable. When the females of the department were reading that Zodiac book and discussing their experiences—gobbling up everything it said like it was the Word of God—she was the most inquisitive, wanting to know the sign of her ideal "Soul-mate." It turned out that since she is a "Virgo" (that figures), she is the only one "compatible" with—as the astrological psychologists' put it—the "partying Capricorn" male. She is nice looking, with long, silky, auburn hair and a cute, medium-brown face. However, there are two elements that he observed that signaled "Don't even think about her": She's too young (only 20, and acts every year of it), and she kicks it with Deidra and the whole clan of wild wolfettes.

"What about yourself?" he questions out of politeness.

She giggles and claims to be "Fine," as she looks over his reading material. "Can I ask you something?"

Sure she can ask, but he may not answer. He glances to the side, surveying her babbling friends at a table out of ear's reach. He goes on the defensive, expecting a provocative question. "Sure."

"Are you a preacher?" she asks innocently.

Mel chuckles a little as he ponders what he imagined might be the query. "No. Not at all. Why do you ask?"

"I always see you reading the Bible and I thought that you had to be a preacher to read it that much," she says, leaning against the table.

Mel didn't realize he was being watched or noticed. He figures Deidra must've told her something, but he really doesn't care. "I like to read the Bible, and plus I'm in a Sunday school class that's really enlightening, so I have to study."

"Really? What church do you go to?"

"I go to Love of God Missionary Baptist Church," he says, somewhat intrigued about where she and the conversation are going. "Do you go to church?"

"I used to go on Easter when I was a kid, but I haven't been to church since my grandmother died four years ago. She went to Reverend James Meeks' church: Salem Baptist on 118th and Indiana," she says, taking a seat that she's more than welcome to. "I don't know about going to church. I believe in God, but it's so many religions out there that claim that their god is the real god, that I'm totally confused. Like my cousins: they're Jehovah Witnesses' and they want me to go to Kingdom Hall with them, but I haven't, because they seem so weird to me. They don't even celebrate Christmas, and I know I love to get Christmas presents."

Mel laughs out and tells her "I hear you," as he leans forward on his elbows to listen more intently.

"What's the difference between Jehovah Witnesses and Baptist Churches? They both go by the Bible. Do y'all believe the same thing?" she shoots all at once.

Mel is surprised at how serious she is about the subject. Although she has limited knowledge, she's very sincere. Unfortunately, he's not prepared to give her a full answer. "I really can't tell you a lot about them, but I know what I believe," he says with boldness as the Holy Spirit takes over. "I believe that Christ died for my sins and that based on my faith, I have salvation."

"Don't all religions say that they have salvation? How do you know for sure?" she queries for an answer like a heat seeking missile searches for fire.

Mel pauses and takes a deep breath, like his father does when someone poses a question to him about his faith. Maybe it's spiritually hereditary. It's important to let the Holy Spirit have His way, without putting his two cents into it. He addresses her when his lungs fill up: "I can't speak for other religions, but I can only tell you what my experiences have been. It may sound hard to believe, but the Lord communicates with me personally," he says, a puzzled look spreading over her face. "It's not necessarily an audible conversation like we're having—vivid, none-the-less. When I'm troubled or unsure, or even if I need to be cheered up with an encouraging word, the Lord speaks to me. Often times, I can open my Bible to a particular scripture that addresses a need, without flipping through it or looking in the glossary. Other times, He'll speak to me in a song on the radio or through a minister on TV.

"Like once, I was reading the Defender and I came across an article about an anniversary and concert this church was having. The subtitle read 'Have faith: God doesn't forget His children.' I was at a low point in my life. Things weren't as smooth and easy flowing as I wanted them to be. I had moved into a new apartment six month's prior and I was struggling to pay the rent and the utilities—among other things. At the time, I was in school and I thought I was going to have to drop out and get a part time job just to make ends meet. That was the devil trying to keep me from getting the education that the Lord wanted me to have. I was depressed and unsure if He even cared what happened to me one way or another. My rent was already late that month, and I was going to fall two months behind. I won't even tell you what I had in the refrigerator, because it was empty—with the exception of a half loaf of bread, milk and mayonnaise. The article quoted the pastor, saying *'the Lord always provided for me, even if it wasn't when I wanted or expected something—He was always on time when I needed Him. When things didn't go my way, I knew that the Lord's will was perfect and that He's able.'*

"I read it on a Friday, said a prayer of faith that moment, and took my mind off of things, somehow. That following Monday, I got a grant check for $968 from school, which I was told I wouldn't get. That meant that I was going to be eating choice meals that whole month—as opposed to mayonnaise sandwiches—and my rent wouldn't fall two months behind. You can imagine that I was riding high, but that was only the beginning. Two weeks after, I found out that out of a gazillion applicants, I won a $3000 scholarship from the American Institute of Certified Public Accountants. And to top it off, the week after, I got a raise from my job, which made things a lot easier to keep up with, and I was even able to get my first car. The reason I know it's the Lord is because scripture backs me up—or rather, my experiences confirm what the Word says. It's not just a coincidence that this is what Sunday's lesson is about," he says, sliding the book across the table to her.

As she skims over the book, the first shifters come down for their afternoon break, making the cafeteria sound like a playground at lunchtime. A band of long-winded, loud-mouthed females park just behind Mel.

She finally says, "I've tried to obey the Ten Commandments, but I tell a lie here and there, not to mention the times me and my boyfriend—ex-boyfriend as of last week—slept together. And is abortion really murder, because—between you and me—I had one last year and I feel real bad about it?" as she stares down to the side with a concerned expression.

Mel smiles at the opening as he gets up and sits beside her with his Bible, praying silently for the Holy Spirit to guide him to the right passages. Mel opens right to James 2 and 10 (he thanks the Spirit in his mind) and points it out to her, emphasizing, "If you break one commandment, you've broken them all, and God knows I've broken quite a few today alone. On the way to work, I went to bed with a young lady I saw on the bus stop," he says, to her surprised, *'no you didn't pick up a prostitute on the way to work'* expression, as if this "holy preacher" is so above and beyond sin. "Not literally, but in my heart—for a split second, I wanted to sleep with her, but I caught myself before I became obsessed with it. And then I was throwing mental daggers at people because I didn't want to be bothered. And I'm not trying to say that I don't sin in actions and speech, but sin is sin is sin, whether deeds, thoughts or words."

She nods in understanding.

"Now let's clear something up and turn to the books of the law: Exodus, Leviticus, Numbers, and Deuteronomy," he says, turning to the ten commandments, then on to some of the other laws in the other books. "As you see, there are more than ten commandments."

"I'm seeing that," she says, amazed.

"There are actually over 400 laws. I couldn't even name 20 of them for you. Now tell me, who can follow all of those laws?" he begs, without giving her a chance to answer. "Now as far as abor..." he starts, pausing as he notices that she's distracted by the women at the other table, who've gotten louder. He considers recruiting them for the choir, because their voices could easily knock down the walls of Jericho. "You want to go to the conference room?"

"Yeah, let's do that."

They gather their things and relocate to the quieter room, out of sight and out of mind from the world. It's airy and bright, even though there are no windows. Mel is excited and glad that he has his Bible with the King James translation and the parallel New International, Amplified, and New American Standard versions. The KJ can be confusing and unclear. He wants it to be plain to her as she reads it. He sits at the head of the long conference table, and she sits on the same end just to the side.

"As I was saying about abortion," he says as he opens it up again, this time flipping to a page that he highlighted in Ecclesiastes a while ago. "Here we go: *'As you know not what is the way of the wind or how the spirit comes to the bones in the womb of a pregnant woman'* tells that the life begins in the womb, and as a backup scripture, Isaiah 49 and 5 states, in part, *'he who formed me in the womb to be his servant'*. So life begins in the womb, according to scripture."

She stares down, rubbing her bare arms—like she's wiping dirt away—stating, "I killed my baby" as the guilt and cool air overcomes her. Tears form in her eyes as she says, "I need to go to church and get to the point where you are."

"Going to church is all well and good, but it's no guarantee of salvation," he says as he takes his blazer off and hangs it on her shoulders. "And if you look up to me as a role model for Christianity, you're actually looking down. I'm still growing and I have a long way to go, but I won't reach that point until I leave this world."

She reasons, "You have it together, you know the scriptures, you're nice and you have this line of communication with God. And you're so religious. If you're not a good example of what people should be like, I don't know who is."

"From that standpoint, I'm no better than you," he insists. "Everybody can have a line of communication with God. It's called prayer. I haven't been blessed because I'm such a good person. And I'm definitely not saved because I'm good or religious. If I were given what I deserved, I would've been cast into hell a long time ago. The grace of God saves me through my faith in Jesus Christ."

She shoots him a puzzled look.

He starts flipping through the Bible again and comes to the 23rd chapter of Luke. Then the Spirit takes over and starts breaking it down: "A person can have salvation and no religion whatsoever. Jesus saved one of the criminals on the cross just before he died because the criminal realized *who* He was, and had faith in Him, illustrated by his request to be saved. Now here's a non-religious guy that didn't even get baptized, yet he was saved. And over here in Galatians, the Apostle Paul tells us that we are put right with God by our faith in Jesus Christ, not by obeying the law and being religious. At the same time, a person can be as religious as the Pope and still not be saved. Religion is what we see, but God sees what's in the heart. A good example are the frontin' Pharisees that Jesus addresses in Matthew: on the outside, they appear good to everybody, but inside they are full of hypocrisy and sins. Best believe Jesus told them where their destiny is. So as far as me being religious, it means nothing if my faith is absent and my heart is wrong."

"So it doesn't matter if I go to church or not, as long as I believe in Jesus?"

"Well, not exactly. Jesus loves the church and is coming back for it. Religion should be the manifestation of faith, not the other way around. James here tells us that our faith should be put into action, not just words," he says as she reads it. "And over here in the book of Hebrews, it says that we should not give up meeting and going to church to fellowship together. One of the purposes of going to church is to worship and praise God with fellow believers, in order to draw strength."

He notices that she seems a little apprehensive and uneasy at the mention of a church service as they both pause a moment while she digests everything he fed her. She's wrestling with some issues as she's being convicted.

"I don't know if I can be a Christian, because I like to go to the clubs and stuff like that. It would seem like my lifestyle would contradict my claim to be a Christian," she pouts.

"Let me tell you, if we all waited until we were perfect, the churches would be empty. It's a growing process. Nobody is expecting you to turn into a saint that walks on water immediately. Look at me: I've been in the church all of my life; my father is a pastor; and the Lord has always spoken to me, but I didn't really start taking it serious until this year. You're actually the first person I've witnessed to in-depth," he says to her delight as she smiles. "And the twelve disciples were common men when Jesus called them. They didn't say *'let me go to Theology school first'* or *'let me first get rid of my bad habits'*. They came as they were. You like the club scene and all that...don't you know the Spirit will purge you of that desire to go club jumping? When I moved out of my parent's home, I started cussing like a sailor, and I loved cussing. But then the Spirit left a sour taste in my mouth—literally—every time profanity slipped out. I liken it to the taste of vomit. And as much as I love the pleasure that sex brings, the Lord took the comfort out of it for me. I can still enjoy it, but I can't have peace in doing it outside of marriage. And make no mistake about it, the itch is still there."

They both laugh at that.

He points out to her that God is Spirit and must be worshipped in spirit and in truth; then they go over to Galatians and he shows her where Paul stated that a person receives the Spirit by hearing and believing the Gospel; and the last scripture he shows her is the eighth chapter of Romans (since she is in awe of his line of communication with God), where it says that the Spirit comes to us in our weak state and prays for us and pleads with God in groans that words can't express, when we don't know what to say, "which is often with me," he adds. "And since God knows the thoughts of the Spirit, and the Spirit is for and in accordance to God's will, your line of communication can always be open, too."

Mel checks his watch, realizing that her supervisor may notice that she's about 15 minutes late. "Well, I'm not going to hold you, and to emphasize that I'm not trying to recruit you to my church, but to the body of Christ, I need to ask do you believe in Jesus Christ as your Savior—or do you need to study it some more?"

She looks him in the eyes and says, "Yes and yes. I believe that He's my Savior and I would like to study the scriptures with you some more."

Mel could barely contain the joy and the excitement that he feels on the inside, even though his countenance is very serious. "Would you also like to visit my church home or go to Bible class on Wednesday nights? You would love the Pastor, who—as I said—is my father. He's real down to earth and knowledgeable."

"I don't mind visiting, but I don't know if I want to join yet," she says with a little hesitation. "Wednesday nights are bad for me. I have an evening class that night. Can I just study with you on my lunch break next Wednesday?"

Mel is so honored that he just smiles for a few moments as she beams with him. "That would be great. We can do this again next Wednesday. I'll give you a Sunday school book when I get back upstairs, and we can either go by what's in the book or let the Spirit lead us," he says, pausing to collect himself. "Before we go upstairs, I would like to pray with and for you—you don't mind, do you?"

She shakes her head.

"Okay, I want you to repeat after me to start, and then I'll just pray over you, okay?" he verifies as he faces her and extends his hands.

She nods as tears well up in her eyes and grabs his hands.

"Let us go to the Lord...Lord"

"Lord"

"I acknowledge that I am a sinner"

"I acknowledge that I am a sinner"

"and I believe that You died for my sins"

"and I believe that You died for my sins," she sobs.

"Lord"

"Lord"

"I ask that you forgive me of all of my sins"

"I ask that you forgive me of all of my sins"

"and I accept You, Jesus"

"and I accept You, Jesus"

"as my personal Savior"

"as my personal Savior"

"Okay, let me go on from here, Karen," he says through her silent weeping. "Heavenly Father..." he says as the rest is untimed, unrehearsed and unremembered.

When he finishes, they embrace.

"Thank you," she whispers in his ear.

"Glory be to God," he says, patting her on the back. He could actually hear the angels in heaven singing and rejoicing. High is the only word he could think of to describe his feelings at the moment. As they collect themselves and their things, he asks, "What are you studying?"

She smiles, wiping her face. "Would you believe Accounting?" she quizzes.

"Really? That's what I majored in."

"I heard you when you mentioned winning a scholarship from the American Institute of Certified Public Accountants," she says, adding, "That means that you can also tutor me in that, too."

"Sure, no problem. I can give you a few pointers and help you with it. Where are you going?"

"Right now I'm at Harold Washington City College, but I plan to transfer to Chicago State in the fall."

"Cool. That's my alma mater. I can even talk to some of the professors and tell them to look out for you when you get there. And if you ever need a job reference, just let me know."

They both just smile at each other as they head out the door and float upstairs. Mel never thought that anything could compare to the feeling of falling in true love, until this moment.

Mel kills the last three hours of his day meeting with his team, monitoring and making phone calls. At the end of the day, he gathers in the parking lot with Greg and Reggie from MIS.

"So what's up, Mel? Who did you bring in for me?"

"We're bringing in the first one, no thanks to Miss Man."

"The queen's reign would've ended today," Greg says.

"You must be talking about Jackie," Reggie suggests.

"Who else?" Mel asks. "Anyway, he didn't like either one of the ladies—because believe me, I vouched for both of them. The second one didn't have any skills. All she knows how to do is look good."

"That's what you hire her for," Reggie comments. "At least long enough for one of the real men to get to know her. Then you could cut her loose."

"I'm saying. You can hire her to sit on your lap all day. Hang her on the wall," Greg seconds. "C'mon Mel, you need to raise the morale in the department...brighten the place up. You could've given her share of work to those fat motormouths that talk all day."

"She would've been nice to look at during the day, but it was only one spot, and I don't think we did bad with the first one. We could've ended up with another he-wannabe-she," he says as Jack happens to strut past to his car like a proud pussycat, still wearing a red regretful face, although Mel apologized to him.

They all look at him in disgust. "I oughta put a crown on the queen," Greg threatens loud enough for him to hear, but he's smart enough to ignore him. "Dumb bitch. I still got a score to settle with him/her/him."

"Just make sure I'm there to see it. He'll need somebody to pick him up off the ground...and then knock him back down and step on him," Reggie says.

After shooting the breeze for a shift, Marcus and Felix join them.

"Thanks for moving me away from that Tasmanian Devil Bitch—excuse the French," Marcus blesses.

"You're not talking about 'Go to Hell' Gayle," Greg inquires.

"She called herself getting an attitude because she thought I wasn't doing anything. I was writing something up because my computer froze, and she had the audacity to tell me to get on phone. I told her to put on a muzzle."

"Then she went back to kindergarten on you," Mel inputs.

"I know...I told her to."

"She's the first person I got into it with," Greg touts. "She tried that same thing with me, and I asked her if she's ever tasted some knuckles. She told me to go to hell, like she tells everybody, and I haven't felt any gale force winds since."

"I can see how you can want to hit her," Reggie adds.

They end up evaluating every female that comes out of the building, occasionally flirting with some of them. Greg and Felix even heckle a couple that happens to be walking through the area. Greg spots Brent coming towards them from a block down. "C'mon...hit him," he urges an unknown driver as Brent crosses the street. "Shoot. Some people just can't drive."

"Let me borrow your keys, Melvin," Marcus requests.

"Why?"

"So I can mow him down."

"I don't want him splattered on my bumper," Mel jokes as Brent finally makes it to the group.

"What's up, fella's?"

"Nothing," Felix confirms. "I have a joke: A little girl came running into the house crying her eyes out and cradling her hand. 'Mummy, quick! Get me a glass of cider!' she wailed. 'Why do you want a glass of cider?' asked mum. 'I cut my hand on a thorn, and I want the pain to go away.' Confused, but weary of the child's whining, the mother obliged and poured her a glass of cider. The little girl immediately dunked her hand in it. 'Ouch! It still hurts! This cider doesn't work!' whined the little one. 'What are you talking about?' asked her increasingly perplexed parent. 'Well, I overheard my big sister say that whenever she gets a prick in her hand, she can't wait to get it in cider!'"

Mel can't even bring himself to smirk.

As they yuck it up, Deidra comes strutting pass. They all get quiet. Mel and Greg ignore her, Reggie speaks to her, and Brent, Marcus, and Felix follow her behind with their eyes. When she gets out of earshot, they comment on how desirable she is.

"Every man's fantasy," Felix comments.

"I'm a man, I say," Marcus cuts in.

"Well, I guess I'm not a man, then," Greg states.

"Ditto," Mel seconds.

"You sure proved that, Melvin," Brent remarks. "I don't see how you could turn that down if you were. I would tear it up," Brent affirms.

Before Melvin could respond, Greg cuts into him like he's been waiting for the opportunity. "Your jungle-fever ass wouldn't do nothing with that shrimp-fried rice grain between your thighs."

"You're just mad because you couldn't handle her when you had her," Brent retorts. "You really must be lacking on the goods," he says, cupping his crouch.

"Okay. I'm lacking," Greg agrees. "I tell you what: either you're shedding or something kinky is going on with you and your mutt. Talk about bondage and bestiality." Everybody observes the excess dog hair all over Brent's clothes and buckles over in laughter as Greg continues: "You like your animals submissive, huh? Chaining that dog to the bed. Did y'all get tied up? Tell us Brent—inquiring minds want to know—is it better than the goats? Ba-a-a-a-a-a-a-arf-arf-arf."

"Yeah okay," Brent says with a slight grin as he reddens over.

Greg rolls on: "It'll be interesting to see the offspring. I guess y'all are going to have buppies. Melvin correct me if I'm wrong, but didn't Mosaic Law state that anyone involved in animal sex should be put to death?"

Marcus and Reggie are actually rolling on the ground.

Brent continues to grin uncomfortably as he starts to resemble a walking blood cell. "You got me," he concedes, walking off with his tail tucked.

"That's right: take your heathen ass on before we stone you to death," Greg enforces. "And remember: Next time you challenge me to a verbal battle, don't come with dog hair all over your clothes and your tongue tied, 'cause I'll show you no mercy. And bring more than one stale joke!"

It takes them about an hour for their breath to come home to their lungs. They roll away chortling, and Mel is still giggling when he makes it to church for the business meeting. He is about an hour late and he heads straight to the bathroom, since the mayonnaise from the chicken sandwich earlier was a bit spoiled and is moving his bowels. A couple of gentlemen come in as he relaxes in the stall. He recognizes one voice as that of Donald, and the other person is Trustee Smith. They're talking about that "whore" Lorraine, who is upstairs making a big fuss. Their talk takes a gossipy twist when Donald comments that he believes that her brother is a Vice Lord and that Smith should be careful not to let his daughter get dragged down. That's ridiculous. Mel has observed and talked to Harold, and there is no indication outside of his rough look and environment that he gangbangs. As if his faithful attendance to Sunday school and his participation in the choir are just a cover up. He buses it by himself to get to church. Mel shakes his head when they leave out, oblivious to his presence.

When he walks in, Lorraine is just finishing a heated statement. Mel takes a seat in the back next to Earl. "What's she talking about?" he questions.

"She lambasted the board for being stingy with God's money—and she's right," he states. "She also testified that an angel in the midst of all of the devils, sent her a money order for $675, which allowed her to pay her rent and fill her refrigerator for the week."

"Is that right?" Mel verifies.

Earl nods. "You missed everything. We started thirty minutes early."

"Shoot."

After going over the plans for the next quarter, his father dismisses. Mel maneuvers his way to the front to get the financial reports and other information. Before he makes it, Lorraine intercepts him and pulls him to her. "I know you're the angel in our midst," she whispers in his ear.

Mel smiles and asks, "What are you talking about?"

"I saw what you were tithing that day in the office and I did the math."

Mel just shakes his head, stopping short of lying.

"Listen Melvin, I really appreciate it. God is going to really bless you abundantly for what you did. I will never forget it and neither will He," she says, pointing up.

"I've been the beneficiary of God's benevolence throughout my life, so just give Him the glory."

"God bless you," she says through teary eyes, as she gives him a tight hug.

Chapter 13

By the grace of God, Friday has arrived. The week was longer than the month of February. It was busy, and today is going to last about a week. Last night, Mel attended a concert featuring Vernita's church choir, and some of the songs are still ringing in his head. She knows she has the lungs to uplift a corpse. They ministered well after one in the morning, and the energy enhanced Wednesday's highlights. Not only did Karen keep her word to be faithful and come to the Bible study, but she also brought one of her girlfriends—Harriett Freeman. On their way to the conference room, Marcus asked where they were going—which opened another witnessing door. When Mel told him, he invited him to join, and he did. The study group is up to five people from a two-person concept. They had a good discussion about the voice of the Lord. He explained that many people expect and want an audible voice from the sky, and ignore the inner voice and the outer signs. He likened it to a person's faith that is limited to what's visible to their physical sight, often covering their hindsight—forgetting what the Lord has done for them. Many testimonies were flying that session. To close, he encouraged them to learn the scriptures, in order to recognize and distinguish the voice of God from their own thinking.

Mel called Greg at home from the cloud he was riding on, and invited him. He promised to try to make it when he came back to work. As the Father would have it, Carmen—who started that Monday—is scheduled for lunch at that time and has agreed to be a part of it. However, Satan was busy at the same time. Jackie pulled some strings and got LaShawn hired. Mel didn't let it take his joy though.

Mel contemplates the piles of work he has to do today while he listens to his "Sounds of Blackness" tape in the parking lot. Monitoring, scheduling, one-on-one coaching, testing and grading are on the morning's agenda. After "Everything is Gonna be Alright" finishes, he cuts the ignition off and says the "Serenity" prayer—with a little improvisation to fit the day. Mel dreamed about work last night (what a waste of sleep). Sometimes it seems like he never leaves the job. What a way to feel after only two months. He realizes that the people he works with has a lot to do with it...a few people anyway. Standing just outside the door to the building are some of those people now, yacking and smoking like they're at a nightclub or beauty shop.

Tensions are high. Morale is low. Tempers are short. Faces are long. Everyone is feeling overworked and underpaid, which seems to induce bad attitudes and hateful dispositions. And the irony is that they seem to take it out on Mel and the other supervisors, as if they're cracking a whip from an executive chair. Three straight days going on four of 95 plus, humid degrees didn't help matters. Somebody is liable to detonate, blowing the whole department up in the process. He strains out a "Good morning" to the girls—ladies—just as he gets near them.

Deidra doesn't reply, and Gayle lets out a dry "Hey". Devita questions, "Why isn't it a casual day today?"

"If it was left up to me, it would be casual day everyday. Take that up with your manager," he says, squeezing by them and holding his breath as he walks through the wall of smoke, since none of them bothered to move.

Felix jumps through the closing elevator doors just in time to tell Mel a dirty joke to start his day off. "A young guy walks into a talent agent's office and says he wants to be in show-biz, so the agent says 'O.K. kid, show me what you can do.' The kid tells some jokes, sings, juggles on a unicycle, swallows flaming knives etc. The agent was impressed, so he says 'I can do things for you! I can get you on TV! Your name will be in lights! By the way, what is your name?' The young man replied 'Penis Van Lesbian.' The agent couldn't believe it and said 'Sorry kid, but you're gonna have to change your name...nobody's gonna hire you with a name like that.' The young man refused and walked out. Months later, he returned to the agent, so the agent asks, 'Are you still looking for work? Have you changed your name?' The young man hung his head low and said 'Yes, every agent in town turned me down because of my name, so I've changed it.' 'Great' said the agent. 'What is your name?' The young man replied 'Dick Van Dyke.'"

Mel just shakes his head and announces through a plastic grin, "The mouth of fools poureth out foolishness" as he exits the elevator. He greets the few people in the department that arrived early and goes to the Men's room. It's about ten minutes before start time and almost everybody is dragging in. Mel checks his voice mail to see who called in, and to his surprise, his father left a message for him to call.

David answers the phone. "When are you going to get a job?" Mel interrogates.

"When are you going to get a wife?" he retorts.

"I bet you and your mouth won't be using my car again. You still owe me some teeth for smoking that junk in it."

"Joke. It's just a joke," he insists. "Speaking of wife, have you heard from Memory?"

"Put Dad on the phone."

"Seriously. Dad bailed her out of jail yesterday."

"What?" he questions with a touch of amusement.

"She got arrested for driving without a license, and she didn't have any money to post bail, so she called dad and he bailed her out."

Mel chuckles a little. "Let me speak to him," he demands through his silent laughter.

"Hello."

"Hey Dad."

"Melvin, I need you to stop at the bank and get the statement of account and make the deposit before the bank closes this afternoon."

"All right," he agrees. "Is that it?"

"That's all. I just wanted to make sure you did it before the bank closes."

"Okay," he reaffirms as he can barely contain the glee he felt at knowing that Memory was arrested. "I heard you bailed Memory out of jail yesterday."

"Yes, she didn't have 100 dollars with her," he verifies. "So I spotted her the money."

"I wish you had called me first...I would have paid you 200 to leave her in there."

His father doesn't respond to that.

"They should've given her the chair," Mel vents.

"For driving without a license?" he questions.

"Maybe a flailing would've been more appropriate." Mel can sense Dad's frustration.

He tells him "Make sure you make it to the bank before they close."

"I got you," he says.

The day just got a little easier. He knows it's wrong, but he feels a little appeased. Assuming that everyone is in, he tackles the team and department totals first, which takes up about an hour and a half of his morning. So far it's smooth...not as busy as anticipated and no incidents yet, and the day is a quarter over. The tea is running out of him, so he takes a washroom break. When he gets back, he'll knock his monitoring out.

As he exits the bathroom, he spots Greg casually walking in...wearing Bermuda shorts, shades, sport sandals and a T-shirt with an explicit message on it. Here they go. Mel just shakes his head, praying that he's coming in from a break or that he called in to Teresa. He can hear some of his co-workers making an issue out of it.

Nope: he hasn't signed on today. Nope: He hasn't called in, he notes, getting off the phone with Teresa. Two hours late and he's violating even the casual day dress code on a normal day. Great. He's trying to get fired. Mel wishes he were on Teresa's team when he calls him into his cubical.

"C'mon man. What's up?" he quizzes.

"Whatcha mean?" Greg questions with a smile.

"Are *you* trying to get fired, or are you trying to get us both fired?"

"You talking about my shorts?"

"I'm talking about the shorts, the shirt that somebody is going to be offended by, the sandals, the missing socks—take the shades off, because that's how you jack up your peripheral vision," he says as he takes the initiative and removes them. "And then you're two hours late. I thought you were my boy."

"I am. We still down like that. I thought it was casual day today. It should be. You know I was out yesterday. I thought that since it was so hot and so busy, we would be able to dress down."

"If it was a casual day, you'd still be in violation."

"I was going to put on some socks, man. I missed my bus this morning and..."

"Don't tell me about last night's escapade. I understand and I sympathize with you, but understand that I'm going to have to write you up. And it's nothing personal, either."

"I know man. Do what you have to do. We still cool," he insists smugly.

"I'll give you a copy later and I assume that you won't be signing it."

"You know me, Dawg," he confirms. "Are you going to monitor me today?"

"Naw, 'cause I may have to fire you if I do," he says. "That's it. Go put on some socks, G."

"Aiight," he says as he bounces up.

Mel watches him rhythmically walk to his seat as if he's treading to some music. What is he going to do with him? The coolest brother in here is becoming the biggest headache. He pulls out his headset and monitor sheets and starts listening in on some calls. To his surprise, the first four people he monitors do everything perfectly. They are making his day a good, easy one. His first call was quite hilarious. Mychal Rand has a voice that's unreal and...bogus. Sounds like a combination of PeeWee Herman and Barney the Purple Dinosaur. Apparently, the first person he called thought so, too. Mychal had to put the call on hold for something, and apparently didn't press the hold button. The woman told her associate in the background: "You oughta hear this guy: he sounds phonier than a three-dollar bill." Mel almost fell out of his seat as Mychal hung up and came whining about what happened. Mel gave him a pass on that call. He'll monitor Denise (who's sitting close to the water fountain all the way on the other side) and call it a week for monitoring. She usually gets distracted by the traffic to and from the fountain, so he's warned her that if she can't stay focused, she'll have to move.

The first two calls are excellent, despite a visit to the cooler by one of her girlfriends. There are no long pauses (indicating a muted phone) or any "could you repeat that please" or "could you hold on please". She is serious today, or maybe she hears the infamous echo and senses that she is being screened. Whatever. He decides to listen to one more call, just as he spots Deidra floating over to the cooler...followed by Greg. He watches them and isn't really listening to the call until Denise puts it on hold, apparently to quickly check something, because she doesn't even look up at them, and immediately gets back on. Mel turns to make notes on his sheet for her, when he hears screaming on the receiver and in the department. Denise puts the caller on hold as Mel looks back there to see Deidra shouting at Greg. Denise gets up to restrain Deidra, because it seems like she's about to jump on him. Greg just looks as smug as a bug in a rug as Mel rushes to them. Deidra is livid...and wet.

Teresa comes out also, and soon there's a small crowd as Deidra continues to spew venom at Greg. "You stupid bastard...see if you get away with it," she shrills.

"Calm down, Deidra," Teresa pleads.

"That asshole threw water in my face."

Everybody looks at him briefly as he complacently utters, "It was an accident", and refills his mug with water.

"Accident my ass. Just wait 'til you see the accident I have on you," she threatens, unsuccessfully attempting to go after Greg again as Teresa and Denise hold her back.

"Let's take this to the conference room," Mel interjects, realizing that since a few of the employees haven't put their calls on hold, the dispute could be heard on the other end. "Go ahead of me, Deidra. Follow Teresa, Greg."

Everybody knows that Greg is crazy enough to do something like that. He's certainly dressed for the part. With this ugly scene—coupled with his clown outfit—he's almost as good as gone. It doesn't help that he and Deidra are mortal enemies. He almost seems nonchalant about it. Mel even thought he saw him smirking as he walked past. Just as Deidra gets to the door, he notices a musty, slightly funky odor. It's so dense that a cloud can almost be seen around Deidra.

Mel calls human resources when they get in the conference room to let them know what's going on and to have a representative sit in on the meeting. It doesn't take big bad Joan from HR long to make her way up. This is their opportunity to get rid of him. Greg slouches in the chair, cool and collected, while Deidra is still fuming and foaming. Steve rolls his red, fat head in also.

"Okay. Would you like to tell us what happened?" Mel queries.

"He came and threw water in my face. That's what happened," Deidra huffs. "And I want y'all to fire his ass, because he's always starting..."

"Slow down, slow down," Steve jumps in. "So he just came by and threw water in your face? Did he actually say anything to you?"

Deidra pauses and glares at Greg as her eyes get watery. "Yes, he said something to me. He said that I smelled like last night's sex and that I need a bath...and that's when he threw the water."

Mel has to bite his lip to keep a straight face as Greg jumps in. "That's not what I said. Get the story right."

"That is what you said."

"I didn't."

"One at a time," Steve says. "Let her finish, Greg."

"I am finished. I told you what he said and did."

"Like I said, that's not what I said."

"Well if you didn't say that, what did you say? This is your turn to tell your side of the story," Steve says.

"First of all, I didn't say she smelled like last nights sex...that's something a white person would say. I said that she smelled like hot sex on a platter," he states with too much boldness as he sits up in his chair. "Has anyone gotten a whiff of her today?"

"You're flirting with termination, Greg," Steve warns.

"I'm flirting with death by suffocation. I can't breathe in her presence. I think y'all should do something about her, otherwise I'm going to talk to my lawyer about hazardous working conditions."

"Now isn't the time to be joking around," Steve says.

"Does it look like I'm joking?"

"One more comment like that and I'm going to call security."

"While you're at it, call the hazardous waste department and have them come clean girlfriend up."

Steve picks the phone up and says, "Yes. We need you to escort a former employee out."

"I don't care. I'll walk myself out," he says as he gets up from his seat. "And to show it's nothing personal, I'll help y'all correct the problem," he says as he dumps his cup of water in the face of Deidra again. "Now go douche, bitch."

Mel can't believe it. He's too shocked to laugh. Deidra's mouth hangs open as she can't believe that he had the gall to do it again. Her feelings are hurt so bad that she doesn't even go after him. Steve turns a darker shade of maroon, Joan just looks on in disgust and Teresa comes over to comfort Deidra. It is quite a scene. Part of Mel feels bad for Deidra, but another side is saying *'serves you right'.* Steve lets her take the rest of the day and Monday off, if she needs it.

Greg really outdid himself. As it turns out, he left his resignation on Steve's desk. It was a very explicit letter. He let him and the whole company have a piece of his dirty mind. He already had his desk cleaned out. He didn't even sign on for the whole morning. Instead, he spent his last day passing out invitations to his retirement/birthday party at the Clique and getting on Deidra's nerves. Why he went to such extremes is a mystery to Mel. Did he get another job or did he just get fed up? Steve wanted Greg's records anyway.

When Mel went to his desk to get them, he checked his messages. Greg left one—apparently right after he left the building—telling him to "Meet me at Boobies tavern after work." He also asked how he liked the show, insisting that she had it coming for a long time. Mel just smiles. He had an early vibe that fireworks would explode today, but he didn't realize it was going to be an all out war. At least it wasn't boring. Now Mel is truly eager to get off to learn the method behind his madness.

When Mel walks in the dark bar and spots Greg, he starts laughing uncontrollably. Greg smiles and gestures for him to come over to his table. A lot of people from the department are gathered around, unwinding from the long week, talking about the exciting day and resting their standard, professional English in favor of a more relaxing vernacular. Mel isn't going to stay, because he doesn't drink and he doesn't like to be around a lot of drinking people.

"You should've seen you in there trying not to laugh," Greg says as he shakes hands with him. "I bet you thought I just went totally stupid up in there."

"Awe man," Mel manages to say through his hysteria. "What's up with that? What's your story?"

"Awe homey. I got the settlement from the accident. I'm living large."

"You got it?! I guess drinks are on you," Mel jokes.

Greg kept mentioning the accident he was involved in three years ago and that when the settlement came in, he was out with a big bang, but Mel didn't realize how serious and close he was to getting it. A pick-up truck rammed into the back of his car...gave him whiplash and really messed his back up. There was a hold up because the insurance didn't want to take care of it, since Greg was driving on a suspended license at the time. Apparently, the insurance got tired of fighting it.

"Drinks are on me. Get a virgin Piña Colada. It's cool, Dawg," he says with an excited slur.

"Aiight," he submits as he calls the bartender and orders. "So whatcha gonna do now that you're retired and don't have to work? How much was the settlement?"

"Melly Mel, I got two huned fidy left over after medical and legal expenses. I'm going to Disney Land," he says jubilantly as the table busts up with him.

"Straight?! Two hundred fifty thousand?!" Mel asks in envious disbelief.

"No. Two huned fidy thou. And when I get back from Disney Land, I'm gonna to get that 'Vette that's long overdue. I been on the bus ever since my Cutlass got wrecked. And then I'm gonna get a three flat and move outta Mom's."

"I heard that."

"And that's not even the good news."

"You mean there's more? Did you win the lottery?"

"Close. I got accepted to John Marshall."

"You mean you've been accepted to law school?!"

"You didn't think I was just gonna blow the proceeds on cars and drinks, did you? I wouldn't let Spark off that easy. As soon as I pass the bar, I'm gonna sue them muthafuckas dry. Hopefully you'll be gone by that time."

"I'll be out of there. If not, I'll just come work for you."

Mel is so excited for him that all he can do is laugh and clasp hands with him. He knows that he has a degree in Management like himself, and he did mention law school in passing once, but Mel is totally surprised by his revelation. It feels like it's a victory not just for himself, but for Mel and every brother that gets a raw deal in Corporate America.

"You know I'll hook you up. Just make sure when I take them to court, you vouch for me."

"Definitely," he says as he jokingly rubs his fingers together and collects his drink from the waitress.

"Listen...you coming to my party tomorrow night at the Clique?"

"I don't know man. You know that's not my comfort zone."

"Not the Comfort Zone. The Clique," he says, pun intended. "I know you don't hang out like that, but just stop through. Who knows, maybe you'll meet the girl of your dreams."

Mel can only smile and shake his head at that.

"Deidra won't be there."

"Well in that case, I'm there, dude."

Earl agreed to go at the last minute (hitching a ride with Mel, since his ride is in the hospital in intensive care with major transmission problems), and when they arrive, Greg is going to work on one of the manufactured divas in the Jazz lobby. She is brown skinned with short, styled hair and—like most of the ladies who frequent the Clique—has on a tight, black mini dress that leaves little breathing room and nothing to the imagination. Greg is tucking his pen in his pocket when they spot each other. Mel throws his hands up to the side as if asking 'what now', as they peer in through the clear security glass, where the fleshy security guard checks ID's. Greg gestures for them to come on in as he says something to the young woman and comes over to the door. Although his demeanor and manly profile vouches for his age, Earl is still carded. When Mel gets to him, he looks longer and harder at his—as if he doesn't believe him. Greg slides up and says, "He's with me, AJ", and 'AJ' reluctantly gives him his driver's license back. It is about 10:30, so Mel and Earl have to pay $10 to get in, which Mel really doesn't want to do.

Mel introduces Earl and Greg to each other and asks, "What was wrong with that security guard?" as they drift from within ear's reach.

"He's good at his job. Remember, you and Marc have the same first name tonight. Elephant man doesn't forget a name, either."

"Where is Marcus?" Mel asks.

"I told him to wait up by the table so it wouldn't be too suspicious. Robocop shouldn't sweat you no more. Y'all can roam if you want. I'm going upstairs."

They follow him upstairs. Mel wants to know where they are camped out and he doesn't want to roam alone. The Jazz hasn't started yet, however, loud music with a lot of bass is blaring from the dance club upstairs. "Family Affair" by Shabba Ranks is playing, and when they get to the top, they find no one on the dance floor yet. It isn't as packed as it's going to get, and they all know it.

Greg points to Marcus sitting at one of the bars, talking to a lady of at least 35. "Your boy is getting started already," Greg says to Mel. It must be good, because he's wearing a sly grin while leaning up close to her. He's facing their direction, but he doesn't acknowledge them. They proceed to their high table next to the stairs leading up to the other level of the floor and close to the photo set. Several balloons are tied to one of the stools, with a "Reserved for Gregory" sign in fancy letters in the center of the table.

They aren't seated a minute before a sexy waitress in black skin short-shorts and a white blouse comes over and takes their order for drinks. Mel passes on this round, Earl orders a Heineken's and Greg requests a Long Island Iced Tea with a "touch of Adrien ass." Of course, Greg knows her—in a very intimate way. She agrees to give him a private celebration later in the week. "Adrien is actually pretty nice. Somebody that you would fall in love with and marry," Greg declares as she walks away.

"You know that's right," Earl confirms. "She is *real* nice."

"You know her, too," Greg questions with amusement.

"I knew her when she was just a patron here," he brags.

They both guffaw and slap hands.

"So why does she associate with you two if she's so nice?" Mel questions.

"Because we treat her nicer, if you know what I mean," Earl claims.

"Tell him again."

"That figures," Melvin says. "So how many women in here do y'all know?"

"I know most of the waitresses," Earl says.

"I spoke to a couple of freaks downstairs that I'm working on. It's about three or four up here that I know," Greg states.

"Let me put it this way," Earl declares. "I may have to start wearing a disguise."

"Or find another spot," Greg interjects as they both roar with laughter.

"So in other words, y'all have been consuming and excreting your share of ladies like gluttons up in here."

"That's what I'm talking about," Greg says as he lights a cigarette. This is the first time Mel has seen him smoke. "I already met my quota in the Jazz section. Now all I gotta do is collect a few up here and make my rounds in the Comedy Clique, and I'll call it a happy birthday."

"I know I'm not on a diet," Earl says as he leans over to Mel and whispers, "How long are you going to be on your flesh fast?"

"I told you...as long as it takes," he confirms as a well-endowed cutie struts past. "But between you and I, I hope I don't have to wait long."

"I hear you."

A few more of the people from the job pour in (including Reggie) and some of Greg's friends outside of work, as everyone gets aquatinted.

"What time does the Jazz start?" Melvin asks. "You know I ain't no dancer and I'm not trying to be the butt of nobody's joke."

"I think about 11:30—around that time. You and Reggie can go down and chill in a little. Reggie, you gonna do some steppin' tonight?"

"As soon as I get some food and liquor in my belly," he replies as he gets up and starts towards the stairs where they came in. "I'm going to order something to eat. You want anything Greg—Melvin—Anybody?"

Mel throw his hands up and shakes his head 'no' as he scopes the place out.

Greg answers, "I'm straight, Reg," as his eyes follow a woman that walks past in a black, form-fitting dress and high heels. "I got an appetite for something else," he says as he rises and pursues her.

"I'm going to walk around for a minute," Earl says as he takes off.

Almost every other table is occupied, and the dance floor is still empty. The DJ is playing "Brand New Flava in Ya Ear" by Craig Mac. No wonder everybody is still sitting. It's too dark to read or see the whites of somebody's eyes from a five yard distance, but the hour glass silhouettes and big butts of all the women walking in is unmistakable. Mel slowly turns and takes in the whole scene from his stool. Just over his left shoulder on the upper level he spots a woman facing him, but can't tell that she's looking down at him until the disco light flashes and reveals that she is and that she's missing a front tooth. He quickly blinks away as the waitress returns with their drinks, just as Greg comes back.

"Thank you, darling," Greg says as he puts his cigarette in the ashtray and takes a sip. "You sure you don't want anything, Money? It's going to get hot up in here pretty soon."

"I'm cool now. I'll get something later," Mel says. Besides, he just stuck some Double Mint in his mouth and he is savoring the flavor in case he gets the chance to talk to somebody. Not that he is expecting to find a girl to take home to momma (even if he needed her approval) in here, but he sure isn't out for a one-night-stand—which is the main reason people come here.

"Your boy has a thing for them mother figures," Greg says. "I wonder what his ol' girl thinks of these older women he talks to."

"What?" Mel asks as he leans forward to hear what Greg is saying. This is one thing he hates about coming to clubs like this—you have to yell as if a person's hearing-aid is malfunctioning to be heard and get all up in somebody's sour mouth to hear what they're saying.

"I bet his mother has never met any of these older ladies he talks to!"

"I doubt it. She would probably kick both of them in the butt. I know when I was that age, my mother would!"

"I heard that. They be kinda fine—is it that bad for them at that age?"

"I guess so. You figure they're peaking and brothers their own age are on the decline," Mel says as he gets distracted by a woman walking by their table with her cloths painted on. "He's peaking with her and he can be as mature as an older guy sometimes. He's definitely as smart. I mean they're not that old anyway. I could see if they where gray and wrinkled. Shoot. Look at her. She could pass for somebody our age or somebody who birthed him at an early age."

"I hear you," he says as he looks over at them. Marcus is putting his pen back in his shirt pocket and starts over towards them. He's wearing the same goofy grin, and when he gets halfway to them, he does a Fresh Prince skip. "Mature, huh?"

"He could've done a cartwheel," Mel counters just as he makes it over. "So how old was she?"

"Thirty-six. Count em. Not sixteen. Not twenty-six. But thirty 'call me bad' six," Marcus announces. "I'm a man, I say. I'm a man."

"Damn," Greg says as he shakes his head in disbelief. "I don't believe in role models, but you mine," he declares, slapping his hand while cackling.

"I could use a drink now. The vets can sure drain all your Mac juices," he says as he looks at Mel's surprised expression. "Relax boss. I'm talking virgin drinks. Remember, I'm the designated driver and I don't like liquor anyway, so don't write me up. Where's the waitress, G?"

"She'll be through in a minute. It's on me and I'll give you five points for that, so you up five to two, which means I'm gonna have to Mac extra hard tonight. But I'll catch you though—mark my word."

"I'm gonna take it easy for the rest of the night. Maybe I'll mess with somebody my own age," he says as they both look at him. "NOT! Where's Reggie?"

"Ordering some food with his fat ass," Greg says.

"Damn, wassup with all these people just sitting down? I sure be glad when they get on the dance floor," Marcus says. Very few vacant tables remain and people are still flooding in. The DJ is playing "Juicy" by Notorious Big when he blends "The Bus Stop" into it. That's when Marcus' wish is granted. A few of the women yell, "Heeeyyyy!" as they prance to the dance floor like they are under the spell of the song. "You coming Greg?" Marcus asks as he gets up.

"Naw. I can't get with the national fat ladies' anthem. The two times I tried, I got my feet stepped on by 300-plus pound women. These are three hundred-dollar shoes covering some sensitive corns. I ain't in the mood to get kicked out so soon, because there would definitely be a riot up in this mutha if somebody steps on my snakes. I'll pass, Marc."

Marcus struts on to the dance floor, gyrating to the beat and bobbing his head. Almost immediately after getting on, he is engulfed by females as he moves with the flow that reminds Mel of a square dance with rhythm. A woman with a red spandex dress comes over, gives Greg a hug and asks him to take a picture with her. It's Katrina: a friend from one of the many clubs he frequents.

"I'll be right back, Mel," he says as she leads him up the stairs by the hand.

Mel just nods.

This is definitely not his idea of a good time. He pulls out his watch, only to find that they've been here only forty five minutes. The night is already long. If only the church congregation could see him now. It's not so much that he's worried about what they would think, it's just that he feels as awkward and uncomfortable as a dislocated elbow. He can't dance, hates liquor, and doesn't feel comfortable club Macing—or lying. What's his purpose for being here? He'd rather be at home in bed, reading his Bible. It's hard for him to think about abstinence with all of the naked women floating around. If he gets the right hint, he will talk to one—maybe exchange numbers, and who knows what else (maybe a fine woman will take him home and rape him)—but he's not going out of his way to meet anyone.

As he cases the place again, he notices that his shoulders are tense, so he takes a deep breath and tries to relax, although the paranoia that everybody is watching him has a tight grip on him. He wishes somebody *would* watch him. The flash from the camera startles Mel and makes him blink extra hard. That's another thing he hates about these places.

They would be reserved at a table right by the photo set. He looks at Greg. Now he has five women in the picture with him—all of them are centerfold fine. There is one sitting on each of side his lap, and the other three are draped on his shoulders like an extra layer of clothes. Must be nice. If it wasn't for the Word and Mel's word, he would be frolicking with fornication, too.

Karen walks in with a few of the other females from the company and greets Mel with a hug. She's wearing a black pants suit with platform shoes. Although it's not the most appealing outfit on a woman in Mel's opinion, she looks nice in it. "I bet I get you on the dance floor," she challenges as she takes a seat next to him.

He gives her a doubtful grin and glance. "Good luck."

"I'm surprised to find you here."

"I'm surprised to be here. I call myself just stopping through to wish him a happy birthday. I'm not going to be here long."

"Well enjoy yourself. I know I am, since I'm trying to stay away from the clubs after tonight," she says looking around. "I call myself paying a surprise visit to your church tomorrow."

"Really," Mel says with excitement.

She smiles and nods. "You're going to be there, aren't you?"

"Are you kidding? I'll be the first one there repenting," he laughs.

"Good, because I'm going to try to make it to Sunday school," she confirms as she spots Greg at the bar. "Let me go wish Greg happy birthday," she says as she heads toward him.

Marcus, Earl and Reggie come back simultaneously and start mingling with the other people. It's midnight and the place is jammed with the nocturnal activities that Mel tries to avoid. Their group is all over the place eating, dancing and drinking. Earl mentions that he saw Donald and LaTonya walking around downstairs. Great. At that, Mel lets Earl—who is a little tipsy—know that he is going to cut out shortly. All Mel needs is for Donald to spot him in order to go back and spread it around the church. Not that he has any business here with LaTonya (if they're here together), who is six years shy of the legal age limit for entrance into a nightclub.

Earl agrees just as Mel is yanked from his stool by LaShawn Alexander—one of the customer service reps—and dragged to the dance floor. Mel resists as much as he can without making a scene, but she isn't hearing it. Before he knows it, he's on the dance floor feeling like the center of the universe. Instead of freezing up, he swings his arms and rocks to the bass sound—not knowing what he's doing—just trying to blend in. To his surprise, no one pays much attention to his awkward movements. He relaxes a little, even though he wishes that she didn't do that. After a couple of songs that he doesn't really hear because he is too shocked, they leave the dance floor and head back to their seats. He's smirking, wishing there is a paper bag laying around that he could put over his head as everyone in the group teases him.

"Now was that bad?" Karen asks.

Mel just shakes his head. Surprisingly, he's relieved and a little comfortable, although he's past ready to leave. He folds his hands in front of him, because he doesn't know what else to do with them, and avoids eye contact with everyone as the paranoia of being stared at torments him. Just as his vital signs slow back down to normal, Earl grabs him at the shoulder and offers, "Aren't you ready to go," as he pulls him to the side.

"What?!" Mel asks, stunned by the sudden urgency.

"Isn't it your bed time?" he questions as he gets right up in his face.

"You had too much to drink," Mel declares, turning around, only to have his heart, pulse and breathing shocked still as he comes face-to-face with a passing Memory. Everything seems to come to a complete stop—the dancing, picture taking, eating and merrymaking—except for the song: "Something's Going On" by U.N.V. Of course, she has Ponytail on her arm as her eyes meet his and she flashes a slight grin. For that everlasting moment, he wishes that it is him on her arm. The moment passes, and the moment after he feels all of the same emotions from three months ago. They come rushing back at the same intensity. He thinks about hanging around for another hour, but he knows that he can't stay here. There is a strong possibility that he will see something that will make him snap. Residual feelings remain, but there is an abundance of bitterness that outweighs them. He turns around to Earl, who is looking regretful, and announces, "Let's go." Earl doesn't protest, and after bidding farewell to everyone, Mel leaves without looking back at her.

Chapter 14

Nothing has changed about the registration process at Chicago State. The lines are still long and the advisors are still slow. It's about 80 degrees outside. Without air conditioning and with the crowd factor, it's a saunasish 99. A few people complain in line—talking about how ridiculous this is and how they should get it together—while most stand mum, waiting patiently in the constipated line. At the last minute, Mel decided to enroll for the fall semester as a student at large. The tuition reimbursement forms had to be turned in the previous week and Mel decided to take Speech and TV production—under the guise of a marketing focus. Mel arrived later than he intended, so he's paying now. He took the day off for the purpose of getting up here before the underclassmen and getting the classes that he needed, but the covers wouldn't let him go this morning. The best sleep comes when he knows that he doesn't have to get up and the alarm clock isn't set.

He threw a couple of suits in the dry cleaner's and mailed an admission application to Columbia for the Spring semester. He will probably enter as a student at large, since they have a lot of classes to choose from and he's still unsure about his area of focus. Just before he came in to register, he bought a sausage sandwich from Wendy's that he now regrets, because it's engaged in battle with last night's lasagna and peach cobbler from Vernita. If there was a law against inducing gluttony, she would get a life sentence for addicting him to homemade meals. She knows that she can throw down with Italian almost as well as she can spit a sweet tune out of her mouth.

He stands just outside of the doorway behind about 40 people. The view directly in front of him is captivating though. A pair of daisy dukes hugging some of the nicest buns at CSU is sticking out and glaring at him, saying, *"You want to squeeze the Charmin's but don't."* A set of long, firm, chrome legs extends smoothly from the denims, as if in competition for attention. Not a single scratch. Looking them up and down makes him intoxicated and lustful enough to map out an approach to use to get her in the bed. When there's a juicy romp-roast staring him in the face after months without meat, it's easy for him to forget about his Christian morals.

He clears his throat and clumsily shuffles the class schedule and other forms as he eyes the back of her pinned-up, silky hair. Judging by her side profile, she's a bronze beauty—about an unofficial 11 on a scale of 1 to 10. She's wearing red lipstick—not to much though—and she has the blackest, longest eyelashes. If looking good is feeling good, he's hurting like a broken nose and she's soothing like a hot bubble bath on a cold winter's day. Mel didn't bother dressing presentable...just a pair of Levi's—which are too hot—dirty Nikes and an old Bulls T-shirt from the first championship year that he cleans his car in. He doesn't even remember putting on deodorant. Is that his stale underarms he smells? Now he's self-conscious. His breath is sour, so he covertly pops in a stick of DOUBLEMINT.

If he attempts to break the ice with small talk or a corny line (So, what are you taking this semester; please tell me you have Speech 203 and 208), she may get ghetto loud and ignorant: *'None of your damn business' or 'Naw, I ain't got no class with you—if I did, I would drop it, now please go cremate your dead lines, because they're starting to smell.'* The desire to get embarrassed is absent, so he decides to look and lust in stealth. So what's behind that fine face? A God-fearing woman that's faithful and submissive to the man in her life; a feminist, spoiled brat that cuts out if she doesn't get her way; a smart aleck bitch on a broom, waiting to tell somebody off. So many possibilities. He's curious, but not as curious as the kamikaze cat. He's still a little sore from the Deidra incident, even though his desire to find a good woman is still strong. She probably isn't his type anyway. Her club bunny profile hints that she has many men at her disposal.

After a year, they finally get close to the front, where somebody from his high school days who he's not too crazy about is floating around. Troy Nelson: the class clown and one of several tormentors from Mel's dark days at Lindblom. Apparently, he spots him and heads over his way. If he tries to cap on him, he may deck him with a chair. Surprisingly, Troy comes over and catches the woman in front of him off guard. Her name is apparently Angela. How fitting: an Angel. Troy gives her a hug and they excitedly catch up on the latest with each other. They talk about their mutual friends (Jennifer got pregnant by Derrick—Natasha's husband—and she's gonna keep the baby and Natasha is going to stay with Derrick; Reggie got caught trying to rob a newsstand, and is in counseling for crack addiction; Cindy and Buck are getting married next week, but they'll probably be getting a divorce a week later—with the way they fight all the time; Shawn was on Jenny Jones last week, for a show titled "My Boyfriend Is Sleeping With My Brother", and he came out of the closet on national TV). And she—the Angel from Heaven—broke up with Marvin...what a fool Marvin is.

"We grew apart," she says. "We still talk sometimes and we're still friends, but our lifestyles conflicted. He wanted to go clubbing all the time, and I liked to go to church. I wasn't comfortable at the clubs and he hated church with a passion."

Mel's love for her blossomed at that moment. Now if Troy would start walking until he falls off the edge of the Earth, the setting would be perfect.

"What a shame...You sound like you can sing."

"I'm in the choir, as a matter of fact."

"Sing for me baby," he says seductively.

"Now now. It comes from the heart and you know my heart is reserved for Jesus and that special man in my life. Sorry. No serenade today."

Mel wants to laugh and tell him to get lost, but he holds his peace, because Troy knows how to make people feel like flea feces.

"Damn. How can I be down?" he asks as he throws his hands up to the side. "What church do you go to, so I can hear that voice of yours?"

"Christ the Solid Rock Baptist Church, on 83rd and South Shore Drive."

That's right around Mel's house. It's a medium size church that he hasn't been to...yet.

"Are you singing Sunday?"

"Nope."

"What about next Sunday?"

"I don't know. You'll just have to come and see."

"I ain't in the mood for a preacher, so I'll pass on that. I don't want to be unpleasantly surprised if you don't," he says, with a hint of contempt for the church. "What classes are you taking?"

"I'm trying to get Intro to Managerial Accounting; Business Law; Child and Adolescent Psychology and this stupid Biology class," she says as she fumbles through the class schedule and registration forms.

"I know what you mean. You a business major?"

"Accounting, so Biology is unnecessary."

Mel gets excited at hearing that, and shocked when Troy says out of the deep blue, "You might want to get with this brother," as he nods towards Mel. "He's an accounting brainiac."

Mel embarrassingly simpers and nods as she turns around and questions, "Oh really?"

"What up, Mel," Troy says as he extends his hand. "You still into that accounting?"

"Not really," he says modestly without thinking as he shakes his hand. "I got my Bachelors in it and another Bachelors in Management, but I'm here to try out Communications—TV production specifically."

"So those numbers finally caught up with you and drove you a little crazy? It looks like you loosened up a little, too," Troy jokes—mild for what he's known for.

"Yeah, you can say that," Mel says nervously as Angela looks directly in his face, wearing an expression of admiration. Did somebody crank the temperature up?

Troy spots one of his frat brothers (he's an Alpha) and with a "Talk to you later" to them, he jets out. And Mel is left standing there, facing Heaven on Earth in all of its glory, as the split moment of silence and nervous hesitation seems like an hour of conceited muteness.

"When did you finish up?" she asks.

Mel stumbles over his tongue and makes a thousand statements in one exhalation: "For accounting? I finished in '91. My management degree two semesters later. What about you—How long do you have?"

"At the rate I'm going, I'll be here forever," she says as she flashes the prettiest half smile and rolls her eyes in jest. "I've been going part-time for a couple of years and then I took a semester off here and there. I'm classified as a lower level junior, so theoretically I have about two years left. It's hard to schedule things, when you have to work full-time, too. And then I have a family that I have to take care of."

"I can understand that. You have kids?" Mel probes.

"No, but I might as well, since I spend a lot of time with my sister's three kids. I have no regrets about that, but I'm glad they're hers and not mine. My grandmother suffers from Alzheimer's and has been up and down in the last few years—mostly down—so I have to care for her too since I refuse to put her in a nursing home. Those places are like concentration camps."

"I know what you mean," Mel says empathetically as he tries to hide the excitement of falling deeper in infatuation with this childless, Nubian beauty. "Work is a heavy enough load to deal with. People add to the load. I admire you for that."

"Thanks. Hopefully I'll be finished before my ten-year high school reunion," she jokes as a spot opens up at a clerk's station. "This is definitely a good start. See you later," she says with a wave as she fades off to the table.

"Okay," is all he can utter, with hopes that he sees her *sooner.* He has a sinking feeling of helplessness. Perfect woman, imperfect timing. He grows ardent as he watches her back—waiting for another station to open up, so he can catch up with her. Opportunities like this don't come along often. She could be the answer to his prayers, so he prays in silence: *"Please, Lord, let her be the one. I still won't sleep with anyone until marriage."*

Just as a station becomes available and he takes a seat, she rises and goes to the cashier to pay. His head follows her as she walks all the way across the room.

"How are you," the stout, worn out clerk asks.

He turns around and hands her the forms. "I'm okay. What about you?" he returns as his head does a 180 degree'r to watch Angela.

"Just fine," she answers without looking up as she puts his information in at an unacceptable pace. He turns to her and she's drinking a diet Pepsi while she looks at her screen. The urge to knock the can from her mouth is almost as strong as the anticipation of talking to Angela. She finally tells him that his two classes are available (D-uh. As if everybody is breaking their neck to take TV production).

"Thanks," he says as he springs up and purposely walks towards her—seemingly in slow motion—with his heart racing and his palms leaking. There are a million things that he wants to say to her—wants to know about her—but his mind is cluttered with possible dialogue yearning to come out. The last thing he wants to do is freeze up and make an off-the-wall utterance. Focusing with tunnel vision on her, the walk is labored and uncomfortable. He cusses under his breath as another lady gets in line directly behind her.

He's only a step off, because she steps up to the cashier and bends over (what a view) and writes a check. Fortunately, she has to wait for a receipt, so he still has another chance. He lingers back, not getting in line so he can pull her to the side. As she hands over the check and steps to the side, Mel floats over inconspicuously. The Devil must be playing tricks with him, because he gets a few feet from her and a couple of her girlfriends come over and strike up a conversation with her. Mel plays it off and fades back. He never approaches a girl in a group. Never. Now he's getting frustrated and impatient as he flips through the class schedule in order to look occupied.

Her receipt comes back quick and she darts out of the door. Mel almost has to run to keep from losing her. Just before he gets to the door, he stops briefly in his tracks as he notices that she's on the phone in the hallway. And she's looking right at him. That long moment makes him feel awkward, causing him to shift into stupid, avoid her eyes, and walk past as if he's going to the rest room—like a hypocrite. He'd be the loudest griper if a woman who was interested in him was playing the "avoid eye contact" game. It's one of his pet peeves and he just did it. After he turns the corner, he realizes that he does have to use it.

"Shoot," he groans in frustration when he gets to the urinal. He's blowing it big time. It would be a different thing if she was unapproachable and mean spirited. But she seems to be just the opposite. If it was an ignorant woman, he would be making a fool out of himself.

After using it and washing his hands, he takes a deep breath and resolves to go and talk to her no matter what. Determined as ever, he bolts from the washroom and turns the corner to where the phones are—expecting to see her—but she's gone. He looks around in a panic and runs to the registration room. After scanning it, there's no sight of her, so he quickly trots to the exit to the parking lot. Through the glass door, he can see her getting into what looks like a late model, black Daytona. Just a second, a step, a nerve off and she peels off. In twenty minutes, he developed one of his biggest crushes and had his heart crushed. Too much drama at once. It's a long shot, but maybe he'll see her again on campus. Better yet, he'll visit Christ the Solid Rock Sunday. That means five and a half long days and six nights of the wettest dreams, since it's only Monday.

After he paid his tuition with one of dad's personal checks and took his ID picture, Mel floated all the way across campus to the bookstore, oblivious to the circulation of students all about. He muses about lakefront walks and picnics in the park; carriage rides downtown and dinner on the Chicago River; Gospel plays at the Regal and snuggling on cold winter nights, watching rented videos—or watching each other. Marriage, kids (about six or seven on her body), and a happy life would follow. He even made up a hymn in his head titled "Angela." The lyrics are simply "Angela Angela Oh Angela". He's past the clouds, orbiting the Milky Way. If he had gotten her phone number, he would be flying around Heaven with the rest of the angels. It's a good thing there were no trees in his path, because he would've walked right through them.

Of course he will have to get to know her first, but intuition tells him that in their brief exchange, he heard all he needed to hear. The rest is all about compromise. If she wants him to pierce his navel and tattoo his face, he will be a radical, Holy Ghost filled, PK with a hole in his belly button and the face of a clown.

Before he realizes it, he is browsing in the bookstore. "You need help with something," one of the female clerks asks.

"That's okay. Thanks," he voices without thinking as he strolls the aisle of imprinted sweat clothes. He peruses through several colors of athletic wear, when he comes to his favorite color combination: burgundy and gold. He holds a large pair of sweat pants up to himself and considers buying two pairs (one for him, and an identical pair for Angela) with matching hooded sweatshirts, but decides against it—for now. He hasn't gone completely crazy...yet.

He grabs a large sweatshirt and starts towards the book section, when he half hears, "I thought Chicago State's colors were green and gold."

He casually turns around, not realizing that the statement is directed at him. A woman with yellow and orange construction garb on and a girlish countenance about two arm lengths away stands sifting through the clothes. They're the only two within voice reach. Apparently, she just got off, because her jeans and work boots are dusty and she's still wearing a hard hat. She looks like she could be funky. Is there construction going on on campus?

"Looks like Loyola's colors to me. You sure you're in the right place?" she questions with a slight grin as she peeks up at him, holding up a green and gold sweatshirt.

He can't believe she's tripping on school colors, like this is high school. She must be a freshman. "Yeah, I'm in the right place," he mutters, slightly flustered because of the brief disruption of fantasy.

"I'm just messing with you," she quips. "I saw you grinning from ear-to-ear and I thought I would bother you. You don't have to stop smiling on account of me."

"Oh. I'm not tripping. I was just deep in thought."

"Um hm. Must be a really special girl. I know that type of smile. Say it's not," she demands as she faces him.

He notices how her chestnut brown eyes compliment her ivory complexioned, pudding face. "To be honest, I forgot what I was thinking," he lies, a little embarrassed by his ignorant reception as he starts blushing. "Just something silly, I guess."

"Yeah okay. I'll go with that," she says, smiling impishly.

For a long moment he pauses, struggling to come up with something cerebral to say, and pulls out something stupid like "So...you work in construction, huh?"

"No," she denies as she drops her smile. "I'm an account executive for a large-chain, European clothing manufacturer. This is the gear I wear to sell potential clients on our top line."

"Ha-Ha-Ha. Just call me Joe Gump."

"Of course, I direct traffic on construction sites. What gave me away? I was hoping I would be inconspicuous," she says as she lightly slaps him on the arm. Her touch sends a nervous chill through his body that makes him shudder slightly, as if her hands are charged with electricity.

"So what are you taking," he says, jumping to another subject.

"Oh. Let me see," she says as she fumbles with her books and checks her schedule. "I'm taking Biology and Speech."

"Speech? Which one?" Mel queries.

"Speech 203 on Saturday afternoons."

"Really? That's when I have it. Are you in 201 in the Harold Washington Hall?"

She checks her schedule and beams, "Yes" after she verifies.

"Is this the book?" he asks, pointing at a book in her arm.

"Yeah."

"Let me go get it before they run out of used ones," he says as he starts to the section. "What are you going into?"

"I want to be a nurse."

"Really? How long do you have to go?"

"This is going to be my first year, but I came out of Whitney Young in '87, so don't think I'm fresh out of high school. I got married and had a son after I graduated and, of course, I had to start working full-time."

"Oh yeah," Mel says with reservations about hearing her life story. Even if he was attracted to her and she wasn't married, she wouldn't be his type: he's not trying to get with somebody's momma.

"I moved back home the end of last year and I thought, *finally I've got the chance to pursue this dream.* I've always wanted to be a nurse, but of course, it wasn't happening with a family and all. I'm really excited about coming back to school."

"I can imagine."

"I don't know what to expect...I wanted to take more classes, but I want to take this first semester slowly, so I can get used to studying again. My regret isn't the path that I took, but that I gave my dreams up. For the longest time, I didn't seriously think about going back and doing this; I just sorta accepted my lot in life." She continues from the textbook section all the way to the counter, passionately detailing how excited she is about being back in school. "And what are you going into?"

"Who me?" he questions as his gears get caught between dense and dumb. "I already have degrees in Accounting and Management. I'm thinking about changing careers, so I'm taking a couple of courses that are along the lines of visual communications."

"That's a long way from Accounting."

"I know. You wouldn't believe how *not me* the field is. It's too bad it took me eight years and over $20,000 in tuition and other expenses to realize it. If I like it, I'll just go to graduate school for it."

She just nods her head in understanding as they reach the counter. He lays his books and clothes down. As the cashier rings up over $90 in merchandise, he digs into his pocket for his wallet, only to discover that he only has ten dollars. "Awe shoot," he says as he throws his hand over his mouth, remembering that his money was left in his jacket that he dropped off at the cleaners.

"What's wrong?"

"I left my money in my jacket pocket. I'm sorry, but I'm going to have to come back and get this tomorrow," he embarrassingly tells the patient cashier. He turns to his classmate and declares, "I'll see you in class Saturday" as he rushes out the door, hoping the cleaners recovered it and are honest enough to return it.

"Okay. See you."

"Earth Angel" by Anita Baker goes off way too soon for Mel's liking as he pulls in front of his house. Homey comes in with him, jumping at his bag of Pepe's, so he immediately pours some nuggets and water in his bowls. He releases a long sigh and silent prayer when he sits down to eat. The cleaners recovered his money and he decided to treat himself to "Natural Born Killers" at Ford City. He window-shopped, bought a religious T-shirt, the Kirk Franklin tape and some chocolate chips from The Cookie Factory. He took the scenic route home (a drive through the Loop, then local down King Drive, Cottage Grove and Lake Park Avenue to South Shore Drive) and listened to the tape while eating cookies. He just so happened to drive by Christ the Solid Rock on his way to Pepe's. After he finishes his Tacos, he scrubs down in the tub, and reads his Sunday school lesson. Before he knows it, he is on his knees closing his day out with an optimistic prayer. After he asks that "Thy will be done", he crawls into bed and smiles himself to sleep.

"I'm telling you, it's hitting the fan," Earl says. "You should've seen the choir stand: it was more singers in the audience. The tension up there was brick thick. That choir is a war zone and somebody's going down, soon."

"Reverend didn't address it during service?" Mel questions as he cruises down 95th Street on his way to Chicago State.

He ran into Earl at the 79th and Yates bus stop on the way home from the CEDA office in Hyde Park. His GT is in the shop—again—because of a bad alternator. CEDA informed him that he should get a decision in the mail within two weeks. They assured him that he qualifies and will likely be approved for the assistance. He prays that he will, since he only has about $1000 saved, $700 short. Since he is up and out, he might as well pick up his books from Chicago State, so he agreed to give Earl a ride to the El station. During choir rehearsal that Friday, Lorraine and Harold were late because of a bus delay. Gene didn't care and tried to fine them both. Brenda stepped in and told him that he didn't have the authority to fine anyone and that they were *pardoned. They exchanged a couple of pleasantries before Gene walked out—along with about half of the stars in the choir stand. A fourth more sat out Sunday.*

"What could he say that hasn't been said? You could tell that it was on his mind, though. He had a 'Lawd have mercy on me and these trifling people' expression. It wasn't too bad to me. Ray got down on the keyboard, Lonnie smoked on the drums, the choir sang to God, and I didn't miss the devils one bit. Good riddance I say. Now I can get a chance to work on my song with Ray."

"Umph," is all he can muster out.

Sunday came and went down as a big disappointment for Mel. He had a very spirited prayer the night before and taught a good lesson that morning as the fill in for Deacon Lewis. Then he set out for Christ the Solid Rock, ready to profess his love and propose to Angela. He was charged and puffed up with bravado all the way up to the door of the sanctuary. When he opened the door, there she stood, close enough to smell her breath; close enough to kiss. That's when his day came crashing to earth. She greeted him with a glancing smile and he lost his voice; the bravado was popped out of him in that instant and he took a seat in the second row to the back, just in front of the ushers. The sermon was probably good, but he missed it as he sat petrified in the back. After service, he observed from an inconspicuous distance as she chatted briefly with her fellow members. Then she dashed off just as quick as a snap. He spent Labor Day laboring over Sunday. He was so glad when Tuesday came around—although he had to go in to work for the end of the month inventory. That meant only five days before Sunday.

"At least people are not focusing on you being at the Clique anymore," he consoles.

"Well, I really didn't do anything immoral when I was there," he retorts with a bit of edge. *On the way out, he met eyes with Donald and knew right then and there that his presence at the club would be the top story at Love of God. Sure enough, in Sunday school Trustee Smith inquired where he was that night. Mr. Smith never asked about his whereabouts. Donald probably didn't wait until he got home to call and tell him. They were just trying to discredit his character any way they could. Later, his father told him that people were grumbling about his presence at the club. Mel confessed and promised, "I'm not going back again, anyway."*

"Whatever happened to the *WO*man I saw you with in the Merchandise Mart?" Earl fishes.

"Vernita is doing fine. She sent me a plate of her barbecue for Labor Day. Now stop being nosy."

"Just asking, Cuz. She seemed like a nice lady," he says as he holds in his laugh.

"Yeah right. She seems like a juicy bit of gossip for you."

"Oh—speaking of juicy gossip—guess *who* was picking up Connie Shaw from school two days ago?" he questions.

Mel doesn't even answer, because he doesn't care about high school affairs.

"Don *Juan* Bradford."

Mel gives him a questioning glance.

"That's right. I saw her get in the car with him when I was passing on the bus. I guess he has a ministry for high school girls."

"He has a lot of nerve," Mel mumbles to himself through clenched teeth.

"Not to mention a lot of kids," Earl seconds. "And a wife."

"Had the nerve to trick on me when he's creeping," Mel snickers as he shakes his head.

"I hear you. I would tell his wife, but with her giving birth three months ago, I don't want to instigate. She may kill the baby," he jokes.

"You think he's doing something illegal with those young girls?" Mel questions.

"Let me put it this way: I'm sure he's not schooling them on Bible principles. The question is 'does anybody know besides us'...specifically his wife, Pastor, Brother Smith and Harold."

"Harold is big enough to knock a hole in his head, isn't he?"

"You know it. I wonder if my man Smith will still be chummy with him if he knew he is giving his little girl an internship on the birds and the bees."

Mel just giggles at the thought.

"By the way, is that brother of yours graduating?"

"By the grace of God, yes," Mel testifies. "Now that you mention it, he has a class with Connie."

"Is that right?"

Mel nods as he comes to the stop. He lets Earl off at the El station at 95th Street and heads on to school. When he gets to the Robinson University Center, he gathers a couple of copies of Tempo (the CSU student newspaper) and reads a bulletin board advertising books for sale and upcoming school events on his way into the bookstore. He made sure that he had his money this time and is thankful that they still have the sweat set that he had picked out the prior week. When he gets over to the book section, he doesn't see any used books, so he collects the new ones and is about to head to the cashier, when a familiar voice says, "Somebody played hooky Saturday."

He turns around and has to do a twice over, because at first he doesn't recognize the young lady before him. After a two second study of her features, his eyes blatantly pop out of his head and his mouth hits the floor when he realizes it's the woman that he chatted with the same day he registered. She looks two hundred percent different, though.

"Oh. How you doing," is all he can manage to say as he struggles to remember the name she never told him or he never asked for. At the moment, he doesn't know what his name is.

"I'm fine. Bet you didn't recognize me without my work clothes on. And where were you Saturday, Melvin?" she queries with a charming grin.

He finds himself fumbling over words and a little embarrassed. Last Monday, she looked like a homely caterpillar; Today she looks like a butterfly fresh out of her cocoon. She's wearing a brown, laterally-stripped, form-fitting summer dress with thin beige leather sandals; Her hair is a beautiful, reddish brown and a little past her shoulders; And the body: it is so curvaceous and luscious, he can't believe it's real. He's going to have to repent when she's out of his sight, because as long as he sees her, he's fulfilling all of his deepest fantasies with her in his heart. The blood pressure of his manhood is rising. She's breathtaking. That may explain why he's hyperventilating. And the killing part is she knows his name.

"Oh...I was...I had to do something. Something came up at the last minute. Did I miss anything?"

She continues to smile that *smile* at him. "The instructor assigned another book," she says, holding it up for him.

"Not another book."

"Yep. Another one...and I got the last used one. Sorry."

He watches her full, red lips and hangs on every little word and punctuation mark that comes off of them. "I'm sorry, but I don't even know your name, and I feel a little goofy since you know mine," he says abashedly.

"That's okay. I'm Cherelle," she says, entrancing him with that simper. "I saw your name on your registration forms and I remembered it."

"Nice to meet you, Cherelle—formally anyway," he says as he extends his hand forward and his memory back ten years to one of his all-time favorite songs (I Didn't Mean To Turn You On) by the artist of the same name, who he considers one of the most gorgeous creatures to ever walk the earth. They have the same physical features, but they are arranged differently. Never the less, they're both fine. He notices how soft, yet firm her hand is when he shakes it, not to mention the electric-like charge she sends through his body again. *Did she mean to turn him on?*

"Nice to meet you, too. You're looking kinda' jazzy today, with your cute tie. I like that clean-cut professional look. You're ready for the world with that outfit," she flatters.

He blushes uncontrollably. "I'm surprised you recognized me *in* my work clothes," he says as he grabs the other book the instructor requires.

"Is that where you're heading?"

"Nope. I'm headed to the cashier—this time with my money," he jokes as he gestures in the direction. "Just got off...actually I got off a couple of hours ago and I just made some stops before I got here. I'm do to crash land any second, so be prepared to catch me. My caffeine tank should be on empty."

She giggles at his humor. She's so cheery. "You work the night shift?"

"Are you kidding? I was just filling in for another supervisor for inventory. I could never do this on a permanent basis. I like to sleep at night."

"You're a supervisor?"

"Am I?"

He pays for his books and strolls across the campus with her...not going to any particular location, just walking and having a good conversation. They settle on the ledge of the Harold Washington Hall, talking about everything under the watchful eyes of God. "...and that's why I stopped breeding: it was too emotionally draining."

She nods with that last statement, looking interested in his every statement. "I love dogs...used to have a dog when I was a kid. It got ran over by a truck."

"That's too bad," he says sympathetically. "And you never got another one?"

"At the time I didn't want another one just to replace him...he was like a family member. When I was ready for another dog, I went through changes as far as my family is concerned. I mean my daddy was out of work and we had to keep moving from apartment to apartment, and then my parents were on the verge of getting a divorce, and things were just so hectic," she says as she looks down, for the first time she doesn't look cheerful.

"I can understand," he says in a low, soothing tone as he studies her facial expression, pausing for a while to watch the other students roam over the campus. Suddenly, he realizes that he's extremely hungry and very much awake now. He knows under any other circumstance it would be a long shot, but he asks, "Are you hungry?"

"I usually don't eat until lunch time, but yes, I could go for a snack."

"You want to go to the Original Pancake House on 87th with me?"

She eyes him and smirks a little. "Sure. I'll go. Are they still serving breakfast at this time? What time is it?"

Mel pulls out his watch and says, "A quarter to eleven."

"That's a nice watch."

"You think so," he quizzes, recalling the source of it as they both rise and trek back across campus to his car. "Let me tell you the story behind this watch..."

Along the way to the car, he observes people looking enviously at them. A couple of guys are peeking at her first, and then glance at him, determining that he is her good thing that she isn't letting go. Just as they pass them, he notices their heads U-turning and stealing a peak of her succulent hind side. It is oh so nice. He almost forgets about his infatuation with Angela. A group women along the way are overtly scoping her out (probably thinking some snide thoughts about her), and then they stare him down with competitive interest. He is loving the attention. There wouldn't be a fraction of the eyes directed at him if he was walking by himself. Cherelle seems unaware of the attention she is drawing. She's an excellent conversationalist.

"...and so the watch is all that's left of our relationship. Sometimes it reminds me of her; sometimes it reminds me how late I'm running. It doesn't bring back painful *memories*...no pun intended. I'd be lying to say that I don't miss her, but I consider myself over her and I wouldn't go back with her," he says as they get to the car. "This is me right here."

"This is a cute car," she says as he leads her to the passenger's side. "What kind is it?"

"It's called a Dodge Stealth," he proclaims proudly as he closes her in. He's surprised and pleased that she isn't familiar with it.

When he starts the ignition, "Tomorrow" by the Winans comes on the tape and he turns the volume down so they can continue talking and hearing the music at the same time.

"You told me you got married right after high school...are you still married?"

She's looking out of the window in a seemingly pleasant daydream. "That's my favorite song," she says, pausing briefly while he pulls out of the parking lot and onto 95th Street. She starts back up after the song finishes. "I married my high school sweetheart a year after high school. We both had big plans...or fantasies, depending on how you looked at it. Johnny planned to be a big-time lawyer after he finished up at Northern, and of course I wanted to be a nurse. I found out I was pregnant the week before he left for school. I told him to go ahead and I decided to wait and get ready for Chuckie."

"That's your son's name," he slips in as she pauses during her methodical recount.

She nods. "I named him after my father, because Daddy doesn't have any sons."

"Do you have any sisters?"

"Two younger sisters: Dameeka, 15 and Eunice, 19."

"You're the oldest? So am I. Did you have it as hard as I did?"

She smiles at him and nods in agreement. "He finished college in five years and took time off to spend with us. He got a job as an account executive—he studied marketing—and we moved into a townhouse. I was sure we were on our way to living happily ever after. Things were going well—or so I thought. He was a good father and husband for about a year. Then he changed and started going on these 'business trips' and staying out all the time. I didn't have a problem with it though, because I figured it came with the territory. Then I found out that he had a girlfriend while he was at Northern and they had a daughter and a son together. That bothered me, but what bothered me more is that he started going to Atlanta to see her. I guess he really was taking care of business," she says dejectedly while trying to be facetious.

"I was willing to work through it and even forgive him...I tried to get him to go to counseling at my church, but he refused and told me that he wasn't happy in the marriage. Well, I knew it was me, so I tried my best to hold on to him. I started doing things that I thought would make him happy, like inviting him to baseball games—he loves baseball and I hate it—going out on the town more, because I realized that maybe we didn't get out enough; going out to nice restaurants—even though I felt my cooking was better and cheaper. I even went dancing with him, and I don't dance at all. I was willing to walk through fire to make it work, and I feel like I did...I feel like I've been burned. But he was just as determined to end it, and he did."

"I'm sorry to hear," he says sincerely, seeing how discomforting it is to her.

"He started slapping me around," she says matter-of-factly without any hints of bitterness. "The last time he hit me, he used his fist and slit my lip. I had to have twenty stitches to close it up. That's why my lips are so big now."

His eyebrows go up, because he can't imagine someone hitting this mild mannered creature. He's even more surprised at how casual she is about it.

"So you're divorced?" he questions as he glances at the ring.

Apparently, she catches him and says, "The ring is a deterrent for unwanted creeps, not that it works...And no, I'm not talking about you. We're in the process. The only thing left is his signature. I was holding out for the child support arrangements, but I decided that if he doesn't want to pay it willingly, I don't want him to pay it at all. I moved back home last year, so the townhouse is all his. I don't want any alimony from him. I don't even wear his name anymore: Duncan. It never even sounded right anyway. It reminds me that I've been dunked," she jokes.

"I'm surprised that you didn't take him to the bank."

"It wasn't necessary to combat ignorance with ignorance. After all, this was somebody I loved and planned to spend the rest of my life with.

I felt that he loved me in the beginning, but he fell out of love and moved on. It wasn't right how he did me, but he's going to have to deal with it later on down the line somewhere."

"And you don't have any ill will for him?"

"Nope. There are scars, but I forgive him."

Mel looks over and shakes his head in disbelief at finding someone with a heart similar to his. "I'm amazed at you," he says as he pulls into the parking lot. "You're a better person than me, because I went through a lot, but I don't know if I could've gone through that."

She forces a smile through her gloomy account and they get out. When they enter, the hostess gives them the option of smoking or non-smoking. They look at each other and simultaneously say, "Non" and laugh. The hostess grabs two menus and leads them to a window booth. The restaurant isn't as crowded as it usually is. Mel usually gets take out, because the line for seating is longer than he likes (it didn't help that he was usually alone).

After skimming the menu, he decides on his usual. He looks up and is captivated with the way her eyes jump from side-to-side like little coconuts as she studies the menu with her chin resting lightly in her hand. After a few moments, she looks up, catches him gazing at her and chuckles, "Am I taking too long?"

"No. No. Take your time. I was just daydreaming," he says sheepishly as the spunky brown waitress comes by and rescues him.

"Are you ready to order?" she asks, flashing a smile at them. Mel gestures to Cherelle and she orders a ham and cheese omelet. He orders eggs, links and buttermilk pancakes. "And what will you have to drink?"

"I'll have an orange juice, please," Cherelle says.

"And you?"

"May I have a large glass of milk."

"Sure thing," she says as she collects the menus and darts off to the front.

For a few moments, they sit in silence. It's not an edgy, uncomfortable silence that comes when there's nothing to say. They're both relaxed and comfortable around each other. She studies the place while he gazes out of the window.

"What's the difference between this place and the International House of Pancakes? It would be easy to get them mixed up."

"The color and a slight variation in the name. This is black owned and operated in a black neighborhood and a good example of how black people support black merchants."

"Amen to that."

"I thought I *was* going to the International House of Pancakes when I first came here. Then I went out past 95th and Western and noticed the difference in the name," he says with a slight chortle. "I haven't gone out there for breakfast since."

"I heard that," she says as they both pause and smile like giddy teenagers. She rises and says, "I have to go to the lady's room."

He points her to the front: "Right behind the cashier."

He watches her behind as she walks past. Now he has a desire for breakfast in bed. It doesn't take her long to get back, and when she passes, he gets another glimpse...a real good look.

"Let me go wash my hands," he says as he heads towards the front. He grabs an African-American Reader newspaper from the pile on the bench by the exit before he goes in. After he sets the paper down on the faucet and turns on the water, he glances at the scripture (just as he had been peeking at Cherelle) that is on the cover. He's immediately convicted by Galatians 5:24. He says a silent prayer, asking forgiveness, strength and guidance.

When he gets back to the table, the waitress is setting the food out. "Perfect timing," he says as he takes his seat and lays the paper on the bench. Cherelle gives him an expectant look. "What," he questions.

"Just waiting for the magnificent grace."

"Oh. Okay," he says as he bows his head and gives the grace. "How did you know that I say a prayer before I eat?"

"Well, considering you are a deacon and that you have an intimate relationship with God, I just knew that you would give thanks before you stuffed your face," she says, cutting into her omelet.

Mel just sits there petrified, staring at her.

"You ask how do I know? I'm psychic," she claims as she takes a bite and ignores him.

He continues to gaze at her in disbelief.

She looks up and grins. "You visited my church a couple of months ago...Saving Grace?"

"Oh. Okay. You go to Saving Grace, huh...800 North Laramie, right?"

She nods. "I saw you praying during the devotion and I've never heard anybody lay it out to God like that. It was *so*...real. It's not to say that when other folks pray it's not real, but yours seemed so sincere. It really touched me. If there's anything that you know how to do, it's pray."

"Really? I never gave it much thought," he says, somewhat dumbfounded.

"That's what I mean. Some know what they're going to say...have it all scripted. But yours was so spiritually based. It wasn't even long, but it was powerful. Where did you learn to pray like that?"

"I don't know. For the most part, I've always prayed—or should I say talked—to God like that. I couldn't really give you a formula. The only thing I can suggest is to be yourself and be real with Him. Umph. I never thought my prayers were moving. As a matter of fact, I was always bashful about praying in front of people. I would rather pray alone any day, but when necessary, I'll pray in the presence of others."

"Whatever it is, keep doing it that way."

Mel humps his shoulders and shakes his head. "So what do you do in the church?"

"I'm a nurse," she says with pride.

"But of course," he jokes as he commences with his breakfast.

They eat in silence, occasionally commenting on how good it is and making other brief utterances. When they finish eating, they chat briefly. The waitress brings the check and Cherelle grabs at it as Mel snaps it up. She looks bewildered.

"How much did mine come to?"

"My bill comes to $11, which covers both of us."

"You don't have to pay for me, Melvin."

"I know I don't."

"I'd feel more comfortable paying for my own."

"I would feel insulted if I didn't pay for it. I invited you, remember. There're no strings attached, but I mean if you feel that you have to return the favor, I guess you'll have to take me out to eat some other time, but it's not necessary."

She goes along with it in silence, adding, "I'll pay the tip then, and don't argue with me on that."

"Suit yourself."

In the car, Mel can feel a touch of tension in the air, and doesn't know if it is because of the disagreement with the check. "Where are you going now?" he asks, breaking the silence.

"Well, I'm going to visit an aunt that stays a block away from Chicago State. And pretty soon I'll have to go pick up my son."

They pause as he pulls up to the light. "Do you want me to drop you off there?"

"That's okay. Thanks anyway."

"I didn't offend you did I...by paying for the breakfast?"

"Un uh. That was very nice. There's nothing offensive about a gentleman. I'm just a little preoccupied with a situation at my home. I'll tell you about it later."

Mel breathes a sigh of relief. "Where should I let you out," he questions as he approaches the school.

"The library is fine. I'm going to talk to the Board of Governors first, and then I'm going over her house."

When Mel arrives at the parking lot, he gets a little jittery about his next question. He doesn't know how to read her, so he procrastinates. "Well, thanks for joining me for breakfast."

"Thanks for having me. We must do it again sometime."

"By all means," he says grinning at her nervously. "So...can I call you sometimes."

She looks at him and smirks as she reaches into her purse for a pen. She scribbles her full name—Cherelle Morrison—and the number on a sheet of her notebook paper, rips it out and hands it to him. "So...are you going to give me yours?"

"Oh yeah," he says as he pockets the trophy and writes it on the notebook, at her urging.

"Okay Mister Adams," she confirms, looking it over. "I'll give you a call sometimes, too."

"Yeah. I look forward to talking to you and seeing you in class."

She smiles and lets herself out. "Thanks again for the breakfast."

"Anytime."

She gives him a playfully suspicious glance and walks off. He cheats a little, sneaking a long look at her rear before closing his eyes. "Mercy," he says as he pulls off.

Melvin finds himself grocery shopping after he left the school. He has gotten down to a juiceless refrigerator and a steakless freezer, which will not do. Sale or no sale, he gets everything he wants and needs, estimating the total to be around $50. He is about to checkout, when he remembers that when he runs out of food, Homey usually runs out at the same time, so he heads to the pet aisle.

When he turns the corner, he can't believe who's—or what's—in his path. The Angel. A tadpole instantly forms in his throat and grows into a bullfrog as he considers turning around, but she glances over at him and smiles. "Help me Lord" he murmurs as he gets up to her.

"Can you help me get this bag in my cart?" she requests.

"Sure," he says as he lifts the 40-pound sack and loads it in her cart. *Does she want him to drink her bath water, too?*

"Thank you," she says as she studies his face. "You go to Chicago State, right?"

"Um hm," he nods as he loads up on a couple of 40-pound bags that are on sale.

"Melvin, right?"

"That's right. I'm surprised you remember," he blushes. "And you're Angela?"

"That's me. So how are you doing?"

"I'm okay if you're okay."

"Well then, that makes us both okay," she confirms as she examines his groceries. "My, are you having a party?"

It will be if she—and only Angela—shows up. "No, not really. Just shopping for myself for the next two weeks."

She smiles as she assumes, "You must have a greedy dog."

"Yeah, he can put away some food," he says, shifting from side to side.

"What kind is it?"

"A Rottweiler."

"Really? I have a German Shepherd."

"Oh...so we both have dogs of German descent," he observes.

"Yeah. You think they're Nazi's?"

"Not mine. He's too black for words."

"I hear you," she laughs. "So are you ready to check out?"

Only if she is. "Just about."

"Okay, let's go."

Anywhere she wants.

His intestines are doing flips as he walks to the checkout counter with her. Words are popping into his head as he anticipates the "right" thing to say.

"So what are you doing for the rest of the day?"

"I didn't have anything planned," she says as she peers at the tabloids. "What about you, Mister party man?"

"I wasn't planning anything, either. Probably just rest up for church tomorrow."

She flashes him a strange look and asks, "Didn't I see you at Christ the Solid Rock last Sunday?"

He laughs. "That was probably my twin," he jokes. "Yeah that was me."

"I thought so, but I didn't know you well enough to start talking to you," she confesses. "So what church do you go to?"

"Love of God Baptist Church."

"Where's that?"

"It's on Calumet, right off of 63rd Street."

"Isn't it that big church with the two buildings?"

"That's it."

"Oh...Okay. I've never been there. I'm going to have to visit sometime."

It would be better if she joins and becomes a part of the first family. "Have you had any accounting classes before?" he quizzes.

"I had some in high school, and I struggled to make C's."

"Well, if you need any help, I can tutor you at no cost."

"Thanks. That's sweet of you. I know I'm going to take you up on that offer," she promises. "Of course, I can't tutor you, but if there's anything I can do for you, let me know."

Mel's mind goes to the gutter with that proposition. *What can she do for him? She can start by rubbing whipped cream all over his body, and then she can end by licking him clean.*

After they pay for their stuff and walk out to their cars, Mel contemplates another uncomfortable situation. Things were going well so far, so he figures why not? "Would you like to catch a movie tonight?"

She gives him a puzzled look and hesitates. "I don't know...um. Tonight?" she snickers uncomfortably.

"Well, if it's inconvenient, I understand. I just thought since neither one of us had anything planned, that maybe we could get out of the house."

"Well," she mulls. "How about if you give me a call at about five or so and I'll let you know."

YES! "Okay. I'll call you this evening," he says as he pulls out a pen from his pants pocket.

She writes it down on a torn paper bag. "Okay Melvin," she says as she hands it to him. "I have to make sure I can get my neighbor to watch my grandmother for the evening. Give me your number, so I can call you if I find out sooner."

Gladly. He gives her the digits, bids her farewell and sings "Angel" by Angela Winbush all the way home.

He was home thirty minutes when she called and said that she could get away. They decided to go to the show that evening, and Mel was too frantic. Mel scrubbed down, clipped his whiskers, and conditioned his hair. He searched his closet for an outfit, finally deciding on a black, short-sleeved, button-up shirt, purple pants and black, leather bucks. He felt perfect. Everything felt perfect. The only thing left was to have a perfect time and then get married. On the way to pick her up, he bought a single red rose from the gas station and placed it on the seat of his car.

When she opens her front door, he discovers that she can go to a higher level of beauty: her hair is curly in the front and down her back. She is wearing—really wearing—a black summer dress with a split up the back (Mercy), a white blazer and black sandals. Unbelievable. He takes every breath-taking inch of her in. "You look real nice."

"Thank you," she says. "So do you."

He beams with pride and hope. *Does he hear wedding bells?*

Chapter 15

"What's that smell?" Angela questions as she turns her nose up.

"That's my new cologne: Fumé. You like?" Mel jokes.

She shakes her head while frowning.

"As long as you don't light a cigarette, we're cool."

"I don't smoke."

"I know you don't. It's a joke. I got gas on my hands on the way here and it'll be a few hours before the smell is gone."

She doesn't say anything as Mel pulls off. He's not as geeked up as he was on the first date, two weeks ago. Perhaps it's because it could be considered a telling, bad date. Not that either one of them did anything wrong. It just fell hard and flat. It was like he took a match to the 35 bucks. A day spent in a dark closet would have been more stirring and worthwhile. He doesn't really know exactly what went wrong, but he's trying to stay loose on this date. They're going to Ford City to see "Forrest Gump" and maybe have dinner at Old Country Buffet—almost a rerun of two Saturdays ago.

On paper, they are so perfect for each other that it almost seems like a waste of time to go through the drama of courtship. She's compassionate (gave a buck the windshield washer on the street, even though he didn't wipe the window), introverted (hardly ever goes out, this marking the second time in six months), and affection starved (she said that she would love to be married, but only to the right person). Their birthday's are even so close—just three days apart—that if astrology were added to the equation, they would be ideal for each other. He gives her a few brownie points for being a devoted Christian. However, she's not too holy and celestial to where she is unable to comprehend human nature.

They both had rough childhoods (so did he and Memory). She relayed how her deceased father didn't even let her go out until she was almost out of high school. She didn't even go on prom. After she graduated, she immediately started working and moved out. Mel picked up signs that her father may have abused her. He found it odd that she would describe him as jealous when she would look at a boy. She said he died a year after she left home.

It is also ironic that they both have similar experiences with relationships. He's starting to consider that nine out of ten people have probably suffered the same heartache as him. She said the main reason she broke up with her last boyfriend—Marvin—is that he was messing around with a girl that she went to school with. She gave him a choice, and he picked Carolyn, and that's when they grew apart. She is smart, pretty (fine), and spiritual. All of the qualities that he would list on an order form for the woman of his dreams, but the dream is fuzzy.

After watching the movie without really saying much (he likes it that way, although it was somewhat unnerving), they head over to the restaurant.

After ordering, she mentions an old friend she bumped into: "Today I went to the store and bought some ice cream and Iraninto an oldfriend from highschool. She'sgetting marriedtomorrowand her fianceowns the store.Sheused tocome toschooldrunk andhighallthetime. I remember she passedout on thegymfloor andtheschool calledtheambulance..."

She goes on as Mel studies her mouth with wonder. This happened the last time and Mel attributed it to nervous excitement. He missed "Speed" because she chattered throughout the show. He vowed to ignore her comments during "Forrest Gump" and it worked, although it didn't last. Now he's coming to the realization that her mouth is like a run away freight train without a conductor.

When she gets off of the "Friend-at-the-store" tale, he casually asks, "Are you going to Midnight Madness?"

"Imaygosinceit's the firstone.It shouldbe prettyexcitingwiththe stepshowandall.IwonderwhatkindofteamisChicagoStategoingtohavethisyear."

"What do you think of Craig H..." he tries to ask, before getting cut off.

"Ithinkhe'llbeagoodcoachHe'sgoodfortheschoolasfarasattractingpeopletothebasketballgamesbutIdon'tknowifhe'llhelptheteamwinanygamesMaybeiftheyshootasgoodashedidwhenhewaswiththeBulls..."

"You like basktetba..." she cuts in again before he can finish the statement.

"IlovebasketballIusedtoplayitwithmycousinsatonetimeThatwasinmyTomboydayswhenIusedtofightboysandclimbtreesandstufflikethat..."

"What do you think of black sports..." He was going to say black sports agents, but he doesn't bother, as she takes off again.

"Somesportsstarshaveforgottenwherethey'vecomefromIt'sliketheym akeitandjustsaytoheckwiththecommunitytheycomefrom..."

It is becoming a chore to listen to her. He is wondering where is the button to turn her off. Does she have Energizer batteries? Is she a talking doll with a pull string longer than the equator?

"...MaybeonedayIcanworkasanaccountantforsomeoftheblackathletes OnedayIwouldn'tmindactingorsomethingalongthoselinesDidn'tyousayyo uwantedtobeanactoratonetimeDidyouever considermodelingImaygetaport foliotogetherandstartmodelingDoyouknowhowmuchtheymakeTheymake moreinadaythanalotofpeoplemakeinamonth..."

She converses like a drunk man would drive on a straight path: swerving from side to side, jumping from subject to subject. It is like talking to a hyperactive third grader. She just keeps blurting out vacuities nonstop. She asks him something and cuts him off with another question before he can even answer the first one. He endures another hour of her mouth and leaves the restaurant drained and fatigued from listening to long boring commentaries about nothing. He thinks that she is rude in their discussions, although she probably doesn't realize it. But how does one tell someone to shut up? When he drops her off at home, it is a little after 12. He gives her a formal hug and starts questioning whether he heard wedding bells or just his ringing head.

Today is the second presentation for speech class, and Mel squeezed out all of two minutes to show how to operate a video camera. Pretty dull in his opinion, but what else could he do. Cherelle is demonstrating how to take blood pressure. And Mel is her prop. She caught him off guard by asking him at the last minute.

They talked a couple of times on the phone, and he concluded that he likes her...in a sibling way. Not much was revealed during their conversations, but she is easy to talk to. She is as reticent as he is, but—like him—when she speaks, her words have meaning and not just sound. She's decent, charming and old fashioned (just like himself). She has reverence for God, often compliments Mel on how well he carries himself, and doesn't believe in men wearing earrings (even though Johnny got his left lobe pierced after they married). He hasn't seen her any time outside of class since their first breakfast, and with the exception of a possible movie together, he really doesn't expect to "date" her. Outside of crediting him with being nice, she shows no inclination of wanting to get involved with him. Besides, she has a son and she isn't divorced yet.

When she announces 120 over 80, he is pleasantly surprised. He was sure it shot up once she touched him, because his heart started drumming rapidly. Once again, she sent a charge through his body when she touched him. Does she have electricity flowing through her veins? She had the whole routine down: she was clad in a white, nurses uniform—including the hat; she stuck a thermometer in his mouth (of course it was sterile); and she even handed him a prescription for fun and relaxation, along with a Blow Pop. Needless to say, the instructor—Ms. Kronkite—thought she did an excellent job and awarded her an overall A.

"I was impressed," he says with the sucker hanging out of his mouth as they exit the room. "That was a good presentation."

"Thanks. I'm glad you thought so...and I'm definitely glad Ms. Kronkite thought so, too. I was so nervous."

"Get out of here. You seemed so at home."

"You didn't feel me shaking?"

"I thought it was me."

"Why would you be shaking?"

"I was worried my pressure was a little high. That's what aced it for you—my clean bill of health. You know Kronkite is concerned about my well being—maybe not my grade point average, but she's definitely concerned about my health."

She gives him a proud smile and rolls her eyes at him. "She is a hard A. I thought my first one deserved at least a B overall. I couldn't believe she took off so much for coming up ten seconds short. And I just knew that yours was an A. To me, yours was the best out of the class."

His face flushes over another shade of black, because he's too dark to blush.

"So I take it you're going over your aunt's house," he assumes as they get to the exit.

She nods. "I have to take her equipment back."

They both pause, seemingly waiting for the other to say something to keep the conversation going. She takes the lead.

"What are you doing today?"

"You mean what have I done today? My day is over. I'm going home to relax. Why?"

"Well, I was wondering...my family is having a barbecue birthday party for my daddy. We just decided to invite some friends and family over. No big deal or anything. Just a little eating, and some of my relatives will be drinking—of course—but that'll be confined to the back porch. If you're not up to it, that's okay..." she rambles on.

"I would love to go," he cuts in to her surprise as she beams like the desert sun. "What time is it?"

"They started this morning, but I'm going to stay over at my aunt's house until 6:30, and then we're going to go together."

"Oh. You want me to pick you up?"

She flashes a modest glance. "Are you sure that's okay?"

"Of course. Why go in two cars, especially since you're the only person that I know? I'll pick you up at 6:30."

They both pause again, waiting for something else to fall out of their mouths to justify their continued companionship. This time he initiates.

"Can I give you a ride?"

"It wouldn't be a problem?" she quizzes.

Mel shakes his head and grabs her arm. "C'mon." She smiles and follows him to the parking lot. "So what's the dress code?"

"Well, casual. It's not a formal event. You can come as you are. There'll be people dressed down to shorts and jeans tonight, and even gym shoes."

"So are you going to wear that nurses uniform."

She just smiles and rolls her eyes.

"What are you wearing then, because I don't want to seem like an oddball?"

"I'm going to wear a summer dress and sandals...like the one I had on when I was picking up the second book."

Mel's manhood throbs and his jaw locks down on the remnants of the candy coating and into the gum at the thought. "What color is it?"

"It's like a beige with green and tan strips."

"I don't know if I have anything that goes with that..." Mel catches himself making the insinuation that they are a couple. "I mean, I don't have anything along that casual line. I guess I may wear jeans."

"Don't worry about it. You're fine with what you have on."

Mel cuts her a vetoing look. "I'm not wearing a Chicago State sweat suit. I'll just rent a tux and leave it at that."

"Then you'll make me look bad and underdressed."

Mel passes her a questioning glance. He could never make her look bad. He pulls up in front of her aunt's house and they pause again, as if there's no security out of each other's presence...as if there's no assurance that the vibe will be there again. They take the chance.

"I'll see you at 6:30."

She smiles and nods as she exits.

Mel immediately went up to the church for his deacon's and trustee meeting that he was already 20 minutes late for. He holds his peace and secretly urges the long-winded members to stick a sock in the issue they keep going over like a broken record. After an hour of babbling, they dismiss and he rushes home to check his closet for something to wear. He doesn't feel good about anything he has, so he sets out for Bachrach's in Ford City. With all of the clothes he has that people deem sharp, when he's trying to style and profile, they always seem outdated. It takes him all of 15 minutes to decide on an outfit and a pair of shoes. He settles on a shadow gray, short-sleeve, knit shirt, charcoal gray, loose-fitting slacks, and a pair of black loafers—all for $200. He wasn't planning on a new outfit any time in the near future, but he didn't realize that he was going to be trying to leave an impression so soon. Although he wasn't going to go to the barber for another week, he figures a fresh fade would enhance the whole profile. By the time he washes up and conditions his hair, it is time to pick her up. To be safe, he calls and is ordered to "Come on."

He doesn't have to get out of his car when he pulls up to the house. They are coming down the walkway before he comes to a complete stop. Mel almost forgets to brake as he watches Cherelle descend toward him with the grace of a dove, her aunt in tow. Although he was expecting her to be breathtaking, figuring he would be prepared to play it cool, he finds himself hyperventilating and sweating it out as she gets to the car.

"Melvin, this is Aunt Jeannie...Aunt Jeannie, this is Melvin."

Aunt Jeannie sticks her head in the car and inspects him. He's surprised at how young she looks. She can't be over than 30. They can actually pass for sisters. The resemblance is stronger than ammonia.

Aunt Jeannie is a slim with curves in all of the right places. A true woman, oozing with femininity.

"Hello Melvin," she says jubilantly.

"How you doing, Aunt Jeannie?"

"I'm fine...and call me Jean. It's nice to meet you," she says as she takes a seat in the back. "He is handsome, Cher," she shamelessly proclaims.

"Thank you," he says modestly as his face flushes along with Cherelle's. He's never seen anyone that shade of red, but it looks nice on her.

"So Melvin...Cherelle tells me that you have an interest in communications or some kind of video production," she probes.

"Yeah. Right. I'm just sampling some classes to see which direction I want to go in. I'm also considering some type of visual communications or computer graphics. Something artistic and creative," he says with pride.

"I hear you're in Corporate America...that's a big change of heart, isn't it?"

"Oh yeah. Make no mistake about it. My focus for all of those years has been on business management and accounting, but it's not something that I feel I can do for the rest of my life without going crazy with boredom. Then that glass ceiling is a big factor, too. So here I am: taking the first step to a career change, and I must say I'm excited about it."

"I know what you mean. It's hard to imagine me staying in nursing until I retire. That's why I'm going to be enrolling in law school next year."

"Really? I have a friend I used to work with that's going to John Marshall next year."

"That's where I'm headed."

"What a coincidence...we're both in the process of switching fields."

"Yeah. Miss Cher here can't understand it, but who knows, once she gets into nursing, maybe she'll go into politics or something. I decided to go into something that I'm good at and comes natural: Arguing. The gift of gab is an art form...ain't that right, Cher?"

Cherelle just rolls her eyes at her and smirks.

"I hear you. I think that I have an eye for the black experience that doesn't get broadcast in the media."

"I know what you mean. Let the white press tell it, every black woman is on welfare and every black man is a criminal. That's why I don't watch the news anymore. I can't relate to what they show. I've never seen a car-jacking or a drive-by. It's because of that image that a lot of black people—black men in particular—get pegged as crooks, even though they may be innocent."

"You're all right with me, Jean."

"I like you too, Melvin. You're a good, positive brother. We need more men like you. Do you have any brothers?"

"I have a younger brother that's not quite like me."

"Oh well. Maybe he'll grow up to be like you, and then we can hook up," she jokes as they all laugh.

Jean and Mel hit it off well and chatter all the way to the party. She relaxes him from an evening being spent with strangers. Normally, he's not comfortable around someone as sassy as she, but she has a touch of flair and earthiness that makes her just a plain, funny character to love. He hopes that the rest of the relatives are as easy to get along with as she is.

"Now you're going to meet some crazy folks tonight, Melvin, but don't be intimidated...they're all harmless."

"Are they anything like you?"

"Not even close. When God made me, he broke the mold."

"I'm not going to leave you hanging, Melvin," Cherelle interjects.

"Oh...it's no problem."

"I know how it can be stressful around a bunch of strangers. I'm not going to keep you in there that long, either. If you can survive the interrogation with my big, bad daddy, you'll be home free. Whatever you do, don't smile in front of him."

Mel's eyes get big.

"Stop messing with him Cher...you're liable to scare the man away."

"Melvin knows I'm kidding. You'll like Daddy a lot. Just be yourself."

Mel just nods as he exits the Eisenhower expressway at Independence. He keeps a watchful eye out as he comes to a stop at Pulaski. He turns on Pulaski and notices the area looks like a wasteland...as if a bomb was dropped in the area. There are bad spots on the south side, with the run-down buildings and debris scattered on the streets, vacant lots with shattered liquor bottles and weed gardens, and the drug selling and gang-banging trash. It is in most cases restricted to patches in almost every neighborhood, but spread out enough. What Mel observes is a whole community of depression and poverty. Apparently, Jean notices it too.

"When are you going to move out South, Cher? It looks like the aftermath of a nuclear holocaust over here."

"It's better than it looks on the West Side. Besides, once I get the means, I'll move somewhere better."

"Once you get the means? Come move in with me. You practically live there anyway. That way, you'll be closer to *Melvin*. Why have him travel across the city just to see *you*?"

"I don't mind," he interjects.

"Thank you, Melvin," Cherelle says as she turns around and rolls her eyes at her. "You know I can't live under the same roof with you anyway."

"Awe, you didn't have to go there."

"You know I'm joking. I just want to be close to daddy, because I worry about him sometimes over here. I don't like him over here alone."

"Alone? He does have a wife and two younger daughters still living under his roof. Correction: three daughters. I'm going to have to talk to Janice about putting you out."

"Mom will never put me out."

"Do you forget I've known her for 36 years, so there's a stronger bond between us. Don't challenge me. You'll be out and on the South Side begging Melvin for a place to stay."

"Yeah right," she says as she shakes her head.

"I know I'm right."

Cherelle just forces a smile and mumbles under her breath as Mel approaches Roosevelt Road.

"You're going to make a left the third block after the light, Melvin." Mel proceeds to turn down the block. "All the way to the end of the block and turn down Springfield...it'll be the yellow house on the left."

"As if the man can't read the address. Besides, the house is gold," Jean antagonizes.

"Anyway," she says as Mel pulls in front of the two-story, frame house. "This is home Melvin. Are you nervous?"

"I can't breathe."

"Better give him mouth-to-mouth, Cher."

"C'mon Jean...stop embarrassing me," she pleads.

"Okay. I'll chill out."

"Thank you."

As they exit, Mel notices a porch of men (about 10 deep) across the street who are looking intently at them. They start giving catcalls to the ladies. Cherelle cuts them the nastiest glare. Mel could see heat seeking missiles come out of her eyes.

"When are y'all going to call the Department of Streets and Sanitation on them?" Jean questions.

"You mean the Animal Welfare?" she corrects.

"I meant what I said. Looks like riffraff to me. What do you think Melvin?"

Mel chuckles.

"I just have a problem with rabid dogs living across the street...if they get too close, I know Daddy will shoot them."

"They're not dear to you, huh?" Mel wits.

Cherelle looks at him and says, "Please. I have a problem with things that sell drugs to kids. Daddy has been trying do something about them for the longest, but to no avail."

"Neighborhood Pharmacists, huh?"

"You know it," Jean says as they get up the stairs.

Just outside the door, Mel can hear the commotion inside. When Cherelle gets it open, the laughter blares out. About five middle-aged men with hard, yet cheerful faces, are in the dark living room, watching the Lennox Lewis/Oliver McCall fight. Apparently, McCall just KO'd him in the second round, as evident by the replays flashing across the screen. Actually, they're paying more attention to each other than they are to the television. Everyone is barking out armchair color commentary at once. Instead of breathing air, there is cigarette smoke to inhale. They all have beer cans in their hands as they have a merry time.

"Hey now!" Jean shouts. "Where's the birthday boy at?"

"Downstairs playing cards," one of the brothers shouts.

"I'll catch up to you later, Melvin. Relax and have some fun," she says as she dashes off through a doorway.

"Excuse me," Cherelle pleads. "Excuse me, please."

"Don't you see we busy here," another jokes.

"I want you all to meet someone," she says as she leads Mel over to them. "Everyone, this is Melvin. Melvin, this is my Uncle Reuben; this is my other Uncle Troy—who used to take me to the circus all the time; this is Robert, my cousin; this is my Uncle Arthur."

"Art for short," he adds.

"This is Uncle Levi."

"Just like in the Bible," Levi comments. That is the first thing that came to Mel's mind when the name came out.

"And this is my cousin, Lorenzo," she finishes.

"How you doing Melvin," Lorenzo asks as he extends his hand.

"Make yourself at home Melvin," adds another one, whose name Mel has forgotten that quickly. He thinks it's Cousin Trent—or something like that. "Have some beer and some fun, brother."

"Thanks," Mel responds to the invitation to fun, although he'll pass on the beer.

"Where's Momma," Cherelle asks.

"In the kitchen," Lorenzo says.

"Well, I'll see you guys later. I'm going to let Melvin meet the rest of the family."

"Aiight."

"Nice meeting you Melvin."

"Stay up buddy."

"Okay fella's," he says as Cherelle ushers him into the kitchen, where Jean is gnawing on a rib, about seven other mid to old women are sitting around a table—some smoking, others drinking beer, all gossiping—a younger lady who resembles Cherelle (actually, she may have a slight edge in looks over her—slight, but noticeable), that he assumes is one of her younger sisters, and a short, thin lady, who's a Xerox of Cherelle and Jean. No mistaking who she is. With the exception of a few gray hairs mixed in with the reddish hair, a couple more shades of yellow in her complexion, and a few wrinkles around the eyes, she's the blueprint of Cherelle. Rather attractive, Mel notes. Greasy food is everywhere. All kinds of barbecue and sauce litter the countertops and stove. Mel is in hog heaven.

They don't notice them when they enter as Cherelle interrupts: "Momma, this is Melvin: the classmate I was telling you about."

"How are you Mrs. Morrison," Mel greets as he leans over and embraces the lady who's standing all of about twelve inches.

"You're the one who said that powerful prayer. Now I remember your face," she says with a warm smile as Mel giggles and tries to downplay it.

"That's what Cherelle keeps reminding me of."

"Ain't nothing wrong with that, honey."

"We need more righteous men," one of the women interjects to the laughter of the rest of them.

"This is my sister Eunice," she introduces as Eunice gives him a suspicious smirk—as if she knows something good and secretive. If there is one thing he determines from that moment about her, it is that she's a big flirt. Cherelle introduces all of the ladies by name, and as soon as he repeats them in his greetings, he forgets them.

"Help yourself to the food, Melvin. Make yourself at home," Mrs. Morrison extends.

"I'm going to fix him a plate," Cherelle interjects. "First I want him to meet Daddy."

"Uh oh. She's trying to spoil his appetite," one of the boisterous women exclaims.

"Well at least his food won't come back up," another jokes.

Mel is starting to run a temperature.

"You know he wouldn't like that, will he," Jean adds.

"Stoppit. All of y'all," Cherelle pleads.

"Yeah," says Mrs. Morrison. "He'll like Melvin a lot."

Everybody—except Mel—smirks in silence at the obvious inside joke as Cherelle tows him past them, towards the back. A clan of people are gathered on the back porch, frolicking and cussing with their alcohol and smokes. She leads him down some stairs, where the unmistakable sound of the pre-preacher Al Green is blasting through the muffled chatter of more partygoers. It looks like someone dumped a truckload of dry ice on a flooded, checkered tile basement floor. There's a flashing disco light, which illuminates the smoke and the nice finish. The area is spacious and about five couples are rocking from side-to-side, intoxicated from love, glee, and liquor. It looks as if they could pass out any moment. Others are gathered at the bar and around the record player in the back.

"This way," Cherelle says as she turns into a room with a dingy blanket covering the doorway. Inside, a serious card game is going on. Normally, the room serves as the Laundromat. It is well lit and cramped.

Cherelle holds up her hand and gestures for Mel to wait, as four men sit concentrated around a card table surrounded by a handful of spectators. Three of the players look like bar room brawlers after a long day's work, and a smaller one with his back to Mel is hard to read. The fellow just in front of the smaller man is about Cherelle's complexion and has a beard to get lost in. He's wearing a lumberjack shirt and his hairline is receding. No doubt about it: Mel can picture him playing Santa Claus to Cherelle.

After the big dude to the right of the little man puts his last card down, the dwarf of the group slaps down his card and demands, "Get up from the table."

"Awe man. This the luckiest niggah," says the giant to his left.

"All of y'all just get up from my table. This my table."

Cherelle touches the little man on the shoulder and interrupts his declamation. When he turns around, she hugs him around the neck and plants a kiss on his cheek. "Happy birthday, Daddy."

"Thank you, Cherry. You just made it happier."

"I want you to meet a friend of mine," she says as she waves Mel forward and hooks his arm. "This is Melvin. We're in the same speech class," she announces as Mr. Morrison shifts his chair around for a better inspection.

The first thing Mel notices is the left hook extending from his arm, then the wooden legs just under the table catches his eyes before he meets Mr. Morrison's deep dark browns. He's a twiggy man with a deep voice and a welcoming, exultant smile. Mel almost laughs at the conflicting mental expectation and actual picture. He was expecting the big bad wolf with a shotgun. Mr. Morrison is actually the only one at the table that doesn't have a can of beer or cigarette and the mass of Paul Bunyon.

"How you doing, Deacon Melvin?" he asks as he extends his hand.

"I'm okay. What about you?" he retorts as he wrings his firm hand.

"Fine," he says nodding his head approvingly. "You play Spades, Melvin?"

"Well, not..." he stops as Cherelle elbows him.

He turns and orders the big Santa stand-in to "Get up little brother," before Mel can even accept the invitation.

Cherelle whispers in his ear while her father is occupied with securing a seat: "Go play...he would be insulted if you don't. He just wants to talk to you. I'll help you if you don't know how to play."

Mel reluctantly steps around the table. Cherelle pulls up a chair to the side of him.

"It's your deal, rookie," one of the bigger guys declares in a gruff voice as he slides the deck over to him.

Mel's temperature immediately shoots through the ceiling and his voice goes on vacation. He gets a flashback to his first college biology class that he was two weeks late for.

The professor had a test waiting for him, and it wasn't multiple choice. A ten question essay test that was worth 20 percent of his grade. Normally, Mel was able to BS his way through with rhetoric, but he didn't know nothing about anything on the paper that he just stared heatedly at for about ten minutes...like he's staring at the cards in his hand now. A classmate slipped him a sheet of paper that he hoped was an answer sheet. Close. It was a note stating that he could "reschedule the test if he wasn't ready. I had him last semester." He immediately walked up to the front and whispered to the instructor that he was unprepared and—if at all possible—could he take it some other time. Sure enough, the professor granted him a stay. He ended up getting a C on two nights of studying for the test.

Where is his pass coming from now, in a card game that's impressionable to old man Morrison? Beads of sweat build up on his head, as every hundredth of a second seems like a minute. Cherelle—sensing that he doesn't know how to shuffle the cards—grabs them on cue, cutting them and dealing 13 to each player, with Vegas gambler precision. She explains, "The object of the game is to win as many rounds—or tricks—as possible...Our goal is ten," as she arranges the suits and number rank for him. "Do you understand the value of the cards?"

Mel nods reluctantly.

"The spades are the highest ranking suit—the markings are the suits—followed by the hearts, diamonds and clubs. The Ace is of the highest value; the two is the lowest. The lowest spade can capture the highest ranking card of any other suit. You and Daddy are partners," she emphasizes. The instructions sound simple enough to him as she continues to go over her quick tutorial.

"I thought this was a game of two partners, not three," the big burly man on the right joshes as he takes a swig of his brew. "Somebody go tell my wife to come down and advise me."

"Stop messing with his concentration," Mr. Morrison interjects in an earnest tone, but in a facetious manner. "Just don't throw the wrong card out, 'cause I'll have to put the hook in you," he threatens as he shakes the hook at him.

"Daddy," Cherelle appeals.

Based on the two-minute crash course, Mel is thinking three of hearts. "You should throw out the three of hearts," Cherelle urges in his ear. He lays it out with a nervous hesitation as he looks at Cherelle for approval. She smiles and nods.

The bidding goes on until the last bid falls on Mel. He lays down an ace of spade.

"Ain't this about nothing," the man on the right states.

Cherelle claps triumphantly as Mel is oblivious to his victory.

"You sure you're not hustling us," he queries.

"No sir. This is the first time playing. Give Cherelle credit for her coaching abilities."

"I think they're both in on it. I think we should hook them both up," the other man suggests.

"Melvin is just too good for you old folks. It's time to retire," Cherelle brags.

"It's time to cut the cards again. Let's see how lucky you really are, Mister Melvin," the guy on the right challenges.

Mel and Mr. Morrison commence to win three straight hands...and have a ball doing it. Mel notices that Mr. Morrison isn't a man of many words, but he is warm none-the-less. Not a drop of profanity comes out of his mouth. There is nothing intimidating about him. As assurance, Mr. Morrison jokes, "You're always welcome here as long as you keep bringing home the victory", after winning the third time. Ickey, the Morrison's next door neighbor, is the big guy on the left. He seems as quiet and calculating as a snake. His arms look like lethal weapons. Mel imagines that he could have been a gladiator in another lifetime. He doesn't say much of anything and wears a blank expression throughout, even when the table is yucking it up. Mel is reluctant to win against him. It's not like he is trying so hard. Mel replaced one of Mr. Morrison's younger brothers: Martin Morrison. He remained in the background with his beer and cigarette as he cheered for Mel. The man to the right is Cherelle's uncle—one of Mr. Morrison's other younger brothers—and is appropriately called Big Will. He's as round as a giant beach ball. And he has one of the most elating, wheezing laughs. Mel laughed with him because he sounds so funny. The object of the laughter is secondary. He keeps the table upbeat and noisy. Come to find out, Big Will is a wayward deacon.

"Woe unto the man that crosses the Lord's deacon," Big Will announces as Mel wins another game. "In my faithful days, I was highly favored with the good Lord...still am," he confesses between swallows of Miller.

"That's it, show your appreciation by drowning the Spirit out," Mr. Morrison teases.

Big Will pauses before continuing. "Whatever you do Melvin, keep the line open with the Lord, and keep it clear. My problem is my line of communication has alcoholic interference...you know what I'm saying," he says without giving anyone a chance to comment. "With that interference comes distorted spiritual discernment. Once you start second-guessing the Holy Spirit, anything can happen. In my case, I started chasing other brother's wives."

Mel nods at his candid advice. Although he figures it's a given, he's learned a long time ago to regard the given. The last time he slighted some advice, he ended up being taken for $5,000 cash that still pains him to this day. After all, it was supposed to be towards the remodeling of his kitchen. To this day, it's still in a mess.

Just as Mel passes Cherelle the cards, a dark he-man with menacing eyes, relaxed hair, and a neatly trimmed beard connected to his side-burns slides through the blanket and makes the rounds with everyone, and is greeted like a dignitary. If pride has a host, it just walked in glowing superciliously as if he has been dipped in oil. "I'm IT" is shrouded by his pseudo-humble presence. He's wearing a black vest and black slacks, and stands out like a diamond on top of a mound of coal. When he gets to Cherelle, they embrace. Correction: He bear hugs her off the ground, like a grizzly would. Perhaps because Mel is used to being considered average height at six feet, that the man-bear looks bigger than life. He finds himself trying not to look at them as they talk, hoping that he's another cousin. Although he's not facing them, he keeps a critical eye on him, like a stingy child who has given permission to another kid to play with his prized toy would. It's not like she is "his", but Mel couldn't stand the attention she is giving him, although it is brief.

"Let me introduce you to my friend. Melvin..." she calls, getting his attention. "Melvin, this is my friend Clarence. Clarence, this is Melvin. We grew up together. He used to live on our block," she offers.

Mel finds himself questioning why he's back as he rises and wrings hands with the brick wall. Mel has never given a weak handshake...always firm. His father always told him that a firm handshake is a sign of the sincerity in a man. He's said often that it's a sign of a real man. Clarence is real sincere, because it feels like he is crushing Mel's fingers. "What's up, Mel," Clarence asks.

The name is Melvin, especially to strangers. "Nothing much. How you feel," he retorts.

"Can't complain, man. Can't complain at all."

"I hear you."

"Let me go grab a plate and brew and I'll catch up with you later Cherry."

"Okay Clarence."

Mel cringes at the sound of that pet name coming from him.

"You still haven't eaten yet, Melvin."

He shakes his head.

"I'll fix you a plate after I shuffle the cards," she says, and does it in haste. "You can whip them without me, can't you?"

Mel humps his shoulders indifferently.

"Sure you can. I'll be right back."

Just like that, she is gone. Surely, she will run into Clarence. He doesn't like the thought. He especially hates the possessive feeling he has over a woman that he isn't sure how he feels about. As if he has the right to feel that way. After all, he was out with Angela—the woman he made up in his mind was his perfect match before they had a good conversation—last night on a date that he can only describe with a sound: YAWN. He's not even sure if this is an actual "date". The card game isn't fun anymore and he still finds himself on top. He is relieved when Big Will decides to call it the night and Mr. Morrison takes a break. He is tired of sitting in the chair and smelling cigarette smoke and beer. He is actually eager to see what Cherelle is doing. It doesn't take long for him to get his answer.

Clarence has his hand on her shoulder as he addresses her at the bar. It seems like she is eager to get away, and when she spots Mel, she picks up a plate and breaks away. Mel plays like he doesn't notice them and heads up the stairs. Before he turned, he saw Clarence looking in his direction and feels his competitive glare burning through his back.

"Melvin!" she shouts over the everlasting Al Green music. He ignores her. She catches him in the middle of the steps and offers, "I'm sorry, Melvin. Clarence stopped me and insisted on catching up on everything."

"That's okay," Mel lies.

"Daddy had cancer and had to have his legs amputated three years ago," she mentions in a tone slightly over a hush.

Mel's eyebrows go up and jokes, "Don't worry...I still won't cross him the wrong way."

Cherelle smiles at him and playfully slaps his arm. "Well, do you want to eat up here?"

"That's fine," he says as they proceed and park at the kitchen table.

Jean is in the same spot doing the same thing. He wonders how such a small woman can eat so much. She should've been filled to the top of her head by now. Mel forces himself to finish the ribs in no time while Cherelle bounces around the house talking to other guests. He hasn't developed a liking for cole slaw and potato salad, so he disposes it as he always does when he goes to barbecues, and settles in the living room where Big Will is entertaining the guests with his laughing. Mel is ready to go. The only thing missing is an excuse. He sits oblivious to the chatter going on in the room, when one of the patrons jokes that Big Will corrupted Mel.

"No. He's a righteous man. Didn't touch no alcohol and didn't even know how to shuffle the cards," Will compliments to Mel's embarrassment.

He giggles it off and turns around to catch Cherelle coming around the corner from the basement with Clarence right behind. She's wearing a nettlesome frown as she takes a seat with Jean. A thwarted grin of disconcertion is plastered on Clarence's face as he comes towards Mel and rests right beside him. His glow is dimmed.

"I hear you're studying video production and communications," he offers.

"Yeah, I'm taking a couple of classes at Chicago State to see where it can take me."

"I hear you. One of my partners has his own business along those lines...videotaping weddings. It's actually quite lucrative for him."

"I hear it can be. I'm looking to possibly produce films. Depending on what kind of taste the classes leave in my mouth, I might pursue a Masters from Columbia. I'm just in a 'wait and see' stage now."

"Cherelle tells me you have a Bachelors in accounting."

"Yeah," he says as he looks back in Cherelle's direction, trying to contain his self-consciousness. What else did she tell him, and why? Does he know his social security number, too? "Imagine after six years of schooling you decide that you want to do something else."

"I know what you mean. I studied finance and economics at Howard, and for my graduate work I majored in Psychology. I knew that I didn't want to work in a bank and I don't think there's such a thing as an economist," he confesses, as if Mel asked.

"You ever consider teaching?"

"Nope. Don't have the patience for it."

"I hear you. That's why I didn't go that route. So have you finished up your Masters work?"

"Yep. I work for the FBI."

"Straight? That's good." Mel *is* impressed.

"It's interesting, brother...profiling criminals. Often cases against them rest on my evaluation. I tell you, I've come across some real live one's in my short days with them, and I've only been with them for a little over two years," he boasts.

"I can imagine," he says, nodding his head and twisting his face with mixed admiration and nausea. Of course cases will rest on "HIS" evaluation.

They listen in on the discussion that has turned religious. Will is talking about how God speaks to people—in his drunken state.

"I don't believe in God," Clarence confesses. "Cherelle tried a long time ago to sell me that BS, but I was too strong willed for that. I mean, consider the source of this wisdom now...his wisdom comes from the bottle. And he's supposed to be a deacon," he says caustically.

Before Mel could respond, not that he had a response—just a look of disdain—Cherelle cuts in between them, leans over and asks Mel "You want to go out for a while?"

Mel rises, bids Clarence farewell with "Later man" and a raised fist, and follows her out of the door with a coat of satisfaction. The air is cool, fresh and still as the noise from the inside is muffled out.

"Whew. It's good to get out of there."

Mel yawns and agrees in silence.

"I'm going to have to hide those Al Green 8-tracks," she says as she strolls by his side. "It played for the whole two hours we were there."

Mel just laughs as he lets her in the car.

He collapses in the driver's seat and reclines back slightly. His head is pounding to the beat of 'Love and Happiness.' "You have a Tylenol?"

Cherelle rambles through her purse and pulls a coated one out. "You up for the drive-in?" she asks. "I want to see 'Forrest Gump'."

Mel's eyes pop open. No way. The only thing he's up for is the next morning after a good night's sleep. "Where did you get all of this energy from?"

"I'm actually too tired to talk...I just want to get away from here. There's only so long I can be around all those people. And then when all the smoke clears and the music stops and the people leave, whose job is it to clean up? Of course it's mine, and as you can imagine, I'm looking forward to it."

"I know you are."

She takes a deep breath and lets out a long, loud sigh. "They're going to be at it all night and I want to lay down," she says wistfully. "Tonight is a celebration of sorts for me too: my divorce was finalized yesterday."

"Congratulations."

"Thanks, but in all honesty I have mixed emotions. I'm officially free from Johnny, but how do you celebrate the end of something so sacred...something that was supposed to last forever? Everybody else seems to be more thrilled about it than me. I mean it was like they were making you and Clarence out to be competitors for my affections. And would you know that that fool played along with it," she says with a chuckle. "He actually had the nerve to ask me to move to Cleveland with him. Can you believe it?"

Mel humps his shoulders and shakes his head as he strains to keep from grinning.

"He actually asked me to marry him a few minutes ago," she says incredulously.

"Well, did you accept? He seems like a nice guy that had it on the ball," Mel fishes, knowing the answer, but lacking the juicy details of the rejection that he's lusting. He wants to know all of the rust spots of the Man of Steel.

"Are you kidding. First of all, I hadn't seen him since I've been married, which is over six years...and that wasn't long enough."

"Ouch."

"Secondly, he was my first boyfriend, and I do mean *boy*friend—as in we were still in eighth grade. Since I wasn't doing any grown folks business, he spread himself around to others—claiming that I should be honored to be with him, since nobody else would. Mind you, he's still a *boy*...so proud and arrogant. My divorce isn't even 24 hours old and he's asking me to marry him, talking about *'out of all the women that I have a chance to marry, I want to marry you.'* I couldn't believe I was hearing the same line he gave me in grammar school. Tonight he showed me that he has no class. He doesn't even believe in God and can't stand my belief in Him. I mean, what is he going to do when things get rough and divine intervention is the only solution? He's too proud to pray, mind you."

"So what did you say?"

"Say to what?"

"His marriage proposal."

"Melvin!" she laughs. "I told him to go back to Ohio and stick his head in the ground. You're so silly. Why do you think I wanted to get out of there?"

"I didn't know what you did. All I heard was how ridiculous he was. For all I knew, you could've accepted and been having second thoughts about it."

She looks at him like he has two heads. "Can we go?"

Mel starts the ignition and pulls off. They ride in silence for a few blocks. They get to Pulaski and Mel turns right.

"So where are we going?"

"Well, I'm going to bed...and you can go home, because I know you're beat, too. Make a left and you can drop me off at this motel on Roosevelt and Karlov."

Mel looks over at her and raises his eyebrows. "What?" he asks, pulling over to the curb.

"Drop me off at the motel. I gotta get some sleep. Now."

"What about Jean?"

"Jean's staying overnight and she's getting a ride with one of our cousins."

"Why don't you come to my house," Mel hears himself inviting. "I have an extra room."

"Well," she contemplates. "I'm going to have to get back over here in the morning and that's a waste of time."

"I wouldn't mind."

"I know you wouldn't, Melvin. You're so nice. But I think it would be convenient for both of us if I just stay here. I appreciate it," she says as she pats his hands, sending the same mesmerizing jolt of electricity.

He gapes at her as she smirks impishly.

"What?"

"I'm not comfortable leaving you there by yourself."

"I'll be okay. I'm only a few blocks from my house, and I know most of the people in the area by face."

"Well how about if I stay here the night with you."

His proposition wipes her smile straight as she can't contain her surprise. "Melvin...you don't have to do that."

"I know I don't, but I would feel better if I did."

"I don't know, Melvin..."

"Are you afraid I'm going to try something? I'll give you my word that I won't."

"I know you won't," she retorts, somewhat snappy. "I mean, I'm not worried about you trying to take advantage of me. I know you're sincere, but I don't want to inconvenience you, that's all."

"This is what I want to do," he says. "I would be inconvenienced if you say no, because I will be worried into a sleepless night."

They gaze into each other's eyes before she finally smiles and says, "Let's go." Mel requests a room with two beds, but the attendant informs them that they only have single beds available and asks if they would like separate rooms.

"We'll take a single room," Cherelle interjects, without giving Mel a chance to consider it. She collects the key and leads the way.

The room is dry and chilly, which makes her feel underdressed and the air conditioner out of season. Mel kicks off his shoes, which have tortured his feet all evening, and switches on the TV on his way to the bathroom that he has bypassed for the last four hours.

Cherelle is sitting at the foot of the bed, hunched up with her arms folded and her shoes off. "I laid a towel on the floor because it's a little wet," he states as he pulls off his drenched socks.

"It's wet over by the air conditioner, too."

"I guess it isn't Holiday Inn, is it?"

She shakes her head with a smirk as she heads to the bathroom. Mel adjusts the thermostat to warm and runs through the channels before settling on "White Men Can't Jump". It's about 15 minutes into it, which will have to do tonight. He sits at the head of the bed on top of the covers with his back against the headboard. Cherelle emerges with her hair pinned up.

"Have you seen 'White Men Can't Jump'?"

She peeks at the TV and shakes her head as she crawls under the covers. "It's freezing in here," she says as she curls up into a ball.

"It'll be warm in here in a minute," he says as he catches the suggestion. "I just adjusted the thermostat."

She doesn't respond as Mel gets a little uncomfortable by the silence. He ponders what the congregation would conclude if they knew he is in a motel room with a woman. They wouldn't believe him if he told them nothing happened. They would just draw their own conclusions, like they did when they found out he went to the Clique.

"I'm glad you're here, Melvin. Thank you for staying with me tonight," she testifies.

"Hey...I just want to help you celebrate."

She smiles as she continues to look at television. "I cried when I wasn't able to talk to you last night," she confesses. "I felt so lonely...I felt abandoned...like nobody cared whether I lived or died last night. I knew the day would come, but I didn't know it would sting as bad as it does."

"I can imagine."

She shifts her head and her hair comes untied, but she doesn't bother putting it back up. "When I was a little girl, I wanted to be a wife and a mother more than a nurse. I still want to be married, but I don't know if I have anything left to give. I don't even know if it's worth the trouble, but I hate being single."

"I know what you mean."

She soughs and looks up at Mel with wet eyes. "Do you believe in destiny?"

Mel looks down at her in her vulnerability and strokes her hair without thinking. "I used to. When Memory told me I was her soul-mate one week, and then the next week she was with someone else, I started doubting if two people could come together on the same accord...with the same level of affections and devotion. I don't know what to believe now. When it's all said and done, it's all in God's hands, and I certainly don't know what God's plan is for me."

Her eyes drop as she ponders the point, and then jump back up to him. "Do you think that if God has a path mapped out for you, but you go a different direction, that you'll eventually end up on the path of righteousness?"

Mel stops stroking and says, "Yes, I believe that no matter what detour we take, we as His children will be on the path of righteousness."

"Well, do you think that if God has a mate for you and you go with your own program, that eventually you'll end up with that person?"

"Technically and theologically I believe that, but in all honesty—God forgive me—I don't know if I believe it for my own life, because I believe that the mate God had for me—and not Memory—is long gone. But then again, with my limited way of thinking, I don't know if she was who God chose for me. In hindsight, it looks perfect, but something kept me from marrying her in the first place. I don't know if I was looking for a sign or a confirmation from God Himself, but I couldn't do it. I really don't know what to tell you Cherelle. After all, I'm still in recovery myself."

Cherelle looks at him intently through glazed eyes. They're silent for a long moment, until she thinks she wants to say something. "Melvin..." she pauses.

He peers down at her and starts running his fingers through her hair again. "Yes," he urges.

She lays quietly as she gazes up at him. She opens her mouth slightly to speak, but nothing comes out as she looks away and blinks the tears dry. "I'm sorry," she says, turning over. "I lost my train of thought. I'm just too tired right now."

Mel is left hanging and decides it's a good time to turn the TV and lamp off.

He crawls under the cover with his cloths on, turns his back to her and says a short, silent prayer. He opens his eyes and stares at the moon lit curtain while the heater hums away. The warmth from her body causes him to feel something more than rising flesh as he lies motionless. He closes his eyes and searches his soul for the meaning of the vibe, drifting off and getting lost in a blissful blackness. When morning comes, the covers are helter-skelter, the room is a sauna and Cherelle lays on his chest. He forgets his answer when he opens his eyes. He studies the room for a while, when he feels her shift. Suddenly, she jumps up, which causes him to jump, too.

"I'm sorry, Melvin," she says, rubbing her eyes.

"Sorry for what?"

She doesn't answer as she strolls to the bathroom.

Mel gets up and stretches. He is galvanized, like he breathed caffeine during the night. His body is lively and well rested. His mouth is tart and he has the taste for toothpaste. He slips on his dry socks and his stiff shoes. Cherelle comes out of the bathroom with her brow wrinkled as she reaches for her sandals and rubs her hair back. "What time is it?" she questions hoarsely.

Mel picks up his watch from the dresser and announces, "A quarter to seven."

"I have to go," she claims as she gathers her purse and the key.

The short ride to her house is silent as she yawns every few seconds. When he gets to her curb, she thanks him and makes it to her door in a haste. When she gets it open, she turns and waves. He puts his thumb to his ear and his baby finger to his mouth, and she nods and lips, "Tonight" as she steps in.

A few of the choir members came back, even though Gene stayed AWOL. Many parishioners commented that the choir sounded more spiritual. Go figure. During the service, LaTonya got dog sick and had to have an ambulance come and wheel her to the hospital. They were still running tests when Mel last checked. When Mel got in from church that evening, a message from Cherelle was waiting. She called right after he left for Sunday school, thanking him for staying with her last night and apologizing for seeming abrupt and rude. After making the rounds at the hospitals and nursing homes, and having dinner at his parent's house, it was well after ten. It's against his religion to call someone's house after ten. He didn't appreciate that type of respect until he was the receiver of a late night call.

When he called Rita's house just before 11 two years ago, her mother answered. Once she determined that it wasn't an emergency call, she read him in one ear and out the other about calling at any time of night. Not once did she raise her voice, but she was loud and clear. She addressed him in an even, monotone: "Other people live here and like to sleep after ten because they have to work. It's very rude to call at a certain time of night just to talk. Unless it's an emergency, please don't call at this time of night again. I'll leave a message for Rita. Good night." She didn't wait for Mel to return the closing. He remembers the irritation Ms. Wright must've experienced when Darlene called him at 11:30 during one of their flings. He had just dosed off and remembers thinking that it must be one of his relatives in a dire situation. He forgot what she said and what she wanted to talk about, but he remembers it was so trivial that it made him too mad to fall back asleep. He hasn't answered the phone after ten since then. He'll talk to Cherelle tomorrow.

Mel slept long and hard, waking up just before the alarm clock went off. A solid eight hours wasn't enough for the weekend he had. He drank his tea before washing up, and he finds himself perked up. The morning sun shins brightly and provides him with a breakfast substitute. This can't be a Monday. Everybody should experience a spiritual boost like this. Feeling rejuvenated and blithe, he finds himself driving down 76th Street towards South Shore Florists'. As long as he is in a festive mood, he might as well try to spread it. On impulse and as if it is a mental condition, he sends a dozen red roses to Cherelle, just because it feels good to do. The note in it reads: ***"'How hard it is to find a capable wife! She is worth far more than jewels!' I guess some people don't like jewels. Fret not, because with or without a no-good husband, you still have your worth. I hope you have a blessed day. Melvin."*** He smiles as he drives off and forgets all about the seeds of joy he sowed.

The morning proceeds without incident. He makes it to lunch ahead of schedule, with no casualties. The calls are coming in at a pace that satisfies the projections, but don't wear the operators out. Since he didn't bother bagging a lunch, he is going to have the Caesar's Salad that is on the menu. This is the only time he'll eat lettuce, and he eats it in abundance when he does. After Mel wolfs down his lunch, he retrieves his Bible from the car.

Deidra is sitting in her car, smoking a cigarette two rows over and he unexpectedly passes by her car just as she sniffles. He stops and notices that she has a wet face from crying. The window is half cracked, with Toni Braxton playing low. That split second his carnal mind rejoices, saying, "Serves her right—whatever it was...she had it coming to her" and urges him to gloat, but he has no more animosity towards her. At that moment, he truly forgets about what happened between them in the past.

"Are you okay?" he asks sincerely.

She turns startled and wipes her face when she realizes Mel—of all the people—sees her in a wounded state. "I'm okay," she insists as she tries to keep her "nothing-can-fade-superwoman" image. "I just had a rough time this morning, Melvin."

"You sure," he presses.

She nods her head, but her eyes are blood red from crying. It looks like more than the morning rush. "I'll be okay."

"Okay," Mel says as he reluctantly leaves.

When he gets back in the building, he asks Jack does he know what's wrong with Deidra. He said Deidra called and said she would be late. Mel ponders what could be wrong and sends a plea up for her well-being as he goes into the conference room to read. He is so disturbed by the sight of a downtrodden Deidra, that he can't focus on his scriptures. Now isn't the time to study: it is time to practice.

"Give me an opening Lord," he says, and no sooner than he gets it out, the door opens and Deidra staggers in. She collapses on the sofa, weeping insuppressibly.

Mel springs up and embraces her as her sobs grow louder. "It's going to be okay," he says, rocking her gently. Then he does something that is so not him, but it comes naturally all of a sudden.

"I want Je - sus to walk with me, I want Je - sus to walk with me, with me; All a - long my pil - prim jour - ney, I want Je- sus to walk with me," he croons softly. *"In my tri - als, walk with me, walk with me, In my tri - als, walk with me, walk with me, When the shades of life are fall - ing, Lord, I want Je - sus to walk with me."* The words that he doesn't know have a soothing

effect that settles her down. He rubs her back and starts humming the tune as his spirit proceeds to sing: ***'In my sor - rows, walk with me...When my heart with - in is ach - ing, Lord, I want Je - sus to walk with me. In my trou - bles, walk with me...When my life be - comes a bur - den, Lord, I want Je - sus to walk with me.'*** For no explainable reason he chose that song. All he knows is that it was on his mind, he knew the tune, and it worked.

Her body relaxes as she whispers, "I need some tissue."

Mel hands her the handkerchief from his jacket pocket. This is the first time it's come in use, and she wears it out blowing her nose into it. She leans forward and covers her face with her hands. Mel places his hand on her shoulder and informs her, "You don't have to talk...just take it easy."

She nods and lets out a loud sob before regaining her composure. Mel pulls her into his bosom.

"He was so rough," she says in a steady voice. "He hurt me bad."

"Who hurt you?"

She doesn't answer.

"What happened, Deidra? Who hurt you?"

She shakes her head and whimpers, "I don't know."

"Deidra...what happened?" he urges.

"He took it."

"What do you mean?"

"I was raped," she squeals as she breaks down again.

Mel feels his heart sinking in a puddle of quicksand as he squeezes her. He is experiencing her sorrow on a secondary level. Her helplessness is consuming him. Part of him feels responsible. After all, he originally prayed to see her downfall—although he took it back in the next breath. He starts wondering if he can curse and then retract a curse. With his mind going in different directions, an intense prayer of strength starts pouring from his mouth. When he finishes, she has a distant stare, but she is silent. Mel uses the inter-company phone to call human resources, who calls the police and paramedics.

As it turns out, she had a flat on her way home last night and a guy helped her get it changed. When he turned down a financial token of appreciation, she thanked him and turned to get into her car. That's when he jumped on her and brutalized her in the back seat. The man was a monster. She has a few lacerations on her vagina and a few bruises on her body from trying to fight him off. He also sodomized her. The physical wounds will heal quickly, but it is hinted that she may be off for a while to recuperate emotionally. Deidra walked out with her head down and her air of steel cracked. It hit Mel hard. At the height of his anger, he wouldn't wish that on NO woman, and he questions whether his emotional appeal was granted. In a matter of seconds, her self-confidence was snatched away. Her spirit was crushed. She walked out like a zombie. If she can't put the pieces back together, she might as well be the walking dead. Teresa has to leave on emergency, so Mel stays late. When he gets off, he heads over to his father's house for some understanding.

"I can't say that it was a curse. I do know that there are consequences to walking in sin...and yes, for putting your mouth on God's anointed."

"I didn't want that to happen to her. I said some things in anger and pain when it happened, but once I calmed down, I retracted it," Mel explains. "I've prayed for her many days...not out of duty, but out of love. Doesn't that count for something?" he wonders.

"Sure the fervent prayers of the righteous availeth much," Pastor Adams confirms, adding, "but you must also realize that all things work together for good to them that love God and are called according to His purposes. I can't tell you what's the purpose behind every tragedy or misfortune. But I do know that God is in control, despite what appears bleak and chaotic to the human eye. You have to trust Him...and believe that your works of righteousness will bring righteous benefits. Don't think for a minute that it was a coincidence that the young lady came into the room with you—the man she slandered. God prepares us for situations like this. And best believe, he prepared you. You could've spoken and acted in the flesh, but you didn't. You were meek...you were submissive to the Spirit. Therefore, she was able to see Christ in you."

Mel nods at the reasoning. It makes sense, but he is still disturbed.

"Listen: When you eat a healthy meal, trying to nourish your body—and in your case, trying to gain weight—do you see the results immediately?"

Mel smiles and shakes his head.

"Of course you don't," he declares as he leans forward in his chair. "In the beginning, you're usually going through a period where your body is being purged of a lot of wastes. For some, the results are more visible than with others, but the results are present. You had a chance to minister to her needs, and you fed her well. You may not see the results now or ever, but best believe that since she was fed, there will be positive results."

Mel nods in content.

"By the way," his father starts. "LaTonya is pregnant."

"What?" Mel questions as his eyebrows and suspicions jump.

"Nine weeks."

Mel pauses as he recovers from the shock. "Who?" he questions in a hushed tone.

"Well, Lorraine called me this evening with Harold on the line, and he denied ever touching her. In fact, he claims that he's a virgin," he states.

Mel's eyebrows rise a little more. "Do you believe him?"

His father nods as he leans back. "I sure do."

They stare in mutual, perspicacious silence at each other, before Mel hears himself confiding, "I have an idea who may have done it."

His father doesn't discourage or urge him from speaking.

"I saw Donald in several compromising places with her. I even thought I saw them in action in the church. Maybe nothing is up, but it didn't look right."

His father just nods and closes his eyes as he takes a deep breath. "Why do you think I put him off of the deacon board?"

Mel's eyes pop out of his head. "You knew?"

He nods. "I caught him in the nurse's room with his pants down and her mouth where it shouldn't have been, if you know what I mean."

Mel's brains start oozing out of the eye sockets. "You mean they did it in the church?"

"Just as bold as if they were a married couple at home...on the Sabbath."

Mel's mouth is on the floor now as he sits perplexed.

"I told him to get himself together behind closed doors, so it wouldn't be a big controversy, but he was too proud to repent. We'll see what comes out in the wash. In a case like this, an investigation isn't always necessary."

"Unbelievable," Mel says as he shakes his head.

He's as dumbfounded as a bat-bludgeoned drunkard when he leaves. The revelation brought him to the realization that in his short life, he hasn't experienced all of the unpleasant surprises. His father fed him well though, but he'll have to wait a while for the benefits of the message. He picks up a Checker's hamburger on the way home. By the time he gets home, the burger and fries are an afterthought. When he gets in, he can hear Cherelle's voice on his answering machine, but can't make out the message as she hangs up. He *69's her and she picks up on the first ring.

"Cherelle?"

"Hello Melvin."

"I'm just walking in. What's up?"

"I was just calling back because I wanted to talk to you before I went to bed," she says as she lets out a short, relieving sigh. "Thank you for my roses...I was so surprised to get them. They're beautiful."

"Oh," he says as he remembers that he sent them. "It was my pleasure. I'm glad you liked them."

"I was worried that I scared you away Sunday morning. I just didn't feel like going home to clean up."

"Oh no. I understand. It was no problem."

"I slept real good that night. I was burned out," she rambles excitedly. "It carried over into Monday. But when I got back from taking Chuckie to school and making some runs, the deliveryman was walking up my steps. I was so surprised when he said he was delivering them to me. That was the sweetest thing...it made my day...my week...my year," she expresses. "Well since you brightened my life, how was your day?"

"Well, it was quite eventful, to say the least," he says somberly as he goes on to explain what happened. "...So I'm on somewhat on a guilt trip."

"I can understand that," she says sympathetically, adding, "but you can't hold yourself responsible."

"That's what I'm trying to convince myself of."

"There's a scripture in Job that states how God calls men to repent. Of course that includes women, too."

"What chapter is that?"

"I believe it's the 34th...let me see," she says as Mel can hear her flipping the pages. "It's the 33rd chapter and verses 27 through 30."

"Let me get my Bible. Can you hold on?"

"Sure."

He runs upstairs, retrieves the study Bible from his office, and gets on the cordless phone as he parks on his bed. "You said Job 33," he confirms as he opens to the scripture and skims over it. "I wasn't familiar with that passage," he states as he finishes.

"That's one of my favorite books."

"When I first read the story I was depressed."

"It is kinda sad at first, isn't it?"

"Yeah. Tell me about it," he agrees as he slips out of his work clothes and into his shorts. "I like the parables in Luke...that's how my gift of reading was manifested. The first thing I ever read was the scripture when Jesus blessed the children. When I'm down, I go to that passage. That's my roots."

They share testimony after testimony and discuss intimate areas of their lives. He paces the house as he nervously opens himself up to her. He ends up in front of the television, but couldn't tell what was on if his life depended on it. After they talk about everything under the moon, the sun rises and he finds himself in a zone comfortable—or maybe urgent—enough to go to the bathroom.

"Are you running bath water?" she questions.

"Nope. I'm using the toilet. Those supersonic ears of yours don't miss a whisper, do they," he jokes. "They're probably so sensitive they can hear my thoughts."

She chuckles with him.

"Do you realize that it's going on six, and we've been on here since 10:30?"

"Time flies, doesn't it?"

"You got that right. I don't know if I'm going to be able to wake up to go to work."

"Who said that I was letting you go? My mind is being stimulated and I'm not about to stop."

"You said that like you meant it."

"I did. You're nice to talk too. I've never talked on the phone this long."

"Neither have I. What did we talk about anyway?"

"I don't have a clue," she states. "However, I will let you go...but not for long. Talk to you tomorrow night?"

"Why not tonight?"

"You need time to recover, darling."

"You underestimate my endurance," he teases. "Tomorrow is a good idea, though."

"Goodnight."

"Good morning."

"I stand corrected."

Mel is surprised that he made it through the day on one cup of tea and without even an urge to close his eyes. He snoozed for two hours after he got off the phone with Cherelle. The day went by in a minute and he didn't stay a second over. Claretha gave him the confirmation he needed to acquit his conscious of the rape. She sent him an Instant Message with a scripture from John: ***"Jesus Answered, Neither hath this man sinned, nor his parents: but that the works of God should be made manifest in him."*** She added: "If we all got what we deserved, we would have been in Hell. Don't feel responsible for Deidra's misfortune. Instead, continue to keep her lifted up in prayer and let the Lord give her the comfort she needs." Mel didn't even tell anyone at work about his guilt trip. He could only reply with a "Thanks."

Out of an obligatory urge, he calls Angela, since they haven't spoken since their last outing. He figures that since he is alert and has some energy, he might as well put it to use and see how she's doing. The minute she answers, he regrets it. He asks her how things were, and she takes off.

"TodaywehadatestinBiologyandtherewasacheatsheetgoingaroundTh eProfessorfounditonthefloorbythegarbagecanandgaveeverybodyazeroan drescheduleditfornextweekIcouldn'tbelieveitIstudiedallnightforthattestan dbecauseofafewignoramousesIcouldn'tgetcreditforstudyingThatmeansI'm goingtohavetostayupallnightagainThat'sashame..." She goes past infinity on the subject. With an occasional "Uh huh"; "Okay"; "Yeah"; "I hear you", Mel gets two sentences in during the eternal, 15-minute conversation. When he gets off the phone, he feels like he had been dragged through a desert. He decides right then that unless he is suffering from insomnia, he isn't going to call her again. Maybe subconsciously he knew that calling her was better than counting sheep. He yawns all the way to the edge of his bed. At 6:30, he says a quick prayer. When he rises from his knees, it is 7:30, ending his long weekend with a pacific, 12-hour slumber.

Chapter 16

Mel has been going from eight last night until seven in the evening on a ham sandwich and a can of Hawaiian Punch, so he's currently running on fumes. He is in good spirits: his gas was turned back on Tuesday and he took a long, hot, gratifying bath at home for the first time in five months. Yesterday's call meeting with all of the players turned up a lot of dirt. Donald had been going with both Connie and LaTonya for about a year—playing them and their families against each other. Connie told Harold and Lorraine the whole story before they were all summoned. LaTonya—at the urging of her father—fessed up and admitted that Donald was her lover. It took three men to restrain Trustee Smith. Donald—who was brave and stupid for showing up—was excommunicated on the spot. Reverend and Trustee Bradford were salient by their absence, though. Donald had no one to back him up. Pastor Adams pulled Smith into his office and somehow convinced him to not press charges. Trustee Smith also expressed sorrow at how he allowed Donald to play him against Lorraine and Harold and begged their pardon. It was all well. LaTonya and Connie even made up.

On the drive home, Cherelle and Italian Fiesta are the only things on his mind. When he gets in, he orders his pizza, lets the dog out (who's been holding it all day), jumps out of his clothes and into his shorts and T-shirt that he'll sleep in and calls Cherelle. They haven't talked in two days and it seems like two weeks to him. He is growing attached to her. She answers on the first ring.

"Hey you," he says, relieved to finally hear her voice.

"Hi Melvin. How you doing?" she asks, with a touch of distress in her voice.

"I'm fine. What about you?"

"It's been a long day."

"I have all night and I have big ears."

"Okay. Hold on a second," she says as she lays the phone down.

"Hello, Melvin?"

"Yes?"

"This is Eunice: Cherelle's sister."

"Hi. How you doing?"

"I'm good. I just wanted to tell you what your flowers did to Cherelle. The girl was already crazy about you. Now she's totally insane about you."

"Oh really?" Mel questions with skepticism.

"I'm serious. Nobody has ever sent her flowers before."

"Wow."

"I think you're good for her...keep doing whatever you're doing, because it's making her feel real good about herself."

"I'll keep that in mind," he says with a chuckle.

"Okay. Here comes Cherelle, so I'm gonna go now."

"Okay," he says as Cherelle picks up.

"Melvin?"

"I'm here."

"What did my crazy sister say to you?" she interrogates.

"She just asked how I was doing."

She pauses in disbelief as she changes the subject. "Anyway, that was the glass company outside. Do you know one of these drug dealers over here threw a brick through the front window."

"No! What happened?"

"My father got into an argument with them again. A few threats were directed at him. Then they left. We didn't see who threw it, but I'm sure it was in connection with the earlier run-in. Right now I'm so mad I could go kill one of them. What if one of us were standing in the window?"

"I know what you mean. That's a shame. Did you call the police?"

"They left a few minutes ago. They had the one that threatened my father, but he said he didn't know anything about it. I wanted to take the cop's gun and shoot him in the mouth for lying like that. Had the nerve to threaten my father. I'm so upset, I don't know what to do."

"Just talk to me. I don't want you to go to jail for murder. We wouldn't be able to talk on the phone all night anymore and I wouldn't be able to take you on prom next year."

She giggles. "Oh Melvin. I'm sorry. I've been going on about these knuckleheads. How was your day? How is Deidra doing?"

"It was kinda tight, only because there's not enough time in a day. Deidra is taking it easy. She's going to be off for about another week. I talked to her earlier and she sounds better."

"That's good to hear. I hope she recovers mentally. The physical scars will go away, but it's something scary to deal with."

"I can imagine. Never in a thousand years would I have thought that something like that would happen to her. She seemed so confident and strong willed."

"That means nothing when it gets physical. A lot of women are mentally strong, and some are physically strong, but their physical strength is nothing compared to a man's."

"Now I don't know. You're kinda stacked and you're no weakling. I think you could probably deliver a nice punch to the jaw."

"You know I'm not a fighter. I'm not even a good debater."

"I'm sure you can hold your own," he says as he struggles with his mental image of her. He's been thinking about her so much, that her face is an ever-changing blur in his head. They continue to talk and he forgets that he's hungry and ordered a pizza.

"Is that Homey barking?" she questions.

"I don't believe you heard him. He's outside. Those ears of yours are too keen for me," he jokes as he gets up to see why Homey was fussing. Just as he gets to the window, he sees a long Buick speeding off, and that's when he remembers, "I ordered a pizza and I forgot and left the dog outside!"

"Your dog didn't eat the pizza man, did he?"

"No. But he just pulled off, which means I'm going to be hungry tonight. I oughta eat the dog."

"Why don't you just order Chinese instead?"

They both laugh as Mel gets a craving for fried rice. "What are you doing?"

"I'm talking on the phone with you."

"I mean are you planning to do anything tonight?"

"No. Why?"

"I'll be over there in about 20 minutes. Be ready."

"Okay."

Forty minutes and 20 miles later, they are eating combination-fried rice on the top floor of Royal Pacific overlooking 22nd and Wentworth. The radiance from her face is a beacon in the dim, empty restaurant. A few more patrons gather on their private deck, as if drawn from the dark Chinatown street like moths by the glow she emits. They are both dressed down in the already faded sweat suits that they bought when they first met in the Chicago State bookstore. For the rest of the evening, they laugh and cherish each other's company. When they leave, they throw a penny in the eel and turtle pond at the bottom of the restaurant.

"So what did you wish for?" Mel asks.

"I'll let you know if it comes true. What about you?"

"Same O. When I get it, you'll be the first to know," he says as he ponders his wish and prayer that he will get a sign that indicates it's okay to fall in love again.

"I still can't believe you came and got me."

"You're the one who distracted me and made me forget that I ordered a pizza and left the dog out there, and then you had the nerve to suggest Chinese. So don't go there Miss Thang. Besides, I was dying to see you."

She smiles and blushes as she takes his hand in hers as they stroll back to the empty parking lot. He deactivates the alarm and hands her the keys. She gives him a questioning look.

"Tonight is your first driving lesson."

"Really?" she questions with a surprised grin.

"Um hm," he says nodding his head as he opens the door for her and gets in on the passenger side. "I keep the parking brake on and the car in neutral, so you can just turn the ignition. Be careful when you start a strange stick, because some people leave their cars in gear, and if you start it without clutching, the car will jump forward."

She nods and starts it up.

"The first thing is to take the parking brake off," he explains as he points to it. "Now, with your left foot, press down on the pedal all the way on the left—without doing that, you can't shift the gears—and push the stick into "1". Now, with your right foot, gently press the accelerator."

She revs the engine and then eases off.

"Okay, now what you want to do is take your foot off of the clutch."

She lets up all the way, causing the car to jerk and shut off. Her eyes pop out of her head as she smirks nervously.

"That's okay. I wanted you to do that so you could relax."

She rolls her eyes and smiles as she starts it up again.

"Now, clutch down, shift into gear and gently accelerate. This time, while you're revving, ease up off of the clutch so you can feel the power going to the wheels."

The car starts rolling forward.

"That's it...ease up and as you ease up, give it just a little more gas at the same time."

She does and it gets more power as her face beams with excitement.

"Okay...now what I want you to do is shift to another gear, and to do that, you're going to press the clutch, shift down and into the "2" slot, accelerate, and ease off the clutch. You got it?"

"Yes," she says, nodding eagerly.

"Now try it."

To his surprise, she does it smoothly and gets the timing thing down instantly. She drives around the parking lot for a few minutes while Mel teases her. He instinctively kisses her on the cheek, causing her to blush all over. Then he demands, "Now kidnap me."

She just giggles away.

"Hello. This is Melvin speaking..."

"NO! Your name is mud and I already paid this. Don't call me anymore or I'll sue your ass," the customer says, slamming the phone down as if it is going to do damage to Mel. He didn't even give him the account number. One of the agents transferred the call and failed to get the information. It's been that type of day.

"Have a good day, too," Mel says mockingly as he signs his phone off.

He's tense, his clothes are sour from sweating it out all day, and nothing would be better than Cherelle's presence for the rest of the day. It was so busy, Mel had to actually do some heavy customer service today. He must have taken over 20 stressful calls. That head set was like an umbilical cord permeating his head with screaming, irritating, nasally, East Coast voices. To make the headache worse, Sandra came in saturated in some floral scented perfume that somebody's grandmother would wear. He got a whiff when she walked past his desk and it felt like somebody was sticking a pin through his temple. It was loud, dense and durable (the smell actually stayed hours after she left for the day). To top it off, she did it two days in a row, which prompted over a dozen complaints about allergies and nausea. He wanted to fire her, but he put out a memo instead (making sure to be sensitive about not embarrassing her), encouraging employee's to lighten up on the fragrances, otherwise some restrictions could be added to the employee handbook.

The spontaneous date to Chinatown was just what he needed to take his mind off of work and every other hectic thing in his life. It was hard to take her back home last night. She's so nice to look at and talk to. A repeat would sure be welcome. He prays that she's home as he dials the number. Her father says she's been out for about two hours, and he doesn't know when to expect her. That's one unanswered prayer. Mel stuffs his briefcase to the point where it's as heavy as a cement bag, but since it's Friday, payday, and quitting time, he feels feather light as he floats out of the department, carrying with him a little disappointment and anger from the last call.

He lets the eager crowd off the elevator first rather than getting stampeded. As he turns the corner, his eyes immediately focus in on Cherelle among all of the scattering Spark employees. That's when he notices how tired his face is from frowning all day. He tries to keep the serious front as he walks towards her, but her smile just pushes it to the back and out of sight as he grins with relief and thanks Jesus.

"I thought you might want to do something after work today," she says, giving him a hug. "How was your day?"

He looks her up and down approvingly. She's wearing a long, blue denim dress with a white, short-sleeve shirt underneath and sandals that show her pretty red toenails. Her hair is wavy in the front, with a bang just over her eyes, and the back is in a thick, long braid that looks like a rope. "It just got real good," he flatters.

She glows as they fly off to the car.

"How was your day," he asks as he pops in the Take 6 CD.

"Fine and getting better. I studied all day long and decided the best way to start the weekend, would be by spending time with you. You and the Lakefront were really on my mind all day."

"Ditto," he says smiling, with nothing else to say as they cruise down a light Jackson Avenue to the Lake.

Caressing her hand is a natural reaction, so he does it like it is his constitutional right. The weather is still a picture perfect 75 and the weekend never seemed more promising. Even if the weather was chaotic and the Apocalypse started, the space around them is sound. She has brought him good fortune. Any other day, there wouldn't be a parking space within ten miles of the Lake, but he pulls into one with their names on it right across from Grant Park. He doesn't realize how beautiful it is at the Lakefront, until he gets out and takes it all in from a short distance away. They get out and stroll through the park, oblivious to the people and traffic around them. Occasionally, they will mention something meaningless. The moment is meant to be enjoyed, and they both respect it with a comfortable silence. He forgets that he barely closed his eyes last night, and he doesn't notice how fatigued his body is. Like a dream, they wind up on Randolph without even realizing how they made it that far. They're just there and park on a bench.

"You may have to carry me back to the car," Mel informs her when he realizes how far they've come.

"I have the will to carry you, but I don't think I have the strength," she says as she pulls out a big bag of popcorn. "I guess I'll have to stay here overnight with you, huh?"

They smirk at each other as she starts tossing kernels out to the pigeons. Pretty soon, they're surrounded by the bold, hungry birds. He hasn't orally committed to her, and she hasn't put her stamp on him, but being with her just seems right. And even considering any other woman feels so wrong. Guessing about their status is aggravating and leaves the door open to hurt feelings.

"Where are we going?" he queries from Kenosha.

She gives him a puzzled look.

"What are we doing? I mean, what are we? I know we're friends—I guess...I mean...what are we becoming?" he stammers, not knowing how to put it in simple terms without the fear of scaring her away.

She chuckles at him and offers, "We're siblings in Christ," tormenting him a little.

"Siblings in Christ?"

"Yep," she says as she proceeds to feed the pigeons nonchalantly.

"Oh," he agrees in order to spare himself the possible embarrassment of pouring out his heart, although he's not at all satisfied with the answer.

"Silly," she says as she elbows his biceps. "I don't believe you were going to go with that answer."

"I wasn't going with it..."

"Yes you were. You were just going to be content with being siblings. So you were going to risk letting some other guy step into my life and sweep me away? I'm mad at you now."

"No. No...I wasn't going to just let you go like that. I just didn't want to put any pressure on you to be with me."

"Pressure? There's no pressure. I love being with you."

Mel grins at that and runs a fever as he loses control of his heart and tongue. "Listen...I was just trying to say that I love spending time with you, too. I know we just met and all, but I'm really liking you a lot and I can't stand the idea of you being with any other man. I know I don't have control over my feelings or yours, but I'm just scared of walking that path alone. I don't want to get crazy about you and the feelings aren't mutual. And that's not to say that my spending time with you and feeling a certain way is contingent upon you feeling the same way and..."

Before he can continue, she puts her finger on his lips and tells him to "Shhh."

She grabs a handful of popcorn and throws it out. Then she turns to him with glazed eyes and a serious expression and addresses him: "I don't know exactly how you feel about me or where you are as far as your feelings are concerned, but I can tell you that I'm close to the end of that path—as you put it—and perhaps you may have to catch up with me or eventually walk another path. I know that I'm falling in love with you. From the moment I saw you at the front of my church praying, I was drawn to you like no other man before—and that includes my ex-husband. When I saw you in the bookstore the first time, I was so excited I didn't know what to do or think. That sparkling smile just glorifies God's galaxy; You're blacker than the abyss. And I just love black. I was in awe. But the second time, I felt that you were an answer to a prayer. I feel that you are my destiny.

"At the same time, I'm a realist. I know that a lot of men don't want to get involved with a woman with children and I realize that you may be one of those men—which I respect totally. What I don't appreciate is men who put on a front, like it's not a big deal that I have a son, when all they want to do is get me in the bed. I don't see that in you and that's one reason why I'm falling hard for you. I'm not looking for a father for my son, but whoever I get involved with and marry will have to be a father to him, because the man—*my man*—is supposed to be the head of me...the head of the house.

"To answer your question, I'm not sure what's going to become of us, but while we're getting to know each other, you don't have to compete with no other man, because I know what I want and I'm not trying to settle for less. Now let's enjoy getting to know each other," she says as she seals it with a gentle kiss on the lips, shattering all of his inhibitions.

Mel didn't know words could make him inebriated, until he says something goofy like "So you're not going to give me any. You'll feed these birds that like to mess on my ride, but you won't feed me. Just neglect me. In other words, I have to compete with the birds."

"Nope. Birds win hands down."

"Chirp tweet," he sounds as he opens his mouth.

She tosses one in and asks, "Do you have the taste for seafood?"

"Yeah, I could go for some. What do you have in mind?"

"A king's treat for you, as opposed to this bird food," she says as she gets up and pulls him up by the arm, dominoing the pigeons back. "I need you to take me home first. I'll pay for the gas."

Mel looks at her like she should be in a straight jacket.

Unbelievable. Mel has to slap himself to make sure he isn't dreaming. Cherelle cooked in his broken kitchen and on his stove (she cleaned it off before she started—like there wasn't nothing to it). After they left Grant Park, he took her home to get her cooking utensils and seasonings. Then he took her to Market Fisheries on 71st and State. She bought some crab legs, popcorn shrimp, catfish and a live Lobster. They stopped at Blockbuster and rented Gladiator, which Mel found hard to concentrate on, because he was in such a perfect world. Movies take him away from reality, but he didn't want to leave the world he was in—ever. And she wanted to pay for the gas. If she treats him any better, he will have to sacrifice a limb to even be worthy.

Before he brought her home, he stopped by his parent's house and introduced her to them. As usual, Dad was pleasant and friendly. Mom, on the other hand, threw him a curve ball. Out of all of his girlfriends he's introduced her to, she has never been warm to any of them. She even gave a lukewarm reception to Rita. She hated Memory's guts...or that's the way she acted. Memory always tried to warm up to her, but

Momma was always abrupt and curt, like Memory had just shed her snake skin in the living room. Maybe it was her motherly sixth sense or something. He was expecting her to curse Cherelle, condemning her to eternal damnation after finding out that she was married before and has a son (which Mel wished she didn't disclose to her), but instead, she welcomed her with open arms. They actually hit it off—almost better than Mel and Cherelle did. Mel stood mute and perplexed as they laughed and joked with each other. She even gave her a hug as they left and said she hoped to see her again. He thought that maybe it was an omen, but he just shook the idea out of his head and counted his blessings. She treated Cherelle better than she treated him—her own son—but he wasn't complaining. That made dinner even better.

Did she tap-dance all in that seafood or what? She claimed this was her first experience with lobster and that he had to serve as a guinea pig. Mel was a masochistic lab animal, because he was begging for more of the tormenting morsels. She could put Red Lobster to shame. His taste buds weren't biased either. A few minutes ago, she took him to the land of bliss with a back massage. She gave him the shock treatment from her hands. He wonders how many volts go through them. And to top it off, while she was cooking, Homey snuck upstairs and wagged his tail stub at her while she got down. She didn't panic. Instead, she casually called Mel in there. When he got in there, he couldn't believe she was petting him. Homey doesn't like mankind outside of Melvin. He couldn't stand Memory (not that Mel blamed him).

She comes back into the living room wearing a pair of his shorts that hang low and an oversized T-shirt. She's spending the night with him and they're going to school together. The dream continues as she gently collapses on top of him. Maybe he'll never wake up.

Three weird encounters occurred after Mel dropped Cherelle off at home after class: A guy that used to bully him in high school; a dude who made him the butt of his cruel jokes from his first job at Burger King, and Darlene. It's almost as if he talked them up.

Cherelle verified her sister's story about her never receiving flowers from a man. She also stated that she was ridiculed for being the ugliest girl in the class at one point. Not once did she complain...just recalled. Mel tried to comment on how gorgeous she looked, and she kept playing it down, stating, "I was the girl nobody wanted to be seen with" or "I was everybody's scratching post and litter box," and that "Scary Sherry" was her nickname. Mel was quick to point out that he traveled the same dirt road. He still didn't understand why he ran across them all in the same day. The answer came in the sermon just delivered by Reverend Williams at the prison, titled ***"Touch not my anointed,"*** *which focused on how a curse follows when a person puts their hands or mouth on God's children. The scripture was taken from* ***Genesis 12:3 (And I will bless them that bless thee, and curse him that curseth thee...),*** *with a reference to* ***Galatians 3:29 (And if ye be Christ's, then are ye Abraham's seed, and heirs according to the promise).*** *It was short and deep. Mel found no pleasure in knowing the consequences of his tormentor's deeds, though. In fact, his enemies' downfall grieved him and adjusted his outlook. As opposed to praying for the destruction of those who do wrong by him, he has a heart to pray for their salvation. After all, he doesn't have to ask God to take care of them, for His Word says that they will reap a curse for sowing ill-will to God's child.* As they extended an invitation to the inmates, Mel reflects.

Harvey Griffin was no different than the rest of his high school classmates. He was like an icon for the abusers. He was a Gangster Disciple, football player, Heavyweight wrestler and everybody's—except Melvin's—Homey. And because Harvey treated him like public enemy number one, everyone else followed suit. Once, Harvey tripped him as he walked to his seat in the cafeteria. He had a plate of pasta and a large lidless cup of fruit punch on his tray. When he got up, Harvey dared him to jump. He could've retaliated Karate Kid style, but then he would've been beaten into ground beef to everybody's amusement. There was a strong possibility that no one would've broken it up, so Mel decided to keep his limbs intact and wear his lunch for the rest of that day. In study hall, Harvey would slap him across the head and roast him daily. Most of the school adopted most of the nicknames that originated from him, such as "Grease Monkey," "Grape Ape," and "Black-ass Bullfrog." Often he would hear the girls from the school talk about how ugly he was. What hurt more than anything, was that a handful of them said it because of peer pressure. At one time, a couple of them thought he was "cute." He felt like a freshman for four years. Harvey made him want to die.

When Mel walked out of Walgreen's on 71st and Jeffrey, there was Harvey...in the parking lot selling Streetwise. Often, Mel prayed for the day that all of his enemies would be delivered to him and at his mercy. When he saw the once chiseled-from-granite, "Most Attractive Man" in the class hawking the newspaper for the homeless—with barely enough weight to anchor him from a gust of wind, sunken eyes and soiled clothes—he felt no urge to gloat. He looked worn and ghastly, like his diet consisted of laxatives and vinegar. Harvey glared at him and then blinked away without acknowledging that he knew him. He didn't even thank him for paying two dollars for a paper that sells for a buck. It didn't matter, though.

It was much the same torment when he worked at Burger King downtown on State and Congress. It was like he was a career Butt of the Jokes. Sidney Harris was especially ignorant. When Mel started, Sidney had three years seniority and was all the way up to $4.15 an hour. That only added to his conceit. A day never passed that he didn't brag about how many women he had (he was twenty-one years old and preyed on high school girls). Sidney made him want to kill. When Mel saw him walk into the barbershop after a hard day's work with the same uniform on, he almost laughed and jacked up his lining. After all of those years, he hasn't earned a white manager's shirt or a solid blue crew-leader's jersey. He was still in the ugly, dark-orange shirt. The irony is that Sidney snickered at Mel when he saw him in the chair. Not a greeting. A sneer. It made him appreciate his hard work and perseverance—which is a gift from God—in the face of adversity. While he has come a long way, some of his peers are stuck in neutral on the upside of a hill.

As if seeing them on the same day wasn't enough for the mind, he ran into Darlene at the Jewel on 87th and the Dan Ryan. She had some bitter-sweet news he could've done without. She asked had he heard about Memory. Of course he hadn't heard about or seen her since that day in the club—which was the day after she got arrested. Darlene informed him that Memory is five months pregnant by model Roger Walton. Mel didn't know Roger was a model. Come to find out, Memory was his publicist. Anyway, Roger is married, and apparently he fired her after she told him. When Darlene told him that Roger was giving her the cold shoulder, she actually sounded sympathetic. When Mel questioned her feelings, she said that she didn't take pleasure in seeing Memory get dogged over the way that she was. That was the biggest surprise of the day. She even suggested to Mel that maybe he should call her. Mel didn't comment on that, but he did consider it.

When he was coming up, everyone close to him kept emphasizing that it didn't matter what people said or thought about you and to pay it no mind. That sentiment is true in theory, but in practice, it's just a cliché. When it all boils down, it did and does matter what people think and say. It does have an affect on the psyche. Enough people told him that he was less than zero, so he felt worthless. Mel was hurt by a lot of what was said and done. How could he ignore something that he was aware of? However, in retrospect, he realizes that his weeping endured for a short night, and wishes that those that crossed him could experience his everlasting joy.

Pastor Adams lays his hands on an inmate name Marcel, who testifies that he's been in and out of prison throughout his life, stating that the next time he gets out, he won't be coming back. After he gets through praying for him, the high yellow inmate with youthful looks requests the mic to sing a song. Five minutes remain, and the guards don't object. Marcel closes his eyes and sings, **"I've Been Redeemed"** off key and with power, as many of the hardened, stone-faced prisoners break down. Redeemed indeed.

Chapter 17

Business is better than anticipated for Spark. Sales are up, and in turn, delinquent accounts are up. They didn't have the ad out of the newspaper a good two months, before they had to readvertise and bring in about ten new collection representatives. Human resources contacted some of the applicants that responded to the last ad and set up interviews with them. Mel interviewed five of the prospects in the morning and could understand why they weren't called in the first hiring blitz. A white guy didn't have the typing skills, but he did have a year and a half of credit experience. His resume indicated that he was attending Moody Bible Institute, taking some enrichment classes. When asked about it, the gentleman confided that he's preparing to possibly do some mission work in South America, which meant that his days at Spark would be numbered. He got a recommendation for hire from Mel, because of his honesty.

There was an Italian female with no collections experience—just extensive telemarketing experience. She was very outgoing and had an aggressive disposition. Her resume indicated that she was a finance major at Roosevelt University. She had potential, so Mel gave her a recommendation, and informed her that she would be called in for a second interview. When asked why she left her last job, she was honest in confessing that she was fired for insubordination, explaining that her immediate manager had a vendetta against her because she wouldn't go out with her.

The last interview of the day would have been hired based on her attractive appearance alone if she had just a smidgen of sales or collections experience. She was in her second year at Olive Harvey (19 years old), her three-year background was in data and order entry and she claimed that she was interested in going into communications. After a little probing, they both concluded that she wasn't qualified for the position. The disappointment immediately registered on her face and it touched his heart. As a consolation, he offered to pass her resume to the order department that was also hiring. She beamed with excitement as he informed her that their interview will be deemed a recommendation for hire for the order department and that she would be called within a week for the second interview.

When he escorts her to the elevator, Marcus was getting off. It was funny the way their eyes met. When the doors closed behind her, Marcus mobbed Mel.

"Did she get it?"

"I recommended her for your department, and believe me, I had you in mind when I did it, too."

"Man, I owe you," he says grinning from coast to coast. "You're late for Bible study," he informs.

"That's Right!" Mel blurts. It's five minutes after the start time. "Meet me down there," he says.

He gathers his Bibles from his desk and zooms to the elevator. He doesn't know what he is going to discuss today. He read over some scriptures the weekend and Monday, but nothing stimulated his spirit. He determines that it is a case of improvisation and ad lib, which is okay as long as everybody is on the same spiritual page. When he opens the door, he knows that it is going to be a special session.

"Praise the Lord," he says upon entering.

"Praise the Lord," they all responded.

"How is everybody doing?"

Everybody affirms that they are blessed.

"Well, it's good to see that we have a first-timer today," he acknowledges. "And what a blessing it is to have you with us, Deidra."

"It's a blessing to be here," she confesses through a radiant smile. "I would like to thank the study for all of the prayers on my behalf. It was very uplifting."

"We were glad to," Carmen confesses.

"Praise God," Karen adds.

"If you don't mind, I would like to make a request," Deidra says.

"Anything that we can do," Mel promises.

"Well, as you know, I was in group counseling," she admits. "And while I was there, I met many other women who went through the same thing and are having a harder time coping. A lot of them haven't turned to God, and I just wanted to say a prayer on their behalf."

Mel smiles as he nods his head. "That would be perfectly okay," he assures. "Would you like me to lead it, or would you like to lead it?"

"If you don't mind, I would like to lead it."

"I don't mind at all."

"I would like to request a prayer, too," Carmen interjects. "My brother is scheduled for open heart surgery, and I would like to send a prayer up on his behalf, before he goes under the knife."

Mel nods and approves it. "Is there anyone else that would like to request a prayer?"

Marcus raises his hand and blurts, "I would like to pray for a stronger relationship with God and for the salvation of my brother, who's addicted to crack."

Karen requests a prayer for her "ex-boyfriend that just found out that he has a form of lung cancer."

"I would like to intercede for my whole family...we just lost my great grandmother, and some of us are struggling with the loss," Harriett announces.

Mel pauses as he nods at everyone's request. Now he understands why he couldn't focus on any particular area. "Okay," Mel says. "Here's what we're going to do: We're going to go around and allow each individual to send a prayer up. Now this isn't a competition. God knows what's in the heart before it comes out of the mouth. Don't worry about how long it is or how articulate it is. Just talk to the Lord in your own way. Take your time and petition the throne of grace. After everyone gets through, I will say a closing prayer on behalf of the whole class. We'll let Deidra open it up, and then we'll just go around the table until it comes to me."

"Praise the Lord," Carmen says.

"Is everybody okay with that?"

They all smile and nod simultaneously.

"Okay, lets join hands and look to the Lord."

For 45 minutes, they are all on one accord. The Spirit of God is in the room and in each individual as they all speak with the Lord in their own way, as one. Mel has never experienced anything as powerful as the six souls joined together in a non-religious setting—petitioning God on behalf of others. Every prayer is fervent and real. A couple of people break down and start sobbing. They all praise God throughout. Some are longer than others. All are filled with the individual's own language. Each is equally powerful. Mel closes it out and pleads on behalf of everybody in the room by name and the people that they interceded for, and he finds himself praying on behalf of Memory, Harvey and Sidney without premeditation. When he says, "IN THE NAME JESUS, I PRAY.

AMEN," everyone lets out a loud Amen and gives a strong minute of praise as they hug each other.

"That was awesome," Marcus declares.

"Yes it was," Carmen seconds.

"Did you feel the Holy Spirit?" Karen queries.

"I still feel Him. GLORY!!" Harriett shouts.

Deidra just smiles as she wipes her face.

Mel gathers his things while everyone pours out. Deidra hangs around, and when they are alone, she thanks him.

"The Lord is really going to bless you," she says. "You're always so gracious and just genuinely nice."

"Well, thank you. But I'm still being worked on just like everyone else."

"You've been a real blessing to me. You just can't imagine."

"Give God the glory."

"Melvin," she says and pauses. "I did something real mean to you and I never apo..."

"Ssshhh," Mel says as he puts his finger to his lips. "All is good between us. The fact that you turned to Jesus is good enough for me."

She smiles and embraces him. "Thank you," she whispers.

Mel headed straight to Cherelle's house after work. They are planning to attend Midnight Madness at Chicago State. He was so glad to get out of Spark. Jackie was on her weekly period today. One of the women brought in a candy sales sheet for her daughter's school. It's against company policy to solicit or sell candy or anything along the lines, but Mel didn't see any problems with it. He actually bought four buckets of gummy bears. Jack peeked it going around and wrote her up. Mel wanted to kick his butt, but good. He has managed to make the whole department despise his vexing presence (including the other three supervisors), which can't be a good thing. Everybody is just sitting and waiting for a comet to fall from the sky on top of him. Mel unwinds and kills time on Cherelle's living room couch with her and some pictures.

"Who is this?"

"That's me when I was in third grade."

"That's you?" Mel questions with amazement. "You were funny looking," he laughs.

Cherelle slaps him on the arm and cuts him a disapproving glare.

"You were cute though," he recovers as he flips through the pages of one of her photo albums.

He met her youngest sister—Dameeka—and she looks just like Cherelle did when she was a child. Dameeka is very reserved, and from what Cherelle told him, a genius. If nature runs its correct course, Dameeka is also going to be a combination of beauty and brains like no other.

"Shouldn't we be going soon?"

"Yeah, we can go."

"Let me go put on my clothes," she says as she dashes upstairs.

Mel looks through the photo album at all types of pictures from different eras of different people. He studies the people he's familiar with and gets lost in the photos of Cherelle...especially the post braces pictures when she really developed into a pleasant dream. Chuckie comes down and sits right next to Mel with one of his books.

"Hey Chuckie. How are you, Buddy?"

"Fine," he answers bashfully.

"What you got here?"

"My book," he claims, showing him the orange cover with a tiger on it.

Mel reads the title to him: "'THE tiger WHO WORE WHITE GLOVES'...Can you read it?" he questions as he takes it and sits him closer to him.

He nods his head as he looks down.

Mel turns to the first colorful page and asks, "What does this say?"

"There was once a Tiger terrible and tough..."

Cherelle walks up and beams, letting Chuckie finish the last page.

"...and satisfied with his strong striped hide."

"Time for bed, Chuckie," she announces. He doesn't protest as he gets up and obliges. "Say goodnight to Melvin," she instructs.

"Goodnight," he says stoically as Cherelle leads him upstairs.

"Goodnight, Buddy. See you later."

Mel is left smiling by his innocent charm. Chuckie reminds Mel of himself when he was a child: humble, respectful, and intelligent, although some of his humility has been depleted by some of his accolades. He actually reminds him of his adult self, too.

He notices that Cherelle still has the flowers—which are a bit decrepit—and vase that he sent about a month ago. They rest next to one of the many photos of her in the living room. This one is a prom picture with a galactic, star-studded background. She's posing alone in a solid pink strapless dress with matching pink shoes, and her smile just accents the whole picture. Two cockroaches dance on the corner table next to it, but Mel ignores them as Cherelle comes back down in her Guess jeans and Chicago State sweat shirt.

"You know," he ponders. "Out of all of these pictures of you in here, I don't have not one."

She looks at him bewildered and states, "You never asked," as she picks up the frame from the table and pulls an identical picture out. "You like this one?"

"I love it."

She sits on his lap and writes on the back of it: *Don't 4get that I got sick just 64 this picture ☺ 2 ♥Melvin♥ "♥The Black King♥" Adams♥ One of the sweetest persons on the face of the earth♥ I have learned 2 really l♥ve and appreciate u even though we haven't known each other long♥ I thank God everyday 4 blessing my life with such a beautiful spirit and I hope that our friendship will continue 2 grow n2 something that will last 4ever♥ 4 your i's only. L♥ve Cher♥*

She puts her red lip imprints on the back and then she imprints Mel's cheek. As big as Mel's vocabulary is, he couldn't come up with anything to say to her. He just examines the picture and beams with honor.

It isn't quite John Thompson. Craig Hodges will have to do. It sure isn't Dick Vitale. Some guy name Jimmy "In the Gym" Smith has the honor. They are in Chicago—a long way from North Carolina and the Tar Heels. Although it's the Cougars of Chicago State, the excitement is just the same as Midnight Madness at one of the nation's powerhouses. If the crowd is indicative of the home game audience in the future, there will be sellout crowds for the first time since they jumped to Division I. Mel and Cherelle have floor level seats next to the announcement table. They arrived shortly before eight—just before everybody poured into the gymnasium. The Jammer: Dave Michaels from 106 Jams, sat right next to them at the table.

"Call in sometimes, brother," he says to Mel as he gives him and Cherelle a cassette single by PMD. "I'll remember you."

"Thanks man. I'll be shouting at you from time to time," Mel promises.

The first event is the celebrity basketball game featuring local celebrities and entertainers, such as singers M-Doc, Stevie 02, DJ's Steve "Silk" Hurley, Lil' Rod and EZ Street and a couple of exotic dancers. As the players warm up in the crip line, BJ Thomas comes strolling by with a giraffe and stops to talk at the scorer's table. He nods at Mel when he spots him. "What's going on Mel," he asks, extending his hand.

"Nothing much. How you feeling?" he replies with a shake.

"I'm blessed man. I'm blessed."

"This is my friend, Cherelle," Mel introduces. "Cherelle, this is BJ Thomas. He's a writer for the Defender and a few other papers. We belong to the same journalism organization."

"Oh, that's nice," she comments. "So are you here on assignment?"

"Nope. Just here to enjoy the festivities," he says. "Mel, I don't know if you've met Malcolm Johnson. He's with the CABJ, too."

Mel stands up to shake his hand and looks to the sky to meet his eyes. "Another MJ. I thought I saw him playing for the Bulls," he jokes.

"Not quite there yet, Homey," Malcolm laughs.

"Give him about four years, and then he'll need body guards to walk down the street," BJ interjects.

"So are you playing tonight?" Mel asks, seeking to know his basketball affiliation.

"Don't tempt me. I'm actually here covering the event. This was one of my top five choices. Ricky Birdsong and NU have a little more to offer though."

"So you're in your first year at Northwestern?"

"Yep."

"You don't recall that guy that qualified academically but was always catching it from the press and the law for his bad attitude?" BJ fishes. "They dubbed him Malcolm X."

"Okay," Mel exclaims as he recollects how the troubles of MJ were well documented. "Now I remember. The X man...Didn't you get into a fight in a game last Christmas?"

He laughs. "Is that the only impression you have of me?"

"I just thought it was funny how the photographer snapped the shot just as you connected to ol' boy's nose."

They all laugh.

"Well Mel, we're going to push on," BJ says. "I'll probably see you at the meeting next month."

"All right. Peace out," he says.

"Nice meeting you," Malcolm says to Cherelle. "Stay up, Melvin," he bids as they fade away.

The game is about to start as the teams gather at their benches.

"I didn't realize he was that short," Cherelle mentions of the stripper known as Chocolate Shake, who was just introduced.

"You *know* him?" Mel questions with a touch of jealousy.

"I know *of* him."

"So you haven't been acquainted at some bridal shower or club?"

"Please," she says. "I didn't have a bridal shower and I wouldn't be caught dead in a strip joint. Some of my old friends, on the other hand, have told me some wild tales about some of them."

"Um hm," he mutters.

"Besides, I wouldn't want any chocolate that's been passed around and nibbled on by all types of people. You haven't had a lot of women tasting you, have you?" she questions as she snuggles up to him and sticks her nose under his ear lob.

"I didn't know I was edible," he laughs.

"Of course you're edible...like gourmet chocolate. And Cherrelle sung it best: you look *good* to me," she purrs as she licks his ear lob.

Mel chuckles as he heats up. "I think I'm melting," he quips. "And you know chocolate is kinda' sticky when wet."

"Just the way I like it," she says, eyeing him alluringly. "There's nothing like lapping hot chocolate."

He opens his mouth for a comeback, but he's void of words...just full of desire. The crowd is what saves Mel. If they had some privacy at that moment, his promise would be broken. He breaks free of her stare and focuses on the game.

She leans over and whispers, "I'm sorry."

"For what?" he asks as he keeps his eyes on the floor.

"For tempting you," she says. "I shouldn't be talking to you that way."

Mel smirks uncomfortably as he switches topics. "Did you know M-Doc in high school?"

"I don't know him now," she states. "Which one is he?"

Mel points him out to her.

"I told you I was a nerd back then. I didn't keep up with that 'In' crowd."

"This guy at the job went to school with him, too."

"Melvin."

He looks her way.

"Do you accept my apology?"

"Your apology is unnecessary. I wasn't offended...just a bit enlightened."

"Enlightened? Are you mad at me?"

"Of course not. It's just that I realize that it's not realistic to not desire you in that way. Regardless of what I say, I can't fool myself into thinking that I can control my urges for a long period of time."

She grins softly.

They remain silent for the rest of the game. At half time, Xtaci performs two love ballads, and Mel finds his hand wrapped in Cherelle's. They sit hand in hand until Hodges leads his team to victory with 16 points. Immediately after, the Greeks put on a step show that gets the crowd even more charged. The AKA's go first and are the only sorority to perform.

"Have you thought about pledging?" he asks, breaking the silence and her grip as the AKA's finish their routine and leave the floor.

"Nope. That's not my thing."

Mel nods as the Kappa's prepare to perform. They are out in numbers tonight, whooping it up with each other in brotherly love.

"John is a Kappa," she mentions as they put on a colorful rendition of a ring battle. "And guess what your good friend Clarence is?"

"He has Q-Dog written all over him."

"You know it," she confirms. "Did you pledge?"

"Please," he begs. "Did Rodney King ask to get his brains beaten out?"

After the Greeks step for what seems like the whole night, with the well-choreographed Sigma's winning the competition, the actual intra-squad game is finally ready to be played. The crowd counts down the last ten seconds to midnight, and the team comes storming out as the season officially starts. They put on a dunk show before the hit and run scrimmage.

After the game, Cherelle got her picture taken with Craig Hodges and they stopped at Harold's Chicken before heading to Mel's house.

"Chuckie likes you," she says between bites as Mel licks the mild barbecue sauce off his fingers at the kitchen table. "He's so bashful, that he normally doesn't come out to socialize with anybody—even some of his family members."

He smirks at her.

"I saw the way you showed interest in his reading...his father hasn't even done that," she adds.

"He's a nice kid. It's easy to get along with him," he says as he grabs his mess and trashes it.

He heads upstairs to the bathroom and changes into his shorts after washing up. Cherelle emerges as he fixes the linen on the bed in the guestroom. She leans up against the chest of drawers and studies him.

"I'll have you tucked in in no time."

She flashes a gentle smile at him.

When he finishes, she takes a seat on the bed as he pulls out the long T-shirt that she brought over during one of her previous overnight stays. He runs downstairs and turns everything off. She's in the same spot when he returns, sniffing the single, long-stem red rose that he strategically placed just under the pillow, and reading the card that was next to it. The card included an invitation to a play next month at the Regal Theater (the tickets have yet to go on sale, but he'll be sure to have choice seats). Her clothes are neatly folded on the dresser as she sits barelegged at the foot of the bed. He notices a distant look on her face and waves his hand in front of her eyes. "You okay?"

She nods.

He looks at her for a moment and takes a seat next to her. "I would give you a penny for your thought, but I don't have change. How good is my credit?"

She smirks slightly.

"What's on your mind, Cherelle?"

She closes her eyes, shakes her head and lays back. "I was just thinking..."

"I could see that."

She sits back up and faces him. "I'm going to take Chuckie to the Aquarium next Saturday and we would love for you to come, but I don't want you to feel obligated to be a father figure to him."

Mel turns away and studies the floor.

"You don't have to go. I won't hold it against you. I will spend time with you that evening, regardless of whether you go or not, but spending the whole day with you is appealing, and I know Chuckie..."

"I'll go," Mel announces monotonously.

Cherelle calms down and verifies, "You sure?"

Mel nods. "Personally, I don't understand how a man can walk out on something that he created. What if God walked away from man, like man walks away from his children?" Mel ponders as he lays back. "I guess I would have to be a father who turns his back to his child to understand."

Cherelle gently places her hand on his head.

"You're too good to not take the risk of opening my heart up to you. I'm almost expecting a big, unpleasant surprise from you...you seem too special to be real...and I feel so unworthy of you. Why else would a man walk out on a beautiful woman?" he philosophizes. "It's almost as if when I open my eyes, you will be someone totally different. Is it safe to open my eyes? Is it safe to be in love with you?"

She lightly brushes her lips over his and then lays beside him. "Thank you for the rose," she whispers in his ear. For the rest of the night, nothing else was uttered, there was no movement, and he kept his eyes shut.

The computers were down throughout the company for the whole day. Management was having a heart attack and the representatives were having a party. The company was crippled. It was a real headache for Mel, and a bad time to hear commentary on black men from the "experts". "Nigga's" this and "Nigga's" that poured out of their mouths. The whole realm was covered: Nigga's only want white women; Nigga's are gay; Nigga's are cheap; Nigga's are weak; Nigga's commit crime; Nigga's are the cause of world hunger; Nigga's created diseases; Nigga's brought sin into the world. Nigga's Nigga's Nigga's. They talked as if black men—or "Nigga's," as they were called throughout the discussion—are a separate race from the black woman. It's when they got on the topic of "Nigga's" in the correctional system and how they have influenced the rise in female inmates, that Mel had to leave in order to keep from going off on one of them, because there's no reasoning with the perpetually ignorant.

On the panel: Devita Harper, a.k.a. Devilina, the main advocate of African-American men sticking to African-American women ONLY. Also the biggest hypocrite in the galaxy (Not only is her taste in the Euro-Hispanic look, but her first child is by a—gasp—WHITE MAN); Kimberly Lott, the freak of the century (word is she has had a few encounters with the same sex, but since she didn't like it, she decided to stick with group heterosexual activity); and "Go to Hell" Gayle, the linebacker from Notre Dame that knows from experience with every brother in heaven, hell and on earth, that the black male is cheap, in jail and endangered. Let her tell it, if it wasn't for black women like her, they would've gone down the drain a long time ago. Down the drain is a much more appealing alternative to Gayle. She also claims that they're just born dumb and can't help themselves. Mel would like to believe that she's actually Charles Murray or Richard Hernstein in disguise.

To give them the benefit of the doubt, he realizes that the subject has weighed on his mind lately. With the recent publication of the Bull—or Bell—Curve by Murray and Hernstein—which supposedly justifies the oppression of black people because they are naturally less intelligent than white people—subconsciously he's been in a semi-funk about black and white people. That was a good lunchtime discussion with the fella's the day before. His participation in the prison ministry fueled the rage. It is really a sad sight: black men being in the majority in the prison community. At the same time, it is encouraging to hear some of the testimonies of the inmates that turn their lives over to Christ as a result of their chains.

And Brent: the midget bigot. Monday, Mel went up to the sixth floor to get clarification on a report, and had to walk pass the marketing department. Not only were the representatives playing nerf basketball (if that went on in the Mel's department, they would've replaced the whole floor), but he heard them—along with Brent—mimicking a stereotypical black person: "Yo yo yo...Pass da bawl befo Ah blast ya," went Brent. Then later on, he had the nerve to try to have a conversation with him, not realizing that Mel overheard him. Marcus, Nelson and Reggie were sitting at the table with them in the lunchroom. When Mel mentioned that he was interested in possibly pursuing a career in video production and how he had put together a rough documentary on mating Rottweilers, Brent—who was sitting across the table from him—stuck his two cents in and emphasized, "I can make home movies." Mel stood up, leaned towards him—only a whisker away from his face—and countered through clinched teeth "I betcha kin pass 'n dunk 'n shoot too. But are ya down wit a wun ate sev'n? Kin ya hang wit da brutha's 'n da pen? Wassup, White Boowee?" Brent turned crimson with fear welling up in his eyes and—wisely—didn't respond.

Needless to say, when he leaves work Wednesday, he is emotionally ill and fuming. He thinks it's a good idea to go over Cherelle's house and whine to her, not realizing how much pressure has built up. He dumps the frustration on her as they sit on her porch under the quarter moon and in the cool breeze.

"It's like opposition is coming from all directions," he laments. "Even from sisters."

"Don't take it personally," Cherelle encourages, gently rubbing his back. "I'm in your corner."

"Don't take it personally?" he questions as he somehow manages to tune out her positive comment. "How in the hell can I not take it personally when it's coming so frequently from women the same color as me?"

"It's not coming from me," she reasons as she draws her hands back. "And it's obvious they don't know you and countless other good black men like I do."

"That's really not any consolation when everybody is attacking me and my brothers, including my own mother."

"Well I take it back then," she casually concurs.

"See what I mean," he antagonizes.

"You're tripping."

"What," he says, his voice rising a notch. He is already intense and louder than normal, now he's shouting at her and doesn't realize it. "Why are you patronizing me?" he questions as he stands up. He doesn't give her a chance to answer as her mouth drops and her brow wrinkles up at his tirade. "Stop acting like this is all in my head...like I'm overreacting. Have you ever been a black man before? Of course not, so don't make light of the situation. I don't need that from you," he says, pointing a finger at her.

She clicks her lips and folds her arms as she shakes her head and rolls her eyes at him.

He continues: "I don't care about you getting an attitude. I've been getting everybody's attitude all week, so one more doesn't matter to me."

"If it doesn't matter, then why are you yelling at me?" she retorts.

"Because you're being ignorant by belittling what I'm going through."

"I'm not belittling what you're going through and you don't have to yell at me," she sobs. "I don't deserve this," she pules as she springs up and starts for her front door.

Mel catches her by the arm as she gets the screen door open. "I'm sorry," he apologizes.

"Let me go," she whimpers as she tries unsuccessfully to jerk her arm away.

"I'm sorry, Cherelle," Mel desperately whispers in her ear as he embraces her. "I didn't mean to jump on you like that."

She stops resisting and buries her wet face in his chest as she squeezes him. The weeping continues for a few moments as he rocks her and pleads with her to pardon him.

"Do you forgive me?"

She nods.

He kisses her on the top of her head. "I won't do that again," he promises, feeling like a pig's behind. "I love you. Do you still love me?"

She nods again.

He gently pulls back, peering into her downcast eyes. "I'm going to go now," he announces as he uses his thumbs to wipe away the tears on her face. "I've done enough damage. Don't you want me to leave now?"

She shakes her head as she gazes up at him.

She doesn't move as he kisses her lightly on the lips. She remains in the same position as he skips down the steps to his car: arms folded under the chill of the autumn breeze.

He toots his horn and she reluctantly waves as he pulls off. He sighs and shakes his head. "Good for you, Mel," he chastens. "You're about to drive away the perfect woman."

He slows to a stop as he gets to 14th and Harding and wipes his tense brow. Staring straight ahead, he replays the day's events in his head in that long pause, realizing that he is guilty of what he accused the ladies at the job of doing: bashing the innocent along with the guilty few. When he gets home, he's going to call Cherelle and apologize again. Damn. How can he rip into his comfort zone? It must be a build-up of testosterone.

As he reflects on the flowers and card that he will send to her tomorrow, he's startled back to reality when someone slams into the side of his car, another guy jumps on top of the hood, and two more run around the front, fleeing from a plain clothes, gun-totting white man—presumably an officer—who's in hot pursuit. Mel thinks for a split second as they cut into a gangway and shots ring out. He has his video camera. He was planning to tape the Bible study for testimony purposes for his congregation, but he had to cancel because of the chaos.

Without weighing the risks, he pulls over to the side, scoops his camera from the back and jumps out, running after them while switching it on. Once he gets to the edge of the building, he kneels and cautiously peeks around. The officer is hiding behind a dumpster as Mel focuses the lens on him against the backdrop of the dead end alley. He jumps back slightly as the flare from another fired shot indicates that the dudes at the end are going for blood. The cop fires two shots back and sparks fly as his bullets ricochet off the wall. Mel picks up a shadowy head peeking from behind a garbage can. Suddenly, one of the guys darts across the way, firing three shots. The officer fires one shot and the man crash lands.

His comrades shout, "Dedrick's hit," as they run from behind the can firing, forcing the cop to stay sheltered. One of the guys reaches down and grabs something by the fallen assailant, then darts through the wall. He can hear a creaking door slam shut and sirens closing in. Mel draws back and saunters back to his car. A few residents peep out of their windows as the lights from the approaching squad cars illuminate the street. He lays the camera on the back floor and pulls off, ignoring the traffic signal that kept him there long enough to catch it in the first place.

"How are you," Mel questions as he hands Cherelle the pink roses and the handwritten, apologetic card.

"Fine," she says, embracing him. "I didn't know if I would see you again."

"I got your message last night, but you know I try not to call anyone's house after a certain time. It was late when I got home," he confirms. She apologized for her part in the argument—whatever it was. She sounded so sad and repentant. "You weren't in any way at fault yesterday...I was a total idiot and I'm just thankful that you're forgiving enough to even talk to me."

"No, I should have let you vent," she insists. "I didn't have to get sarcastic when I knew you were under pressure."

"Look," Mel says as he plants a kiss on her lips. "Don't argue with me...I was at fault and I will not have you taking any blame. Understand?" he questions through a sly smile.

"Yes," she says with humility.

The midday news is on and the top story is last night's shooting. Mel is wound up so tight from the previous day, that he called in sick. He was up all night examining the video, which came out crystal clear. He heard several news reports already, when Cherelle brings it up.

"There was a shooting a few blocks away from here after you left," she announces as they take a seat on the sofa. "One of the guys from across the street was killed by a cop."

"Really?" Mel questions. He didn't know it was one of the same fella's.

"It was actually the one that Daddy had the argument with before the brick came through the window," she confirms as the report states that several witnesses said that the white cop shot an unarmed black man in the back. "I'm surprised he didn't have a gun with him. I saw him showing one off to some kids before."

"What do you think of the cop that did it?"

"I have mixed feelings, but I don't think anyone should shoot a person that's not armed, unless you're protecting yourself. I think he should be tried just like any other person would be in a situation like this," she says with conviction. "Between you and I, the cop is known to hassle black people. Once he stopped Johnny for no reason. You and I know that he pulled him over because he was a black man in a luxury car."

Mel pauses as the report states that the cop has been reassigned to a desk job until an investigation is conducted. "Is anyone else here?"

"Uncle Willie is in the basement, but he shouldn't be coming up here."

Mel takes a deep breath and states, "I want you to see something," as he pulls a videocassette out of his inside pocket. "Put this in the VCR."

As the view of the alley comes into focus, she immediately recognizes, "That's right on Harding." Then it registers, "You were there?"

He nods.

Her brow crinkles as the shoot-out unfolds and she recognizes the sky blue Charlotte Hornets jacket that "Clifford always wears" and the raspy voice of "Peanut" as he shouts that "Dedrick's shot." She didn't recognize the other shadowy figure. As the tape blacks out, she gives Mel a silent, befogged look before asking, "What are you going to do?"

Mel shakes his head and humps his shoulders. "I don't know."

She leans forward. "Melvin, you have to..." she starts, before Mel cuts her off.

"I know what the right thing to do is, but I don't feel right doing it. Truth is the Christian way, but sometimes it's hard to be a Christian and a black man. Lately I've been struggling with black and white; light and dark; right and wrong. It seems like there should be a gray area, but I know it's an illusion. Right now, I'm not spiritually strong and I need you to bear with me and stay by my side. As my lady and sister in Christ, I need you to send a prayer up on my behalf, because I've quenched the Spirit and I have been too ashamed to talk to the Lord," he says, looking down.

Last night, he unleashed some of the testosterone. He could have made a fortune at the sperm bank. That left him mentally desolate, as if His Spirit left him. The devil was in his head. Instead of releasing some of the rage, it just added depression to the problem. All the while, Cherelle was on his mind, and the thought of her felt good.

She doesn't say anything for a moment as she peers at him with concern and places her hand on his knee. Without getting his consent, she firmly clutches his hands and petitions the throne of grace for her man. Mel is moved as she lays it all out for him. When she says, "Amen," they sit quietly as the TV continues to broadcast the incident. Without her mentioning it, he knew that she is in his corner no matter what he does. When a commercial comes on, she addresses what was mentioned yesterday.

"I think you should talk to your mother."

He glances at her and she looks back.

"I'm concerned about your relationship with her," she mentions. "Yesterday, you said that she was against you like everyone else. I find that hard to believe."

"You obviously don't know her like I do," Mel shrugs. "And how do you know that I haven't tried to talk to her throughout the 25 years I've been on this earth?"

"You're right. I don't know her like you do and I don't know how you communicate with her," she calmly offers. "But from what I can see, she's nicer than you give her credit for."

"You only met her once and how long did y'all talk? All of 15 minutes," he snaps.

"I've talked to her since then."

"Oh really? How's that?"

"I called her up a few times."

"Is that right?"

"Yep. And I like her like my own mother."

"Umph," Mel grunts.

"And you know what else? She loves you to death."

"And just how do you know this?"

"She told me."

Mel pouts as he avoids a rerun of yesterday and locks his jaw. Part of him is testy over them talking without his knowledge, especially since he can't have a civilized conversation with her himself.

"Don't be offended, sweetheart," she says as she snuggles up to him and wraps her arms around his neck. "All I'm asking is that you at least try to grow closer to her and bring down the walls. That's all."

"It's hard to talk to that lady," he whines.

"I know it is, honey, but can you at least try, for me...I would appreciate it."

She's good. "All right. I'll try," he resolves like a preschooler that was conned into eating his vegetables.

Honor thy father and thy MOTHER: that thy days may be long upon the land which the Lord thy God giveth thee. The first commandment with promise; the first commandment that Mel learned; one of two commandments that he's kept (thou shalt not kill is the other—although he's gotten dangerously mad at folks throughout his life). It wasn't anything easy. The mother part of the equation is as hard as taking a deep breath after being punched in the belly. Often, he would bite his tongue and hold his breath to keep from saying the wrong thing to her. He prays for guidance as he heads over there, realizing that the potential to finally break that sacred commandment is great. He's planning to tell her everything that he ever wanted to tell her, and he's not going to be denied and he's not pulling any punches. Okay. Maybe he won't tell her to go to Hell or that he can't stand her, but he will address their relationship—or lack of one.

As he speeds down the Dan Ryan, he charges himself up by recalling some of the nastier things she's done to him. *Once, she smacked the fire from him up at school because he was late that same day that she paid a surprise visit. At the time, he had perfect attendance, was on the National Honors Society and honor roll, and had a reason, that she didn't bother hearing (he had to go back home to change after he was splashed with mud from a speeding car). She was waiting for him in the hall as he came rushing in. It came out of deep space and had him seeing stars. There were only a few witnesses, but it still stung to the heart. He was already dark. His face was charred another shade of black on the left side. He hasn't forgotten or forgiven that. Then, of course there were the "fun" restrictions: NO going to games; NO television on school days; NO close, frequent associating with the heathens (which meant that he didn't have too many associates); NO R rated movies; NO leaving the house without the address and phone number of where you're going to be; NO being late coming home (not even a minute late); NO fast food; NO breathing without permission; NO thinking without permission; NO living unless "I" say so. Mel's temperature rises as he starts grinding his teeth. The indifference to his many accolades didn't help. It seems like he could give his life as a sacrifice for the world, and it wouldn't faze her. She would probably find fault with him some kind of way. More than all of the harsh treatment and restrictions and indifference to doing the right thing, he resents the preferential treatment she shows towards David.*

If he hacked off the heads of a preschool Sunday school class, he would still be her baby. He could do no wrong in her sight, despite doing nothing but wrong. He smokes, drinks, comes in when he pleases, cusses like a drunk pirate (although not normally in her presence, he's slipped a few times), talks back to both of them (if Mel thought about giving the lip service that David does, he would've needed a tooth detector before the words got out of his mouth), and for the most part worships the devil with his hedonism. Mel remembers when David asked Momma to get his ear pierced. She said no. What did he do? He went out and got both of his ears pierced, and got his chest tattooed for good measure. What did she do? She balked briefly and tucked her tail. What the hell?

Mel is seething as he pulls in front of his parent's home. He wants to beat them both: David for being so damn disrespectful, and her for not putting her foot down deep into his shallow butt like she would've done Mel. He sits still long enough to calm down to a civil level. When he gets out, he's almost in tears as he stomps to the door. This is not going to be pretty.

He lets himself in and he can hear her in the kitchen (where she usually is when he pays a surprise visit) washing dishes. With purpose, he marches in and takes a seat at the table without speaking. She looks over at him as he gazes befuddled at the wall.

"Would you tell me if I was adopted?"

She casually turns the water off and stares at him. "Would I tell you if you were adopted?" she repeats.

"Yes," he snaps. "Would you tell me if I was a stepchild; not a product of the same parents as David. Would you tell me if I was adopted?"

"What is this all about?" she questions calmly.

"C'mon Momma," he says with agitation as he rises. "This is about 25 years of fourth class treatment at your hands. This is about a blatant lack of sensitivity and respect from you. This is about a lack of motherly love towards me—in actions at least, because you'll tell anybody that listens that you love me. You even told me a couple of times," he says as he paces.

She dries her hands, faces him from across the room, and leans against the counter, as it seems like her face is straining to comprehend what he's saying.

"For the life of me I can't recall if and when I've disrespected you. My conscious is clear on that. For my whole life I've been too busy trying to please you and make you proud of me to show you any type of irreverence. If I have, I sincerely apologize from the bottom of my heart," he says as he pauses and places his hand on the wall, leaning and still muddled in divers thoughts. "Nope...nothing comes to mind. But if you like, I will write you an apology in blood for being born."

Her face is a little calmer as she shifts her head up. She remains silent while he continues, shifting from first to fifth gear in intensity.

"What can I do to please you? You treat my friends like a loving mother would treat her own kids, but you treat me like a bald bastard with no morals. And the favoritism you show towards David is too ridiculous to even go into. You don't even chastise him for disobedience. He raises all kinds of hell and you embrace him. He shows no regard for your authority and you reward him. I bled, cried and sweated to try to please you and I got contempt from you...even to this day. You don't even praise me for the effort I put out. You've NEVER praised me. Never. So yes...I pose the question again: Am I a stepchild or what?" he asks as he looks intently at her. He doesn't give her a chance to respond—not that she was intending to—as he proceeds to rip into her. "How come you didn't just flush me down the toilet when I was born, because that's the way you've treated me my whole life: as waste that you wanted to discard...wanted to flush down the toilet," he says, pacing back to the table to catch his breath.

She just continues to stare at the spot he was standing in. Her sentiments are an enigma blanketed with an expressionless mask. It is quiet for a brief five minutes. The serenity of the eye of the storm doesn't last. Mel erupts again, this time with more potent venom.

"You make me want to die," he snickers through clinched teeth and a halcyon tone. "If it wasn't for Cherelle, I swear I would leave town and probably never call you again. You wouldn't have to deal with me anymore. But unfortunately, she likes you a lot, which is understandable since you show everyone but yours truly the utmost love. If it weren't against God to hate somebody, I would hate you. But you know what? Lord forgive me, but I hate being your son," he says as he rises.

She doesn't answer as they peer at each other, as if facing a reflection.

Her muteness sends a surge of disdain through him that comes out of his mouth in the form of a repetition: "I HATE BEING YOUR SON!" he shouts, poking a finger at her as he storms past. The door slams. She just stands motionless, eyeing the spot where he just mirrored her.

The knock on the door didn't sound urgent—sort of dull and dilatory—but it was three o'clock in the morning and it woke Mel up out of his sleep. It was all the better, because he was having another nightmare about how he went off on his mother. If she ever made him feel like waste, he made himself feel like something even more despicable. From the moment he got outside, he felt lower than a worm. He will apologize to her, because he hasn't had any rest since. Besides, he was wrong. It's a good thing the dog wasn't outside, otherwise whoever it is on the other side of his door may have ended up fertilized on the lawn. He eases to the door and peeks out in stealth, just in case it's someone he doesn't want to acknowledge. It's a dreary eyed David. He opens the door to catch him as he staggers in laughing a wheezing laugh. "Mel," he slurs, and then starts tittering hysterically.

"What's the matter with you?" he questions as he leads him to the sofa and slams him down.

He just giggles even more.

Of course he's toasted. He smells like a distillery. Mel has never seen him like this. Mel checks to see if he has any bruises on him and if there are any visible signs of trauma. He appears to be okay. Then, like a bolt of lightening, his memory comes back and he peeks out of the front door. "Where's my car?!"

David's laughing turns into sobbing as his face breaks down and he starts weeping.

"Oh no!! C'mon David!!" he yells as his temperature rises to the boiling point and his body starts quaking. He takes a deep breath as he grits his teeth and asks, "Are you okay?"

David nods.

Then Mel has the urge to make him unokay as he paces to the kitchen for a glass of fruit punch.

Momma threatened to put him out; Dad almost lost his religion (it took every ounce of spirituality to keep profanity from coming out of the same mouth that he preaches the gospel with); Mel killed him with his anger. He will repent later, after he's buried. They all yelled him into sobriety. If he was having a hangover, they cut him loose and he was falling in a bottomless pit of fussing. David was so humble and woeful. If it was somebody else's car—like his parent's—Mel would've felt sorry for him.

When Melvin went to look at his car, he was expecting the worse. And he got it...and then some. From the door to the taillights, it was all good, but from the windshield forward, it was a bad dream. Mel could only laugh when he saw it, because the only other urge was to do to David what David did to the car: ram him head first into the cement viaduct post at 67th and King Drive. A state of the art designed, aerodynamic masterpiece of a car was reduced to condensed scrap metal. TOTALED. And David wasn't insured, so Mel's rage may not have peeked yet. Judging by the looks of the remains, David was definitely traveling at warp speed. He's fortunate that the engine didn't blow up or come through the dashboard. For David's safety, Mel is grateful. But he's still angry enough to kill him.

When his father dropped him off at home, he said nothing during the trip. He wondered if he knew about his blowup. While he was in his mother's presence, she proceeded as if nothing negative was said. She even addressed him by name and seemed to esteem him. "Melvin, if the insurance doesn't take care of it, I will make sure you get it replaced," she assured. Needless to say, Mel felt very uncomfortable being around her without the apology being offered. He wanted to do it in private, since he acted ugly in private. He will when he gets the opportunity.

Mel prayed before he picked up the phone to call his insurance. He needed the strength to press on if they told him he was out of luck and out of wheels. After taking some of the information, the representative told him that an accident report would be necessary. He called his instructor and informed her that he may not be in class, and then he left the message for Cherelle that he may have to cancel the date. He called his mother and told her to bring David to the police station on 71st and South Chicago. Filing the report was no picnic. They had to wait an hour while the officers tended to two other people. It seemed like they were either purposely going as slow as they could, or they were filling the forms out for the first time. When they finally got to them, Mel was in a funk. The officer was even funkier with his callous disposition. Two hours of his life wasted. When he got home, there was a message from Cherelle. She said to call her at Jean's house.

"Hello."

"How you doing, Jean?" he asks. "May I speak to Cherelle."

"Sure you can, Melvin."

"Hey Love," Cherelle greets.

"Hi there. I take it you got my message from earlier."

"Yep. Sure did."

"I don't think that I can do it today."

"I understand. Is everything okay?"

"Yes and no. I don't have a car at the moment, thanks to my knuckle-headed, beer-guzzling brother who played demolition derby with it."

"NO!" she says. "Is he okay?"

"So far. That could change for the worse, depending on what my insurance says."

"Well, I hope everything turns out for the better."

"I just feel bad about having to cancel out, but right now I'm a ball of nerves."

"That's quite all right. We can do this some other time. I'm just glad that no one was hurt."

"Yeah, so am I," he contemplates. "Well, it's been a crazy morning and I'm going to take a nap and unwind."

"Can I come sing you a lullaby?"

"Sing me a lullaby?" he questions reluctantly.

"Yeah. I'll leave Chuckie over here."

"You're serious?"

"Of course. I want to see you, even if you are going to be asleep. I won't bother you...I just want to be in the same place as you."

"Wow. I'm flattered."

"So can I come?"

"Sure."

The day isn't too bad. In fact, it is a very good day. Cherelle bused it over to Mel's house. A fine woman busing it over to Mel's house in the 90's? He must've been fantasizing. Thirty minutes after she hung up, the fantasy stood before him. He was so honored, he couldn't sleep. She gave him and the day new life. After he laid down—with her by his side (she actually fell asleep while he watched her)—they got up and went to see "Hoop Dreams" and "True Lies" at the Burnham Plaza just south of downtown. It was a pleasant surprise to find that she enjoys action movies, and amusing that she was so sheltered and reserved growing up, that she didn't recognize many of the west side shots in the movie. But even more rewarding than their mutual cinema interests, was Mel's career vision after watching the basketball documentary. Before, he was torn with indecisiveness and unsureness. Now he knows what direction he wants to go in and that paled the events of the day. Afterwards, they dine at Giordano's up the street. Mel literally forgets the day's events and gets lost in her.

"So you mean to tell me you wouldn't have left Arnold if he was neglecting you?" he interrogates as they get to the counter to pay the pizza bill.

"I didn't leave Johnny."

"Good point," he contemplates as she steps in front of him to cover the tab.

"I owe you," she declares, rendering him speechless.

As they start up the stairs, he desires to know everything about this wonderful woman and how he can compliment and protect her. "Tell me...what are your biggest fears?"

She stops at the top of the stairs in the lobby. "My biggest fears?" she repeats, taking no time to ponder as they exit. "My biggest fear is seeing something happen to the people in my life and not being able to do anything about it. I don't worry about myself...I worry about others."

"Others...like who?" he fishes.

"Like my father, Chuckie, my mother and sisters. All of my family," she declares with closure as they pause at the corner of Jackson and Wabash. "And of course, you," she whispers through her soft smile. Mel almost dissipates under the scrutiny of her brown eyes, but she spares him by announcing, "I need to make a couple of calls."

When she fades back into Giordano's, he beams with the blessed assurance that he is in the company of an angel. As he hovers on the corner, he notices a man in rags taking a slumber next to a paper cup. Without a request or a second thought, he sticks a ten in there with all of the coins and says a silent prayer on behalf of the sleeper, hoping that he's also having a pleasant dream. Cherelle walks up and surprises him with a soft peck on the cheek. Mel gives her a questioning look.

"That's for being so beautiful," she declares boldly. "You don't have to do the things you do and be the way you are."

Mel chuckles bashfully and claims, "You just bring out the best in me," as they float hand in hand to the subway.

Big Will is out south and agreed to bring Chuckie back home. The only reason Cherelle didn't go home with Melvin is because she agreed to work in the kitchen at church and she had to be there at the crack of dawn. Which is for the better: they wouldn't be able to restrain themselves tonight. He confides in her how he cursed his mother out and how his conscious wore on him like a mad ape. Surprisingly, she is understanding and insists that it was probably no way of getting around it since it had built up. She does encourage him to make amends, and assures him that his mother probably understood. She doesn't tell him if she spoke to her again.

"I'm going to probably take a week off since it's close to the end of the year," he predicts as the Douglass train zooms through the darkness of the West Side.

"Why not wait until the holiday season?"

"Everybody usually takes off at that time."

"So you don't want to be part of the crowd?"

"Well," he contemplates. "It depends on who's in that crowd."

"Just me and Chuckie," she claims. "I was planning to take him skating and to see the Nut Cracker at the McCormick Place."

"Well in that case, I'm in."

She squeezes his hand, which elicits a big grin. When they reach her stop, they stroll the 15 depressing blocks to her house since the bus wasn't coming, oblivious to the drug community along the way. When they reach her door, there's a penitent pause as they stand only a breath away from each other.

"You want to come in?" she asks in a hushed tone.

"Yes, but I need to be getting back home," he whispers back.

She nods as her eyes glaze up. "Well, can we do this again next Friday?"

"By all means. I've been wanting to see The Lion King," he grants. "And this time, let's bring Chuckie."

She clamps on to him and plants a soft kiss on his lips. He gives her a long squeeze and reluctantly releases her. "Be careful," she warns.

"I'll be okay."

"Call me when you get home."

He nods as he backs up, still smiling and still suspended in air. He's so high, that he finds himself giggling and talking to himself when he reaches Pulaski, still unwitting to the element that he is in.

"Heh heh. I'll call you before I get home, heh heh," he giggles under his breath. He observes the ground as he eats up the sidewalk.

Cars go by unnoticed, and there's about two square blocks of space per person on the street, which makes it comfortable to chat to himself without having to worry about the crazy house being called on him.

"Yeah. You're lucky you didn't stay overnight...might've ended up with a Melvin III."

As he passes the alley just before Taylor, he notices a figure to the right side. He glances at the dirt colored face of the man and keeps going with his same smirk. Three paces later, his heart jumps out of his mouth and his smirk collapses as he goes under the viaduct. Didn't he see a clone of that dude three blocks ago on Roosevelt? As he starts peeking over his shoulder, he can hear the light steps quickly bearing down on him like an avalanche, and just as he turns his head to see behind him, the ice-cold glock is on his cheek.

"Don't even think about runnin'," the raspy voiced man warns as he skips to the front of Mel. Their eyes meet. "Fuck you lookin' at? Don't look at me, mothafucka," he hisses, slapping his face with hot, sour breath as Mel's eyes drop to the pavement. "Now empty yo' pockets and don't hold out on me, 'cause if you do, I'll empty this mothafucka in your head" he threatens as he sticks the barrel right in his nose.

There's Cherelle, inside the dark chamber, smiling at him. Oh how he loves her so and longs to see her, even though he left her just ten minutes ago. She's looking nice in her wedding gown. She said 'I do' and she gives him a namesake. Memory has a place in there too, with Mister Ponytail by her side, grinning at him. He hears his father preaching one of his many sermons that applies to his life; Momma is fussing and David is being flip at the lip. He finds his niche in video production and he is happy. The congregation is coming together as a unit...as one body in Christ. The church is purged of the toxic members. Finally. The Bible study group is growing in knowledge, rejoicing at how intimate they were with the Lord. Deidra confesses Christ as her personal Savior and Marcus found a serious girlfriend his own age. Karen is baptized at his church—crying as she went down into the water, like she did when they went into prayer. And Homey lives to be an old gray stud.

Smelling the gunpowder, he obliges, pulling his wallet out first and tossing it to the ground, and then he removes his Rolex and hands it to him. The man's hands are bony, clammy and jittery.

Mel's eulogy is auricular. Some in the congregation are happy to see him go home. Most are sad. His mother isn't even present. Maybe she's too distraught. Maybe she doesn't care. He still hasn't apologized to Momma. There is no wedding to his true love. Cherelle lives the rest of her life waiting for that glorious day when they will be reunited. He left without leaving any offspring. It should be a divine law against a man dying without leaving any children behind. The video remains a secret and his car is junked. The insurance got off easy. There is so much life ahead. What a waste.

Before he knows it, the man is snatching the watch from his hand, scooping the wallet up and trucking out like Carl Lewis. For something that lasted all of fifteen seconds, it seems like that gun was in his face for eternity. Mel has tunnel vision and he starts forcing his breathing. He's nine blocks from Cherelle's house and six blocks away from the El train. By instinct, he heads back to Cherelle's, although he's almost too numb to walk.

She opens the door in her housecoat, wearing the same captivating smile.

"I couldn't get enough of you, so I came back," he jokes.

"Oh Melvin," she says, hugging him.

"By the way, can you spare some bus fare...I was just robbed."

She pulls back and gives him a *'beg your pardon'* once over.

As the President addresses all of the first-line supervisors from every department in the company, Mel's mind is omnipresent (with the exception of the meeting), and he hates being everywhere. *He's had better weeks. Nothing else happened since the robbery, but the after-effects of last week's events crept up on him like the shadowy character that stuck him up. Out of habit, he still reaches into his pocket to check the watch. Every time he pulls out lint, the reality of the last remnants of Memory being gone would make his heart ache. He could have pawned it, but it meant too much to him. Not that he was hoping she would come back to him...the watch had the opposite affect that she intended: it kept his mind off of her when he would look at it. It's absence sent him into a deep depression. He even started second-guessing his emotional longing for Cherelle, who graciously made sure that her uncle dropped Mel off at home that night. He started wondering if it was just lust-laced infatuation. After all, he never wanted to join a ready-made family. Why is he compromising now? And he still hasn't apologized to Momma.*

Mel tries to focus on the sales figures the President is going over, but the only thing he sees when he's not daydreaming, is Jackie, who's sitting right across the conference table from him. His ugly mug evokes visions of snatching him by the collar and slinging him out of the window. Oops. There is no window in here. Just white walls and bright white lights. It has the ambiance of a hospital. The perfect setting for a nap. The caffeine is losing its power. Maybe because he has gotten up to two cups a day as a substitute for sleep. He's a junkie. Right now, he's fading. His eyes remain open, but his mind is blanking out. The dream is what's been tormenting him the whole week...waking him up in the middle of the night, attacking his conscience. The cop's life is turned upside down by the false evidence. Mel has the key to open the truth and exonerate him. That same key would lock another black man up, adding just a small hundredth of a percent to that rapidly growing number of caged up brothers. Right is right and wrong is wrong. Why does right feel wrong and wrong feel right?

The prompting of "Questions?" from Mr. President snaps him out of his trance/snooze, and he's angry at his trifling ass brother and the insurance company that's dragging their feet. Mel wants to beat the stupidity out of David every day that he's on public transportation. He must give some credit to the insurance company, though. When he "honestly" informed them that he wasn't driving—that his brother was driving—the claims representative urged him to take the out that she was offering him (when she asked who was driving, he told her his brother was. She asked him again, and again he gave the same answer. She asked him if he was *sure* that he wasn't driving instead of his brother, and he said he was positive—"I have to be truthful about it even if I am out of a car"). She appreciated the truth and said that she would take care of it, although it may be a couple of weeks before some progress is made. And he still hasn't apologized to Momma.

The week was torturous, and he is thankful that it is coming to an end. When the meeting lets out, it is quitting time. He is regretting that he agreed to go out with Cherelle and Chuckie today. She said that she would meet him downtown at the Afrocentric bookstore since she will be in the area anyway. What he really wants to do is go to bed and wake up next summer. It must be nice to be a bear. He checks his Email, and is surprised to have a document from an outside source. The address is **GMAN@aol.com**. He opens it and a grin immediately spreads over his face. It reads:

> **What up, Mel Dawg. Could you spare a couple of dollars? What's going on at, uh...what's the name of that place that I used to work at...Spark. How are things at Spark? My place is waiting at John Marshall. I start in two months and I'm actually kinda eager. I'm trying to get into that mode of heavy reading, and believe it or not, I started reading the Bible—everyday. I found some interesting verses in there that you're probably already familiar with: The King's heart is in the hand of the Lord; he directs it like a watercourse wherever he pleases—Proverb 21:1; For if you remain silent at this time, relief and deliverance for the Jews will arise from another place, but you and your father's family will perish. And who knows but that you have come to royal position for such a time as this—Esther 4:14. As you can tell, I'm studying the Lord's will. It's pretty interesting. This may sound strange coming from me, but I also sent an apology to Deidra. We talked briefly on the phone and she said everything was cool. It's amazing what time away from Spark can do to the heart. Anyway, send a shout out to Marcus and the rest of the fella's and slap Jacquelyn for me. Peace out.. Greg.**

Mel snickers as he imagines Greg reading the Bible. It's inspiring to read how he made amends with Deidra. He always thought that he had too much pride to say, "I'm sorry." More importantly, Mel knows that he has to do the right thing. And he will. But first, he heads to his stall for a talk with the Lord. For the whole week, he's been giving God the silent treatment. Now it's time for a change of heart and disposition. And he still has to apologize to Momma.

Cherelle and Chuckie are waiting outside the bookstore when he arrives. It has been a week since they saw each other, and with the exception of yesterday's confirmation, they haven't spoken on the phone since Sunday when she was checking to see how he was doing in light of the robbery. That was six days too long to go without seeing her. She never looked more glorious. Her hair is pinned up with a band in some type of beehive style, with an explosion at the top like a waterspout. She is wearing a red leather jacket, black stretch pants (Mercy), a black sweater and black, high-heel, lace-up boots. Chuckie is matching her, with his black jeans, gym shoes and Bulls cap. When Mel gets up on them, he can only grin loudly as he takes her in. She always steals his speech.

"You look nice," she compliments. "But then again, it's been a week since I saw you. You would look nice to me even if you just crawled out of the mud," she says as she gives him a warm embrace and a soft peck on the cheek.

"Hey buddy," he says to Chuckie.

"Hi."

"You ready to see a good movie?"

"Yeah."

"Well let's get this show on the road," he says as they head in the direction. "I miss you," he confesses to her.

"I miss you, too."

"I decided to do the right thing."

She glances and smiles at him.

When they get to the theater, Mel orders a big bucket of popcorn and three pops. He asks Chuckie where he wants to sit, and he points all the way to the first row. Just watching Chuckie beam with excitement is worth the price of admission. He has never seen Chuckie as outgoing as he is now, and it is a pleasant surprise. They stay until all of the closing credits disappear in the sky.

"Are you hungry?" Mel questions as they step out in the lobby.

Both Cherelle and Chuckie shake their head.

"Well," he says reluctantly. "I guess I can take you home now."

She steps up to him and whispers in his ear, "I would feel safer if I spent the night in your arms."

Mel chuckles. "I don't know Cherelle...you look real dangerous tonight. Like a Black Widow."

She turns her head down and bats her eyes at him.

"And she has me trapped in her web," he says as they hook arms, walk to the bus stop and board the Jeffrey bus that is just arriving. When it passes the Museum of Science and Industry in Hyde Park, Mel points out, "We're going there tomorrow" to Chuckie.

Chuckie looks awestruck at it.

Cherelle looks at Mel in admiration.

When they make it to his house, he switches on the television out of habit and lets Homey out. When he gets back into the living room, Cherelle and Chuckie are grinning impishly.

"What?" Mel questions.

"We have a surprise for you," Cherelle announces.

"A good movie, enough popcorn to satisfy my tummy, and a sleep-over with my two friends...What more could a man have?"

"Close your eyes and you'll find out."

Mel closes his eyes and he can hear them moving around.

"You can open them now," she announces.

When he opens them, Cherelle is holding Chuckie up close to him and Chuckie has a gold pocket watch swinging in front of Mel's eyes.

Mel starts giggling. "Oh my God," he says. "You didn't have to do this."

"Sure I did. Now you won't lose track of time and now I can put you under my spell," she jokes.

"I'm already under your spell."

They both get silent and serious for a moment, as their body language is loud and clear.

"Thank you Chuckie and Cherelle. I love it."

"You're welcome," Chuckie announces as he hands it to Mel.

Mel examines it, admiring the embossed cross on the outside cover with his finger and reading the inscription of his name on the inside cover. He closes it shut and gazes at Cherelle.

Cherelle takes a hint and announces, "It's time for bed Chuckie" without taking her eyes off Mel. Although Chuckie isn't tired (kids have an abundance of energy), he doesn't protest, as if he understands. After tucking him in, they come back downstairs. Mel is still choked up, so Cherelle switches topics.

"See the book I got," she says, pulling a novel out of her purse. "My middle name is Toni, and I realized that I haven't read anything by Toni Morrison, so I said why not try 'Song of Solomon.'"

Mel's mouth is just hanging open as he stares trance-like at the cover art.

"Are you okay."

"Don't go anywhere," he says as he jumps up and darts upstairs. Just as swiftly as he left, he comes flying back down with his Good News Bible in hand. He flops down, flips the pages, and tells her to "Read the highlighted scripture."

"Women of Jerusalem, I am dark but beautiful, dark as the desert tents of Kedar, but beautiful as the draperies in Solomon's palace. Don't look down on me

because of my color, because the sun has tanned me," she recites. "Okay, I see what you're getting at. This cover is an illustration of the verse. Interesting that you would pick up on it so quickly."

"That's not all," he promises. "Read Matthew 16 and 16 through 17."

She flips to it and reads: ***"Simon Peter answered, You are the Messiah, the Son of the living God. Good for you, Simon son of John! answered Jesus. For this truth did not come to you from any human being, but it was given to you directly by my Father in heaven."*** She gives him a questioning look.

"My Father in heaven told me the truth about you...this truth didn't come from my flesh. The book is a sign...a confirmation. And the truth is you're the one," he says as they get lost in each other's soul.

Chapter 18

A trail of coed clothes extends from the door to the king size bed: black boots and brown bucks just inside the door; white cotton footies and black dress socks inches away; navy-blue, loose-fitting Levi's alongside black stretch pants at the foot of the bed; black sweater and a beige tinted, button-up shirt balled up in a Tobacco, suede blazer on the chest of drawers. The linens are on the side of the bed. Just like the clothes, Mel and Cherelle are coupled, wrapped up in each other like strands of braided hair. "Saturday Love" by Cherrelle plays low on his clock radio.

The night was exciting and the outlook on life is promising. Mel and Cherelle were almost inseparable after Midnight Madness. They graced each other almost everyday with excitement. The irony is that Mel enjoys giving most of his time to her. He has even grown attached to Chuckie. If that is an indication of what family life is like, Mel felt that they were wasting time and passion. Saturday promises to be a joyride after class: the Museum is first, followed by the Aquarium and then on to the Planetarium. He finds it hard to believe that she has never been to them. They will never run out places to go, since she has been deprived of the cultural and tourist sights of Chicago. They will dine at the Old Country Buffet that evening and drop Chuckie off at about nine. Together they will watch a Blockbuster movie in the evening and close the day giving praise.

After Cherelle put Chuckie to bed with the prayer: "Now you lay me down to sleep, I pray the Lord my soul to keep; If I die before I wake, I pray the Lord my soul to take," life seemed to start fresh. "It" happened and there wasn't any resistance. Mel made it to the mountaintop again, but there is a major difference this time around: He is still up there and he can almost touch the sun. The Promised Land sure looks good as he tans over from the warm and glorious union. The land is surely flowing with milk and honey. Not only is Cherelle a good lover, but they are walking the same path at the same pace, and for that, she didn't need a lot of bedroom gimmicks. Mel ponders "Is a rock hard penis stronger than the Spirit" again, as he lays petrified on his side with Cherelle snuggled neatly in his arms. "Of course the Spirit is stronger" he reasons, but it was more than a moment of fiery desire.

Legally, they haven't eloped. The paper and jewelry will come soon, not later. And if a ring makes an engagement official, then they're unofficially betrothed. With emotions so strong and mutual, formalities are all that remain. Mel didn't break his covenant with the Lord: he made another one. They both vowed to the Lord to unite as one: husband and wife, for better or for worse; richer or poorer; in sickness and in health; till death due them part. God is their witness. Christmas marks the ceremony. They decided since it was never truly festive for either one of them, they will break the trend in a big way. It isn't official, but their consciences don't convict them. "It" was beautiful: pledging love to each other in front of the Lord in an hour-long prayer of praise and thanksgiving.

The only black-mark on his mind is the tape of the shooting. His soul wouldn't give him rest, and he finally gave in. Earlier in the day, he decided he is going to turn the tape in to the news and the lawyers for the officer. As the clock hits 2:38 in the morning, he drifts into a deep, dreamless sleep in which he's never felt as content, complete and happy before. Although he doesn't realize he's alive, he knows he doesn't want to ever wake from the amazing peace.

The ringing phone has such a sudden urgency, that he reflexively picks it up. "Hello," he curiously blurts as he checks the clock. It is four in the morning. At that moment, he realizes that he experienced an hour and a half of perfect peace.

"Hi Melvin. Can I speak to Cher—it's an emergency." It's Eunice, and that realization brings with it a touch of equilibrium. Her voice is hardly pressing. She must be calling to tell Cherelle that she can't watch Chuckie. Their schedules are so rigid because of his age and their work timetables.

"Hold on," he says as he sits up, turns on the lamp and nudges Cherelle, who seems to be in a deeper slumber, but wakes up immediately. She squints, trying to focus. "It's Eunice."

She takes the phone and says a dry, "Hello," pausing as he slips on his shorts and drags to the bathroom with his eyes closed.

Just as he makes it to the hallway, she lets out a blood-curdling wail that pierces the still morning air like a storm siren and rocks the walls of his house like a tremor. Mel's eyes open up as if he sniffed a pneumonia cap. He runs back in to attend to her, only to be brushed to the side as she bursts out screaming—almost steamrollering him as she flies down the stairs with the bed sheets in tow. She's going so fast, that it doesn't seem like her feet are touching the stairs or the floor. It really is an emergency. Mel has never heard anything as ghastly as her scream. Although it's obvious that the angel of death has claimed someone near and dear to her, it doesn't register immediately to Mel. He wants to believe it's something else, possibly a case of mistaken identity or an accident in which her beloved is in critical condition at worse. But there is no mistaking: it was the wail of death.

He nervously follows her down stairs, not knowing what to expect as he notices that she shed the covers on the steps. He turns on the living room lights, and hears her sobbing in the kitchen. When he finds her, she's collapsed in a kneeling position on the floor, as if she is having labor pains. She is still naked from the love escapade three hours ago. With every exhalation, she howls in distress like an animal being mutilated and every breath she takes is strained and agonizing like an asthmatic's in the midst of a severe attack.

"What's wrong, sweetheart?" he queries with concern as he gets on the floor and puts his arm around her.

She pushes him away as she gets up and staggers to the corner where she collapses into a ball. "I can't breathe," she manages to blurt between quick, short breaths.

Realizing that she's hyperventilating, he stays a few feet back as her face reddens and tears spill. Mel eases towards her and sits next to her. He notices that she's still clutching the phone and starts rubbing her back. She probably doesn't realize she has it in her hand. Mel gently pries it from her fingers.

"Hello?" Mel checks to see if Eunice is still on the line.

He can barely hear her weeping on the line as she tries to explain what happened. The only thing he can make out is "daddy" and "killed". Cherelle's moaning made the rest inaudible.

"OK. I'll call you back," he says, realizing he needs to tend to the living—he needs to tend to his woman.

Cherelle buries her head in his chest and howls, "They killed him Melvin—they killed my daddy."

She continues to groan uncontrollably as Mel squeezes her tight, because there's nothing he can say that could make it better. She's breathing better, but the wound is so fresh and deep, that he almost wishes it was physical so she could go into shock.

"They killed my daddy," she says repeatedly as he gently rocks her tense body from side to side. She moans in cadence to the swaying. It's unreal and eerie. Humanity seems lacking in what he hears. The sound is unearthly, like a weeping phantom.

The bond between Cherelle and her father was too strong to be defined with words. It was expressed openly with no inhibitions. Cherelle wasn't the boy that Charles wanted to be his namesake, but she might as well have been, because he loved her just the same—not like a boy, but like a child that came from his loins.

Once, when she endured a typical day of verbal torment from her classmates about the way she looked, she thought that she had reached the point where she couldn't take any more and was planning to end it once and for all with daddy's gun. It was a Friday, which was fight day at school, and she had a couple of girls spit on her and a few boys push her down and throw dirt in her face. Before the clock hit four (she usually got home at 3:55 on the dot), she expected to have a bullet lodged in her head and lay in an everlasting sleep. She couldn't imagine a lower valley.

She came home crying, not expecting her daddy to be home. Apparently, he happened to get off early that day. When he tried to find out what was wrong, she tried to hold back the tears and cover up her pain, but that made her even more hysterical. What she didn't realize was that her father knew what she went through, even though she never told him or anyone else in her family. She didn't want to tell him, because she knew that he loved her more than life and she was afraid that he would come up to the school and make a scene uglier than herself. That day, he sat her on his lap and cradled her like a baby. She just broke down and spilled her guts, telling him everything she went through that day and practically her whole life, expecting him to go up to the school and whoop every single one of her classmates. To her surprise, he just kissed her on the head, smiled and said, "Let's go for a ride."

She just knew the destination was the school, so she was shocked when he pulled up to the beauty salon. It didn't dawn on her that he was taking her there to get dolled up. She couldn't believe it until she was getting out of the seat with a new hair do, a manicure, and a complete makeover. It was the happiest day of her miserable life. And it didn't stop there. The next stop was the mall, where he took her into Carson's for a new formal dress and a pair of shoes. It was pink with ruffles and the shoes were white patent leather. She never had an outfit like that on Easter, let alone on a typical, hot summer day. When they got home, the day got better. He told her to get dressed in the new cloths and he did likewise in one of his best church suits: They were going out.

He took her to the show to see "The Wiz" and afterwards, they went to Pizza Hut. The day's earlier experience was totally forgotten by the time she got home that night. It was a fairy tale. And it continued the next morning when he took her to get a puppy. For once, she felt good about herself. What made it even better was that it wasn't just a one-weekend event. Every Friday after, they ritualistically went to the show or bowling and then to a Pizza place, since that was her favorite food. It went on until she had her braces removed, filled out and met her ex-husband in her third year of high school. She remembers it like it was yesterday. She wishes it were yesterday. Now she's ugly again.

After a few moments that stood still, she begs, "Let me go," as she squirms in his arms.

That baffles Mel. "Just relax, Cherelle. Just relax. I got you," he insists, his clutch tightening.

Her tone gets serious, yet pathetic as she claims, "I feel dirty. I can't breathe." Her grieving starts to escalate into all out hollering as she pulls away from him and lays on her side in a fetal position. "I'm being punished. Instead of fornicating, I should have been home with my daddy. Now he's gone and it's all my fault. I should have been home," she sobs.

Mel can't deceive himself. Although now isn't the time, and although he needs to be strong for her and bear her burden...he realizes she's experiencing an emotional hurricane and what she says shouldn't be taken personally, but he can't will the emptiness full. That statement cut through his heart. He's never felt this helpless. If he could work a miracle and bring her father back, he would. If he could take his place on the death angels tally sheet, he would. But the facts remain: her father is gone, she's hurting like hell and there's nothing he can do about it...except pray. He places his hand on her bare hip and prays,

"Lord have mercy," with the faith of a mustard seed as Cherelle continues to groan her heart out.

"What's wrong, Mommy?" Chuckie questions, catching Mel off-guard. Kids are not blind and easily fooled, especially this one. He knows something isn't right about his mother sitting on the floor as naked as the day she was born, crying her eyes out, and her boyfriend sitting next to her with a sagging face, but Mel figures he doesn't need to hear it right now.

"Go back up to the room, Chuckie!" Cherelle yells, before Mel could give him a false reason for the excitement.

His face slowly breaks down from the perplexed look to reveal his hurt feelings as he stands motionless and lets out his own long wail that's louder than his mothers', which makes her more uneasy...and which makes Mel more uneasy. He sucks in a deep breath, pauses and screams again even louder.

"Stay here," he whispers to her as he jumps up quickly and scoops Chuckie up and heads back upstairs. When he gets to the bedroom, he cradles and consoles him into the contentment that the matter is not as serious as it seems. "Shhhhh. It's okay. It's okay. Mommy is just having a bad dream."

He doesn't say anything and seems to be pacified by that explanation. Then Cherelle comes staggering up the stairs, moaning like a person would moan if they lost their best friend, and Chuckie gets excited again as she passes the room with the subtlety of a Tornado. She slams the bathroom door behind her and Chuckie screams, "Mommy!" as Mel picks him up again and carries him downstairs.

Mel thinks and talks fast as he assures him "Mommy is going to be fine," and quizzes, "So Chuckie, do you like the Power Rangers?" in an effort to take him to a more pleasant atmosphere.

Chuckie just nods up and down.

"What about the Ninja Turtles?"

He nods again. Mel got lucky, because he doesn't think he put all of the adjectives in the name and he didn't know if they were still the super heroes of choice.

"Do you know what's coming up really, really soon?"

Of course he nods.

"What's coming up, Chuckie?"

"Christmas," he says with the enthusiasm of an immovable object. So far, he isn't following Mel there and Mel knows he's in trouble.

"Don't you want to talk to *my* daddy? Let's call my daddy," he says as he picks him up and carries him on his hip into the kitchen.

The phone rings four times before his mother picks up. "Momma, is dad in? I need to speak to him. It's an emergency."

"You know your father is fellowshipping down state," she advises.

"Oh no," he says, remembering that he went to East St. Louis to visit and conduct a revival for his boyhood friend.

"What's the matter?"

"Momma," he exclaims, exasperated and desperate as he sits Chuckie down, walks to the other end of the kitchen and whispers into the phone. "Cherelle and Chuckie are over here and Cherelle just got news that her father died and she's taking it hard and I don't know what to do or what to tell Chuckie."

"I'll be right over," she says without hesitating as she hangs up before he could confirm.

Cherelle grows louder, Chuckie becomes nervous, and Mel goes insane. Chuckie wasn't going for the small Christmas talk. Mel was addressing him, but as he was talking, Chuckie kept looking up towards the stairs as the moans echoed throughout the house from the bathroom. Mel has to admit, it takes his mother less than six minutes to arrive. When he answers the door, she's in a full-length coat that she's holding together with her hand. She has her nightgown on underneath. Homey is at the bottom of the stairs looking perplexed. Mel forgot he left him out last night. It's a miracle that his mother got through him.

"Where is she?" she asks, but Mel didn't have to answer, as she is quickly saturated with the sounds of sorrow. She proceeds up the stairs and tells him to "Just talk to him some more."

Mel waits for her to make it into the room and then obliges, telling him tales from his childhood and how good God was and is. He is about to go into the story of Jesus when, suddenly, just moments after his mother reached Cherelle, there is silence in the upper level. It's like going from night to day with the snap of a finger. It is truly a Godly act. He can't imagine what she could've said or done, but he is grateful. He continues with his dissertation of how God sent his Son, Jesus, to save him and everyone in the whole world, trying to enlighten him about the real meaning of Christmas. Before he could finish, he realizes that

Chuckie knows all about the real meaning behind Christmas. He ends up enlightening Mel on a couple of things.

His mother and Cherelle—dressed in the clothes they ripped off earlier that night and carrying Chuckie's stuff—come down a few minutes later, talking casually to the amazement of Mel. It's as if nothing happened as he takes his ears off Chuckie and listens to them.

"Honey, don't let Satan lie to you, because you know the devil is a liar," his mother claims with authority.

"Yeah, I know he is," Cherelle agrees with a double dose of assurance.

"I know this is hard, but you and your family are going to have to pull together to get through this. You really should go and see about your mother as soon as possible."

"I am."

"I can keep Chuckie and I'll let Mel drive you in my car," she turns to Mel to get his consent out of respect for him. "Mel, do you mind doing that? If not, it's okay. I can take her home and talk to her family."

She doesn't have to ask him if he will take his woman home. That's a given. However, he is honored by the consideration she shows him.

"I'll drive her," he says as he dashes upstairs to put on his clothes. Mel is positively astonished by what he saw and heard the last couple of minutes. Not only did she get Cherelle to calm down (how, is a mystery that he hopes to solve soon), but for the first time in his life, he felt like his mother was truly respecting him. Love was subjective, but respect was always an issue. Perhaps the conversation woke her up, but he is regretting some of the things he said to her. He wishes he could take some of the statements back.

When he gets back down stairs, the miracle continues. Chuckie is dressed and they are talking and laughing about cooking. Mel can only shake his head and announce, "I'm ready," and they are off.

His mother sits in the back seat with Cherelle and chatters on and on with her until he pulls up to her house. She stops talking, closes her eyes and gives Cherelle a long hug, encouraging, "Bear each others burdens and lean on the Lord. He won't let you down. I'll have my husband give you a call and possibly a visit when he gets in and I'll keep you lifted in prayer."

She has tears in her eyes when she gets out with Chuckie. Mel gets out to walk her to the door and she addresses him when she opens it as Chuckie gravitated to David's Game Boy in the living room.

"You really have to support her and her family for a while. Funeral arrangements bring out the worst in black people, so you're going to have to be strong. See how things go, and if it starts to get messy, you need to intercede and lead them in prayer—and you need to let the Spirit lead you. And by all means, don't take anything Cherelle says that may be offensive, personally. She's wrestling with the devil and she's bound to say some things that will hurt, but stand by her. She's a nice young lady—if I had to choose a wife for you, she would be my first and only choice. If you need anything, I'll be here all day and I'll let your father know as soon as he gets in."

For a moment that he wants to pause, they stand and smile at each other. The walls just came tumbling down and so did the tears in her eyes as they embrace like they've never embraced before.

"Thanks Momma. I love you," he utters without thinking.

She put her finger on his lips, telling him "I'm proud of you. Now go stand by your lady friend," as she wipes the moister from her face.

"Okay Momma," he says as he trots to the car.

He feels favored. It's too bad it's in the midst of tragedy. He almost feels guilty to have an open door to a more intimate relationship with his mother on the day the woman he loves and plans to marry lost her dear father. She's grinning when he gets in, so he grins and quizzes, "Why are you smiling?"

"I was just looking at you and your mother. You two are so much alike—that's what's so funny. And powerful praying must run in your family."

Mel looks at her curiously and demands her to "Elaborate," as he pulls off.

She chuckles and grows silent.

She's wearing a perplexing, blank grin as she stares ahead. Whenever she has to say something that's disturbing, she pauses and meditates on it. Neither one says anything as Mel drives along. He pulls up to the stop light at the intersection where the I.C.O. train runs on 71st Street. The warning lights are down and as the train rolls by, Cherelle leans over and gently hugs him and pecks his cheek.

"I insinuated earlier that my father was killed as a punishment to me for sleeping with you. From the bottom of my heart, I'm so sorry for saying that and I hope you won't hold it against me."

"Don't worry about it," Mel blows off, somewhat relieved.

"I like your mother. She is going to make a perfect mother-in-law. You know you have something special when a mother gets along with the daughter-in-law. Johnny's mother didn't hide the fact that she wasn't too crazy about me. But she did hide the reason," she says as she reflects.

"So does that mean that our Christmas date is still on? You weren't drunk with passion?"

She looks over at him and smiles without answering. "I wish I could've given daddy the news. He would've been so happy. Now I have to find somebody to give me away," she says somewhat dejected, not focusing on the real loss.

"I guess that means it's still on."

She just looks at him and rolls her eyes.

"So tell me about this amazing prayer."

"There's not much to tell. She prayed for me in the Spirit, the Spirit came over me and I'm leaning on the Lord right now. I'm still in a lot of pain, but I'm going to have to live with it."

"That's it? I mean, what did she say in her prayer?"

"After she cursed the devil, rebuked a spirit of division, bound up and cast out the spirit of grief, she went into a tongue language, so I couldn't tell you what she said, but it got through. I could literally feel the burden being lifted as the Spirit of the Lord fell upon me like a blanket."

Mel is astounded. "My mother prayed in tongues?"

"You didn't know?"

"I've never heard anybody speak in tongues."

"I believe I heard somebody fake it, but this was real. There was an accent on her words—it almost sounded African—like that was her native tongue...nothing learned or American about it. Another language, not just forced utterances and babbling. It was awesome. The peace that came over me was even more overwhelming. Your mother is a power prayer for sure."

"Ain't that something," he says, because that's the only crutch phrase he could utter.

"And that's not the half of it. I managed to get my clothes on before she got there. When she finished praying, she told me *'don't let the devil lie to you. God isn't punishing you. It isn't about what you or your father did. Everything works for the good of God's glory. We may not understand His ways, but believe His ways are perfect. The Lord knows your heart and your desire to be obedient. He knows you're not perfect...if you were, you wouldn't need Jesus as your Savior. So don't let Satan use your passion and love for your man against you. And by all means, take your feelings serious and go through with what you and my son have planned. God has stamped His approval on it.'*

"I was too shocked. I couldn't believe she was telling me this. The Spirit revealed my fears to her. The first thing that I thought when I got the news was that I was being punished for making love to you last night. Of course, that was the devil talking to me and she was able to discern that. I know you didn't share any of that with her, especially last night...you didn't get a chance. God was addressing me through her."

Mel is speechless now. How come Momma never told him about her Spiritual gifts? Casting out Demons? Tongues? Prophesy? Discernment? Now he wonders can she heal the sick and raise the dead. Mel hasn't manifest any of those gifts. He really needs to talk to her. He leans on his other crutch phrase "Ain't that something," as they drive down a clear Lake Shore Drive in an unstable silence. It seems like there should be some dialogue between them, but there isn't. As long as Cherelle is content, that's all that matters. He has mixed emotions about what he heard about his mother second hand. What else doesn't he know?

Several people are already at Cherelle's house when Mel arrives. Mostly relatives and neighbors. Eunice is still having a hard time dealing with it. Jean sits with her, embracing and rocking in unison. Dameeka talks with some of the other relatives, showing no signs of grief. Mrs. Morrison is holding up, barely. Her eyes are misty, but she is trying to keep everyone else comfortable. The rest of the family is clinging to each other. Casual conversation is going on. No real weeping. No drama. There are even some surges of mild laughter throughout. Cherelle. She is all business. She sits her mother down and makes sure every one in the house is recognized, addressed and consoled. Melvin chats with one of Mr. Morrison's brothers that he met when he entered.

He calls himself Bud and claims to be the oldest child out of all of them as he reminisces with pride and joy some of the times they had growing up in the south before migrating to Chicago in 1942. Mel tries not to laugh too hard as Bud recalls how a bull once gored his brother in the butt so hard that he flew over the fence and couldn't sit on his left cheek for a month.

The phone hops off the hook and people—co-workers, friends, and associates—are in and out expressing their condolences. The morning passes without any conflicts and as noon approaches, it is time for them to go and identify the body. Cherelle asks him to drive her. What is he to say? On the way there, she holds up as she discloses some things about him.

"Before he lost his legs he was a practicing Karate instructor."

"That explains why you worried about telling him what some of your peers did to you?"

She nods.

"That also explains why Johnny is still walking around...because Dad couldn't catch him?"

She smirks and nods again. "His mobility meant so much to him. He took care of his body: didn't drink, smoke or dope. He told me once that he looks forward to having his glorified body, when cancer or accidents won't prevail against it, and he'll get the use of his legs and hand again. You should have seen the hope that beamed from his face when he told me that," she chimes as she herself beams. "It's that faith and hope that kept him going and upbeat. Never did he make an issue out of losing them."

Melvin puts his hand on her hand and squeezes.

"Melvin, they said he was coming from a friend's house when it happened," she says and pauses. "He had just loaned Scotty some money for his phone bill and as he walked passed the vacant lot on Avers, they say that somebody shot him in the chest...twice. He still had his wallet and a gold ring on, so they say it doesn't look like a robbery."

Mel thinks about asking does she suspect that Scotty may have had something to do with it, but opts not to, because he doesn't know him or want to offend her.

"He was shot like a dog," she asserts without emotion. "I don't want to think that Scotty had anything to do with it, but at this point, I don't know what to think."

"I understand."

When they arrive, she pleads with her eyes for Mel to go in with her. Mel viewed his first corpse at his grandmother's funeral when he was five. At the time, he didn't have a concept of death, but he had a spiritually innate discernment of life. The mortician did an excellent job on her...made her look like she was in a peaceful sleep. But Mel was immediately spooked by the wisdom that the body had no spirit. He has reluctantly viewed the dead since that first encounter, but he doesn't go out of his way to. What is he to say to Cherelle? Since they left a few minutes after the rest of the family, Mrs. Morrison, Jean, Eunice and Big Will are waiting when they arrive. As they walk in, Cherelle clings especially tight to Mel's arm. Her whole body is shivering.

"Are you sure you want to do this?"

She looks through glazed eyes at him and nods her head as her forehead reveals several stress lines.

They wait five minutes, when the coroner comes out and leads them through a white hallway and to a monitor. He informs them that they won't see the actual body, but an image of it on the screen. There is no protest. Cherelle's grasp gets tighter as the picture of her father comes on the screen. Everyone stands still in silence for an everlasting moment. It seems like they are waiting on Mrs. Morrison's approval. And she gives it.

She snickers and points out, "He's in there smiling that same smile."

And he is. He has a utopian grin. Mel looks over at Cherelle, who reflects the same uncanny smirk that her daddy is sporting. The circulation in Mel's arm starts flowing again as Cherelle loosens up. The Spirit whispers in Mel's mind ear that he's neither dead nor sleeping, but alive and well in glory. Then Cherelle observes and confirms: "Daddy's got his legs."

When the musician played "Precious Lord, Take My Hand", the family as a whole broke down. It had finally started to sink in that Mr. Morrison is gone, and they all wailed away collectively. Cherelle was rather hushed as one tear eased its way down her smooth face. She teared up occasionally during the days in between identifying the body and the funeral. She insisted that Mel take care of his business while her family worked out the arrangements. He called her throughout the days after he dropped her off from the coroner's office, but she remained strong.

After they left the casket suspended over the grave, most of the family went to the repast at the Morrison house. Cherelle bypassed it, choosing to go over Mel's house instead. She hasn't had any sleep since that wonderful night, which magnified her fatigue and—added to the gapping void in the pit of her stomach from the grief—gave her the feeling of being physically nauseated. Once she got there, her emotional strength came tumbling down. She cried a distressing lake and went into a placid slumber.

"It's really hard to deal with...it leaves a feeling of emptiness to know that somebody is walking around in my neighborhood with daddy's blood on their hands," Cherelle ponders.

"I can imagine," Mel relates.

She slept until late the next morning. Ms. Kronkite excused them both. Mel has missed three sessions and she informed him that he really couldn't afford to miss any more for the rest of the semester. Cherelle said she felt like somebody reached down her throat and pulled out all of her entrails. She was hurting for a big breakfast, so Mel rushed her over to Jackie's Place and fed her until she was satisfied. Surprisingly, she pecked and picked over her food like a bird.

"There's only so much the cops can do when nobody is coming forward. Somebody saw or heard something. Somebody's conscience is convicting them...it has to be."

"I would think so."

"Why hasn't anyone come forward then?" she questions as she runs the knife through the eggs on her plate.

Mel just shakes his head.

"Oh Melvin...what am I going to do? What can I do?" she ponders as she peers dejectedly out of the window.

The Monday following the shooting, the Chicago Defender devoted one column and two inches of reporting to it. It appeared on page four in the Police Roundup. Mr. Morrison's name didn't even appear in it. It was so generic and impersonal, as if it didn't matter. Cherelle was mad at the paper, but Mel informed her that it was common practice. Neither the Sun-Times or the Tribune covered it. Mel called up BJ and asked what's the most that he could do as far as coverage. BJ came through in a mighty way.

NOT JUST A STATISTIC

A day doesn't go by that I, like many other residents in the black community, don't read the Police Roundup in the Chicago Defender. Each time I would read about a senseless tragedy, my soul would weep for the families that were shattered and pray that I won't ever read of a loved one in there.

Behind every account of a lost life (often the name isn't revealed) there's a story about a soul that lived, loved and inspired. Unfortunately, it can't always be detailed in print, which seems to desensitize the human race to this type of crime.

It has gotten to the point where lost lives are only a matter of statistics. My father was one of the many faceless, nameless headlines in the Roundup last Monday.

Needless to say, I was disappointed with the account that didn't even name him. I was already in a world of pain that can't be imagined and I've always dreaded.

However, the Lord has blessed us with many gifts:

1. He has blessed us with memories. Not only do I remember how my father used to take me and my sisters to Great America–simply because one of us wasn't feeling good–and sing us to sleep, but I remember the goodness of my Father in heaven.

2. Our Father has blessed us with forgiveness through Jesus Christ. For all have sinned and fall short of the glory of God; For the wages of sin is death, but the gift of God is eternal life in Christ Jesus our Lord; But God demonstrates his own love for us in this: While we were still sinners, Christ died for us; That if you confess with your mouth, "Jesus is Lord," and believe in your heart that God raised him from the dead, you will be saved. For it is with your heart that you believe and are justified, and it is with your mouth that you confess and are saved.

I'm thankful that I remember how my father taught me that, and how the Holy Spirit has comforted me with the assurance that I will see him again.

It is that assurance that gives me a heart full of joy and peace of mind. It is how I am able to forgive. Unfortunately, my forgiving won't save the person responsible.

This isn't a request for the gunman to come forward; rather, this is a plea for him to repent and get right with God. The advocacy of Jesus is far more influential than the accusations of the prosecutors of this world.

What will happen if you get caught up in the criminal justice system? I don't know. But I do know that the Lord controls the mind of a judge as easily as he directs the course of a stream.

I beseech anyone that was involved or knows anything about it, to get the blood off of their hands. Not only is the fellowship with a good man (he was returning from giving his last dollars to a friend when he was struck down) at stake, but–more importantly–the eternal presence with God.

Before he helped her put it together, they prayed for Thy will to be done. Originally, it was supposed to have an angry tone. It was supposed to be a mad appeal for the capture of the triggerman. The Lord had other plans though. After it was finished and on the way to layout, they prayed again. It appeared in the Weekend edition of the Defender, since that's the one that's read the most. It gave Cherelle some closure, even though the person who killed him remains at large. She just needed to say—in a big way—that I love you daddy one more time.

Chapter 19

Two days before the funeral, Melvin made several copies of the tape and mailed them to each of the television networks, the Police headquarters, and the District Attorneys office. It was broadcast all over the nation that very day. They apprehended Clifford and Peanut a day later and Officer Grimaldi was exonerated and off of suspension. They wouldn't implement the third mystery guy. In his interview, Grimaldi stood with his wife and young son and thanked the person who taped it and sent it in. Mel wasn't even tempted to identify himself as the officer urged the person to come forward so he could recognize, reward and thank him in person. There were those who wanted to see Grimaldi burned at the stake. Melvin would have been an adequate substitute. The risks far outweighed the reward. Besides, doing right is his duty and it would be rewarded in due time. To this day, God and Cherelle are the only witnesses.

Life was so dramatic that he didn't have time to rejoice at the ecclesiastical crop. That first Sunday was spiritually spectacular. Karen was baptized at his church and he missed it, as he spent that day with Cherelle at her church. Deidra showed up, along with the rest of the Bible study group. Deidra said she will think about joining, although she has an inactive membership at another church. Mel didn't press. He was just elated that so many were giving the Lord some consideration.

Earl sung his song: "Open Our Eyes". Everybody says the Spirit took over him and the whole church was on fire. To top it off, Trustee Bradford issued a formal apology to the congregation on behalf of his whole family, and not just for the Donald incident (which he assured is being taken care of through prayer and counseling), but for all of the trouble they caused in the past. He addressed the Adams' specifically, promising to stop butting heads like the goats that they were and to start being meek and working together with the sheep. Mel would have loved to witness that. The next time he crosses paths with Trustee Bradford, he will bury the hatchet that he has been carrying around for almost six year. Word is Donald may be rejoining. He not only had been fasting and praying for unity and a forgiving heart, but he has been interceding on behalf of Donald and pleading for the renewal of his soul.

The sweetest fruit (no pun intended) of the harvest, was Shawn's presence in the Bible study—no thanks to the seeds of animosity Mel stored up. A week earlier, Mel heard his father and two radio broadcasts' that focused on the parables of the lost son, sheep, and coin. The coals on his head burned a ball spot up there. It was ironic that Mel was teaching on how Jesus wants people to come as they are and to depend on Him to change them. Shawn requested prayer for a closer walk with Christ and an obedient heart. Mel was almost in tears when he testified that he wants any and every thing that's not of God to be pulled up and cast out from him.

Lamont's official departure from Love of God was bitter. How sweet it is to know that he's extending his ministry and opening a church. You promised him to not only visit, but to try and get involved with his outreach efforts.

His acceptance to Columbia came in the mail that week with instructions to register the first week in February. Film and Video will be his focus as a student at large, and he's giving serious thought to pursuing a degree in it. He's going to miss seeing Cherelle at CSU, although they'll presumably be married by that time. Speaking of which, Mel not only exchanged the ring, but he upgraded to two karats, which says, "I LOVE YOU" that much more.

On a less than joyous note, Jack was transferred to another facility up in Des Plaines. The department ordered Pizza to celebrate, since it would have been a little tacky to actually have a formal party.

As he prepares to leave, getting an early jump on the Thanksgiving weekend, he contemplates one more unresolved issue and decides that it can't go another day unsettled.

Mel walks in the same way he did a month ago, minus the fire and rage. His mother is stretched out on the comforter in the living room, reading the Daily Word. She is dressed in a pink warm-up suit and looks like she is going to shoot some ball at the park.

She greets him with a warm smile and a "Good afternoon," as she lays her book down and beams at him. "You're off early."

"I scheduled a half-day today," he accounts as he takes a seat on the sofa right next to her. "How are you doing?"

"I'm blessed."

Mel nods as he picks up the Daily Word and looks at the inspiration for the day without actually reading it. "Where's Dad?"

"He went up to the church to help prepare for the Thanksgiving service," she informs. "Maybe you should invite Cherelle to the breakfast tomorrow, since I assume you will be eating dinner at her house."

Mel twists his lips as he ponders the suggestions. "That might not be a bad idea," he says as he stretches out and tries to get comfortable.

"Are you okay?" his mother asks, her maternal intuition detecting his uneasiness.

Mel doesn't say anything as his mother peers at him.

"Are you and Cherelle okay?" she quizzes.

Mel nods as he looks at the dead television screen.

"Do you want to talk about it?" she whispers.

Mel looks at her smooth face that seems to gleam like a night light and blinks away as if it's to bright for his eyes.

She takes a deep breath and picks up her Daily Word, setting it on her lap as she flips through the pages.

"I said some things to you that I regret," he announces with no surface emotion...the opposite of his heated tongue-lashing.

She continues to peruse the book.

He looks straight ahead in shame as he continues: "They say that what's in your heart will eventually come out of your mouth...I don't know how true that is, but if there is truth to it, well I purged my heart of evil and I didn't tell the whole truth. I failed to mention that you did show me love by coming up with the down payment on my second car, and then paying the insurance for me; I also failed to mention how you bragged to all of your friends about me graduating with honors and buying my house, in which you covered the utilities on more than one occasion; Of course I failed to mention how you got up out of your sick bed and saw to it that I made it to Lamont's birthday party when I was in sixth grade. Then there are the countless prayers that you sent up on my behalf that were honored by the Lord...too many to count and too valuable to appraise. I commend and thank you for all of it...and I thank God for you."

He pauses and he gets choked up as he reflects on the pleasant memories that far outweigh the bad one's. "I guess what I'm really trying to say is I'm sorry for what I said, and I hope you find it in your heart to forgive me."

She doesn't say anything. She doesn't even look at him. She just continues to skim over the little book. They are definitely from the same mold. An unspoken understanding is reached. The amendment is made.

The silence is interrupted by the ringing phone, which is sitting next to her. She answers and announces, "He's sitting right here," as she hands Mel the phone.

"Hello," he says.

It's Cherelle. She informs him that the police have a suspect in custody.

"I'll be right over," he promises as he turns the phone off.

"The keys are on the dining room table," his mother says without even looking up.

He smiles and he retrieves them. When he gets to the door, they both grin at each other. There is silence, then he's out the door. She remains in the same spot with the same expression.

Cherelle was excited when Mel pulled up. She came prancing out before he came to a complete stop. Her family left for Missouri that morning. Cherelle stayed because she was planning to fix Mel a big Thanksgiving dinner—a foretaste to marriage. She is silent all the way to the station. Her visage is apprehensive when he comes to a stop. He touches her on the hand, she looks at him and expresses, "I feel funny about this."

"You don't have to go in if you don't want to."

"I'm not sure what I want to do...but I think it has to be done," she resolves as she opens the door.

When they get in, she asks for Detective Torres, who is handling the case and who phoned her. After a short wait, he comes from a long hallway and introduces himself.

"Hi Ms. Morrison. I'm Detective Torres," he says, extending a hand to her. "Can you follow me and I can tell you what we have," he says as he leads them down the corridor that he came from and into a room.

"I'm nauseous and hot," she mentions to Mel as they take a seat in a cluttered office. Mel rubs her back as Detective Torres begins.

"First off, let me commend you for the strength you've displayed in the face of this tragic situation. That commentary had an effect on an eyewitness, who gave us a detailed account of what happened and has agreed to testify. Without your plea in the Defender, we probably wouldn't have anyone in custody."

Cherelle nods at that.

"The guys name is Mark Sanders," he announces as he shows them a mug shot of a mean looking dude with long, over-processed hair. "He has a record of armed violence and sexual assault and he has signed a confession."

Cherelle stares bewildered at the photo.

"The witness was already in custody. Calvin Jenkins—a.k.a. Peanut—was with him when he shot your father," he proclaims. "Apparently, they tried to rob someone when Officer Grimaldi pulled up on the scene...you may be familiar with the story about how Dedrick Simmons was killed in a shoot-out that was caught on video."

Mel becomes queasy and thinks he's having a heart attack.

"Your father was walking by as they were arguing about the gun that was fired by Mr. Simmons in the shoot-out. They felt that he might have heard something, so they shot him so he wouldn't speak up. He was in the wrong place at the wrong time. Mr. Jenkins claimed that he didn't want to kill him and that his conscience wouldn't let him rest after he read your commentary. He actually claims to have turned his life over to Christ."

Detective Torres goes on a little while longer, insisting that the case is airtight. Cherelle sits stoically as he speaks, and Mel is having trouble breathing. He really doesn't hear anything else after he identified the guy as the third man on the tape...the tape that he hesitated to turn in. Wrestling with right and wrong when he knew what was right, cost Cherelle's father his life. It should've been him, because it's almost certain that she will hold it against him forever.

Not one word is uttered on the short ride to her house. Mel can barely drive. At the moment, he can imagine how it feels to try to drive drunk. Cherelle lays against the door panel with her arm covering her eyes. When he pulls in front of her house, he notices that she is tearing.

"Do you want me to come in," he inquires, knowing that she probably doesn't ever want to see him again.

She shakes her head and breathlessly claims, "I need to be alone."

He's too ashamed to look at her as she wipes her face with her jacket sleeve.

"I don't think I'm going to cook dinner tomorrow," she indicates. "I'm sick," she reasons as she buckles over in pain...emotional pain.

Mel knows why. She lets herself out without saying another word and seems to be queasy and unstable as she struggles to make it to her door. Mel watches her all the way in. She doesn't even turn around to wave when she gets the door open. He sits there for about ten minutes and gazes at the door after she goes in, hoping she would come back out or invite him in. She doesn't, which doesn't surprise him.

Thanksgiving came and went. Mel didn't have a bite to eat the whole weekend. He nibbled on chocolate chip cookies and sipped soup from a can for four days. He didn't even leave the house after his mother dropped him off at home that Wednesday night. Thursday he called Cherelle, but no one answered. Of course she doesn't want to speak to him. Mel isn't talking to anyone. Nothing matters anymore. He called in sick for the whole week, because he knows he is the slowest rodent in the rat race at work. He is even giving God the silent treatment, although he is speaking to Him with his mind. Sometimes he wonders if a mind discussion is less honorable than an oral. It doesn't matter to him at the moment.

"I don't ever want to have another relationship again. It's too unpredictably painful. If You were trying to send me a message...that I was supposed to be single and totally devoted to serving you, I got the message. I thought I was doing that. Why did it have to be such a painful lesson, though? Is it wrong to fall in love? It couldn't be, because You are Love. I wish you would take me away, right now. At least when Moses saw the Promised Land, You immediately took him home. How come it wasn't me that got shot? Right now I wish that I had never met her. I wish I wasn't even born. This is the worse feeling in life. If I was wrong for feeling the way that I did...if I put her above you...It felt so right. Have mercy and don't let us cross paths again on this earth. I'm going to get my number changed tomorrow. The sign. I thought the image on the book was a sign. It seemed so obvious. It felt so right. Maybe I should call her again. Never. I called her twice Monday and they said she wasn't in both times. I left a message and the non-returned calls makes it quite obvious that she doesn't want to talk to me. It's like looking at a dead body, with the expectation that it'll get up and come back to life."

The phone rings and Mel ignores it. He doesn't have the energy to listen, let alone talk to anyone. If he can't moan too good audibly, he's certainly not in a frame of mind to chat. He doesn't even mute the sound on the television as the answering machine picks up the call. As he stares zombie-like at the screen, the sound of Cherelle's voice cuts through the noise from the TV, sending a surge of life through Mel's body. He springs up and trips over the coffee table to get to the kitchen phone.

"Hello," he says desperately as Cherelle is leaving a message.

"Melvin?"

"How you doing?"

"I'm okay," she replies in a less than enthusiastic tone.

There's a long pause as Mel is at a loss of words.

"How have you been," she asks.

"I could be better, but I won't complain."

The pause is longer as she lets out a sigh. "Melvin," she calls.

"I'm here."

"Can you come over here?"

"When?"

"As soon as possible," she pleads. "I need to talk to you in person."

"I'll be right there," he promises, hanging up.

It takes him all of 50 minutes to get to her house. He figures that if she is going to officially bury the relationship, he'd rather throw the dirt over it before it starts stinking. She'll probably hand him the ring back, too. This will give him some closure. Besides, he is dying to be immersed in her presence, even if it's for the purpose of saying goodbye.

Her mother answers the door and welcomes him in. "How are you," she questions as she gives him a hug.

"I'm doing okay," he replies as he takes a seat on the sofa. "But more importantly, how are you doing?"

"I'm hanging in there and holding on to the Lord," she says with resolve. "Cher," she calls upstairs. "Is she expecting you?"

Before he can answer, she descends down in her housecoat and some flip-flops. The ring on her finger illuminates the room like a supernova. She doesn't seem like the type who would keep it.

"Can you give us some privacy, Momma?"

Her mother nods and fades to the kitchen.

Cherelle sits on the sofa next to him, but not too close. Her face looks exhausted and her hair is sticking out in all directions.

"You got here quick," she observes.

"Yeah, the buses were timed right and I was already dressed."

She nods as they both pause. "I haven't done any studying," she confesses. "Have you prepared your last speech?"

Mel shakes his head.

Another long uncomfortable pause. Mel hates small talk. The decision is hers. She doesn't have to feel obligated to soften him up before she gives him the verdict. He's prepared for the worst: the death sentence. He just hopes she makes it quick, although there is no way that it can be painless.

"Is your brother off punishment yet?"

"He'll never be off punishment in my book...at least as long as I'm car-less."

She chuckles.

Another hesitation.

She takes a long, loud breath and leans forward on the sofa as she faces him. "Melvin..." she starts.

He looks deep into her eyes, figuring it will probably be the last time. He's braced and his eyes start sweating.

"I don't know how to tell you this."

"Just say it and get it over with."

She looks down and takes another deep breath. "Melvin," she starts again with great difficulty as the words get stuck and her mouth hangs open in a slight smile. She inhales deeply again and blurts, "I'm carrying your child."

His eyebrows fly through the ceiling. "What?"

"I'm pregnant. We're going to have a baby."

Now he has trouble speaking English.

"That's the reason for the dizziness and empty feeling...it wasn't a mental or emotional thing—I was actually sick," she confirms. "I went to the doctor Monday because it was just too unbearable. I should have known, but with the passing of my father and all of the developments, I didn't consider it."

"Oh wow," Mel says as he blinks away and looks down.

"Oh wow is right."

"Where do we go from here?" he mumbles without looking at her.

She squints her eyes at him and the befuddling question. "Excuse me?"

He eyes her and, again, asks, "Where do we go from here?"

She looks to the side without turning her head and verifies, "You did propose to me on that magnificent night, didn't you...or was I just dreaming?"

"You weren't dreaming."

"And if I'm not mistaken, to ease our consciences, didn't we make a vow before God?"

"You aren't mistaken."

"And didn't you give me this ring," she asks, holding it up to his face, adding, "which you insisted was a small way of saying *'I LOVE YOU'*, even though I was speechless because of it's glory and the climatic expression of it?"

"I gave it to you from the heart."

"Well...I guess you're going to have to explain your question, because I don't want to assume that you're pulling out."

He sits back and rubs his palms on his legs to dry the perspiration. "I don't know..." he starts, shaking his head. "I guess it's obvious that you don't intend to leave me..."

"Leave you?!" she questions, cutting him off. "We've just begun something so beautiful...Why would I leave you?"

"Because I could've possibly prevented your father from being killed if I had turned in the tape. When you found out that day, you said that you needed to be alone, and I just didn't think that you would ever forgive me."

"Melvin," she chortles as she leans over and plants a soft kiss on his lips. "When I said I needed to be alone because I wasn't feeling well, I was literally sick and I needed to lay down. I would *never* leave you."

"What about your father?"

"My father is in the presence of the Lord, and in a way I'm kind of envious of him. You figure, he has peace and joy—and I'm sure his soul is dancing and making a lot of noise up there. He doesn't have to deal with the drama down here any more. Besides, you can't limit the power of the Lord. Don't you think that if it wasn't in His will for my father to go, He could have prevented it?" she questions. "He could've struck the shooter down before he fired the shot. He could've sent His angels to deflect the bullet. He could've allowed my father to take the bullet and live to give his testimony. He could've raised him from the dead. I don't understand why it was his time, but I'm not going to worry about it, since I know Daddy isn't. Besides, I have my own heaven to enjoy, right here, right now."

"So you forgive me?"

"Honey," she says shaking her head. "Forgiveness is unnecessary. Remember, a soul went home and a lost soul found Christ, so his living or dying wasn't in vain. But if you insist on going through with a formal acceptance to an unnecessary apology, you are forgiven. Now forgive yourself."

Mel is too honored to talk. He wraps his arms around her like a prized possession and doesn't let go.

Chapter 20

"Happy Holidays!" the caller exclaims.

The all too familiar voice on the other end catches Mel with his guard down. He stutters through his reply. "M-Merry Christmas...h-how are you?" he asks uncomfortably.

Cherelle is sitting next to him watching "Dracula". They decided to stay in since the temperature is below zero. The insurance approved another car for him and Mel anticipates that he'll be on the bus just a while longer. Cherelle knows about Memory, but Memory doesn't know about Cherelle, since they haven't spoken since she told him that "Things weren't working between us." If he wasn't so happy and forgiving, he would've gotten ignorant like he vowed to do if he ever got the chance.

"I'm doing okay." Her normally cheerful voice deceives her, though. Even if Mel didn't learn from Darlene that she is pregnant and that Roger isn't trying to be with her or claim the child, Mel knows her too well to not discern her low spirit. "What's on your wish list to Santa...and were you naughty or nice this year?"

"You know me. I don't have much of a list. Just a lot of intangibles, like peace, love and happiness."

"Sounds like you've been naughty to me," she japes.

"What about you," he shifts. "Are you worthy of a visit from Jolly Ol' Saint Nick?"

"I think you know the answer to that. I just can't wait for the holidays to be over with," she says dolefully. "Is the watch still ticking?" she asks.

What an unfair question. "Let's just say that I haven't lost track of the time," he replies matter-of-factly with a last word tone.

There's a long pause. He's dancing around emotions. The anger, hurt, and love he had for her deluges him with hurricane force and before he can get composed, he hears himself ask, "And how's Roger doing?" He doesn't direct any animosity towards her. There isn't a glint of the sentiments he just felt...just the resolve that their relationship is past tense and life goes on.

It seems like she was expecting the question, because she answers it with the same resolution, although with a slight edge. "Roger is okay. And I guess his wife and three kids are okay, too."

"He's married?" Mel questions along with the prompts and script. He almost feels guilty knowing the answer already.

She doesn't answer, shifting the subject back to him. "What are you doing for Christmas?"

Mel pauses and looks at Cherelle—who's not paying attention to the conversation—and announces, "I'm getting married."

He dreamed of telling her this on many lonely nights since April 21, and he is joyful that he is uniting with Cherelle, but he isn't at all happy about telling Memory—under the circumstances.

Memory snaps back "Congratulations!" as if it doesn't bother her, but he knows otherwise. "Who's the lucky girl?"

"Her name is Cherelle, and she's wonderful," he says as he rises and strolls to the kitchen and out of her earshot. Not once did Cherelle look his way, but it doesn't mean that she doesn't know that it is Memory.

"So you're going to marry your favorite artist...can she sing?"

"Only lullaby's, and for that, I'm a lucky and well rested man."

They pause as tension charges the phone lines. The small talk opens a bag of old pain. A lot needs to be said from both sides, but they don't know where to begin or what to say.

Memory soughs. "How come you didn't hang up on me when you recognized my voice," she asks bluntly.

Mel chuckles as he pours some fruit punch. "Why would I do that?"

"C'mon Mel, let's cut the charades. We can lay it all on the table. I walked in kissing my lover, just before you were going to propose to me. You walked out and I made no attempt to stop you. There was no shame. I didn't even apologize. You have a very thick skin that I've always been impressed with, but I know that it wasn't something that you could just shrug off. I know you better than that, and you know me better than any man. You probably know that I'm pregnant, too."

"I know," is all he can manage to utter.

"I ask again, how come you didn't hang up on me?"

Mel takes a long, deep drag of air and pulls his pocket watch out. "My skin is not as thick as you think. You may not see my pain or emotions, but a lot of things affect me that you don't realize. And yes, I was affected in ways that you could never imagine when we parted. At times I wanted to kill you, and then at other moments I was willing to take you back with open arms and a clean slate. Why didn't I hang up on you when I heard your voice?" he restates with the promise of a detailed explanation. "I don't carry any bitterness or animosity around. We were the best of friends. I planned to spend the rest of my life with you. I loved you...still do, but that doesn't mean that I will take you back. Just like God's love for mankind is unconditional, my love for you was not contingent upon us being a couple. Don't get me wrong. There were many sleepless nights. It took a lot of praying, a lot of time—a lot of quality time with God, getting to know Him again—and a miracle for me to put those negative feelings behind me. I didn't think that I would be able to ever trust anyone again. I was starting to doubt if God's will was for me to be married. Believe it or not, I was seriously considering a life alone, devoted totally to God. But then He blessed me with Cherelle...the miracle. When she came into my life, that's when I realized that I didn't really want anything bad to come to you: I wanted something good to come to me. So you see, my bitterness wasn't about you: it was about me."

A split second of silence lasts a good hour before Memory speaks again. "Can I apologize?"

"It's not necessary. You are forgiven."

She takes another hour of silence to gather her thoughts. "Mel..." she starts and stops, seemingly losing her breath.

"Yes?"

"I respect what you just said and I am sorry for all that happened, but I don't want to lose you as a friend. I don't want you totally out of my life."

"We can be friends."

"But I don't want to offend your bride. Despite what I may have done in the past, I do respect you, and I respect her because she's with you."

"Didn't I say we can be friends?"

"I heard what *you* said, but it may not be okay with Cherelle. If it's not okay with her, I'm going to have to find a way to live with that."

"Well, you're welcome to ask her."

"Is she there?"

"In full effect."

"Can I talk to her?"

"Hold on," he says as he presses the mute button. "Cherelle," he calls.

She emerges in the doorway.

"Telephone. Use the wall phone," he says, exiting the room. He holds the phone to his ear as he takes his seat on the sofa.

"Hello?"

"Hi. I don't know if Melvin has told you about me or not, but my name is Memory, and we were intimate at one time."

"Yeah...he mentioned that you were together for five years. He's told me some good things about you, and of course I've heard the bad and the ugly, too."

"Well, I want to congratulate you on your engagement. I hope that your marriage to him is a blessing for both of you. And I also want to give you a few words of wisdom, if you're willing to hear them."

"I love wisdom. It can only help me."

"I'm glad to hear that. Don't take this the wrong way...I'm not threatening you, but whatever you do, always do right by Melvin...he's a good man and deserves to be treated like the king that he is. And from what he's told me about you, he's blessed to have you, too."

"Thank you. I appreciate the advice and the compliments. And I do realize that Melvin is a good man..." Mel turns his phone off and looks over at her. She's beaming as she winks at him. "Girl, I know what you mean."

Mel tunes the rest of the conversation out as they seem to bond. It's a safe place. He doesn't have to lie about his concern for Memory's wellbeing. Sacrificing his relationship with Cherelle isn't an option, but now he doesn't have to shun her for safekeeping. His heart hurts for her and what she's going through. He's been to that place. He prays that she will have the endurance to withstand the storm and the faith that God's grace will shine on and tan her a darker shade of black.

Order Form

Name:____

Address:______________________________________

City/State/Zip:__________________________________

Phone:_______________________________________

___ copies of Shades of Black	$14.00 each	$________
___ copies of Eyes of Faith	$15.00 each	$________
Please add $2.00 per book for postage and handling		$________
Illinois residents please add 8.75% sales tax		$________
Total amount enclosed:		$________

Make checks or money orders payable to "Terrance Johnson", then send it along with this order form to the following address:

7-Fold Publishing
7732 S. Cottage Grove
Box 121
Chicago, IL. 60619